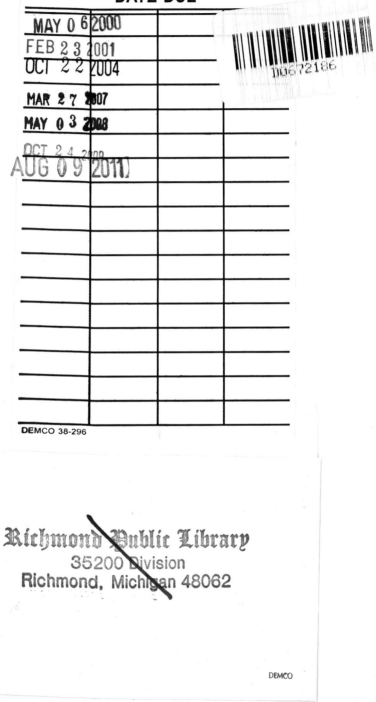

THE DEVIL'S FOOTPRINT

ALSO BY VICTOR O'REILLY

GAMES OF THE HANGMAN
RULES OF THE HUNT

THE DEVIL'S

FOOTPRINT

VICTOR O'REILLY

G.P. PUTNAM'S SONS

NEW YORK

G. P. Putnam's Sons
Publishers Since 1838
200 Madison Avenue
New York, NY 10016

Library of Congress Cataloging-in-Publication Data
O'Reilly, Victor.
    The devil's footprint / by Victor O'Reilly.
        p.   cm.
    ISBN 0-399-14137-5 (acid-free paper)
    I. Title.
PR6065.R65D48   1996   96-34833 CIP
823'.914—dc20

Printed in the United States of America

10   9   8   7   6   5   4   3   2   1

This book is printed on acid-free paper. ⊚

Book design by Brian Mulligan

THE DEVIL'S FOOTPRINT is a work of fiction, but it was inspired by the ever-present realities of terrorism and the dedication of the few selfless people—and their families—who put themselves on the line so that their fellow citizens can rest easier. Mostly their work is unheralded, unappreciated and, up to now—whatever the public impression given—has certainly been inadequately supported at higher political levels. I hope that this will change and that someday their true story will be told. Meanwhile this adventure story is a tribute.

This book is dedicated to Vaugn Forrest, the Director of the real United States Congressional Task Force on Terrorism and Unconventional Warfare, who has helped to hold the line, despite great difficulties, for a decade and a half—and to his wife, Diane.

The current members of that Congressional Task Force are Congressman Duncan Hunter; Congressman Jim Saxton; Congressman Sonny Bono; Congressman James B. Longley; Congressman Michael Forbes; and Congressman Bill McCollum.

With special thanks to the Chief of Research, Yossef Bodanski, and to Don Morrissey and the staff members of the Task Force.

This book is also dedicated with warmth and regard to Maj. Gen. George A. Crocker and the men and women of the 82nd Airborne Division of the United States Army—with particular reference to my airborne mentor, Lt. Col. Tony Tata.

When the going gets tough—those who wear the hard-earned maroon beret of a paratrooper get airborne within hours, seek out the opposition, jump out of perfectly good aircraft, and do what has to be done with élan and no little humor. At times, they pay a heavy price, but it does not stop them. They believe in their mission. They are remarkable people.

Airborne!

NOTE: Readers are welcome to contact me. Best bet is e-mail.
Best option is: voreilly@iol.ie or 100126.1425@COMPUSERVE.COM

My Web page address is: http//www.iol.ie/voreilly

 CONTENTS

 **PROLOG**

TOKYO BAY, JAPAN

SHE HAD LOOKED like a bundle of rags bobbing in the sea.

They would have passed her by without further thought. But they saw for a brief moment an arm had come out of the water that had seemed to wave. It must have been an illusion, because her eyes were closed and she was quite limp when they approached her.

They had hoisted her into the old fishing boat and taken her down to the small cabin below. Her face was cut from forehead to chin and her clothing seemed to have been scorched and burned.

They bandaged her face as best they could. Then they stripped her and wrapped her in a quilt and laid her on a futon. The space was cramped and smelled of rotting fish, but it was the best they could do.

The old man had gone back to the steering wheel and Hiro to the bow to look for more survivors.

Yoshi was left alone with the woman. He stared at the bandaged face, seeing not that but the lithe body and firm breasts and the V between her legs. Her face would be permanently scarred, he was sure, but she had been a beautiful woman.

More than beautiful. Sexual. Strong. Well muscled. Long lean thighs. Unusually prominent nipples. A woman to dream about.

The quilt slipped from her shoulder and he leaned over to pull it up. She was still unconscious. He was sorely tempted to look again, but then his upbringing interrupted him. He had a duty toward this survivor. One day it could be the other way around. You never knew with the sea.

The woman's clothing lay in a heap in the corner of the cabin. Bored, he knelt beside the wet pile and started to examine the items. They seemed to comprise some sort of uniform. There was a shirt with buttoned pockets like the military wear, and the trousers had side pockets and large external bellows pockets that extended to just above the knees. They were used for maps and other equipment, he supposed.

The helicopter must have been military, he guessed. He picked through the pockets. There was a laminated photograph in one of them. It was slightly blurred, as if it had been taken with a telephoto lens. The subject was a *gaijin*, a man in his midforties, he guessed. There was a military look about him.

Yoshi turned the photograph. There was a description on the back in kanji and a name in English: Hugo Fitzduane.

A friend, an exotic foreign lover, a suspect? This was the kind of conjecture the police used. He shrugged and tossed the photograph to one side.

He had half expected to find identity papers in the shirt, but there was nothing. That was odd if she was military, he thought. But then again, he didn't really know how the military worked. The closest he had come to that world was through television.

There was a bulge in one of the bellows pockets. He remembered that they had seemed heavy when they were being removed, but he had paid no attention at the time, thinking it was just the weight of water in the clothing.

He reached into the pocket. The object inside was hard and round. He removed it and stared at it in disbelief.

The object fell from his frightened fingers and thudded onto the floor. The fishing boat heaved in the swell and the hand grenade rolled across the cabin floor and thudded into the bulkhead.

Yoshi's eyes bulged. He knew he should move, but he stayed there petrified, waiting for the inevitable explosion. His heart thumped and sweat beaded on his forehead.

The boat plunged down into a trough and the hand grenade rolled back toward him. He grabbed it and held it with both hands. The pin was still in place.

Shaking, he put the grenade back into the pocket so it would not roll around. Then he checked the other pockets. There was a length of some thick elasticized cord and a long pocketknife with a button on the side.

He pressed the button and a stiletto blade sprang from the handle and locked into place.

What kind of person would carry such things? he thought. What kind of devil have we dragged from the sea?

Yoshi felt a hand on his shoulder. The touch was gentle, utterly unlike the callused hand of his father grabbing him to do this or that. Always work. More work.

This hand was reassuring. It promised only pleasure. Instantly he thought again of the woman's body, of how she would feel under him.

He turned awkwardly, shuffling on his knees. He was afraid, yet compelled to move.

The woman stood there, her face obscured by the bloodstained bandages, her body golden and perfect in contrast.

She must be in such pain. How could she stand there without showing some sign of her agony? No matter how strong her will, she had to feel weak.

The dressings covered not just her entire face but also her mouth. She could not speak. She put her hand behind his head as he knelt before her, and drew him toward her.

Yoshi could smell her sex, feel her skin. He pulled her toward him, paying no attention as the stiletto was removed from his uncaring fingers.

He felt her hand behind his head and he pressed his face into her loins. He sighed with pleasure.

He bent his head still farther toward her. She held him with her thighs for the brief time it was necessary to plunge the stiletto into the back of his neck.

SHIRO came to spell his father at the wheel. They were heading back to Tokyo. Others were better equipped to carry out a search, and the injured woman needed medical attention. It would have been better still to radio for help, but the batteries were flat. The old man really had no time for the newer ways, and quietly frustrated his son's best efforts. The boat was powered by a fine Yamaha marine diesel, but he still used oil lamps for illumination.

Hori smiled to himself. What could you do with such a father but respect him?

The old man selected some fish and his *kogatana* and took them downstairs to prepare. He'd gut and clean them and then they would eat after they had docked. It was easier to cook when the boat was tied up. Meanwhile, he whiled away the time as they chugged in with a little sake. Or maybe quite a lot of sake.

Shiro expected Yoshi to appear shortly after the old man went below, but then reflected that the pair of them might be discussing their unusual catch and probably sharing the sake flask. Well, tempted though he was to shout down for his share, docking the boat demanded he wait for now.

"Yoshi! Get up here, you lazy sod," Shiro called as he brought the boat alongside the dock. You did not have to be too sober to tie a boat up.

Yoshi did not appear, and Shiro felt some frustration. He moored the boat fore and aft and went below.

The cabin was dark and there was a thick smell stronger even than that of rotting fish. The oil lamp must have gone out.

But why were both the old man and Yoshi silent? Drunk and out cold. Well, it had happened before. And there was the woman to attend to. Someone would have to get help. The catch had to be unloaded. There was work to be done.

He fumbled for a match.

In the flare of the flame he saw his father hanging from a hook, his entrails hanging out of his body. He had been gutted.

Then Shiro saw that the hook was not a hook but his father's favorite *kogatana*, rammed through the old man's throat into the bulkhead.

Yoshi lay at his feet, his clothing and the floor around them crimson with blood.

The match burned down to his fingers and Shiro dropped it.

He was quaking with fear, unable to make sense of anything he saw when the stiletto punched under his chin, through his tongue, and into his brain.

REIKO Oshima lit the oil lamp and surveyed her handiwork.

She was believed to be dead and she would stay that way for the time being. Certainly these fishermen were in no position to argue.

She donned her still-wet clothing but supplemented it with various loose garments belonging to the crew. She was now unrecognizable. Her bandages obscured her features and the additional clothing made it impossible to determine her sex.

An old man, an old boat, and two drunken sons. All the elements of an accident.

The hibachi grill was fired with propane. She opened the valve and set the oil lamp at the far end of the cabin.

She had vanished into the backstreets of Tokyo when the fishing boat blew.

She had drunk some sake before she left to help assuage her pain. All she took with her was the stolen clothing and the laminated photograph of Hugo Fitzduane.

This was the man who had killed her.

This was the man she would kill.

BOOK 1

TERROR

 **CHAPTER ONE**

Washington, D.C.

THE CODED FAX arrived as the three were having their breakfast.

The leader's room contained basic cooking facilities, so the group had prepared the Japanese breakfast they were used to. It was a relief not to have to endure coffee with white powder and foods like croissants saturated in fat. How one could function on such an unhealthy diet was a mystery, Wakami-*san* considered.

The fax was decoded by Jin Endo, the most junior member of the group. His face turned gray as he read it, checking for spelling errors before presenting it to the group leader.

He had sworn to die in the service of Yaibo and had meant every word, but to face the fact that this was the day his life would almost certainly end was hard indeed. He was young and good-looking and the juices flowed. He remembered the young blond intern whom he had tried to talk to the evening before. Her skirt had been swept back above her knees, and her thigh, in the crowded bar, had pressed against his. He was Asian and spoke little English, but she found him attractive, he knew.

She worked in the Farnsworth Building for a congressman from Texas. She had given him her number and extension scribbled on a beer coaster. He had said he was a student visiting Washington with his older brother and uncle. He would be here for a few more days. Look me up, her eyes had said, and the warmth of her body had confirmed the promise. But it would be a promise unfulfilled, for he would be dead.

They gave no thought as to why this man, Patricio Nicanor, had to die, but focused totally on how the order was to be implemented. The most important thing, the order stressed, was that Nicanor be liquidated. They *must* make sure he was killed before he had a chance to speak to anyone in the congressman's office, where the T-Group was based. He must be silenced whatever the cost. The lives of the Yaibo cell members were expendable.

The group leader's stomach churned as he read the decoded fax, but his face displayed no trace of his inner feelings. He had trained for many years for such an occasion and he had developed the ability to separate his normal human reactions from his inner self. His initial feelings might be of shock or fear or extreme stress, but he now knew that these were false reactions. His inner self and his fundamental sense of purpose were what counted.

Death was of no significance, for he was as if already dead. What was important would be the manner of his dying. He had dedicated his life to Yaibo, so what mattered was whether his death was in the service of his organization. He would do what was ordered without hesitation or regret.

The fax contained a digitized photo of the target that had been broken up into a dozen segments and then spread amongst the kanji text. It would scarcely fool the computers of the NSA, but it was certainly sufficient to deceive the hotel clerk who had delivered the message.

Endo cut up the fax with a scissors and reassembled the pieces of the picture. What emerged was the picture of a Latin male in his early thirties. It was a clear photo, but it was more indicative of a type than an individual. From the photograph alone they could not be certain beyond a doubt who their target was.

Wakami looked at his senior colleague. Matsunaga-*san* had worked with him for many years. They were the same age and had joined Yaibo at the same time, and their thoughts were as one.

Wakami had not spoken, but Matsunago-*san* nodded. "There is only one certain way of getting the right man, Wakami-*san*. We know where he is going and we know roughly when he is due. We must kill him inside the congressional building as he approaches his goal. That way his guard will be down and we can be certain."

"But how, Wakami-*san*?" said Endo. "There are guards at the entrances and everyone is searched."

"That is a problem we have still to resolve," said Wakami, "but we are not entirely unprepared. There is certainly a solution."

Then Endo asked the question that had been haunting him. He hesitated, and the words rushed out as if they had a life of their own. Immediately he regretted having spoken. This was not appropriate behavior from a junior colleague, and indeed he already knew the answer. But he was young and he was afraid, and he had to ask. His hands, clasped in front of him in a posture of respect as he stood there, were damp with sweat and shaking.

"Wakami-*san*," he said. "How will we escape after we have killed this man?"

Wakami looked at his young colleague with affection. How little the young know, he thought, and how petty are their concerns.

"Endo-*san*," he said, "your concern that you might be taken alive is worthy indeed. You must trust me. I know you will do your duty."

Endo bowed in submission. His bowels had turned to liquid. His life, one way or another, would end this very day. It was certain. He could smell the very skin of the young blond intern, carefree and enthusiastic. She had her whole life ahead of her. He wanted to sob out loud. He straightened and was once again in control. There was a task to perform.

Oshima-*san* trusted him and had initiated him personally. He would not let her down.

THEY entered the outskirts of Washington, D.C.

Twenty minutes later, Warner gave a uniformed guard a wave. It was acknowledged by a nod of recognition, the barrier was raised, and they shot into the basement car park of the Farnsworth Building. It was a mildly handsome but otherwise unremarkable light gray stone building housing four hundred and fifty elected members and their staffs of the Congress of the United States of America.

Fitzduane looked around the drab basement parking area. The place was two-thirds empty. There was nothing to distinguish this parking lot from tens of thousands of conventional commercial-building lots, but still the knowledge that he was now in the very core of the most powerful political center on earth gave him pause for thought.

From this complex of buildings flowed the legislation that made the United States of America.

Fitzduane loved the United States. He was not so sure about its capital.

But the bottom line was that Washington, D.C., counted. It was not a question of whether you liked what they did there or not. The power was real.

Warner hopped out of the car and stretched. Then he came around to Fitzduane's side. The Irishman was still sitting there lost in thought.

"Yeah," said Warner, "it really makes you think when you come here the first time. This really is IT—the House, the Senate, the Supreme Court. All that good shit. The State Department, the FBI, the Pentagon. All those organs of the United States government just waiting to serve.

"It's enough to bring a lump to your throat. You think little old you can make a difference. You go around glowing for a few days, maybe a few weeks, possibly a month or two. And then you start very slowly to understand as the structure starts almost imperceptibly to destroy you.

"It is nearly *impossible* to get anything done in this fucking place. All this talent and ambition, all hundred senators and four hundred and fifty congressmen and twenty thousand staffers and eighty thousand lobbyists cancel each other out. The Founding Fathers wanted checks and balances, and they surely did succeed."

Fitzduane smiled. "Hell of a speech, Dan," he said.

Warner grinned. "You wouldn't believe me if I said I liked it."

Fitzduane walked with Warner to the elevator.

"How is security on the Hill?" he said. "I noticed we weren't stopped on the way in, and I didn't see you show a pass, Dan."

Warner grunted. "Basically, it sucks," he said, "but I guess you can't entirely blame the Capitol Hill police. They are supposed to keep the bad guys out while letting the public in. That is pretty damned difficult. But they go through the motions. If you had not been with me, Hugo, and went in the main entrance upstairs you would have had to walk through a metal detector, and your bag, if you had one, would go through a scanner. But there are ways around that shit. The Task Force thinks security should be tightened, but the politicians don't want to lose any votes. Guess who is winning?"

Fitzduane smiled. The elevator reached the second floor.

LEE Cochrane, Chief of Staff of the Congressional Task Force on Terrorism, glared at his subordinate.

Maurice Isser, a complex hybrid of French-Canadian, Russian, and Jewish origin—now neatly packaged as American—was, at times, a near-impossible man. He got away with it because he was inarguably a genius at both intelligence and analysis. But one of his many quirks was his absolute paranoia when it came to meeting new people. He hated the initial contact at any time, but never more so than when he was not well prepared and softened up in advance.

Cochrane was going to strangle the man. He was going to positively *enjoy* strangling the man. The prospect was cheering.

"Maury," said Cochrane, "all I want you to do is meet him. You can't spend your life as the Invisible Man or peering out of a slit in the stationery closet. Someone is going to wrap a canvas jacket around you and cart you away."

"Why didn't you tell me?" said Maury in an aggrieved voice.

Cochrane looked up at the ceiling, which was of little help. It needed painting badly. The federal budget was certainly not being spent here.

"You were traveling," said Cochrane soothingly.

"Fitzduane," said Maurice, "who is he? What's his history?"

"Jesus, Maury," said Cochrane, "you want history, I'll give you history."

He sighed. "About seven hundred years ago, a Norman knight, Sir Hugo Fitzduane, part of the initial British invasion force of Ireland, quarreled with someone on high and then left the main force and set off for the West of Ireland.

"He fought the bad guys, married a local Irish princess, and found himself an island off the West of Ireland to build a castle on. Duncleeve, it's called. The Castle of the Sword. It says a great deal of what you need to know about the Fitzduanes.

"All these centuries later, a Hugo Fitzduane still lives there. The Fitzduanes seem to be a persistent bunch with something of a—'What I have I hold' outlook on life. And a tradition of arms."

The swivel chair began to turn slowly. Cochrane had Maury's attention.

"The present Fitzduane followed that tradition. He joined the Irish Army and was posted to the Congo with the United Nations. Special forces. His commander was a Colonel Shane Kilmara. His unit racked up quite a reputation for itself. The Congo in those days was something of a bloodbath."

"Ah!" said Maury. "*General* Kilmara these days, I think. Now it's coming back to me. He's turned up all over the globe over the last couple of decades. He is probably the best counterterrorist military man out there."

About bloody time, thought Cochrane. Maury never forgot anything, but he did not always remember where he stored what he knew and the protocol was to help him to find it.

"Kilmara seems to have always accepted his calling as a warrior. Fitzduane was more ambivalent and has always had something of a love-hate relationship with violence. He resigned from the army after the Congo business and then spent the next twenty years as a combat photographer. Cover of *Time*, that kind of thing. Still, you name a war and he's been there. The word is that he's forgotten more about combat than most generals ever knew.

"The word also has it that though Fitzduane is a reluctant warrior he has proven to be *very* good in combat. One of the best."

"The Hangman affair," breathed Maury.

Cochrane nodded. "It was a classic counterterrorist operation, and during it our friend Hugo Fitzduane began to lose his amateur status. He was to find out the hard truth that once you enter the game, it is nearly impossible to leave it alive. A few years later, when he thought the whole Hangman thing had blown over, a hit team of Japanese Yaibo terrorists bent on revenge landed on his island and shot up both him and his young son. Both recovered, but it was a close thing. After he had sorted out that little affair, he realized if he was going to be forced to be a permanent player he had better become a good one."

"I've got it!" said Maury, rising to his feet and beginning to prowl around the office. "This is the same man who set up that counterterrorism think tank. We trade information, but I deal with a man called Henssen, a German, I think."

"Yeah," said Cochrane, "Henssen runs the show on a day-to-day basis, leaving Fitzduane time to pursue his various other interests, which include an involvement with the Rangers, Ireland's special forces. Hugo Fitzduane is a reserve colonel with them and still very close to Kilmara."

Maury suddenly paused in his pacing and froze, his back hunched.

Cochrane sighed. Maury was remembering again that he had not been consulted. It was time for diplomacy or Maury would suddenly make a break for it.

"It was your idea, Maury," said Cochrane, lying, his blue eyes guileless. "Since we're blocked from using U.S. forces, let's find someone else to do the job. So while you were away, we looked and came up with Fitzduane. He thinks he's coming here on a routine courtesy visit, but I think we can persuade him. That is why I want him to meet Patricio."

Maury's interest was engaged again. He picked up Fitzduane's file and studied it intently, then he read Cochrane's notes.

"There is no report here from Patricio," said Maury accusingly.

"Patricio did not like to go into any detail over a Mexican phone," said Cochrane, "nor any U.S. phone, given the currently political climate." He grinned and looked at his paranoid friend. "That is something you understand, Maury. Anyway, relax. Patricio has made it out of Mexico. He rang from National half an hour ago. He'll be here any minute."

"Did he say anything?" said Maury.

"He sounded immensely relieved to be out of Mexico in one piece, and he said he had brought some physical evidence."

"Evidence of what?" said Maury.

"I have absolutely no fucking idea," said Cochrane cheerfully. "He just said that the whole thing was more serious than we had thought, and he added it was the luck of the devil that Rheiman had made it down there. Rheiman meant diddly to me, but Patricio was anxious to get over here, so I figured it could wait."

Maury crashed back into his swivel chair and rotated it a few times, his legs stretched straight out in front of him. Suddenly, he dropped his feet as he centered on Cochrane, bringing the chair to an immediate halt.

He leaned forward to emphasize his words.

"Why should Colonel Hugo Fitzduane, this good-natured Irish aristocrat with his island and his castle and his think tank, go on a mission for us? According to what I read here, he's recently married and he has a young son by a previous arrangement. Why would he risk his life to do the Task Force's dirty work?"

"Well," said Cochrane, "that's the beauty of it. Fitzduane doesn't know it yet, but there's a problem down there he won't be able to walk away from. Remember a certain someone who was reported as being very dead but reappeared in Tecuno? A Japanese connection? A certain Reiko Oshima?"

Maury thought for a few seconds, then a look of perfect understanding came over his face. "A brilliant plan, Lee," he said.

"Entirely your concept, Maury," said Cochrane tactfully.

 **CHAPTER TWO**

THE LANDING WAS not one of the airline's finest.

It belonged to the "any landing you can walk away from is good" variety by a slim margin, but Patricio Nicanor was so relieved to be on U.S. soil that he felt like hugging the pilot and then kissing the world-weary face of the Washington National Airport immigration official who queried him.

Patricio's only baggage was a shoulder-slung carry-on one-suiter. He stopped at a kiosk and bought two foldaway nylon shopping bags and a length of strapping, the kind used to bind and identify a suitcase. He then headed for the rest room and entered the stall reserved for the physically disabled.

He needed the extra space to open his suitcase. The two packages inside, each contained in a thick bubble envelope about the size of a paperback book, had aroused the interest of customs. "Mining samples," Patricio had said, and had opened the retaining clip of one of the packages and pulled out a plastic bag containing what looked like concrete chippings.

The customs man had looked at Patricio's profession, which was written into his passport. "Ingeniero de Minas," it said in Spanish. Samples seemed to make sense.

Obtaining the contents of the two packages had been both difficult and dangerous in the extreme. Patricio wanted to keep them as close as possible until he delivered them to his friends in Congress.

Removing his jacket and working swiftly, he constructed a simple harness that hung each package securely under each arm like twin shoulder holsters. Both strapping and bags were of strong black nylon.

He replaced his jacket. He would look somewhat bulkier, but nothing could be seen. It would be safer to have the items actually on his person.

He reshouldered the carry-on case, made a brief phone call to Cochrane, and found a cab.

They had a funny charging system, he remembered. Zones instead of a meter. What you might call a game of chance if you were a tourist.

WARNER started to emit electronic chirping sounds as they left the elevator on the floor where the subcommittee offices were located. He made a gesture of apology at Fitzduane and reached under his T-shirt for the compact mobile phone that was clipped there.

"You got the Irishman?" said Cochrane cryptically.

"Yo!" said Warner. "We've just got out of the elevator and we are down the hall. I can shout if this thing breaks down."

"Shit!" said Cochrane. "Wiseass!" he added.

"Maury?" said Warner.

"Yeah," said Cochrane. "We've still got a few things to settle, and Patricio's not here yet. Give me fifteen. Maybe prep Fitzduane a little."

"Lee's schedule is running late," said Warner. "I'll buy you a cup of coffee."

The cafeteria was nearly empty. Warner picked a quiet corner.

"The Task Force," said Warner. "Lee asked me to prep you. What do you know about us, Hugo?"

Fitzduane smiled. "I've read your reports and traded information with you. I figured you were worth visiting. Beyond that, I know little."

Warner nodded. "The Task Force was started by Lee. He made a bargain with Congressman Wayne Sanders. Lee would get Sanders elected if Sanders would back the setting up of a subcommittee on terrorism. Lee had come out of Vietnam feeling the U.S. was selling itself short and no one in power seemed to be paying any serious attention to dealing with the threats that were popping up all over the globe."

"Why didn't Lee run himself?" asked Fitzduane.

Warner laughed. "Lee Cochrane suffers from a bad case of integrity. In short, he is no politician, but he is bright and committed and knows his strengths and his weaknesses, so he found another way. He would piggyback right in as close to the center of power as he could get. He might prefer to work in the White House or the Senate, but he's a realist."

"What got Lee focused on terrorism?" said Fitzduane. "It's an abstract to most people. Normally, it is only when you are touched personally that you start to take notice. Then you realize that the world is a vastly more dangerous place than most people like to believe."

Warner nodded. "Lee had a commanding officer in Vietnam he much admired. The guy went on to work for the CIA, got kidnapped by fundamentalists in the Lebanon, was tortured over many months and then hanged. That incident set him off. He also believed various agencies of the United States government did little about it."

"So how do you guys really operate?" said Fitzduane. "Congress is there to legislate, not go hunting down bad guys. The media would have a field day if a bunch of armed staffers started invading sovereign nations and taking out terrorists. Look at Ollie North, and he didn't shoot anyone. Well, not that I know of, anyway."

Warner laughed. "Ollie's heart and head don't always synchronize too well," he said, "but he's not the worst. Look at the *Achille Lauro* affair. The guys who killed the hostage in the wheelchair cut a deal with the Egyptians and were going to get away.

"Ollie got their aircraft forced down. Was he right? I think he was. The United States of America should not sit idly by when its citizens are killed."

Fitzduane drank some coffee. He did not dispute the basic thrust of Warner's argument, but he was having a hard time getting a fix on what a small group of motivated staffers could actually do against the reality of physical threat.

"We're a small group with the great advantage of having a simple mission," said Warner, "and that task is the identification and destruction of terrorism insofar as it threatens this country. And all of the team identify with that mission. We are not riddled with factions and feuds like the CIA and the FBI, or faced with opposing agendas like State or Treasury. Our rationale is not primarily our own preservation. And we care."

Fitzduane's interest was piqued. He was well familiar with the CIA and State situations, but Treasury was a player he had not encountered much previously. "Treasury?" he asked.

"It's a story that makes a point about how we let them get away with it," said Warner. "When the Shah of Iran was in power, the Iranian government was considered a close ally of the West. Better yet, Iran was a major purchaser of Western goods. The Shah wanted the latest and the best, and because he had oil, he could afford it. Along with the tanks and the aircraft and the missiles, the U.S. supplied him with the latest in printing technology so that he could get his profile just right on the Iranian currency.

"Unfortunately, the equipment he bought was exactly the same as that used by the United States mint. Enter the Ayatollah and a bunch of fundamentalists who do not have the West's best interests at heart and suddenly we have a whole flood of crisp new dollars that are so technically perfect they are almost impossible to tell from the real thing.

"It gets worse. The Syrians see the Iranians playing the game and Uncle Sam sitting idly by doing nothing, and they set up a raft of printing presses in the

Bekaa Valley. Their quality is not as good but, hey, they've got volume on their side and they go after the lower end of the market."

"How much are we talking about here?" said Fitzduane.

"We say in our briefings a billion dollars a month because a higher figure is hard to swallow. Actually, we estimate a multiple of that—year after year for well over a decade. We are getting close to talking real money! The situation has gotten so bad that in parts of the world you have to sign each note and leave your address so that they have a comeback if someone down the line complains. So much for confidence in the dollar. No wonder it's worth less every year."

Fitzduane laughed. "So where does Treasury come into all this?"

"We are talking economic terrorism here," said Warner, "we are talking forgery on a scale so huge that Treasury, who will set the Secret Service on you if you so much as photocopy a dollar bill, do diddly. They are afraid if it gets out the dollar will take a dive, so they say and do nothing. Also, the Secret Service are not really set up to invade foreign countries. So we are going to end up changing our currency, but the guys we are up against are bright, so they won't just fold their tents and steal away. Goddamn it, they can now *certainly* afford the latest gear and we have been only too happy to sell them it. The U.S. has a balance-of-trade problem. We need exports. It's a hell of a thing; a hell of a thing. But the bottom line is that the United States government is nearly its own worst enemy."

Fitzduane's spread hands and the look on his face indicated acknowledgment of the validity of at least some of what was being said, but also a mild impatience that the question he had already asked twice had not been answered.

Warner grinned. "Okay," he said. "Let's focus. You want to know what we do and how we operate. We run an intelligence and analysis group based upon a very large network of contacts. There are many people who think like we do in structures like the CIA and State. The structures may be ossified and gridlocked by policy, but individuals have not lost their desire to do the right thing. We have connections as far afield as Afghanistan and as near as down the hall. We link them together, make sense of the pieces, and analyze the result. Then we feed our reports to the right people. Sometimes we get a result. More often we get filed. It's not easy."

"And you also legislate?" said Fitzduane.

"Sure," said Warner. "We work in Congress and that's what Congress does. And within the legislative process we pursue our own agenda. If we strengthen a program that can stem the terrorist tide, that is what we do. We have some successes. Mostly, it's a whole lot of work for very little return. The Founding Fathers did not set up this place to be efficient. That is understandable, but today's threats did not exist when they were around. Nor were they foreseen."

"It sounds like a great deal of work for a modest return," said Fitzduane carefully. "It also sounds exceedingly frustrating."

"Well, Hugo," said Warner, "now you are getting to the real meat. There are some situations where we cannot just sit on our hands like good citizens. Sometimes the threat is so major and the response so minimal that we have to take some action."

"So how does that work?" said Fitzduane.

"We find the right people and light the blue touch-paper," said Warner. "It is not exactly subcontracting—more a case of facilitating." He looked steadily at Fitzduane. "Like right now we have a situation in Mexico."

"No," said Fitzduane flatly. "And this being a political town, that is not—'no' meaning I'm willing to negotiate." He smiled. "Just so we understand each other."

"I think you may change your mind," said Warner cheerfully, "when you have heard a little more. As far as Mexico is concerned, you're already involved. Drafted by circumstances, you might say."

Fitzduane looked at Warner blankly and then shook his head firmly. He had great respect for the subcommittee's counterterrorism reports and he was looking forward to meeting the people who did the work, but that was where it ended.

He could not conceive of any reason why he would want to be involved with Mexico in any way except to visit Acapulco and work on his suntan. That notion did have some appeal given the state of Ireland's weather. Even the snakes had fled because they were sick of the rain.

"No," he repeated, "or as you say over here—'no way!' "

Warner grinned. "You didn't say 'positively,' " he said. His belt began to cheep.

He answered the mobile and then looked at Fitzduane. "Maury has stopped swinging from the chandelier and Patricio has just passed through security. Time to enlighten you, Hugo, about some dirty work south of the border. And then I know you will do the right thing. You may be Irish and your grandmother Spanish, but where it counts you are a true-blue American."

"Lead on, Ollie," said Fitzduane wearily. But his curiosity was aroused, and the Fitzduanes, as a family, were nothing if not curious.

Over the centuries it had killed more than a few of them.

F O R all the talk of congressional perquisites, the Farnsworth Building was a utilitarian structure.

Inside, once you got past the entrance lobbies, it was little more than floor after floor of wide, imposing corridors with rather poky office suites leading off them for individual congressmen. The splendid marbled hallways had been given a higher priority than the humans who worked in the building.

A major corporation would have been embarrassed by the crowded conditions of most of the offices. Typically, a congressman had a three-room suite with a tiny reception lobby and waiting area. One room housed the congressman, the second his chief of staff, and the third as many of his staff as could be squeezed in. If you were a staffer, it helped greatly if you were small and thin. Or even tall and thin. The offices had high ceilings.

"Hugo, the U.S. of A. is run by kids," said Warner as they ambled back to the office. He glanced across at Fitzduane and grinned. "It confuses the shit out of the other side, whoever they are these days. God! Bring back the Cold War. It was so beautifully simple."

Fitzduane raised an eyebrow.

Warner needed no further encouragement. "The workload in this place is ridiculous," he said happily. "The average elected official spends most of his time working on being reelected—on his image—and commuting to and from his constituency. Any surplus time is spent taking his TV makeup off, bogged down in procedure, sitting in meetings, and getting drunk and screwing around because he or she is working so hard. So he hasn't a snowball's chance of actually reading the stuff he votes on, and certainly not in detail.

"Hell, man, consider the numbers and the crazy way this place operates. A single bill can run to thousands of pages. And the House rules are of a scale of complexity that even Machiavelli would admire. And they keep changing."

"So where do kids come in?" asked Fitzduane obligingly.

"Since the elected have not the time to do the job they were voted in to do, the staffers have to do it. However, there is a twist here too. Members do not like being accused of spending too much money on themselves, so they have voted a peanut budget for staffers.

"That means two things. First, few people with a useful body of experience can afford to stay here. As they get older they acquire family commitments, and this is an expensive town. They leave and become lobbyists or head back to the boonies and live on their war stories. Second, staffs are heavily padded out with teenage interns who work for honor and glory and an entry on their CV. They get paid nothing.

"It's a mighty peculiar system. It means the U.S. legislature, if you get right down to it, is operated by a bunch of teenagers working for free. And since the U.S. is *the* superpower these days, it explains a lot. God bless America!"

"So what about you and Lee and Maury?" said Fitzduane. "You're not exactly still in diapers."

Warner halted and faced Fitzduane. "Well, Hugo," he said lightly, "I guess we're kind of unusual."

Fitzduane was getting used to Dan Warner's exuberance, but on this point he did not think the deputy chief of staff was joking. Loose cannon or the right stuff? He had some thoughts on the matter, but it was much too early to be sure.

I T was fortunate that the Yaibo team were already in place.

Wakami's unit had not come to Washington specifically for a killing, but they had been reconnoitering the city for future incidents. They had already checked out many of the government facilities.

These had included the Farnsworth Building. They had been in and out on several occasions and had even visited offices near those of Congressman Wayne Sanders, where the Task Force on Terrorism was located.

They had been able to survey nearly the length and breadth of the capital without hindrance, because they presented themselves not as tourists but as a lobbying group. Since the Japanese were particularly energetic at using the U.S. lobbying system to advance and protect Japanese interests—even when they were quite contrary to American interests—three more Japanese lobbyists attracted no attention at all.

Wakami had even had business cards printed identifying them as "The Osaka Industries United States Friendship Group," and these brought general access.

Senators, congressmen, and their staffers were permanently on the lookout for money, influence, and votes in roughly that order. Everyone knew that Japanese businessmen had money, rice sacks full of it, and that bought influence.

It all added up to a warm welcome for Wakami-*san* and his people. Wakami, who spoke adequate English, had become quite good at making long speeches about mutual friendship in Japanese and having Endo translate in halting English while politicians, their eyes glazed over, stood smiling. Photographs of such events were expected, even encouraged. Lining up a target assassination list, complete with full-color illustrations, had never been easier.

Armed with his copy of *The World Almanac of U.S. Politics,* bought in Sidney Kramers Bookstore, and *The United States House of Representatives Telephone Directory,* given to him by a friendly staffer who fancied switching to a better-paid job as a lobbyist for Japan, Wakami had Endo line up an appointment with Lee Cochrane's office.

Cochrane-*san* might be running the counterterrorism Task Force with minimal staff, but he also had a demanding political role as chief of staff for his congressman. Wearing his political hat, he would see Wakami and his team or at least have him received—if only by an intern not yet old enough to drink legally.

The important thing was that Wakami now had access into the subcommittee's offices, and if a guard at the entrance called up—though that was most unlikely— their credibility would be already established.

He and his people could wait in the subcommittee's reception until his target came into sight. He would delay any meeting until a mythical missing member of the group would turn up. With a bit of luck they would even be given tea. He was not worried about being recognized later.

All three members of Osaka Industries United States Friendship Group quite deliberately had identical haircuts, horn-rimmed glasses, and clothing. To Americans, they would be like peas in a 120-million-population pod.

In Wakami's opinion, it all said a great deal about how the United States regarded terrorism, not that he was complaining. Well, they would learn the hard way. He decided they would go in the main entrance. There was more traffic that way, so the guards would be busier.

That left him with the decision as to how the actual killing of the target should be carried out. Their instructions emphasized that he must be killed and they must be sure he was dead. A dying man could still talk.

To get through the metal detector and scanner, the killing would have to be carried out without either firearms or even the traditional blade. Yet death must be certain and immediate.

There was really only one absolutely foolproof way Wakami could think of.

Finally, Wakami thought about how the members of the team might escape. "Escape," of course, was a relative term.

THE liquid explosives came in as double-walled ampoules of insulin.

The guard at the main entrance had spotted the two containers and the hypodermic on the scanner through the sides of the briefcase, but his voice was sympathetic as he routinely checked the items.

The word "Insulin" was printed on both labels, together with the name of the prescribing doctor and the pharmacy. In that context, the hypodermic required no explanation.

If he had been able to check the ampoules, it would have made no difference unless he had spotted and opened the sealed double wall. There was genuine insulin at the core. It was a useful poison for some situations. Injecting a large dose into a normal healthy person was lethal and hard to detect. The body naturally dispenses insulin into the bloodstream when unduly stressed, and imminent death comes into that category.

The outer wall of the ampoule contained enough explosive to equal the force of a hand grenade.

The guard did not query the other items.

The killing weapon came in as an extension cable for the camera. The cable normally consisted of an outer flexible core and a thin inner wire. Pushing a release at one end pushed a plunger out the other and activated the shutter release. In this case, the ends constituted no more than decorations. The substance was the razor-sharp serrated inner wire.

The other weapons were short "punch daggers"—ultrathin needle blades with a crosspiece making a T, which were clenched in the fist and punched in when stabbing. They were built into each man's briefcase looking like part of the reinforcing frame, with the crosspiece being the designer handle. Each man had one. The blades had no cutting edge but were strong enough when stabbing to pierce even most body armor.

FITZDUANE'S eyes caught Maury's briefly as he entered the room. Maury smiled very slightly and gently, as if it were entirely normal to greet someone while half-concealed behind a drape.

"Hugo, a pleasure," said Cochrane.

Unlike Warner and the other staffers, the marine-trim chief of staff was formally dressed, his shirt white and crisp and his tie regimental. The style was that of a military man in civilian clothes, but the eyes were not just those of a direct man of action. There was a look of introspection here. They were the guarded eyes of a very intelligent man who had seen much to disappoint him but still believed. Fitzduane was mildly irritated at himself for being surprised. He had expected surface polish and competence. He was faced with someone who was more substantial and decidedly more complex.

Fitzduane had read the reports put out by the Task Force on Terrorism. Those who originated them knew—really understood—how their special world worked. And Maury, from what he had heard and read, would not work with a fool. Fitzduane smiled to himself. He trusted he would prove up to the mark.

Maury stayed behind his curtain and said nothing. The situation would have been unusual enough, but the chief of staff's office was comparatively small. Maury was not some discreet watcher from a distance but stood only a few feet away, as if sheer willpower and his very still composure would make him invisible. There was room just for a desk and two scuffed leather sofas with a small table in the middle.

This was a functional place for meeting and talking, not designed to impress. The one exception was a small case containing medals and a photograph of two men in fatigues.

Vietnam. Fitzduane looked at the mementos with mixed emotions. He had been young then, too, and in some ways it had been the best of times. But too many friends had died there.

Cochrane saw Fitzduane's glance. "Not mine," he said. "They belong to the man who inspired all this. His widow wanted me to have them."

"I'm sure you have your own, Lee," said Fitzduane.

Cochrane nodded somewhat stiffly. "The military give them out by the shit-load. They're not what counts. It's what you stand for and what you do. All I did was show up."

Fitzduane nodded. More than many, he reflected.

Standing to one side of Fitzduane, Warner was suddenly struck by the fanciful notion that he was watching the meeting of two knights from the Middle Ages.

Both had warrior stamped all over them. Both were being friendly enough on the face of it, and on the face of it had similar values, but there was still an unspoken competitive element between them. On second thought, the competitive factor probably emanated from Lee. Hugo Fitzduane had actually done the kind of things that Lee merely aspired to do. Of course, Lee had certainly served his time, but that was many years ago. Fitzduane had also been in Vietnam but had had major encounters with terrorism twice—the latter as recently as a year ago.

Lee, the paper pusher, was encountering the adventurer. The chief of staff was competitive from gullet to zatch. It could not be easy for him. Worse, he had to behave himself.

He wanted to enlist the Irishman's help, and Colonel Hugo Fitzduane did not look someone you could lead by the nose. Warner was silently amused. This was going to be fun.

Of course, what two gallant knights like Cochrane and Fitzduane were doing within the confines of Congress was another matter entirely. The Hill was not about daring deeds and gallantry. It was about politics, and that was a cold, reality-based world.

"Lee?" Tanya, one of the full-time receptionists, put her head around the door. "Before you get comfortable . . . There is that Japanese delegation, and Patricio has just arrived."

Cochrane gestured at Fitzduane. "Take a seat, Hugo, and I'll be back in a moment. Dan can introduce you to our friend from Mexico while I exchange pleasantries with our Japanese friends. I gather it is just a courtesy call."

He looked back at Tanya. "Show Patricio in here. I'll see our Japanese visitors in the congressman's office. Have they had tea?"

Tanya nodded. Cochrane grinned. Tanya knew the drill.

"So let's do it," he said. The receptionist backed away and Lee headed toward the door, then waited inside to give Patricio a quick greeting before temporarily ducking out. There were always too many people to see, never enough time, and certainly not enough space. Juggling all the elements was like playing with a Rubik's Cube.

There was no warning.

"What are you . . . Aaagh! My God! My God! They're killing us. They're kill—"

The shouts and short piercing screams were truncated before their full dreadful meaning was understood.

The sounds of people dying belonged to other worlds, not to the paper and verbal wars on the Hill.

They looked at each other uncertainly. There were TV sets everywhere, monitoring Congress on C-Span. Someone had switched into a drama and turned the volume up too loud. It was not real.

Realization came too late.

The door crashed wide open, forcing Cochrane backward and he tripped over the small table in the confined space and then collapsed onto the floor with it upended in front of him.

Warner stood up to help and Fitzduane was blocked.

"Huh-huh-huh-huh-haaaaaa . . ."

The sound of dying.

Patricio Nicanor stood in the open doorway, the expression on his face compounded of shock and horror and fear and pain and something much worse.

It was the look of a fellow human animal *knowing* he was losing his life—and that was elemental and singularly disturbing to behold.

Even as they watched, and that brief moment seemed to take an eternity, his eyes bulged and his throat gaped open in a wet crimson smile.

There was a loud cry of triumph and effort from behind him, and then blood spurted from his torso and his head toppled from his body and rolled toward them.

Patricio's headless body was still erect, his heart still pumping blood, crimson spewing from the bloody stump. Then the corpse was released and slid to the ground.

The killer was suddenly revealed. He stood there for an infinitesimal moment with the bloody steel garrote in his hands and a look of triumph on his face.

Shouts came from the general office, and Fitzduane saw the terrorist begin to turn while letting one end of the garrote fall from his right hand and then reaching into the side pocket of his jacket.

There was the *whumph* of an explosion closely followed by screams of pain that were all the more disturbing for being muted.

Fitzduane's brain fought to process competing messages.

Logic dictated that what he was seeing could not be happening. He was in a safeguarded environment.

Instinct, brutally reinforced by the odors of death, told him that if he did not do something quickly he would be joining Patricio Nicanor.

Survival more than logic was the dominant force on this occasion.

Desperately, he looked around Cochrane's office for a weapon—anything, even a paper knife or an unloaded war souvenir.

There was nothing except an embossed coffee mug.

Anything can be a weapon!

He seized the mug by its base, leaped over the temporarily sprawled figures of Cochrane and Warner, and punched the Japanese full force in the face with the open rim as the terrorist was turning back to Cochrane's office after throwing the grenade.

Fitzduane put everything he had behind the blow. The shock of the vicious impact ran up his arm and jarred his shoulder, and he grunted with the pain and effort.

The mug shattered, virtually exploding.

Shards penetrated the assassin's face. The impact broke both Wakami's nose and cheekbone, temporarily stunning him.

Edged metal slammed into the door frame beside Fitzduane as he ducked in reflex. He realized he would have been stabbed if the first killer's dazed body had not impeded his attacker.

He pivoted, smashed his elbow into his new assailant's stomach, and jabbed with the broken remains of the coffee mug at the back of the hand holding the weapon.

The hand was caught between the blow and the door frame, and Fitzduane was fighting with the force of true desperation.

The man gave a shriek of agony as the bones in his hand were shattered and he lost his grip on the punch dagger.

Fitzduane grabbed the man's arm, the bloody hand dangling uselessly from it, dropped to one knee, and threw the terrorist over his shoulder into Cochrane's office.

Fitzduane then wrenched the strange-looking weapon from the wood. It felt like a woodworker's tool in his hand; the general shape was like a gimlet, but the blade was like a short, thin stiletto.

His movements flowing one into the other, he raised the slumped head of his original attacker with a hard palm blow under the chin.

As his head came up, Fitzduane hooked his right arm around and stabbed the needlelike blade into the man's ear.

The terrorist jerked upright in a horrified spasm as the punch dagger cut into him and his mouth opened as if to scream, but the point had entered his brain before the pain message could be implemented.

He collapsed lifeless like an abandoned puppet.

Fitzduane looked back into Cochrane's office.

The terrorist he had thrown there had fallen on the edge of table that had been lying on its side since Cochrane had tripped over it. The impact had driven the air out of his lungs, and while he lay there gasping, Cochrane had taken his own belt off, made a sliding noose with the belt buckle, and looped it around the fallen man's neck.

The terrorist kicked desperately as the noose tightened, and his one good hand flailed as he tried to loosen the unrelenting grip.

Warner tried to pinion his legs. The terrorist writhed, his strength formidable in his desperation. His legs kicked clear. Cochrane suddenly jerked the noose at an angle with all his strength.

Fitzduane could hear the sound of the man's neck snapping.

Cochrane, his tie askew and his hair rumpled but ever the chief of staff, looked up at Fitzduane. "We're okay, Hugo. Check outside. There may be others."

It was a point that Fitzduane had considered. Reacting to immediate threat had been a matter of instinct. Now he left the shelter of the door frame with some caution.

There were going to be a bunch of trigger-happy Capitol police here any moment, and that thought did not fill him with a sense of well-being. Also, there could be other terrorists. There had been only two waiting in the reception area, but that did not mean that there were not more waiting nearby.

Space was so limited in the offices that his short journey from the door frame of Cochrane's office was through a corridor of filing cabinets. The distance was only about six feet until the space widened, but it represented temporary safety and Fitzduane was not enthusiastic about stepping into the unknown.

But some things just *had* to be done. He had to leave his steel-drawer haven and hope nobody was waiting around the corner with unfriendly thoughts. The image of Patricio Nicanor being decapitated was still emblazoned on his mind, and the unfortunate man's body and severed head lay just behind him.

He moved forward.

There was a cacophony of shouts and cries and moaning noise coming from the general office on the left, but the reception area seemed unnaturally quiet.

He tried to remember the layout.

There had been receptionists working either side behind built-in desks as he came in. One was Tanya. He did not know the others' names. There was a petite brunette in her late twenties. And there had been someone else filing, he seemed to recall. All he had seen was a man's white shirt and the kind of thick hair you have only when you are very young. An intern.

He heard a noise behind him and whirled, the little dagger gripped in his fist, the blade protruding from between his clenched fingers.

Maury stood behind him. He had forgotten all about Maury during the action. The uncharitable thought came to him that it would have been nice if Maurice had intervened earlier, but then he realized that there really had been neither time nor opportunity.

Only seconds had passed, and the leader had initially been cut off from the action by the sprawled bodies of Cochrane and Warner. So he had kept his head and moved when it was appropriate. Of course, Maury, though he was the antithesis of the man of action in appearance, had actually seen more combat than most. He knew about all this stuff, and in this situation that was reassuring.

Maury raised his finger to his lips, indicated right and then at himself. He then indicated Fitzduane and left, and there was a question on his face.

Fitzduane nodded in agreement but felt a chill run through him.

He was getting sloppy. Congress was not in session. He had forgotten all about the empty congressman's office. Because maybe it was not empty, and if he had turned left as he had planned his back would have been to the office. He could almost feel the blade being hammered into his kidneys.

Both men were about to move when they were momentarily brought to a halt by a rivulet of crimson that flowed slowly around the last file cabinet.

Fitzduane was sick inside. He looked at Maury and held up three fingers and brought them down one by one. "Three, two, one, GO!" they mouthed silently in unison, and both moved away from the cover of the cabinets into the reception area and to left and right, respectively.

Tanya lay sprawled on the ground, her arms up in front of her face as if to ward off her attacker. The upper half of her dress was saturated with blood and the material was ripped and torn as if she had been struck a series of blows.

The other receptionist had died at her desk.

She was slumped forward over the computer keyboard, and a bloody hole at the base of her neck showed how she had died.

There was a third body in the main doorway, slain while attempting to flee. The white shirt was now crimson but unperforated.

Fitzduane followed the blood line and saw that in this case the punch dagger had been slammed into the back of the skull.

He felt nothing but sadness. The young should not die, and certainly not slain casually like animals in an abattoir.

Fitzduane moved to the general office.

Several forms were sprawled over their desks and nearly every surface was pitted as if a grenade had gone off.

Unhurt figures rose from behind desks as he looked. Several were bleeding from cuts but seemed otherwise unharmed. Certainly, there were enough fit people to take care of the injured. One was already speaking into a phone.

"Stay here for the moment," he said, "while we check a little further. We've got two, but there may be others."

Maury came out of the congressman's office. "It's clear," he said.

Cochrane emerged from his office, his shocked gaze only loosely focused on Fitzduane and Maury. "He's—I think we killed him," he said, his voice shaky. He looked around, and anger hardened his voice. "Hell, where the fuck is Security?"

He stiffened suddenly as he noticed Tanya and the other two dead staffers. He brought up his hands to his face as if to hide the horror of what he was seeing. "Oh God!" he said. "Oh God! Oh God!"

He slumped on his knees beside Tanya and took her in his arms, though it was clear it was hopeless.

It came to Fitzduane that these were people the chief of staff worked closely with and felt responsible for, and now he had gotten them killed. These were office staffers and interns. This was not what they had signed up for.

Cochrane was sobbing, guilt etched into his face.

Fitzduane hunkered down beside him. "Lee," he said.

Lee looked at him in agony. "Lee," repeated Fitzduane sharply. "How many were there in the Japanese party?"

Cochrane shook his head, trying to focus. "I—I don't know," he said dully. "Two, I think. Does it matter?"

Fitzduane rose to his feet and looked at Maury. "Maury," he said, "can you get me patched through to Security? Tell them the situation here, identify me, and tell them to bring along spare radios, body armor, and weapons. Do you know the right person to speak to? We need some juice here.

"There is almost certainly one other terrorist loose. There is *always* a watcher, and sometimes more than one. You know that. You've been there. I think we should lend a hand. These cops won't have the experience."

Maury nodded as he was picking up the phone. There were several brief verbal encounters in English, and then he broke into rapid colloquial French. *"D'accord,"* he said finally, and put down the phone.

"Quebecois are like the Irish," he said. "We get around."

"Who is he?" said Fitzduane.

"Number two on the Emergency Response team," said Maury. "But how do we know what we're looking for? There are Japanese tourists all over the place—

and the others may not even be Japanese. We could be looking for any race or creed."

Capitol police with drawn guns entered the doorway and looked around uncertainly. Maury's contact had not connected yet.

Fitzduane held up a hand just as one of the policemen was moving forward.

The policeman stopped, though he was far from sure why he was paying any attention to a bloodstained civilian. Yet the man had a definite command presence.

Fitzduane bent down and picked up two pairs of black horn-rimmed glasses that had been placed neatly on the reception table beside two empty cups.

Maury pursed his lips, went into Cochrane's office, and then came back. "Identical haircuts, suits, shirts, ties, and shoes," he said. "A neat and simple trick if you want to avoid being recognized afterwards."

"But which may work in our favor now," said Fitzduane. "Well, it had better. We don't have much else."

A short, stocky, fit-looking man appeared through the doorway dressed in SWAT fatigues. He and Maury had a quick conversation in French before he turned to Fitzduane.

"This is Henri," said Maury, reverting to English.

"Let's go to it," said Fitzduane.

Henri shook his head. "Colonel Fitzduane, I know how you must feel, but it's more than my job is worth. This thing is going to be investigated every which way by more agencies than there are letters in the alphabet, not to mention hearings on security by both houses. If it came out that I had armed a couple of civilians and allowed them to go terrorist hunting on the Hill . . . Well, it does not bear thinking about. I'd be the salami and the system the slicer, and believe me, these people do know how to cut."

Cochrane had now recovered somewhat, though he still looked pale and shocked. He had covered Tanya's upper body with his suit jacket and now stood slumped against a filing cabinet, his clothing soaked in drying blood. He ran one hand wearily through his hair in a gesture made up of both exhaustion and sadness.

"He's right, Hugo," he said. "This is Washington. Simple direct action is not in fashion around here."

FOUR office suites down the corridor, the watcher who Fitzduane had known would be somewhere close, was chatting to the attractive young intern he had met in Bullfeathers.

Jin Endo had felt his job was done when he had spotted the target going through Security at the main entrance, and had phoned ahead to warn Wakami-san where he waited in the committee's reception. He had a note of where the intern worked and headed up to her office immediately, pausing only to discard his weapons in a cleaner's cupboard.

The Farnsworth Building had been sealed off within two minutes of the killing of Patrico Nicanor and the others, and a further cordon was placed around the complex of buildings that made up the Hill very shortly after that.

Everyone within the inner cordon was identified and questioned.

The process took over six hours. When it was over, Jin Endo and his new girlfriend walked free together. Everyone in her office knew that Endo could not have been involved. The police knew the exact time of the assault and Endo had demonstrably been visiting his friend at that time, which also explained his reason for being in the building. Certainly, he was Japanese, but so were over a hundred other people who had been caught inside the cordon and whose tour of Congress had proved rather more exciting than expected.

That night the young intern, shaken by the gruesome details of the incident, allowed the handsome young lobbyist to comfort her. True, he was Japanese just like the terrorists, but you did not blame all Italians for the misdeeds of the Mafia.

Her lover was young and fit, and someone had tutored him well in the art of pleasing a woman. The intern was even younger, but sex was something you got plenty of inside the Beltway—if you were so inclined—so they were well matched. The sex was intense, dangerous, and endlessly satisfying. There was no denying it. Power *was* an aphrodisiac, and working in Washington was all about being close to power. The added aphrodisiac was being so close to death. They had both witnessed the aftermath of the carnage.

FBI agents, backtracking through the evidence, made the connection after four days.

It was only one of many leads, but it rang alarm bells when it was discovered that she had not turned up for work. True, quite a few House employees had taken time off to adjust to the shock after the attack, but most had telephoned in. This particular intern had not, and that was unlike her.

The young intern's family was wealthy, and they indulged their only daughter. After her internship she was due to study international relations at Georgetown University, so she had been comfortably set up in a lavishly equipped condo in Georgetown itself.

The agents had to break into the condo. They found the naked body of the intern, her throat cut, wrapped up in blood- and semen-stained bedsheets in the Deepfreeze.

Of her lover, there was no sign except for a pair of horn-rimmed glasses that turned out to be plain glass.

 CHAPTER THREE

KATHLEEN FITZDUANE, CLAD in a silk kimono that one of Hugo's Japanese friends had sent as a wedding present, leaned on the terrace railing of their borrowed apartment in Arlington and gazed out toward Washington.

Graced with rich auburn hair and long shapely legs, she was the kind of natural Irish beauty who seems almost unaware of her charms. She had an easy laugh and an infectious smile, and there was a caring warmth about her. Right now her face was in repose and there was concern in her eyes.

Directly in front and below her, less than half a mile away, was the Iwo Jima memorial showing U.S. Marines raising the Stars and Stripes on Mount Suribachi after the bloody conquest of the island. In the middle distance was the Potomac and the Pentagon, and beyond that Washington, D.C., itself. Nearby was Arlington National Cemetery and Fort Myer, the home of the Old Guard.

It was a particularly good location to inspire an understanding of American history and, as such, was not an accident, Kathleen was sure.

Lee Cochrane had arranged it, and she had some honest reservations about the chief of staff. He was a little too dedicated for her taste—if that was an adequate word—and she was concerned about her husband.

Hugo Fitzduane had a penchant for causes and a deep affection for America. Hugo and Cochrane seemed like a volatile combination. Indeed, it had already produced a nightmare of violence, though, to be fair, she could scarcely blame Cochrane for that. Or could she?

Kathleen's priorities were strongly influenced by her biological clock. It did not show yet but she was now three months pregnant, and the thought of the man she loved not being there at the birth was disturbing.

Yet in her heart she knew she was helpless. Hugo's ancestors had held—indeed enhanced—their positions by force of arms for many centuries, and the urge to take a stand and test oneself in harm's way seemed to be programmed into him.

But there was a heavy price, and she had witnessed it. She had been there when Fitzduane had been brought in close to death from terrorist bullets.

Later, she had become involved herself when terrorists had taken her family hostage and tried to use her information to kill Hugo in the hospital. They had killed her father, and she still paled at the recollection. She had seen the true face of terrorism, and Hugo was right. It had to be stopped. But by her husband? That was another matter.

It had been a strange way to meet, and though she had fallen in love almost immediately, she had not expected it to work. It was too neat: patient and nurse. Such relationships seldom endured.

But they had gotten married and they were content, and even the shadow of Fitzduane's former lover did not intrude more than was inevitable. Etan had lived with Fitzduane and had borne him a son, but then she had chafed at domesticity and had moved on to greater heights in her media world and Fitzduane had been left to bring up Boots alone. Until Kathleen came along. Now Boots was for all practical purposes her son, and soon there would be another arrival. It was happiness beyond her dreams.

Kathleen smiled at herself. But it was literally true. It was not perfection because it was the nature of life that nothing was quite straightforward, but it truly was—beyond anything she had hoped for in the past.

She smiled to herself as she remembered Fitzduane asleep with little Boots in his arms. This big tall man with his steel-gray hair *en brosse* and his curiously gentle, unlined face and his wound-scarred body, and this tiny cheeky boy, hair all tousled, splayed across his father, totally secure both in his arms and in his love. Of course, Boots—real name Peter—was not so small now. At five he was shooting up like a little rocket, but he was still very cuddly and still liked to be hugged.

Long may it last, she thought, they grow up so fast. If they have a chance to grow up. The shadow of the terrorist threat was ever present.

Hugo had first encountered terrorism by accident, and then curiosity followed by a disgust for what the man stood for had led him deeper and deeper into the hunt for the Hangman. It had all escalated into something much worse than anyone had foreseen, and the fact that they had eventually triumphed was of limited consolation.

With the terrorist's death, he had taken sensible precautions, but, in truth, had thought such violence was behind him. And then had come the Hangman's revenge.

Terror was just a word until you experienced it, and then you knew that it was worse than anything you could have imagined, worse than any nightmare. Because it was not something that you were looking at in fear. *It was reality and it was happening to you.*

Fitzduane had just survived that second encounter, but then he had known that this was something he would have to live with—perhaps until he died. He and his family were permanently under threat.

Any day, some complete stranger, for reasons that made no sense to most civilized people, might attempt—and might even succeed—to snuff out his life.

The day was hot and humid as only a Washington summer can be, but Kathleen shivered.

When she had married Hugo, she knew, she had accepted the nature of the man and of their situation. She supported Fitzduane's decision to become actively involved in counterterrorism instead. But because it was the right thing to do, that did not mean she was happy with it. She wanted a live husband, not a dead hero.

Fortunately, Hugo's counterterrorist work was not an obsession. He did it because it had to be done, but he realized full well that such an essentially destructive activity could have a corrosive negative effect. And that was not the nature of the man. So he actively tried to do work as well that was essentially constructive. And that helped greatly. It gave their life a balance and was interesting in itself.

The threat remained. Rangers—Ireland's counterterrorist unit—now trained on the island as part of a security arrangement that Hugo had made with his old friend and ex-commanding officer, General Shane Kilmara. And Hugo's reserve status with the unit was not just a sinecure. He completed weapons practice and training daily, and was also involved in developing their new strike unit.

Hugo Fitzduane was a man of parts indeed, but, she feared, however he tried to disguise it, the warrior side of him was in the ascendant. But this was the man she had wanted and won, and despite her fears she was at heart content.

She thought of Boots, now staying with his grandmother, and laughed out loud. She missed the little monster, and she knew Hugo did too. He loved children. He had asked how big the little baby inside her was and when she had spaced her hands just so and said it was about the length of a good cigar, he christened the fetus "Romeo/Julietta." The name covered both the options he had pointed out.

But men weren't perfect. He had soon shortened the name for convenience to Romeo. To balance matters out, Kathleen used Julietta.

Neither really minded what sex the new arrival might be just as long as he or she was the child of Hugo and Kathleen Fitzduane.

THE long-wheelbase limousine that had picked up Fitzduane from the apartment had tinted windows.

The heft of the door confirmed his initial impression. It was armored. "Bulletproof" was overly optimistic in a world where armor-piercing RPG launchers were part of every fanatic's standard equipment. Technology, unfortunately, helped all sides.

Based on what Cochrane had said when he had called, Fitzduane expected to see a couple of hard-faced heavies in the front seats. Instead, a quite stunning redhead in her late twenties had ushered him into the vehicle, and when the driver turned he saw that the slim neck and smooth blond hair belonged, not to a rather elegant-looking male with a talented barber, but to a woman as similarly attractive as the redhead.

If this was security in Washington, D.C., he was sorry it had taken him so long to get here.

"Dana," said the redhead with the kind of stunning smile that could blow away a line of marines, "and this is Texas."

The blond head bobbed a greeting. She was otherwise occupied accelerating the limo through Arlington as if it were a sports car instead of multiple tons of armored deadweight.

The dividing panel slid shut. This was a pair who focused on their work, which was currently the matter of keeping his body in one piece. Fitzduane thought there was a great deal to be said for travel. There were some sights and sounds and customs he really did not run across much back in Ireland. Dana and Texas certainly came into that category.

The limousine purred on. The internal loudspeaker pinged tactfully and then Texas's voice cut in. She managed to combine crystal-clear diction with a mellifluous twang.

"Lee asked me to point out Langley as we passed. If you look to your right, Mr. Fitzduane, you'll see the turnoff for the CIA. A short time back, an Iranian pulled up beside a row of cars waiting to turn and went down the line and shot each driver in turn with a Kalashnikov. Four dead. The CIA said it was an isolated incident."

"Wasn't it?" said Fitzduane.

"No, sir," said Texas quietly, and there was a further ping as the speaker shut off.

Fitzduane stopped thinking about voices like corn syrup and wondered again about the late Patricio Nicanor.

The assault was being passed off by the administration as an outrage against the subcommittee by Japanese extremists. The fact that a Mexican citizen had been among those killed had been attributed no special significance. This was an attack by the Japanese Red Army against the United States of America. Señor Nicanor's death was a regrettable accident. He certainly had not been specifically singled out.

It seemed to Fitzduane that being manually decapitated with the equivalent of a razor-sharp cheese wire was about as specific and unaccidental as you could get. But clearly the administration did not want any attention focused on Mexico.

Why not? Because the administration wanted free trade with Mexico, and that meant presenting Mexico as an expanding democracy—which was not exactly the way things were.

And why had it been so important to kill Nicanor before he could talk?

THE turnoff was heavily wooded. The limo slowed and a pair of unmarked gates opened.

The limo entered and halted. The gates closed immediately behind them. They were on a paved drive carved out of the wooded terrain. The drive curved ahead of them and then vanished behind a bend.

"Mr. Fitzduane?" It was Texas's voice. "Could you please step out of the car."

Fitzduane opened the door. He could see no guardhouse, nothing but trees, but he had a definite sense of being observed.

As he looked around, he noticed a hydraulically operated spiked vehicle barrier in front of the limo and a space beyond that, a rather deep space.

Forcing the barrier would not have been a good idea. This place was protected by the equivalent of a moat and who knew what else. Someone was very serious about security; very low key but very serious. The whole approach? Someone with an interesting mind.

"Mr. Fitzduane?" said Texas pleasantly. "When you're ready."

Fitzduane stepped back into the limo's air-conditioning with alacrity. Virginia summer weather was doubtless an acquired taste.

How had these people fought in this stuff? His respect for Grant and Lee and Longstreet and all their good people ramped up a notch or two. This was his mother's country, and it had been hard won.

The car surged forward.

FITZDUANE gazed around him.

He was in a room that screamed military.

Of operations. Of missions planned and implemented and of the consequences.

The V-shaped table, the bank of giant screens, the lectern for the briefer. And the security.

The security here was of the more traditional kind. Armed, uniformed guards outside the door. Dana and Texas had vanished.

He was underground. The limo had dipped without warning. He had been told the Pentagon was like this. You could recognize all the people who really counted by their pale skins. They rarely saw either daylight or their families.

Fitzduane interrupted his musings to examine a large version of the logo that he had noticed on the shoulder patches of the uniformed guards and various other locations as he was ushered in.

In this case the logo was incorporated in an embossed shield that was mounted on the light oak paneling just behind the central chair at the head of the V. It showed a black Vietnam-era Cobra helicopter gunship head-on against a dark blue background. The contrast was slight. The helicopter silhouette was almost invisible. At the base of the shield were the letters "STSF."

" 'Son Tay Semper Fi,' " explained Cochrane as he emerged from a nearly invisible door in the paneling. It hissed closed behind him. They were alone in the room.

Fitzduane did not feel a whole lot wiser. Son Tay had been a famous U.S. raid into North Vietnam during the Vietnam war to rescue American prisoners. The raid had been a military success except that the prisoners had already been moved.

Semper Fidelis. Literally, "Always faithful." The motto of the marines. "Keep the faith," in modern parlance.

Easy to say. Hard to do.

There was a persistent rumor that the CIA had known in advance about the removal of the prisoners but had not told the raiding party. They had not wanted the North Vietnamese to be upset, so went the rumor, because the peace negotiations were at a difficult stage.

Fitzduane was far from sure he believed the rumor, but felt the story said a great deal about the chronic internecine warfare inside the U.S. military and intelligence communities. And that was before the administration and Congress got into the picture.

"STR—the STR Corporation," said Cochrane, "was founded by a Son Tay raider called Grant Lamar. Grant felt there were things that needed to be done in defense of this country that traditional structures were not really well-equipped to do. Too much red tape, too much oversight, too much media attention. His judgment was correct. His operation has been very successful. There are quite a number of companies like STR in and around Washington, but Grant is a major player though little known outside the community. He prefers discretion to prominence."

"An interesting man," said Fitzduane.

"He is," said Cochrane simply, "and he is a friend, which is why we are meeting here. The Hill has become all too public recently."

"It's your party, Lee," said Fitzduane.

Cochrane gave a slight smile. "I hope to change that, Hugo," he said, and Fitzduane felt conflicting emotions. There was the lure of the hunt, which brought a surge of adrenaline, and then there was an interjection of guilt and concern as he thought about Kathleen and Boots and Romeo y Julietta.

There were ventures he should not engage in now that he had a family. No matter how much he was tempted. He had, he knew, a high tolerance for risk, but for those who waited behind it was much worse.

Besides, he wanted to know without cheating which it would be. Romeo or Julietta. Boy or girl?

THE conference room had filled up somewhat, though nowhere near its full capacity.

Dan Warner and Maury were both there. Fitzduane had also been introduced to Grant Lamar, and then Cochrane had said he would introduce other people in the course of the briefing. He wanted to move matters along.

Since Maury was actually sitting down, Fitzduane surmised he must either know all the assembled company or be on Prozac. When Maury got through the initial introduction stage, he was actually quite affable. It was breaking the ice that seemed to freak him out. Yet Fitzduane warmed to him. As he had sensed during the terrorist attack, Maury was sound.

Cochrane, head down, standing behind the lectern to one side of a giant screen, cleared his throat. The sound system was working. The room became silent, expectant. He looked up.

"Three days ago, Patricio Nicanor and five staff members of the Task Group were killed and others wounded. The purpose of this meeting is to cover the events leading up to it, discuss our findings, and to implement an appropriate response. As we know, no action is being taken elsewhere, for reasons which we will be discussing. I shall be covering some ground most of us are already familiar with for the benefit of our guest from Ireland, Hugo Fitzduane. I think everyone here knows his track record in counterterrorist work."

There were approving nods and looks from various people around the table, and then Fitzduane caught the eye of a familiar-looking face. He was sure he had not met the man before, yet the cast of features undoubtedly rang a chord.

The man was in his forties, good-looking if somewhat overweight, with a tousled crop of graying black hair and a thick mustache. He wore half-glasses and looked over them when he spoke. He had the air of an academic. He eyed Fitzduane with some interest before turning back to Cochrane.

"The Task Force came into being because some of us were concerned that the United States of America was not taking terrorism seriously enough. And I would like to add that although as Americans our first concern is for this country, we feel many of our neighbors and friends face the same threats and we should work together to counter them."

Here Cochrane made a gesture of acknowledgment toward the Hispanic-looking academic, and with a shock Fitzduane realized who he was. The man was Valiente Zarra, the founder and head of the Popular Reform Party of Mexico. He was generally considered the one man who was capable of toppling the PRI—the "Pree," the current ruling party in Mexico. The party that had ruled Mexico through fair means, and others decidedly more dubious, since the thirties.

Media reports all described Zarra as "charismatic."

Right now he looked tired, as if he had slept in his clothes, but interested. Even involved. And this *was* significant, because the Mexican presidential elections were only months away and Valiente should have had other priorities than socializing secretly in Washington.

Fitzduane had strong doubts that "socializing" was the appropriate term. He was more of the view that Zarra needed something. Needed it quite badly.

His followers, who worked with the same passion that supporters in the past had worked for John Kennedy, were known as "Zarristas."

The Congress of the United States of America, Japanese terrorists, Mexico, and the Zarristas. It was becoming a decidedly rich stew. Nonetheless, Fitzduane had the strong feeling that there were more ingredients and he could just end up as one of them.

An Irish stew? Personally, he hated the stuff.

COCHRANE was speaking.

"About three years ago, we started paying attention to Mexico and particularly to the state of Tecuno. There was the Camerena affair where a U.S. Drug Enforcement Administration agent was kidnapped, tortured, and killed. Definite links between narcotics and terrorism were established, and the term 'narcoterrorism' came into use.

"The upshot was that more and more terrorist activities and incidents seemed to have some links with Tecuno. However, these were leads were either never firm or merely a link in a chain of locations. It always seemed to be 'soft intelligence.' Nonetheless, connections were established with drug smuggling, money laundering, forgery, and incidents of terrorist violence and political assassination. It began to look to us as if Tecuno was becoming a haven for terrorists, much like Cuba, or East Germany when it was around, or Libya or the Bekaa Valley.

"It did *not* occur to us at the time that Tecuno was becoming much more than this. It was not merely an element in these various problems. Tecuno was the very source of such activities.

"But we might still be in the dark if it had not been for our good friend Professor Valiente Zarra." Cochrane gestured toward the Mexican presidential candidate. "I will let the professor explain his perspective."

Zarra stood up and went behind the lectern. He adjusted his half-glasses and then focused on his audience.

It was true, thought Fitzduane, the man did have something. There was the quality of a leader about him and that intangible called integrity. And when Zarra began to speak, there was also that extraordinary, quite compelling voice.

As a speaker, even in English rather than his native Spanish, well practiced after two decades of university lecturing, Valiente Zarra was dynamite. And charming. And, regardless of his academic background, highly political.

"My friends, I will start by making a confession. In my country we are rightly proud of our heritage, and it is not always a good thing to admit that one was educated for a time in the United States. Well, I attended Wharton for several years and that was how I met Lee. We were at university together. It is something, of course, I try to hide in my home country," he said with a smile, "but it is the reason I am here today.

"My interest in the state of Tecuno, *señors*, started off as a pure matter of politics. What I—my people—have discovered is why we are here today."

He spoke for another twenty minutes.

The punch line made the blood drain from Fitzduane's face.

Reiko Oshima!

It was the name of someone he had been absolutely sure was dead. Whom he had killed.

The name of a Japanese terrorist leader who had been the lover of the Hangman. Who had killed one of his closest friends, Christian de Guevain. Who had been the leader of the fanatical group Yaibo—in English, "The Cutting Edge." Whose people had come within a hairsbreadth of killing Fitzduane and his small son.

Reiko Oshima—also known as "The Lethal Angel."

Fitzduane had seen her die, had seen her helicopter explode over Tokyo Bay as his rounds had pumped into it. No one could have survived that holocaust, he was sure. But the evidence was overwhelming.

She lived.

And if she lived, she was an active threat. She had to be stopped.

The rationale was indisputable. Cochrane and Valiente Zarra were passionate and persuasive advocates. Others joined in. Even Maury fixed Fitzduane with his soulful eyes.

"No," said Fitzduane.

"Hugo," said Cochrane. "You're the best-qualified man to do the job. It is a matter of fact, not opinion. You're the best there is at what needs to be done. We know what this woman has done to you and your son. You know she will try again. You can't leave it."

"No!" said Fitzduane heavily. "I cannot—my family comes first—and that is all there is to it."

KATHLEEN lay back, glowing nicely from the aftereffects of making love.

She had heard that pregnancy could go one of two ways, but certainly she had not found her own ardor diminished, and Hugo, if anything, seemed sexier than ever.

He was, without question, a very passionate man. Since she had found out she was pregnant, he had announced that he was particularly turned on by the notion that their very own little human was growing inside her, and there was certainly frequent evidence that this was so.

There was a whine from the kitchen, and at irregular intervals high-speed chomping sounds as if sand and the tentacles of an octopus had gotten into the gears of the appliance.

Kathleen smiled and then laughed out loud. Since he had been shot, Fitzduane had been forced to take his health very seriously while convalescing, and since then had become a permanent convert to hard daily exercise and healthier eating. The results certainly showed. However, sometimes, Kathleen felt, Hugo carried things to excess. He read widely and had recently discovered "juicing." The health benefits of this were apparent enough, but some of Hugo's blends were a little weird. He liked to experiment.

Frankly, Kathleen would have preferred if he confined this tendency more to their sexual relationship and kept it away from the juicer. He had once juiced raw leeks and turnip, and the resulting concoction had nearly killed them both. Still, he had been learning then. His recent blends were quite promising.

Hugo came into the bedroom clutching two pint glass mugs of a thick, frothy, multicolored liquid that looked as if it should have had a rum base and a Polynesian name and have little umbrellas sticking out of it. Both mugs sprouted bent straws. Fitzduane wore the pleased look of an inventor whose latest experiment has worked, but otherwise not much else except a towel. His hair was still damp from the shower.

Kathleen took her mug and sipped it warily. Hugo was rational on most things, but he would juice, she had the impression, anything that grew. She had strong doubts as to whether the potted plants in the apartment were going to survive much longer. She was sure she had caught her husband eyeing them contemplatively.

"Ummm!" she said. "This is really very good."

"Mango, carrot, apple, celery, kiwi fruit, sorrel, parsley, red peppers, and . . ." Kathleen looked at her husband. "What?" she said firmly.

"Ingredient X," said Fitzduane. "I'm like the Coca-Cola company. I keep my recipes secret. There could be billions at stake."

"Talk!" commanded Kathleen. She took another long sip. It really was extremely good. The straw got blocked and she drank straight from the glass.

"You've got froth on your nose," said Fitzduane. "It's quite becoming when you're naked. It sort of balances out your pubic hair."

"Where?" said Kathleen.

Fitzduane put down his glass. "Working from the top," he said, "if you put a fingertip on your nose and then follow it down over your mouth and chin and between your breasts and then down to your tummy button and keep on going . . . You find your pubic hair. And my hand. And you feel gorgeous."

"That's not quite what I meant," said Kathleen, her voice a little thick as Fitzduane worked on her.

Fitzduane did not reply. At the time he physically could not, since his mouth was otherwise engaged. Later on, as he entered his wife, she seemed, in turn, to be otherwise preoccupied. His nipples tingled as she tongued them, and later on she did other things.

It went on for some considerable time. There was definitely something to the idea, Kathleen thought as waves of pleasure repeated again and again and gradually subsided, that juicing promoted stamina. "What is ingredient X?" she asked dreamingly as she surfaced.

"Your wife has got to be pregnant," said Fitzduane.

"You're a maniac, Hugo," said Kathleen, "and I love you."

"And love doesn't hurt either," said Fitzduane. "But for true ecstasy, you want to add a little broccoli and ginger."

THEIR earlier conversation had focused on Reiko Oshima and Fitzduane's refusal of the mission. And then other matters had distracted them.

Now, after they had made love and eaten, they talked late until the early hours. There was much that Fitzduane would have preferred to keep from Kathleen, but that was not the way it worked. Kathleen, he felt, had earned the right to know. In truth, she did not have to earn anything. He loved her. Their child was in her womb.

"Apart from Lee Cochrane and Zarra, a whole bunch of people talked," he said. "I'll try and summarize it."

"Start with Tecuno," said Kathleen. "I'm curious to know how one state can act as if it is an independent country. Surely the Mexican government would bring it into line?"

Fitzduane smiled. "When is an independent nation truly a separate country?" he said. "It is not as simple as a geographical accident. Mostly, it is people and power and what people can get away with. In essence, might wins. That's history in two words. Look at Ireland. It was four separate self-ruling provinces until the Normans invaded. Then it became officially British and, perversely, united. Now twenty-six counties are independent and Irish, and six counties are British. Is it a coincidence that nearly twenty thousand British troops are stationed in the North? I'm not taking sides here, merely illustrating a point."

"Might is right?" said Kathleen.

"Close enough," said Fitzduane. "Basically I am saying that if you have the will and enough firepower, you can get away with it. Suddenly you are a nation. Strength apart, there are no inherent ground rules to this thing. As General Nathan Forrest said—more or less: 'The secret of success is to be the firstest with the mostest.' "

Kathleen laughed. Hugo believed in doing the right thing more than most people she had encountered in her life, but he liked to talk on occasion as if he was pragmatic. His friend Shane Kilmara was pragmatic. Fitzduane would die an idealist, and she loved him for it. He was old enough to know better, but he would not change. He could assess the actuality of a situation as well as anyone, and better than most. But he was a romantic.

"Mexico is a big place," said Fitzduane, "and Diego Quintana, the governor of Tecuno, is a very shrewd man. On the one hand, he has steadily built up his power base in Tecuno to the point where he can do exactly what he wants, and to further consolidate his position, he is a leading mover and shaker of the PRI, the ruling party in Mexico since before Hitler invaded France.

"Quintana's PRI involvement means that no one will ever move against him as long as the PRI are in power. He is one of the people who run the whole of Mexico, so no one is going to worry too much about his own backyard. Also, you must realize that Tecuno is in the middle of nowhere. People think Mexico City or Acapulco when they think Mexico. Or maybe Guadalajara or Tijuana. Who, outside Mexico, ever heard of Chiapes until recently? Well, now you have a picture of Tecuno.

"Tecuno is Quintana's private fiefdom. Not only is he one of the most powerful men in Mexico, but conveniently his cousin, General Luis Barragan, runs all the police and security forces in the state of Tecuno.

"Quintana is a great believer in family. You want a rough parallel? Think Noriega in Panama or Saddam Hussein in Iraq. The only difference here is that

Quintana has constructed his state within the borders of another. But that does not mean he will keep it there. Tecuno could shoot for independence. It won't be the first time a piece of a large entity broke away. Look at the United States of America. It used to belong to the British Empire."

Kathleen absorbed what she was hearing. Like most people in Western democracies, she had been brought up to believe in the primacy of governments and official structures and institutions and the rule of law, and in her earlier life had not really questioned these assumptions.

But living in Fitzduane's world had opened her eyes. She now was beginning to understand the fragility of so many human institutions, and the many hidden forces that swirled around them—and in so many cases actually dominated them. The public face of power was often not where real power lay.

"It would seem to me," she said, "that Governor Diego Quintana is sitting pretty as long as his party stays in power. On the other hand, if Valiente Zarra gets enough popular backing, then who knows. But can Zarra ever get elected?"

"He could," said Fitzduane. "Mexico needs international investment and access to the U.S. and world markets big time, so a strong group of realists wants to portray the country as a thriving, growing economy with a genuinely democratically elected government.

"That means PRI's traditional approach of playing 'stuff the ballot box' or publicly taking a machete to your opponent and serving him up in tortillas is frowned upon. It makes for bad press.

"Quintana has emerged as the main focus of opposition to Zarra. And Quintana is not the kind of person it is much fun to be up against. Zarra and his people began to get extremely worried. No one was killed publicly, but key Zarristas started disappearing—permanently. Major financial contributors started to get cold feet."

Kathleen pursed her lips. She had, considered Fitzduane, decidedly kissable lips. She was also, he kept on finding, a very sharp lady.

"So," Kathleen deduced, "Zarra decided to do some serious investigation of Quintana. He called upon his old university buddy, gringo Lee Cochrane, for some help, and Patricio Nicanor was sent in to Tecuno to sniff around.

"But why Patricio?" she mused. "Let me think. First of all, he must be a Zarrista—because otherwise why would Zarra and Cochrane trust him?—but secondly, he must have some connection with Quintana which would give him some access. So, since we are talking Mexico, maybe we're back to family. Patricio Nicanor was related one way or another to Quintana or one of his people."

Fitzduane grinned. "Patricio was General Luis Barragan's brother-in-law," he said, "and he was an engineer by training and apparently a very good one. He was also a qualified metallurgist. Barragan needed such a man and naturally turned to a relative. Blood would have been better, but Patricio would do. He was still better than a stranger.

"However, Barragan did not know that Patricio was a Zarra supporter. So Patricio went to Zarra, who introduced him to Cochrane, and together they mounted a series of penetration operations of Tecuno.

"At first, all they got was useful but relatively low-grade intelligence because Patricio was working in a lab in Tecuno City, but then he got moved to a highly classified base in a place called the Devil's Footprint. Nothing for several months, because even senior employees are restricted to the compound and access to the outer world is entirely controlled, and then Patricio made a run for it. I don't know what went wrong, but his cover was blown and the word put out. I guess they had a shrewd idea where he was heading, or maybe he was followed. And the rest you know. It was a nasty way to die, but they were determined he wouldn't talk. And he surely didn't."

"But surely he brought something with him," said Kathleen. "By the sound of it, he was an intelligent man and he was a scientist. He would have brought notes or tapes or negatives or something."

Fitzduane gave a vaguely frustrated shrug. "Two packages were found on Patricio's body," he said. "Clearly, he considered the material important, because they were concealed and strapped to him under his jacket. One package contained a layout of the base and the diagram of what they say is some kind of computerized controller. The other consisted of a small metal bar and some chips of concrete."

"A controller for what?" said Kathleen.

"The lab thinks gas," said Fitzduane. "It controls the precise blending of gas. There is a self-monitoring facility built in and the processes are triplicated, and all three have to agree or the procedure is shut down. So whatever the system is, precision is vital."

"Any idea what gases?" said Kathleen.

"We don't know," said Fitzduane, "except that there are indications that the quantities involved would be substantial."

"Does the layout of the base give any hints?" said Kathleen.

"It might have if it had been completed," said Fitzduane, "but though there is considerable detail of the perimeter fencing, guard posts and the like, most of the explanations are missing. It looks as if he started off with what he could see and was adding the rest as he discovered what different buildings were for. Different pens were used, for instance. Anyway, he never finished it."

"What about the metal bar?" said Kathleen. "Uranium? Plutonium? Radioactive who-knows-what? Something sexy like that?"

Fitzduane smiled slightly and shook his head. "There were no abnormal radiation readings from either the metal or Patricio's body"—he saw the question on Kathleen's face—"nor from the concrete chips."

Kathleen wrinkled her nose in mock irritation. "So what was the metal?"

"Steel," said Fitzduane, "a high-grade but relatively common steel. Maraging steel, it is called."

"It sounds like a cooking process," said Kathleen. "First 'marage' your steel. Then add seasoning."

"That's not so far from the way it is," said Fitzduane. "Though the final use can be less domestic. The stuff is used for all kinds of critical applications—including weapons."

"Gas, concrete, and weapons-grade steel," said Kathleen, "in a heavily guarded remote base. This does not sound like a good thing."

"Maybe not," said Fitzduane. "But they all constitute elements in a high-tech oil research facility—and that is exactly what this is supposed to be."

"What are they doing there?"

"Tecuno is mostly on a plateau," said Fitzduane. "High desert. In that part of the world, that translates into rocky, shale-festooned, waterless terrain. Blazing hot days. Freezing nights. The Badlands of New Mexico, only much worse. Most of the country is deserted since the Tuscalero Indians were wiped out. So what are you left with?"

"Oil," said Kathleen. "I don't just read the backs of cereal packages."

"Oil," agreed Fitzduane. "And a very large quantity of it. Only, some of it is locked into porous rock formations and the big question is how to get it out. So one idea is to force something or other *in* so that the oil comes *out*. Like steam or gas, for instance. Lots of stuff like that, only under high pressure. You are trying to force the stuff out of *rock*, after all. And rock is bloody hard stuff even when geologists describe it as porous. If I hit you on the head with a porous rock you would not be pleased."

"I'd kick you in the balls," said Kathleen, "and with precision. As to all this high-pressure stuff, I assume that is an application for maraging steel."

"So they say," said Fitzduane. "So there's your answer."

"Why did they kill Patricio?" said Kathleen.

"Maybe they didn't," said Fitzduane. "The killers were all Japanese."

"Which brings us back to Reiko Oshima," said Kathleen. "Who is supposed to be dead but seems to have surfaced. Where was she seen?"

"Tecuno," said Fitzduane, "by the CIA."

Kathleen looked genuinely puzzled. "I thought the CIA would not talk to Cochrane's people. They regard the Task Force as an impertinence. A congressional sub-committee should not be involved in counterterrorism."

"That is the official line," said Fitzduane. "But they also read and use the Task Force's stuff. Otherwise, how would they know what Cochrane and his boys are up to? Even more to the point, institutions aren't monolithic. Hell, some CIA even talk to the FBI, though only in parking lots with paper bags over their heads. Or so they tell me."

"This is cuckoo land," said Kathleen.

"It's Washington," said Fitzduane, "a land of shifting alliances. A kind of architecturally superior Wonderland. And Maury is certainly the Mad Hatter."

"So who gets their head chopped off?" said Kathleen without thinking.

It broke the mood. There was a break in the conversation.

"That, unfortunately, we already know," said Fitzduane grimly after the pause. "But who or where is to be next is an open question."

"Why do these people do these things?" said Kathleen quietly.

"Because for a host of reasons we let them," said Fitzduane. "Because they can."

He put his arms around her.

I am glad you turned them down, Hugo, said Kathleen silently. You have done enough. It's not your war. I want you alive with me and our children. I need you alive.

Let someone else do it.

 **CHAPTER FOUR**

CHIFUNE TANABU REGARDED the serried ranks of Kidotai drawn up in full riot and combat gear in the narrow lane and sighed.

In their kendo-like helmets and body armor and shields, it appeared almost as if a company of medieval samurai had invaded suburban Tokyo. They looked truly magnificent.

Unfortunately, seventy-five fine, upstanding members of the Tokyo Metropolitan Police Department's heavy squad was not exactly what she had in mind when she had called for backup.

The good-looking young—very young—police inspector who was her new liaison with the security unit was carrying his protective streak too far. Evidently, he had not much faith in her ability to look after herself, even though he had been briefed that she was a senior agent in Koancho, the Japanese internal security service, and had dealt with more armed terrorists than he had years in the force.

Well, Japanese men. What else could you expect? Sexism did not even begin to describe it. They did not seem to realize that times were changing. A Japanese woman today did not have to set her sights on becoming an office decoration while waiting for the right salaryman to marry. Some even carried guns, and right now Chifune felt very much like using hers on that well-meaning idiot.

She breathed in and out a few times, resolved to keep her temper under control, checked her automatic, and replaced it in the holster in the small of her back. Her suit jacket hung over it nicely. She looked like an elegant career woman in her mid-thirties, she hoped, since that was exactly what she was supposed to be. Not the kind of threat who might alarm the suspect.

On the other hand, if she arrived at the meeting with seventy-five robocops clanking behind her, even the dumbest contact might suspect something.

Inspector Oga, standing beside Tanabu-*san*, chuckled to himself quietly, though there was no visible change of expression on his face except his eyes.

He had first encountered the Koancho agent while acting as bodyguard to the *gaijin* Fitzduane, and since it had been a notably successful partnership, they had been assigned to continue to work together. People continually underestimated the beautiful and decidedly feminine Chifune, he reflected, and quite a few undesirables were with their ancestors as a result. She looked a mere slip of a thing, but appearances in this case were very deceptive. This was one tough and resolute human being. Oga, happily married to a good strong countrywoman though he was, was devoted to her.

Chifune beckoned the Kidotai sub-inspector to come over to her. He was huddled with his sergeants, and there was much saluting as he broke up the semicircle.

She fought to remember his name. She had christened him "Apple Cheeks" for obvious reasons, and *that* she could recall, but it did not seem quite the right name with which to preface a little lecture. Also, to call him by such a nickname in front of seventy-five macho security police would make him an enemy for life. She had enough problems without adding to them. And they were supposed to all be on the same side.

No, a degree of tact was called for, though she would not overdo the pleasantries. This young policeman had to learn. This mission was not riot control, where the main threat was having your armor dented by a brick. Their current targets were terrorist suspects, and that was a serious business. These people could kill you.

"Oga-*san*," she hissed. "What is . . . ?"

Oga leaned toward her. He was used to this. Chifune rarely forgot anything about a case, but she had a terrible memory when it came to the social conventions. "His men call him Apple Cheeks," he said, "but his real name is Noda."

Chifune raised her eyebrows. "Really, they call him 'Apple Cheeks' too? Maybe they are not as dumb as they look."

Oga made a noise that managed to convey the polite disapproval of a concerned colleague both at Chifune's remarks *about* the Kidotai, and the fact that she was talking near them. Oga rated the unit highly whatever his reservations about any individual officer.

Chifune turned to Oga and flashed her devastating smile in acknowledgment of his protectiveness, then turned serious as Sub-Inspector Noda clanked over to her. She had never seen so much equipment on one man. He looked massive in his helmet, body armor, and webbing, but he was probably a mere shrimp.

Sub-Inspector Noda saluted before Chifune could stop him.

"Sub-Inspector Noda-*san*," said Chifune formally, her eyes slightly narrowed. She was furious, but it was important to respect his dignity. Chewing out a subordinate in the brutal manner seen so often in American police movies was not the Japanese way unless there was extraordinary provocation.

She continued. "I appreciate your courtesy, Sub-Inspector-*san*, but behavior which is appropriate in conventional policing is not necessarily practical during an internal security operation. Saluting prioritizes targets. The person who is most saluted is most likely to get shot. These people are not ordinary criminals. They are terrorists, they have firearms, and they use them. You must believe me."

Sub-Inspector Noda-*san* blushed with embarrassment and then went pale as Chifune's words sank in. He looked like a traffic light changing signals. He most certainly did believe this ogre disguised as a woman as she fixed her gold-flecked eyes on his. "Shshsh . . . shot, Tanabu-*san*," he stammered in reaction. "I am sorry. I did not understand."

Chifune began to feel almost sorry for the man. He had been assigned to her to learn, after all, and one had to start somewhere. On the other hand, you did not need formal training to acquire common sense. Mama and Papa Noda had slipped up somewhere. These days no one should be tossed out of the family nest into the police force, of all institutions, without being equipped with some street smarts. Even in low-crime Tokyo. Low crime, after all, was relative.

"It would appear you were not properly briefed, Sub-Inspector-*san*," said Chifune in a mollifying tone. She could feel Oga radiating approval beside her. The sub-inspector's face was being saved. The integrity of the group was being preserved. She was not quite sure how long she could maintain this. She was aware that she had the most unfortunate talent for slipping in a sting at the tail end of a conversation. It was most un-Japanese. Fitzduane had enjoyed it. She missed that man.

"Inspector Oga will fill you in," she said.

Oga was normally a man of few words. This was a longer speech than most, but it was right to the point.

"The senior-agent-*san* and I are due to meet two members of the Yaibo terrorist group in an apartment about two blocks away in fifteen minutes. They say they want to give themselves up. They have had enough. They think we are staff members of a radio station acting as honest brokers. They say they don't trust the security services. In this kind of delicate situation, you don't want a highly visible cordon around the block. You leave it to us, but half a dozen of you, heavily armed and in plain clothes, should stay close and we will be in radio contact.

"If things go wrong, it will be surprise, speed, and firepower that will make the difference. And three busloads of uniformed Kidotai do not constitute surprise. Understand?"

Sub-Inspector Kanji Noda snapped to attention. "*Hai*! Inspector-*san*," he replied. His right hand vibrated, but he did not actually salute. There was hope for this young man, Oga thought benevolently. His own sons were growing. Soon enough they would be Noda's age, and Oga hoped they, too, would enter the police force.

There was the slightly muffled *whump* of an exploding rocket-propelled grenade and then the first bus in the parked Kidotai convoy blew up. Burning fuel and debris showered the narrow street.

A second bus caught fire from the explosion of the first and then sprouted lines of holes as automatic fire swept the narrow street.

An armor-piercing rocket hit Noda's body armor on the left side, plowed right through his body on the diagonal, and exploded just before it exited.

The sub-inspector came apart, as if made from a kit like some medical teaching aid designed to show what was inside the human body down to the entrails.

"Kuso shite shine!" cursed Oga as he leaped for cover in a doorway. The expletive literally meant "shit and then die," and it came to him with some force that he was not even going to have time for the former if they did not suppress the incoming fire.

He saw Chifune flat on the ground behind their parked car. She would be out of the direct line of fire, he thought with some relief, and then he saw her arm come up and flame spurt from her automatic pistol as she fired half a clip into the lock of the trunk.

The retaining latch blasted away, the trunk flew open, and Chifune jumped to her feet and removed one of the long cases from inside.

She was just turning to throw the case to Oga when another rocket hit the front of the car and blew it backward, hitting her below the waist and knocking her to the ground.

Oga ran for the rifle case, grabbed it, and rolled for the protection of the opposite door. Chifune lay with her legs under the rear of the car, motionless. There was blood coming out of the side of her head.

The weapons case had been designed by Chifune and Oga to protect the weapon inside but to allow it, when required, to be brought into action as fast as possible. A hundred-round C-Mag was already loaded. Forty-millimeter grenades were tucked into the retaining pouches of a load-bearing belt.

Oga clipped on the belt, slid a grenade into the under-barrel launcher, and closed the breech. He pulled back the cocking handle and an SS109 5.56mm round slid into the chamber.

Chifune was still lying there. As he looked and was about to run out to her, she raised her head and one arm and made a negative sign and pointed upward. He understood immediately.

Two Kidotai came crashing through the doorway, submachine guns in their hands. They had discarded their helmets and leg armor to move faster. Both looked resolute and experienced. A rookie officer did not, fortunately, mean untrained men.

"Sergeant Tomoto reporting, sir," said one man. "The unit have pulled back out of the line of fire. The men are breaking out heavier weapons and then fanning out to encircle these fucks. Reinforcements are on the way. It shouldn't take long."

"Follow me," said Oga, and he was already running up the stairs as he finished speaking. Chifune's tactical sense was almost always sound. They could see very little from ground level with fire being poured down on them. From a flat roof it should be a different story.

But they had to move fast. He knew them. The terrorists would not stick around. By the time the police cordon was in place, they would be gone. Ambush and run. Kill and hide. Mankind had been doing it since time began, because it worked. The only solution was to react very, very fast and then lay down some serious counterfire.

The roof was not flat.

Oga swore but did not hesitate. The two Kidotai threw him up into the crawl space and he smashed a hole in the tiles. One of the policemen made it up beside him. The second Kidotai, whose cupped hands had propelled up his colleague, headed off to find a window.

Oga, peering out from between smashed tiles, could see nothing from where he stood. He had thought he was pointing in the right direction, but running up flight after flight of stairs was disorienting.

Automatic fire smashed into the tiles and the Kidotai looking through a hole to his left careered backward. He had taken an entire burst in his head.

Oga thought fast. The Kidotai sergeant's hole in the roof was facing the right way, but looking through it risked receiving exactly the same treatment. That was not the object of the exercise.

He smashed out more tiles and then hauled himself out through the enlarged hole onto the roof. Then he looked down, which was a mistake. There was a nominal parapet at the base of the sloped section in case he slipped, but despite the earthquake regulations, it did not look strong enough to stop a Japanese detective inspector. Even one who had considerable interest in continuing to live.

The tiles were nailed onto a matrix of wooden supports. Most of the thin lateral slats were too light to hold his weight, but every two feet or so there was a stronger beam that looked more reassuring.

He thought of ducking back in and making some foot holes, but then realized there was not time. The people he was after would be gone.

He raised his automatic rifle and fired a burst into the tiles just above where he estimated the top lateral beam ran. The tiles shattered and Oga slung his rifle and levered himself up so that he was supported by the beam but able to look over the ridge. In truth, he was too high. He pulled back and lay at an angle so only what was absolutely necessary was exposed. Unfortunately, that was his head.

He felt scared and vulnerable and was just beginning to regret his enthusiasm when he suddenly saw a figure on a flat roof only two blocks away rise to aim a shoulder-fired RPG7 over the parapet wall.

The terrorist seemed close enough to touch. Oga felt that the man must notice him any second. They were monitoring the roofline, he knew from the burst of fire that had killed Sergeant Tomoto.

The terrorist with the launcher was intent on lining up his target below. The sergeant had been killed with automatic-weapons fire, so that meant that almost certainly there was at least one other terrorist armed with an automatic weapon on the roof. Or an adjoining roof. Or moving around.

Oga ducked down and unslung his weapon. It came to him that Chifune was lying there helpless below, and then he moved without hesitation, straightening up so that his weight was fully supported on the bar and then bringing the automatic rifle up to his shoulder and firing as soon as the red laser dot came to bear.

Rounds hammered from the flash guard of the Howa and smashed the arm steadying the launcher before hitting home just below the terrorist's throat. He fell backward, already dead, and as he hit the ground his finger was jarred against the trigger.

The rocket blasted out and blew the water-tank housing into air. The tank inside exploded in a lethal fountain of metal, steam, and water.

A figure scurried out from behind the debris and got up on the parapet, ready to jump across a narrow alley onto an adjoining roof.

There was a split second during which the shot looked possible, but Detective Inspector Oga did not squeeze the trigger.

The thin plank beneath his feet had just snapped and he had instantly dropped an unsettling two inches. There was perhaps thirty seconds' pause while the molecules in the thin laths and tiles debated whether they could sustain his wait. Oga did not dare move.

It didn't help. Tiles and laths snapped one after the other as if in syncopation before he came to a bone-jarring halt on the next, thicker lateral support. That might have been enough, except the building had been erected only a few years after World War II when really any grade of material had to do. And the building inspector was a cousin of the second cousin of the builder. And he was connected with the local *yakuza* clan who just happened to have a load of rather dubious lumber in need of a good home.

The wooden support hesitated, vibrated. And then snapped at a knothole.

Oga was just about to go over the edge when Chifune, her hair matted with blood, appeared through the hole in the roof and grabbed him as he was sailing by. She could well have been pulled down with him, except that the Kidotai held on to her.

As the pair of them were pulled in, Chifune thought more kindly of the brawn of the security police. There were times when she was quite in favor of big strong men. Sexist or otherwise.

THE Tokyo Metropolitan Police Department was *officially* run by the Superintendent General, and he was the man who appeared frequently in the public eye looking authoritative and concerned and dignified and projecting *exactly* the right public image.

In the Japanese tradition of public image and private reality—*"tatamae* and *honne"*—the Tokyo MPD was actually run by the remote and sphinxlike figure of Deputy Superintendent Saburo Enoke, known to one and all within the Tokyo MPD as "The Spider." Secretly, he was also director of counterterrorism.

The Spider had the social warmth of a well-iced dead tuna in the Ginza fish market, but though not liked, he was respected and, where appropriate, feared. No one knew quite how he did it, but the consensus was that he did an outstanding job with the police department. In Tokyo, the crime rate was a fraction of that in other major cities, and terrorism was regarded as being reasonably well under control. Most hard-core terrorists had fled Japan for the Middle East and elsewhere. Most.

Exceptions did not please the Spider. But the context of some exceptions was—he searched for the right word—*complex*. Sometimes exceedingly so. There were forces that the Spider could influence and others that were outside his control. Sometimes that meant accommodating interests that he was privately opposed to. This had been such an occasion. But the Spider believed he could operate most effectively by staying within the web, and to ensure that sometimes sacrifices were required.

Neither the Spider's face nor his body language gave any indication at all of his inner thoughts. The Spider's control was legendary. It was also quite unnerving.

Although the Tokyo MPD had a reputation for integrity, Chifune had initially harbored strong doubts about the Spider. It was only during Fitzduane's visit to Tokyo that she had realized that the Deputy Superintendent of Police was not, as she had originally suspected, an inside man for corrupt politicians and organized crime, but instead was, as the *gaijin* had said, "on the side of the angels."

He did not look like an angel, Chifune reflected. He was very small and somewhat squat and looked almost like a mannequin in his very large and well-padded black leather swivel chair. His tailoring was impeccable but revealed nothing except a sense of order. His one human touch was a penchant for rather elegant designer glasses.

Chifune, on secondment from Koancho, had reported directly to the DSG for over a year. Working with Oga, promoted from sergeant, she had been focused on eliminating the last vestiges of the terrorist group known as Yaibo.

The *gaijin*, Fitzduane, had created the opportunity by destroying the inner cadre of Yaibo and by killing the leader, Reiko Oshima. Since then, it had been mainly a matter of tracking down the small fry—until yesterday.

Yesterday's deliberate ambush, carefully planned and meticulously executed, was more redolent of earlier times when Yaibo had acquired their terrible reputation. They had been the bloodiest terrorist group Japan had ever experienced since the political assassins of the thirties, who had brought the militarists into power, had flourished.

Yaibo had murdered her lover and best friend, Detective Superintendent Aki Adachi. Never a day went by that Chifune did not miss him. She would never forget, nor would she forgive. Her commitment was absolute.

"Tanabu-*san*," said the Spider quietly, and the effect was like a breeze springing up and beginning to thin out a mist. She might not like what she was about to behold, *but she would see.*

Chifune nodded respectfully. This was not proving easy for the DSG.

"It has been necessary, Tanabu-*san*," continued the Spider, "to keep certain information from you despite the fact that it was directly relevant to your work. This view was not mine, but I acceded to it. There were good reasons for this, but I am exceedingly embarrassed. I have your trust, I know, and I feel I have partially betrayed it. It grieves me. It was not appropriate behavior."

"Directly relevant to your work." *Yaibo!* thought Chifune. What could it be? She had read every file, interrogated every suspect, checked every computer record on Yaibo, and talked to every cop with specialist knowledge. So what could she have missed?

"You missed nothing," said the Spider. "No one could have been more thorough and more resolute, but these facts were not in the records. It was a policy decision by certain senior members of the security service. It was felt that it would be better if you were not informed. A confusion of loyalties was suspected."

Fitzduane! thought Chifune. There had been that one night of love before he had returned to Kathleen to marry her. And she had returned to Adachi, who had died so soon afterward. Who had been slaughtered like an animal by Reiko Oshima and her assassins. Her alliance with the *gaijin* had made her suspect in the eyes of some of her superiors. Her loyalty should be entirely to Japan, not confused by an affair with a foreigner. It was a traditionalist view but not entirely surprising. It was also a male chauvinist view, and that was profoundly irritating.

But why had the Deputy Superintendent General gone along with this—whatever it was? He *knew* her. He knew her sense of purpose and her utter commitment. *He* knew her loyalties. Inwardly she sighed. And *she* knew the pressures on him and the accommodations he had to make.

She came originally from that very world. Power brokers; manipulators; unspoken agreements; money politics. All tied to organized crime, with its roots in the chaos of the postwar period and the need to have Japan as a bulwark against communism. So the democratic structures set up by the U.S. government of occupation were flawed. Opposing communism came first—but there was a price to be paid. The public image was that Japan was now democratic, with structures similar to those of the West. The private reality was infinitely more complex and more dangerous. And the Spider had to work within this world. It was reality.

The Spider looked straight at her. She nodded slightly, and he understood. Now she was ready to be told. There was no gentle way.

"Tanabu-*san,*" he said, "Reiko Oshima is not dead."

Chifune's eyes widened. "But . . . *Sensei,* I was there when she was killed, as you know. Fitzduane-*san* and Lonsdale-*san* riddled the helicopter with fire and it exploded over the sea. It was not possible that she could have survived. The aircraft blew apart completely."

"Nevertheless," said the Spider firmly.

Feeling suddenly sick with a terrible premonition, Chifune knew that what he said was true. A hundred questions sprang into her mind.

"Sensei," she said. "How did you hear . . . ?"

The Spider made a gesture to silence her. It was the merest twitch of his arm, but it was enough. He wanted to tell the full story without interruption, and in his own way.

"I have consulted with experts," he said, "as to what may have happened, but, in truth, their opinions are academic, because we know without doubt that she survived.

"The helicopter was low over the water when it was destroyed, and its side doors were open. The theory is that an initial explosion inside the cabin blew her out and into the sea. The after-action reports spoke of multiple explosions. By the time the main explosion occurred, perhaps only a second later, Oshima was almost certainly already in the sea. Alternatively, when she realized that the helicopter was certain to be destroyed, she may have jumped.

"She was picked up by a small fishing boat some hours later. She had disfiguring facial injuries and had minor burns and was exhausted, but she could function. To conceal her survival, she killed all the crew.

"At this point we might have lost track of Oshima completely, except that luck was on our side. Normally, she is extraordinarily secretive and contacts only proven members of the inner circle of her organization. In this case, she was penniless, injured, and on the run, so she headed for the nearest haven, the home of a purported Yaibo sympathizer and right-wing extremist, Shuo Hori. She did not know Hori well, but Yaibo had supplied him with weapons in the past and she had every reason to think that he would be trustworthy.

"As it happened, Hori-*san* was a deep penetration agent of Koancho and had been in place for many years. His main role was to keep an eye on extremists rather than terrorists. No one dreamed that he would come across a terrorist as significant as Oshima. But he is a resourceful man and he responded well to the challenge of what to do. He took her in and cared for her, and when he got a chance he contacted his superiors.

"Our immediate reaction would normally have been to pick up Oshima and that would have been that," continued the Spider, "but Hori-*san* saw Oshima's arrival as his big chance to make a mark, the case of a lifetime. He proposed to his control that he befriend Oshima, work his way into her confidence, and thus penetrate the very heart of the terrorist movement.

"Given Oshima's violent record, it was a very risky strategy. Not only was Hori-*san* personally in danger, but it would mean leaving a known dangerous terrorist loose—and one who almost certainly would want revenge. She had nearly been killed, and many of her group had been destroyed. It seemed unlikely that she would let this pass without a response.

"Hori-*san*'s proposal was referred to the highest levels, where it was considered for several days. The initial reaction was to reject it, but then it was suggested that if Oshima could be encouraged to flee this country, we would have a chance to learn about Yaibo's international network without putting Japanese citizens and property at risk. Of course, this would only work if Hori-*san* fled with her."

Silently furious though she was at not having been included in the operation, Chifune could not argue with either its daring or its logic. It was also quite cynical. The unstated corollary of letting Oshima flee was that if Japanese interests were not harmed and, indeed, advanced, it was of no concern that other nationalities might suffer. But such cynicism was not unique to Japanese security. It was fundamental to her trade in every country.

"A complex operation was mounted to make fleeing Japan seem a highly desirable option for Oshima and her new friend. Normally, such an intensive series of raids might have aroused suspicion of Hori-*san*, but in this case considerable police activity was to be expected. Oshima had been shot and many Yaibo members killed during an attack mounted in the center of Tokyo. A major response from the authorities was both inevitable and expected. The trick was to bracket

Oshima and Hori-*san* without actually capturing them. Thanks to Hori-*san*'s information, that is exactly what we were able to do.

"They fled initially to the Middle East, as expected. Oshima has never stayed in one place for too long, so she and Hori-*san* flitted from Libya to the Lebanon and then Syria, and we received much good intelligence. But then there were some unexpected developments. First, she met a renegade American scientist in Libya, Edgar Rheiman, who was on the run from the U.S. authorities, and then a Mexican general, Luis Barragan, arrived on the scene. He was buying arms and recruiting mercenaries to protect his base in the state of Tecuno run by a certain Governor Diego Quintana.

"He found more than he could have hoped for in his wildest dreams. The American scientist, Edgar Rheiman, had some very specialized weapons expertise he was trying to sell, and General Luis Barragan was in the market and had the necessary capital. And to round everything off, Oshima and Barragan became lovers. All of them, including Hori-*san,* decamped for Mexico and suddenly the operation crossed the line between acceptable risk and out of control. And to make it worse, our agent's ability to communicate from Mexico is very limited."

The Spider paused and sipped his tea, and Chifune understood that it was now acceptable that she should ask questions.

"*Sensei,* I am not sure I fully understand. What is the significance of this scientist, Edgar Rheiman, and why is the operation now no longer acceptable?"

The Spider spoke without emotion for about ten minutes. Chifune's mind raced as she pieced together the elements and assessed the various possible implications. This was not just a case of an operation going wrong. It was a veritable nightmare. It was just horrendous.

She was quite shaken. It then came to her that she was not just receiving a background briefing.

"Tanabu-*san,*" said the Spider quietly, "though the circumstances dictated it, I regret deeply that you were not fully informed earlier. But that is in the past. Now the situation has to be resolved as discreetly as possible." He then told her exactly what he had in mind.

Chifune's heart leaped when Fitzduane's name was mentioned. Then the complexities of the task ahead of her hit home. It was probably the best way to achieve the desired result, but it would be a very difficult operation.

"You may take Inspector Oga with you," said the Spider in conclusion, "and such other sources as you may need will be provided." He indicated a thick file on his desk. "This is the operation file. I think you will find it helpful."

The meeting was at an end. Chifune stood up and bowed respectfully.

The Spider stood up also and returned her bow. This was not the dismissal of an employee but an acknowledgment of a different, stronger relationship.

"Tanabu-*san*," said the Spider. "You must know that despite appearances, I have never doubted you."

Chifune bowed again and left. She felt drained, exhilarated, awed, and confused. She fought to get control of her feelings. The sight of sensible, solid, reliable Inspector Oga was like a breath of fresh air.

"Oga-*san*," she said. "You must practice your already excellent English."

Oga contemplated Chifune's face. It was slightly flushed. There was a mixture of emotions coming from her. Her normal reserve was missing. Whatever had been said by the Spider was rather more than routine. He suspected it might involve the *gaijin*. He said nothing.

"We are going to America," she said.

"North or South?" said Oga lightly.

Chifune's face clouded over as the significance of the mix of Reiko Oshima and Edgar Rheiman hit home. "Probably both," she said grimly, and strode off down the corridor.

Oga, the smile gone from his face, walked after her.

CHAPTER FIVE

GENERAL SHANE KILMARA, commander of the Irish Rangers—Ireland's elite counterterrorist and special-operations force—sipped at his brandy and smiled.

"One of Washington's finer French restaurants *and* a private room. And this from a man who normally forgets to offer me a hot dog, and always forgets the mustard. What is on your mind, William?"

The man with the thinning hair and high domed forehead sitting on the other side of the table blew a smoke ring into the air. Neither man normally smoked, but good cigars were an occasional exception. Both had a weakness for Cuban, and Kilmara had brought a box when he had flown in from Ireland. Since he was received personally by the Deputy Director for Operations of the CIA, clearing customs with such embargoed goods was not a problem.

They had known each other since both the Irish and the CIA had been knee-deep in the Congo in the 1960s. The Congo operation was long in the past—the country had even changed its name to Zaire—but the relationship had endured. Each man considered it more an alliance than a friendship, but mutual regard had sneaked in nonetheless. You tended to learn the true worth of someone over a quarter of a century.

In Kilmara's opinion, the CIA was much maligned. They were very far from perfect and they had their fair share of self-serving bureaucrats, but they had some very good people. Even more to the point, imperfect or not, they were necessary.

William Martin was not quite ready yet to get to the point. "What is the U.S. doing wrong on counterterrorism, Shane?" he said. "You've got more experience than most. I'd value your opinion."

"You already know my opinions," said Kilmara. "Too many cooks and not enough terrorists. Closing down an airport when there is a bomb scare is not counterterrorism. Crucially, your political direction is weak and you don't approach the whole thing at the right cerebral level. You've got to know your enemy, *really understand the fuckers!* Fundamentally, you don't think there is a real threat. The U.S. is too big and too strong. Even if there are hordes of bad guys running around doing their worst, you don't think they can do more than inflict the occasional pinprick.

"And you're wrong. There is all kinds of lethal junk floating around the world these days, and it is only a matter of time before some of it falls into the wrong hands. Nuclear, chemical, biological. It is all available at the right price. That's the downside of the collapse of communism and the introduction of market economies. Everything has a price and the people I am worried about have money. Shit, they have even got credit cards."

He smiled a little grimly. "And they surely have motivation." He sipped some more brandy. "The trick is to demotivate them—in advance. Carrot and stick, both applied with vigor and subtlety. You people don't do that. You wait until something happens and then pursue the perps to the ends of the earth—subject to the political exigencies. A big qualification. That just won't cut it. Someday they will do something and there won't be any earth left to pursue them around."

He looked directly at the DDO. "As I keep on telling you, William, counterterrorism is a serious business. It isn't just jobs for the boys or for a bunch of jocks with guns. Every so often you have got to deploy those little gray cells and then *do something!* Capisce?"

William Martin nodded his head in acknowledgment. He knew Kilmara was right, but the reality of being "*The* Superpower" was that you moved with the subtlety and coordination of a herd of elephants.

Hell, the Pentagon actually had press quarters *inside it* and the CIA was knee-deep in congressional oversight committees. That did not make for preemptive surgical strikes. It did make for an undue focus on ass-covering and gave new meaning to the word *leak*. It also had a disturbing effect on priorities. In practical day-to-day terms, a genocidal war in Africa was of scant consequence. A negative article in the *Washington Post* was serious. And congressional hearings were a crisis.

Given the mandate of the CIA, that was almost exactly the reverse of the way things should be.

It was one hell of a bloody world. But you dealt with the world the way it was. Idealists had notions. Practical people just dealt with the way things were. Which was just as well, because nothing really ever changed.

It was time to focus.

"Hugo Fitzduane," said Martin. "How exactly does he fit into your operation these days?"

"Hugo is his own man," said Kilmara. "But we work together very closely. He has a part-time commission in the Rangers and we train on his island. But mostly he does his own thing. His latest baby is this counterterrorist think tank. They're doing some very good analytical work. Governments don't have a monopoly on talent. Hell, you should know. The agency subscribes."

Martin nodded. "We're concerned about the company he's keeping and what it could lead to. We have enough internal political problems without you people being caught in the middle. A little friendly advice might be in order. Tell Hugo to go and play elsewhere."

Kilmara laughed. "William, you know Hugo. Say something like that and he'll get curious and then you'll never get rid of him. Appeal to his reason, on the other hand, and you are in with a chance. So tell me the problem and I'll see what I can do. Let's start with the Congressional Task Force on Terrorism.."

Martin snorted and then spoke with some anger. "A bunch of congressional staffers have no business at all in getting involved with counterterrorism. That's the job of the CIA and other agencies. Congress should have nothing to do with it. These people even go out into the field, for Christ's sake. They have no right. They should stick on the Hill and do what they are paid to do."

"As I understand it," said Kilmara, "the Congressional Task Force came into being because they identified some serious gaps in counterterrorist work and they consider their oversight role on seeing how a modest twenty-eight billion is spent on intelligence work justifies some examination. Further, they travel because how else are they going to know what is really go on."

"All of that is true, but it's not the fucking point," said Martin. "The underlying fact is that counterterrorism belongs to the CIA abroad and the FBI here and we can't have a bunch of loose cannons screwing up what we're doing."

"Even if they are right?" said Kilmara.

"*Especially* if they are right," said Martin. "And frequently they are. But the end result of showing up the Agency is that we get our credibility damaged and maybe our budget cut, and that does not help the security of the United States of America. And it certainly does not help the work that people like myself are trying to do on the inside. You have got to look at the bigger picture."

Kilmara eyed his cigar, which had chosen to die when he was not paying attention. Cuban cigars did that. He applied a match to the tip and blew smoke while he thought.

Counterterrorism was very necessary, but the effectiveness of the designated agencies was not in proportion to the resources spent. An underlying problem was that counterterrorism had become an industry in its own right, and that meant jobs, money, power and influence, and not a few thriving little empires that had little to do with the ultimate objective.

The Congressional Task Force's problem was that with minimal resources they were showing what could be done. They were succeeding because they were dedicated and focused and the few people they had were of the highest caliber. And their very success was in danger of giving Congress as a whole some radical ideas about what could be done with less money and more of a sense of purpose.

No wonder the CIA, rocked with scandal recently and therefore particularly vulnerable, was upset.

Fitzduane, on a routine getting-to-know-you trip, had stepped right into a turf fight. And Martin had a point. There was a bigger picture. And almost certainly there was a trigger issue lurking around. He thought back over his recent discussions with Hugo. It was fairly clear what it must be.

Mexico.

"Let me float a thought," said Kilmara. "Tecuno. Governor Diego Quintana is your man."

The Deputy Director of Operations, CIA, was refilling both their glasses when Shane Kilmara spoke. Mentally he screamed a loud "Holy shit!" but was pleased that otherwise he had not reacted. His hand was still rock steady.

He looked at Kilmara with his best WASP career CIA man's look. In control; urbane; confident; all-knowing. We talk to satellites. The NSA can break all codes. We know things that you don't.

"You are pouring our brandy on the floor," said Kilmara kindly.

Martin looked down at his faithless hand. It was still rock steady. And it was.

THE DDO looked at his cigar, but there was not enough left to use as a smoke screen. Besides, he had to share this can of worms with someone, and Kilmara was nothing if not trustworthy. And he just might have an idea. And the DDO had drunk just enough to be indiscreet.

"The Agency has been bankrolling the PRI, Mexico's ruling party, for years to keep them strong against communism. To repay the favor, we turn a blind eye at drugs and similar scams, and if some Mexican mover and shaker like Quintana wants to set himself up as a local warlord, that is fine by us. Just as long as he is against communism."

"So Governor Quintana is your man," said Kilmara.

"Well, he was," said Martin. "Now he is so fucking rich he does not need us anymore. But he remains on the books as an asset. He is a psychopath. He makes Saddam Hussein look like a choirboy—but he is *our* psychopath. And experience shows that the Agency needs psychopaths. There are things that need to be done that only people like that will do."

"William, how do you sleep at night?" said Kilmara pleasantly.

"I look at the bigger picture and count the pixels," said Martin, "until the whiskey cuts in."

He stood up and stretched, then walked to the window and looked down at the street below. "So what about Fitzduane, then?" he said. "Is he getting involved or reverting to tourist?"

Kilmara chuckled. "He's becoming a father in six months, so he isn't planning anything foolish. He was asked, but he turned them down. So relax. And that's hot news from the horse's mouth."

Martin left the window and stood with his hands in his pockets looking down at Kilmara, who was still sitting back comfortably. "You know, Shane, just between us, this whole damn thing makes me very uneasy. I'm following policy, but I think those congressional troublemakers are right. Maurice Isser is the smartest damn analyst I have ever come across, and Cochrane, Maury, and Warner make one hell of a team. If they smell something rotten, then they're right."

"But you're not going to do anything," said Kilmara.

"Not a damn thing," said Martin. "And by the way, when is your boy leaving town?"

"You sound like the sheriff," said Kilmara, amused. "Tomorrow all three of us are off to Fayetteville to do a little homework. I am somewhat surprised that Kathleen is coming, but I guess she will tour the area while we go to the exhibition."

"Which Fayetteville?" said Martin. "There is a whole raft of them in this country, all called after Lafayette, I guess. We used to like the French in those days."

"Fayetteville, North Carolina," said Kilmara.

"Uh-huh!" said Martin. "Fayetteville as in right next to Fort Bragg, home of the 82nd Airborne, Delta Force, and other peaceful people."

"The very place," said Kilmara. "Not a high-crime environment like Washington. Peaceful. Lots of young men and women doing healthy things like jumping out of airplanes and learning how to survive on snakes and weevils. And we might do a little touring."

"What's this exhibition?" said Martin.

"A sort of Ideal Homes exhibition, except the booths don't show microwaves and Japanese bread cookers. This one is focused more on my kind of work."

"Which is what these days?" said Martin. He smiled. "Given your advancing years and all." He knew perfectly well what Kilmara did, but was not quite clear what he was leading up to.

"Special operations," said General Kilmara guilelessly.

"MAURY, I have never seen anything like it in my life," said Fitzduane quite truthfully. "That isn't a mobile home. It's a whole way of life. If it was any bigger, it could apply for statehood."

Maury beamed. He loved to travel, and no more so than around the United States. But meeting strangers day after day was a strain. He had designed his own solution and built it himself.

"Power steering; air-conditioning; quad sound; satellite dish; multichannel TV; microwave; dishwasher; three bedrooms; two showers; and four networked computers. All the comforts of a luxury condo, and it travels," said Maury proudly.

"And you can train for the Boston Marathon while running up and down the aisle," said Fitzduane dryly. "Maury, this thing is HUGE! Is it legal? What does it eat? Aah!"

Kathleen retrieved her elbow from her husband's ribs. True, it was the weirdest mobile home she had ever seen, but she and Romeo y Julietta were not averse to some modest adventuring. And if two-thirds of the present family felt like that, well—Hugo could come too. It was democracy. He was outvoted.

Fitzduane had planned to fly to Fayetteville via Raleigh. Maury had pointed out that by the time they had changed planes and hung around the airport for the connection, they might as well drive. Further, he would drive them. He had met Kathleen and it had been devotion at first sight. He was, he had announced, instantly enslaved.

Neither Fitzduane nor Kathleen found any reason to disbelieve him. Maury, once he had broken through the initial contact barrier, was proving to be no fan of moderation. On the other hand, he was a marvelous companion and had snippets of information about practically everywhere and everything.

General Shane Kilmara was more dubious. He had reached the stage in life where he liked a sense of order. But he was prevailed upon. America, he had found, had that kind of effect on him. The impossible suddenly seemed possible.

They set out for North Carolina with Maury acting as a human guidebook. As they passed one Civil War site after another, Kathleen was strangely moved.

"It's all so much and it's all so close," she said quietly. "It has an effect. You can see—feel—why they fought. I'll never feel quite the same about the South again." She wanted to cry. There were reasons why people fought and died, and some of them were good reasons. She reached out for her husband's hand and grasped it, and he put his arm around her and hugged her to him.

General Shane Kilmara, who had seen more of war than most, felt exactly the same way as he looked out through the tinted picture windows.

He had been there before, and he always did. He was reminded of a visit to Arlington National Cemetery just south of the Pentagon and within no distance at all of Washington, D.C. The graveyard had originally been Robert E. Lee's home until a Northerner, disgusted by the bloodshed, had made sure Lee would never return again by using the immediate surrounds of the house in which to bury the dead. The cherry orchards were cut down and it became the National Cemetery.

Not far from the Tomb of the Unknown Soldier, Kilmara had found an impressive monument erected to the memory of the Southern dead and had expressed some surprise. This had started, after all, as a Northern graveyard, and the South were the vanquished. Yet their dead, the enemy, were honored and within living memory of the war itself.

"Don't be surprised, General," his guide, a young lieutenant from the Old Guard, had said. "It's appropriate, sir. You're standing in Virginia."

米 CHAPTER SIX

DANA AND TEXAS watched Maury's custom-built mobile home pull into the forecourt of the Bastogne Inn & Conference Center in Fayetteville with some relief. They had been assigned by Lee Cochrane to keep an eye on the Fitzduane party and had followed them down all the way from Washington. They had not enjoyed the scenery. On the open road they considered that goddamn mobile home too damn vulnerable.

They could not figure out why four sensible adults who all knew they were potential terrorist targets should expose themselves in this way. They had finally come to the correct conclusion that even if you were a target you had to try for some semblance of a normal existence or life would scarcely be worth living. You would be a prisoner. It was the same thinking that had kept the security down to two. Still, however understandable that was, it was tough on your bodyguards.

A vast sign reading "The Spec-Forces Show" was festooned across the front of the hotel. A large sticker in the rear window of a pickup advised: "Special Operations Exhibition—Don't Drink & Drive: You Might Spill Your Drink." Another read simply: "I Don't Brake for Terrorists!"

Dana, who had been driving, glanced across at Texas. "Boys will be boys," she said. "I guess we're in the right place."

Texas rubbed her eyes. Following a vehicle was exhausting. You were not only keeping an eye on it, but you had to both look out for potential trouble and remember your own security. And that meant covering your ass. She had tired eyes and a crick in her neck. A soak in a hot tub was an inviting prospect. It was more likely to be a quick shower. This was a working trip.

"What's the brief?" she said. Dana was the more cerebral of the pair. She handled the paperwork. Texas focused on the action.

"The hotel is an open rectangle," said Dana. "The main block houses reception area, restaurants, and the actual conference center. The two wings at the back house the rooms. Between the wings there is a heated pool."

Texas groaned. "What I wouldn't give!"

"We should be able to work it out," said Dana. "Special security has been drafted in for the run of the exhibition, and the entire hotel is restricted to exhibitors and invited guests for the duration. There is going to be more firepower concentrated here for the next few days than the 82nd can deploy. If there is one place where our clients should be safe, it is here."

"So what do we do?" said Texas cheerfully. "Soak up a few rays and maybe connect with a paratrooper or two?"

"We keep a general eye on things," said Dana, "but we focus on Kathleen Fitzduane. She's only here to be with Hugo, and I've got a hunch all this high-tech killing hardware will pall. She will want to do a little touring, and where she goes, at least one of us will follow."

"What do you think of Kathleen?"

"Nice lady," said Dana, "and very dishy. More the homemaker than the feminist. A good match for Hugo."

"More is the pity," said Texas.

Dana and Texas looked at each other and grinned. Both fancied Hugo.

"Amen to that," said Dana.

FITZDUANE inserted the key in the elevator lock.

They were staying on the fifth floor. Without the special key, the fourth floor was as high as you could go. Well, that was the theory. In fact, all you had to do was travel up with someone with a fifth-floor key. It was not the social norm to quiz everyone else in the elevator as to their floor entitlement. So, from a security point of view, the special key helped—but not too much.

Out of curiosity, Fitzduane had checked the fire stairs access and that had been thought through. You could get *down* the stairs but not back up. The security door clicked shut behind you, and that could only be opened from the inside. Unless you had a passkey, which every cleaner was equipped with.

Security, like most things in life, was a compromise. Perimeter security was much tighter. You could not get in or out of the hotel without a special pass that bore your photograph and thumb print. Armed guards enforced the edict. It was reasonable. There was a great deal of very dangerous hardware inside.

Kathleen had accompanied Fitzduane for all of the first day of the exhibition. Now she was tired and said little. It had indeed been a busy day. From Fitzduane's point of view, it had been fascinating. As to Kathleen's reaction, he was not so sure. Or maybe he was and did not want to admit it. Kathleen was unhappy; in fact, she was downright disturbed.

She lay back on the bed without switching on the light. Some light from the general hotel illumination outside percolated through the blinds, but otherwise the room was in darkness. Fitzduane knew the signs. When Kathleen behaved like this she did not want to be held and caressed, and her thoughts brushed aside. She wanted to think and talk the issue out in her own time.

He sat in an armchair beside the window and waited. Sounds floated up from the illuminated pool below.

Kathleen spoke when she was ready. He had no idea how long it took. It was not important. Her hands were loosely clenched and rested on her eyes. He could smell her perfume from where he sat. Her long legs gleamed in the ambient light in contrast to the prevailing darkness.

"How many booths are there?" she said. "Three hundred, four hundred? And all devoted to the business of killing. Sniper rifles; grenade launchers; anti-tank weapons; laser range finders; radio-detection devices; silencers; night-vision equipment. It is all about the taking of human life, and here are we bringing another small life into the world. I don't understand it. It frightens me. I just can't work it out.

"God knows, I have been on the receiving end of terrorism, but still, I can't make any sense of it. Surely we can find a better way? Is violence the only answer? Are we making a little baby just to have it blasted into oblivion by one of these terrible devices, or maybe it will just be maimed? It is all incomprehensible to me.

"And then, when I meet the people who supply all this lethal equipment, many friends of yours, I find them so nice and charming. They are not horrible war-mongers. They are just ordinary people like you and me. And that is truly terrifying. THESE FRIGHTENING PEOPLE, THESE KILLERS—THEY'RE US! THEY'RE YOU AND ME, HUGO!"

Kathleen's words cut like a knife through Fitzduane. Their real effectiveness stemmed from the fact that these were the very thoughts that he harbored himself.

"I love you, Hugo," continued Kathleen, "but sometimes you make me despair. You're the kindest, gentlest, sweetest man and the most loving father—and yet when I see you with these people talking about the techniques of killing, I feel I have married a monster." She gave a small sad laugh. "I'm in love with a monster. I'm bearing a monster's child. And I have no regrets."

Fitzduane lay down beside her and put his arm around her. They had had this conversation before and he had run out of answers. Fundamentally, there weren't any. Kathleen was right. But in the real world, being right was not enough.

Kathleen snuggled into him. Then she reached out with her hand and caressed him. Soon, none of it mattered.

———

DON Shanley, manager of Magnavox's Electro-Optical Division, watched with mixed feelings as the six special forces troopers left.

They had been drinking beer and telling war stories for the past three hours, and it had been good fun. But it had been a long day, and now all he really wanted to do was have a shower and put his feet up. Exhibitions were hard on the feet. You were standing working all day, and standing around socializing in the evening, and it just was not the way, in his opinion, feet were designed to be used. They were useful appendages and really should receive more care and consideration.

Shanley stripped and stood under the shower, the pressure turned full up. The water needled into him and he could feel the layers of fatigue being stripped away. It was just as well. It was after eleven, but his day was still not finished. An exhibition meant a sixteen-hour day, sometimes more.

Tomorrow, he had additional work to do. He was starting the day with a demonstration of the MAG-600 for a cadre of the 82nd Airborne. The good news about that was that he would not lose any time at the stand, because the paratroopers started so goddamn early. The bad news was that he was not going to get much sleep. All equipment, no matter how inherently reliable, had an amazing knack of letting you down at sales demonstrations. Doubtless, it was the gods playing games.

But interestingly, he reflected, they seemed to play them much less often if equipment was checked out thoroughly and methodically in advance. It was doubly important if the devices had been fiddled about with all day on the exhibition stand. It was impressive how much several hundred pairs of untrained hands could fuck up the most soldier-proof of devices.

Laymen thought you designed equipment for performance. That was the easy part. The hard part was making it stand up to the average soldier's activities in the field. That was not so easy. The military had strange habits. They liked mud and rain and sand and grit and extremes of temperature and humidity. They jumped out of airplanes and helicopters and rattled around armored fighting vehicles. People shot at them with sharp pieces of metal and dropped explosives on them.

All of this was not conducive to good electro-optical performance. No, "Mil-Spec" was not just an arbitrary list of standards. The military were really rough on things.

But it was fair enough, Shanley thought, because they were hardest of all on themselves. And that was hard to take.

Shanley looked like everyone's image of the ultimate professional soldier. His bearing was military. His black hair was cropped short. He was fit and lean, with high cheekbones and a firm jaw. His eyes were blue and piercing and laughter lines showed he could take stress. He was deeply tanned. His demeanor was both confident and encouraging. He had a natural air of command. His voice was a pleasure to listen to, both crisp and authoritative and persuasive. Clothes fitted him as if tailored. He was a man's man and a woman's man. Both sexes automatically warmed to him.

Unprompted, enlisted men automatically called him "Sir." Officers called him "Sir" also, or "Mister" with respect. He had eyeballed Death and he had not blinked. He was ex–Special Forces or some such elite unit. He was ranger and airborne qualified. He was a warrior.

But he had never served. He had come close, but then Lydia had showed up and civilian life had seemed the better option. But he had always wondered.

The irony of Don Shanley was that none of his military traits or mannerisms was affected. All were natural and were innate to the man. Shanley was just ordained by nature to look the part.

It went deeper than mere looks. Shanley also was a crack shot and had a deep understanding of the military art. He knew weapons and tactics and military history, and how the whole terrible business worked, in very considerable detail.

By nature he was conscientious and thorough, and in his value system you should thoroughly understand the needs of your customer. It went with doing the job right.

Shanley was a decent man. Doing the job as well as it could be done was important to him. Work was how he supported his family, and they were everything to him. Lydia and the twins. They were why he did what he did and why he was proud to do it. He also thought it was necessary. The U.S. military were entitled to have the best weapons that money and technology could provide, and he, Donald Shanley, would see that they had them. On that issue he slept easy.

But when he trained men who were about to put their lives on the line, he felt guilty. He felt the need to pay his dues. To serve in a combat unit in defense of his country.

He was an old-fashioned man with simple values. He had a conscience and he cared.

He picked up the phone and called Lydia in New Jersey. This was something he had done virtually every night he had been away since they had gotten married eight years ago. She was asleep, but she responded to his voice with drowsy warmth.

The twins were fine. Sam adored the new pancake recipe. Samantha wanted to play the guitar instead of the piano. The air conditioner had been fixed. All was well with the world. She missed him and loved him.

Shanley replaced the receiver. He had a good job with a fine company, and he had a wife and children he adored. He should be entirely content. And yet something was missing.

He wanted to—needed to—serve.

He swung his legs off the bed and began checking the equipment. Toward the end, he stripped and cleaned the M16A2 and the Barrett. The Magnavox MAG-600, which he was going to demonstrate to the 82nd tomorrow, was an interesting piece of equipment.

It was a thermal-imager sight, which meant it responded to heat emanations. With it, you could shoot in complete darkness or through smoke or fog at quite considerable ranges. Variations of it could accomplish the same task when fitted to a Stinger antiaircraft missile.

One of the most interesting applications of all was the application of the Magnavox thermal imaging technology to driving. Using a thermal viewer fed through to a miniature TV monitor mounted on or in the dashboard, you could drive without lights in the absolute dead of night. Image intensifiers required some light. Thermal imagers required none at all.

Shanley finished the weapons cleaning and consulted his appointment schedule.

A Colonel Hugo Fitzduane of the Irish Rangers and party were due at 3:00 P.M. for a personal demonstration. They had some particular problems they wanted to resolve that sounded as if they were right up Magnavox's street. They wanted to equip a FAV—a fast-attack vehicle—with full thermal capability and wondered if the equipment would take the pounding.

Don Shanley smiled to himself. The Shanleys had come to America from famine-stricken Ireland in the middle of the nineteenth century. Who would have thought then that Ireland would become independent and thrive and prosper?

He was looking forward to meeting this Colonel Fitzduane.

He looked at his watch. It was after one o'clock in the morning. He had given the company an eighteen-hour day. A little personal time did not seem unreasonable.

He put on swim trunks and then slid on a terry-cloth robe and headed for the pool.

The corridors were empty, and when he got outside he could see that most of the rooms were in darkness. For all practical purposes he had the hotel to himself. It was not true, of course, because there was still a night staff on duty, but the illusion was there and he savored it. An exhibition was the unrelenting pressure of people day after day. Well, mostly he liked people, but sometimes he craved some personal space.

Silent in his bare feet, he walked slowly down the path that led though landscaped vegetation to the pool. The vegetation was normally floodlit, but at this late hour the lights had been turned off and only the pool in the center was still illuminated.

The water glowed like the entrance to a magical world. When he dived in, he thought, he would keep on swimming down and the waters would part and mysteries beyond compare would be revealed.

He was just about to leave the darkness to enter the pool area when he saw ripples on the surface of the water. He paused, and seconds later a nearly naked woman emerged from the pool. She did not use the ladder but instead levered herself up effortlessly onto the poolside. Her body was long and lithe and glowed in the soft light.

She was not just fit. She was in perfect condition. Muscles rippled under golden skin, and her figure was showed off to perfection by the minimal black fabric of her costume.

She ran her hands back over her head, squeezing water from her close-cropped blond hair. Her carriage was erect, and something about her posture suggested formal training. If she had been a man, he would have thought military. Ballet? Modeling? No, she had the discipline, but there was too much hard muscle there in the upper body. In this case, functionality ran ahead of appearance.

This woman did not just want to be fit. She *needed* the strength and stamina.

As he watched, she leaned down casually and picked up a towel. She dried her face, and as she did so she turned quite naturally to face in his direction.

"Come on in," she said. "It really would be a cool idea. Don't be shy. It makes me nervous."

Her hands were outstretched. They were not empty.

Shanley looked down at the front of his robe. The red dot of the laser sight rested neatly on his torso. It was not quite central but sat slightly to the left. The red dot was steady.

Rib cage, heart, lungs, and all kinds of other useful bits he was quite attached to in one burst. It looked like a mini-Uzi. Neat trick, that, with the towel.

He stepped into the light. It seemed like a remarkably good idea.

"Ah, Mr. Magnavox," she said slowly. "I saw you on the stand. You were playing with a Stinger missile. Thermal sights, if I recall."

Shanley nodded. She looked at him carefully as if checking, and then the outstretched arms relaxed. He looked at his torso. The red dot was gone. He could feel his heart pounding.

"You don't seem to need them," he said.

HE swam hard for fifteen minutes, notching up the lengths in a fast crawl. He was a strong swimmer. The luminous water was as he had thought. It was another world.

Finally he slowed and turned onto his back to float. Stars glittered in the night sky above him.

She had left earlier. Now she stood there with two glasses in her hands. She was wearing a white djellaba trimmed with gold. The hood was down. She had, he thought, the most beautifully shaped head.

He hauled himself out of the pool, conscious that fit though he was, he was making heavier weather of it than she had. Of course, he was a good ten years older, but still . . .

"I talked to the kitchen," she said. "Irish coffee. Tastes good after a swim."

He put on his robe and took the hot glass. They sat at a poolside table facing each other. His wedding ring glinted in the light as he drank. She wore none, he noticed.

"My name's Shanley," he said. "Don Shanley."

"I know," she said. "I asked. You looked interesting. Married, but interesting."

Shanley smiled. "I'm still married," he said.

She laughed. "You still look interesting," she said. "That doesn't mean I have to sleep with you—even at a trade show where sex seems to go with the territory. I guess I want to talk. I don't know why. It's just one of those nights. I just don't want it to end."

They talked about everyone and everything until the sky began to lighten and there was no choice but to part. They never touched.

"What's your name?" said Shanley just before he left. And then he added as an afterthought, "And rank?"

"Folks call me Texas," she said. "I made captain before I quit. Airborne."

"It shows, Texas," said Shanley. "Thank you. You're a pleasure to meet."

After he left, Texas sat by the pool for quite some time.

✳ CHAPTER SEVEN

KATHLEEN WAS SUBDUED and distant in the morning.

She breakfasted early and lightly and headed for the coast to do some sight-seeing. She wanted to get as far away from Fayetteville/Fort Bragg as possible. The entire area seemed to be making an industry out of preparing to kill other humans, and she found it all depressing. Even the hotel pool offered no relief. During the day it was used to demonstrate equipment used by Navy SEALs.

The military presence was unrelenting. And they were all so damned cheerful and gung-ho about it. She was awash in camaraderie and male bonding, and if she was not careful she would drown.

She loved Hugo and would endure what was necessary given their situation, but it was not her world. She understood that Fitzduane did not enjoy being under threat either, but there was a fundamental difference. Hugo was comfortable with his world of weapons. He was not confined to it, but he functioned supremely well in it. It was something of a shock seeing him this way. In Ireland, on the island, Hugo trained with the Rangers, but it was somehow more subdued. Here it was very American and very extroverted, and she felt the whole damn thing was being rammed down her throat.

She had heard that much of the North Carolina coast was very beautiful. Some totally civilian scenery would be nice. She savored the word *civilian*. It had always seemed such a dull word. Now it carried with it an ethos her heart cried out for.

"You look vaguely shook, Hugo," said Kilmara cheerfully as he found Fitzduane alone having breakfast. "The wife been beating you again, or is it the prospect of yet another warm sunny day? It's disorienting for us Irish. We're like certain types of plants. We expect to get rained on regularly but unpredictably."

Fitzduane did not wear his heart on his sleeve, but Kilmara was someone who was very close to him.

He smiled. "Kathleen is not a happy lady, which is unusual. She awoke *not* in good form and headed as far away from uniforms and military hardware as possible. I think she plans to roam and sunbathe along the North Carolina coast."

"Lucky North Carolina," said Kilmara. "If you don't mind me commenting on your wife, Kathleen looks sumptuous in a swimsuit. Also, she is right. All this military stuff is bullshit. It's fun, but it is ridiculous. And it gets people killed. If I wasn't a general, I would jack the whole thing in. And hell, man, you don't want a wife who wears jump boots in the kitchen."

Fitzduane did not reply to this sally, which was unusual. He normally enjoyed Kilmara when he was being outrageous. There was something else to all this.

Kilmara gave his friend space and focused on his scrambled eggs. Soon enough, Fitzduane spoke.

"Out of the blue, for no reason that I could think of, Kathleen asked me if I ever thought of Etan. Well, the question was so unexpected, I did not dissemble in any way. I told her the truth."

Kilmara was silent under the cover of hunting for some marmalade. He did not really understand American breakfasts.

He was also very fond of Etan, Boots's mother, and had been quite upset when she had opted for a career ahead of Fitzduane. Particularly when she still loved the man. But people were nothing if not perverse. He was also very fond of Kathleen. He thought his friend had excellent taste in women. A Japanese name also came into his mind, but he could not quite recall it. That was the trouble with these military conventions. Soldiers all drank as if there were no tomorrow. Of course, sometimes they were right.

"Some men can sleep with a woman and then wipe the encounter from their mind as if it was of no consequence," said Fitzduane. "You can do that, Shane. I can't."

"Sometimes it is of no consequence," said Kilmara. "Sex should not be confused with romance, though I admit they can overlap. But if you carve the name of every woman you have slept with on your body, you'll end up looking like an old oak tree on lovers' lane. Well, I like my bark pristine. I also believe in concentration of effort. Remember only the good ones—and for heaven's sake, be quick or selective."

Fitzduane smiled.

"So what did you tell Kathleen when she asked about Etan?" Kilmara asked.

Fitzduane took his time replying. "I think about Etan every day," he said. "She is the mother of my son. Every time I see Boots I am reminded of her. I think of what might have been—of what should have been. And it makes me a little sad. She was my lover and she was my friend. I've adapted, but I miss her."

Kilmara's cup of coffee was frozen in midflight. "You said all that, Hugo?" he said. "Holy shit! Someone is going to have to lock you up." He rolled his eyes. "Basic training: Women do not like to be reminded of other women unless you have a ménage à trois. What am I going to do with you!"

"I also said that I have never been happier than with Kathleen and I love her with every atom of my being," said Fitzduane quietly. "And that's true also."

Kilmara waggled his hand and beamed. "Well, for an idiot you recover well." He frowned. "And you did all this over breakfast? Now, *that* is ridiculous."

Fitzduane smiled and then changed the subject. "Where is Maury?" he said.

"In his mobile home," said Kilmara. "He has got an encrypted mobile phone that he talks to Lee Cochrane with. Mark my words. Those guys are plotting."

"What about?" said Fitzduane.

"Think of them as travel agents," said Kilmara. "I think they are still planning to get you to Mexico. They have this thing about Tecuno, and they think you are the best man for the job. Kind of flattering in its way."

"Not a chance," said Fitzduane. "I have enough firefighting to do at home."

"With Kathleen?" said Kilmara, slightly taken aback.

"With Boots," said Fitzduane with a smile. "My sweet little five-year-old son. You know, the one who was found playing with your loaded service automatic last time you were staying. He nearly got it into action, too."

Kilmara went pale. He remembered all too well. Terrorism was something he was used to dealing with, but a curious five-year-old was a higher order of threat altogether. And television made the kids familiar with safety catches and the like. Boots had found he was not strong enough to work the slide and had been experimenting holding the weapon in a vise and using two hands when he was caught. He was an ingenious little monster.

"You've got a point," Kilmara said with some feeling.

ABOUT fifteen minutes away from the main exhibition, live-firing demonstrations were being given in a converted quarry. You could evaluate weapons just so far in a booth.

Fitzduane and Kilmara took the shuttle bus over. They had not told either Dana or Texas, so they felt a bit like kids dodging school. On the other hand, it would have been a foolish terrorist indeed who tried anything.

The passengers were equipped with every conceivable kind of weapon to try out on the range. In addition, both men were armed, though automatics were as nothing compared to the exotic firepower they were surrounded with. Fitzduane reflected that the domestic pop-up toaster might not have seen much development over the last half century, but certainly weapons manufacturers had not stunted their ingenuity.

It was hot in the quarry, and a blazing sun in a clear blue sky indicated that it was going to get hotter still.

About forty attendees were gathered in a rough semicircle behind the firing line. Perhaps a third were uniformed, and the rest wore everything from black T-shirts emblazoned with slogans—matched with fatigues bloused into combat boots—to suits and ties. More than a dozen were women.

"I don't know whether this is fun or horrible," said Fitzduane.

"Watching things go bang. *This* is fun," said Kilmara cheerfully. "When the quarry starts to shoot back . . . *that* is horrible."

There was movement at the firing line, and a man dressed in well-worn but starched fatigues faced the gathering. He wore a DI's flat-brimmed hat as if it had grown with him in his mother's womb.

"My name is Cutler," he said. "You're about to see a demonstration of the Brunswick RAW—rifleman's assault weapon. It's an unusual weapon."

A 5.56 FN Minimi light machine gun, bipod extended, was positioned on the ground beside him with its muzzle pointing toward a sandbag bunker two thicknesses thick about three hundred meters away.

In front of the bunker and leaning against it was a heavy steel armor plate.

"The trouble with the bad guys," continued Cutler, "is that they are not always willing to stand up and be shot at. They don't play fair. They get behind cover like bunkers or reinforced concrete positions that your itty-bitty rounds can't penetrate, and then what the fuck do you do? It's downright embarrassing."

There were smiles from the assembled group.

"We already have rocket and grenade launchers," Cutler went on, "but rocket launchers are bulky and the 40mm grenade does not quite have the punch for a strongpoint. And so they came up with the RAW. Essentially, it is a spin-stabilized elongated ball five and a half inches in diameter—a teardrop shape—that you fire from a launching mechanism that you attach under the muzzle of your personal weapon."

Cutler opened a compact clamshell container and clipped the mechanism and then the projectile in place. The entire exercise took less than ten seconds.

"With the RAW in place, you can still use your weapon as normal. The interesting thing is that for three hundred meters, the projectile's trajectory is virtually flat. Using your rifle sights, where you point it will hit. At longer ranges we're talking indirect fire, but it will go up to fifteen hundred meters."

Cutler picked up the Minimi with the RAW now attached. "As I said, there is no recoil or backblast, so you can fire it standing or sitting or however you want. The bipod is not necessary except to steady your aim."

He then reached out his left hand, turned the RAW activator switch, aimed at the bunker, and fired.

The projectile hissed from its nest under the barrel and then accelerated rapidly.

It looked harmless, thought Fitzduane, more like a well-spun ball than a weapon. But after its initial acceleration, it was extremely fast.

The distant bunker protected by its armor plate could be clearly seen.

And then it just disintegrated, the explosion startlingly violent and more like a heavy artillery shell than a grenade. It seemed an extraordinary amount of destructive power from such a small sphere.

"Well, I'm buggered," said Kilmara. "That little thing does all that damage by itself? You must have set off some explosives in it. You're pulling a fast one, Sergeant."

Cutler grinned. "No, sir," he said. "What you saw is what you got. The RAW is one effective sucker. Ain't technology a wonderful thing. In destructive power, the grapefruit is equivalent to a 105mm howitzer shell."

"Suppose the grapefruit catches an incoming round?" said Fitzduane.

The fact that the RAW had neither recoil nor backblast had caught his imagination. You could use it in a confined space and mount it near anywhere.

"Good question," said Cutler, "but not to worry. The explosive used is insensitive. If it gets too hot it won't explode, and the same applies if it takes a round. We tested it with a .50, and nada."

"Any more tricks?" said Fitzduane.

Cutler nodded. "There is also a dual-purpose projectile that combines anti-armor or bunker busting with antipersonnel capability. You set the range at which it will explode with a built-in display and then it will fire three thousand tiny tungsten balls that will kill or injure everything in an arc with a radius of about a hundred and sixty square meters. The balls have an escape velocity of six thousand feet per second. That momentum will take you through a flak vest or a Kevlar helmet. That's a lot of very destructive metal flying around. It will shred people, soft vehicles, light armor and aircraft—and it's very bad news for helicopters."

He turned and faced another target about two hundred meters away. This time, instead of one bunker, a hundred and fifty combat targets showing a menacing crouching infantryman advancing had been set out to simulate an attacking enemy force. They were in three irregular rows and were spread out in a line over two hundred meters wide and fifty meters deep.

Cutler picked up a RAW munition and fitted it, then adjusted the range on a small LED dial. Then he aimed slightly high. "Airburst," he said, and fired.

Every man in the assembled group examined every target after the demonstration. And every single target had been hit.

One single RAW round.

SOMEWHAT subdued by what they had seen, Fitzduane and Kilmara had a quick lunch and headed for Maury's mobile home to meet their Magnavox contact.

Having a serious discussion at a busy exhibition stand was not easy. Also, Maury's vehicle was more working base than home. In it were excellent communication and office facilities.

Maury liked to travel, but he also liked to work. In truth, he never seemed to stop working. Certainly, one element that underpinned his detailed knowledge of the terrorist world was sheer application.

So far he had spent just one hour at the exhibition. He had done a lightning tour and then returned to his mobile burrow. Military gadgetry was all very well and he kept himself informed, but what really turned Maury on was the live game. Thanks to modern satellite communications, he could play that anywhere—and he did.

Fitzduane found Maury watching the fax for incoming nuggets in the utterly focused manner of a cat monitoring a mouse hole and brought him, protesting, into the meeting with Don Shanley.

Shanley impressed Fitzduane, and he wanted to put the Magnavox man under some additional pressure. Maury was rather good at asking awkward questions.

"What do you guys want to achieve?" said Shanley. "The more I know, the better I can help you."

"You just want to sell hardware," said Maury aggressively. "I hate salesmen."

Fitzduane groaned inwardly. This was not the best way to start. He had in mind awkward technical questions. Downright bad behavior would not be helpful. Still, the only thing now was to go with the flow.

Shanley smiled. "We all have some position to advance," he said. "Personally, I like to think of myself as a problem solver."

Maury glared at Shanley. "What do you know about combat?" he said. "Have you ever served?"

Shanley was tired, Fitzduane had observed. At Maury's question he went pale, as if the remark had struck deep. Given Maury's aggressive approach, Fitzduane would not have been surprised by an angry response, but the Magnavox man showed restraint.

"I know more about my field than most," he said quietly. "I hope that will be sufficient for you gentlemen. As I understand it, your application relates to FAVs. Perhaps we can take it from there. It might be helpful if you work from first principles."

Fitzduane caught Kilmara's eye and made an almost imperceptible gesture. Kilmara took the point and cut in.

"Don, my unit came into being as a counterterrorist force," he said. "Subsequently it was expanded to have an offensive capability. That meant we needed to deploy heavier firepower to deal with armor and other special situations, and pretty soon we ran into problems. Quite simply, our Rangers, no matter how physically fit, could not carry the weight of weaponry and equipment which we considered necessary to do the job. I am sure you know the figures."

Shanley nodded. "A fit soldier is supposed to carry only about one-third of his body weight if he is to remain combat capable—say, sixty pounds odd. In practice, by the time you have added spare ammunition and the modern tools of his trade, the guy—or girl these days—is staggering under a hundred pounds or more. That restricts his mobility and he tires faster. Worse again, he still is not carrying what is required in combat today. The days of a rifle and sixty rounds of ammunition are long gone. Now he is laden with four hundred rounds of ammunition, antitank weapons, explosives, claymores, laser range finders, and—" he smiled—"thermal sights. And there is more. Radio batteries are a real curse. And then there is his NBC kit."

"You've got the picture," said Kilmara. "A single special-forces soldier has never been better equipped or more potentially lethal in the history of warfare, but he cannot carry what he needs.

"Well, I tossed the problem to Colonel Fitzduane. Hugo has a talent for this kind of thing."

Fitzduane could see that Maury was getting hooked.

"Back in World War Two," said Fitzduane, "my father was one of the founding members of the SAS in North Africa. Stirling's idea was to raid behind German lines using heavily armed jeeps."

"Did it work?" said Shanley. "As I understand it, the German Army in North Africa was heavily armored. Jeeps against armor does not seem much of a deal."

"A few dozen SAS destroyed more German aircraft on the ground than the entire Allied Desert Air Force, which contained thousands of men," said Fitzduane. "As to armor, the idea was not to go head to head. In those days, you couldn't destroy a tank with anything you could carry in a jeep. But jeeps were faster and they could hide. And they were devastating against light armor and trucks. As a tactic it worked brilliantly."

"But surely the casualties were heavy?" said Shanley.

Fitzduane shook his head. "Ironically, you were a lot safer in the SAS than the regular army. It was a case of brute force versus speed, maneuverability, firepower, and brainpower. Anyway, with the SAS experience in the back of my mind, I started exploring the idea of a fast, light unarmored vehicle equipped with light but powerful weapons. And pretty soon I was pointed this way. The

U.S. Army might have gone heavy, but some people were pushing at the envelope."

"Chenowth," said Maury. "They made the dune buggies that did so well in the Baja. The U.S. Army formed an experimental division and started playing with converted Chenowths equipped with grenade launchers and TOW missiles and the like. It was political dynamite, because field evaluation showed that a fast attack vehicle, a FAV—which was what they called these things—could, in many cases, outkill not just armored fighting vehicles but also tanks. I've heard kill rates like nine to one and four to one."

Fitzduane nodded. "It gets complicated when you are talking combined arms, because armor does not operate in a vacuum. Add helicopters into the equation and FAVs might not have done so well. Also, the Abrams tank and Humvee programs were well advanced and big money was involved, and no one wanted to lose them. So, for all practical purposes, the FAV experiment was killed. I hear the marines bought a few, and the SEALs certainly took them on board with success, but major development, which was what the program needed, never happened. It should have, because FAV funding would have been chicken feed in comparison to most military programs, but it didn't. That's the trouble with inexpensive programs. There is not enough money in them."

Kilmara smiled. "Well, since we don't have any real budget by American standards, we picked up on the U.S. experience and some work in the U.K. and produced our own machine, but decided to try a slightly different direction. Both the Chenowth and the Saker are wheeled vehicles, excellent for some terrains but no good in marshy ground or snow.

"But we don't have the money to have different vehicles for different conditions, so we decided to go for an unarmored high-speed tracked machine that could do most of what the Chenowth and Saker could do but could operate worldwide. Sand, mud, rocky shale, snow, ice, marshy ground—the Guntrack can go just about anywhere. The intention is to equip it with enough firepower to knock out a tank and handle any immediate aerial threat, and it is the weapons aspect that we are still working on. Want to see it, Don?"

Shanley was not used to generals being this informal. He was a courteous man by nature and had found that around the U.S. Army, a crisp "Sir" did not go amiss. "Yes, sir!" he said.

Kilmara looked at him. "We're an informal culture these days in Ireland," he said. "First names are normal. I'm Shane. He's Hugo, and he—" he indicated Maury—"I think he is mellowing."

"Maury," said Maury. He was looking downright agreeable.

Fitzduane slipped in the video.

The group turned toward the screen.

The terrain was rocky undulating ground covered with outcrops of heather and patches of rough grass. In the background there was a line of hills under a lowering sky that was a surreal mix of menacing clouds and shafts of light.

It was a bleak but dramatic landscape that encompassed an extraordinary variation of shape and line and shade and color. It was stunningly beautiful, and Shanley suddenly realized that this was not just some foreign land.

This was where his roots lay. This had once been home.

A dark shape appeared in the distance. It was hard to make out the details. The silhouette was low and indistinct. The vehicle approached following a zigzag course and across land that would have been impassable in a wheeled vehicle. The sound track suggested that it made surprisingly little noise.

The vehicle came closer and drove parallel past the camera so it could be seen in profile. As it did so, it could be seen that although the tracks were riding over rocks and a generally uneven surface, the upper portion of the vehicle was virtually stable.

The driver locked one track and the Guntrack did a 360-degree turn on its own axis and then came to a complete halt.

It was like nothing either Don or Maury had ever seen. It was a small, low black box on tracks with a wedge-shaped front and what looked like folded-up forklift prongs on the rear. A driver and a gunner equipped with twin 5.56mm Minimi machine guns sat in the front.

The vehicle was steered by left-hand drive. To the right of the front gunner, a Stinger antiaircraft missile was clipped into position. Behind the two front seats was a gunner with an M19 belt-fed 40mm grenade launcher mounted on buffered soft mount attached to a turret ring. As they watched, the rear gunner's station rose on a hydraulic mount to give him a wider field of fire. The entire station then rotated 360 degrees. It then retracted and a slim mast mounting a miniature FLIR monitor rose up and panned in a circle.

"The Guntrack," said Fitzduane, "is the vehicle that the Irish Rangers are beginning to use for special operations. It is not armored in the traditional sense, but it is made from a special plastic that will withstand small-arms fire, and the tracks are a Kevlar and artificial rubber blend. Hell of a good power-to-weight ratio. Accelerates like a rocket and does up to eighty-five miles an hour with a full payload. The weapons fitted can, of course, be varied, but fully equipped with something like you see, it should cost no more than five percent of a tank. As to maintenance, if I can exaggerate just a little to make a point, it can be maintained by the three-man crew with their Swiss Army knives."

The video continued for another fifteen minutes as the camera focused in close-up on individual aspects. Everything from fuel consumption to changing an engine was covered. In fact, it was the attention to detail that was most impressive and ingenious.

The fuel tank, for instance, was of a honeycomb design that could be penetrated by an incendiary round without igniting. The forks at the back could be lowered to pick up a standard NATO pallet holding up to a ton. Guntracks could be linked so that if the engine on one went, the second could pull the first under power.

Shanley and Maury watched with fascination. The sheer logic of the thinking was impressive. The Guntrack had been designed by people who knew the reality of combat.

Maury could still see a problem. "Artillery will make mincemeat of you," he said. "Potentially, there is a terrifying amount of unfriendly metal on today's battlefield, and much of it will cut right through your plastic box."

"The Guntrack is not the ultimate weapon," said Fitzduane. "It is no more than one more useful tool. It is designed for a shoot-and-scoot approach to survival. It is primarily a better way, we think, to get around when you are on the ground on some special operations missions. The underlying idea is not to be detected at all, but if you are detected, to have enough firepower to make the enemy back off while you hightail it out of the area. It beats the hell out of dying."

Shanley had been thinking it through. "How do you use Guntracks tactically?" he said.

"We've found that the minimum practical deployment is two vehicles," said Fitzduane. "Then fire and movement. One covers the other like a fighter pilot and his wingman."

Kilmara turned to face Shanley and Maury. "Well, gentlemen," he said. "Now you know what we are working on. The next question is what you can suggest. Any ideas?"

"More than a few," said Shanley. His mind was racing. What he had seen, if properly developed, was not just interesting. It was tactically significant.

"This idea of a small, inexpensive fast vehicle taking on tanks reminds me of something that happened in Africa. The Libyans tried to grab their neighbor to the south and assembled an invading army of hundreds of tanks. They were beaten by Chadians driving only Toyota pickup trucks equipped with Milan missiles. The pickups maneuvered faster than the Russian tanks could move their turrets. Also, they were so small they were hard to hit."

Kilmara, who had been in Chad advising the Chadians at the time, did not say anything but looked at Shanley with renewed respect. This was a man who did his homework.

"You should look at Dilger's Baby," said Maury cryptically.

Fitzduane and Kilmara looked at each other blankly.

"How does a baby fit into all this, Maury?" said Kilmara carefully. Maybe Maury had finally flipped.

Maury beamed. "You'll see," he said.

WHEN the meeting broke up, Fitzduane checked the switchboard to see if Kathleen had checked in. If she went on an expedition, she normally called during the day to say roughly when she would be back.

There was no message. It was not significant, but Fitzduane could not help feeling vaguely uneasy. He looked at his watch. It was heading toward 5:00 P.M. The exhibition would close at 6:00, and soon after was a barbecue and some entertainment planned by the exhibition organizers for 7:30. The posters announced that there would also be some entertainment and dancing afterward.

Fitzduane had never seen country-and-western line dancers and was mildly curious. Certainly Kathleen, who loved dancing, would like it. As to the parachuting, there was always something morbidly fascinating about watching fellow humans jump out of a perfectly good airplane. Would the parachutes open? Where and how would they land?

It promised to be a pleasant enough evening.

THE North Carolina State Police duty officer contemplated the message slip. A citizen had reported seeing a woman being manhandled into a helicopter that had been parked in a remote clearing in the wooded land that bordered the freeway. The woman had been struggling and then she had gone limp, the witness thought. The helicopter had taken off immediately. Direction? Unknown.

Color of hair? Unknown. She had a bag or something over her head, he thought. Color of skin? The citizen did not know.

Descriptions of the assailants? There had been two—or maybe three. They had been casually dressed.

He could not really tell much else. How close had he been? He had been hiking in the woods and had seen all this as he was walking back. He was fifty to seventy-five yards from the clearing. Something like that. He wasn't real good at estimating distances.

The duty officer called in the dispatcher. "This is pretty thin. What did he sound like? Citizen or crank?"

The dispatcher shrugged. "Elderly, a little vague, but he definitely believes he saw something."

"Why was he hiking in the woods?"

"He said he is a birdwatcher. He was looking for the red cockaded wood-pecker. He's sure about that."

"So he saw all this through binoculars?" said the duty officer, somewhat en-couraged. He had been wondering how much an elderly man could see at fifty yards when peering through the gloom of a forest. Or was it seventy-five yards? It could be a hundred. It could be thirty.

Could you really tell the difference between a woman being helped aboard and pushed aboard? A bag over the head sounded much more like a head scarf to retain some semblance of a hairstyle under the assault of a rotor wash. Not a clear picture.

"Apparently not," said the dispatcher. "They were hanging around his neck, but he just forgot. He said he was too surprised, but he insists that he saw what he described. *Adamant* would convey the degree of emphasis. This guy was all fired up."

The lieutenant smiled and checked the report again. The incident had hap-pened—if anything had happened—forty minutes ago. His nearest patrol car was a good fifteen minutes away. And he was short two men.

"What kind of chopper?"

The dispatcher was getting a little irritated. "I asked him. He's into birds, not aircraft. Single rotor. Civilian paint job, something pale. That's all he knows."

"Did you ask him why he didn't report this earlier?" said the lieutenant. "I don't know what he expects us to do after forty minutes. The helicopter could be sixty miles away by now."

"He had to get to a phone," said the dispatcher. "And then he said he found he hadn't a dime."

The lieutenant shook his head. Where did they find them. He was tempted to log the call as requiring no further action, and then a thought occurred to him. He checked the map again. He knew that clearing. He'd patrolled that area. Hunted around there, too.

"If this is about a kidnapped woman, what would a helicopter be doing in *that* clearing? It's only about a hundred feet across." He looked at the map again and racked his brains. "There's a shitload of other places in the area you could land in more safely."

"Unless you did not want to be seen," said the dispatcher. She waited a beat before adding, "sir."

The lieutenant looked at her. He was good at looks. This one connected. Whatever the witness had said, given Fort Bragg's proximity, it was most likely a military chopper on some damn fool exercise. Still, maybe not. The red cockaded woodpecker was a protected species. The military, much to their chagrin, had been instructed to give the bird a wide berth. The word was they were even printing maps with little woodpeckers printed all over them. Hell of a note.

"Who is the closest?" said the lieutenant. "Richardson?"

The dispatcher nodded. "Sergeant Richardson," she confirmed.

"Tell him to go to the clearing and have a look around. He's got a good eye, and who knows . . . maybe the Russians are invading."

The dispatcher grinned and shook her head. "North Carolina in all this heat and humidity. No chance."

STATE trooper Sergeant Andy Richardson had a reputation for thoroughness. He was not academically bright, but he had learned you could go a long way in police work by just being organized, methodical, thorough, and healthy. And common sense did not hurt either.

He was completing his notes on a minor traffic accident when the call came in. It was not urgent, so he finished the cup of herbal tea he had resting in the cup holder and completed his notes.

He then closed his eyes and meditated for several minutes. It was not exactly police procedure, but his wife Susan was a great believer in cultivating inner peace, and it certainly seemed to work. He did not complete his shift stressed out like many of his colleagues. He could take most things in his stride.

Despite taking his time, he reached the turnoff to the clearing only fifteen minutes after the dispatcher's call had come through. The unpaved access track stretched out ahead of him. The clearing, he recalled, was about a quarter mile away. The forest crowded in on either side.

He was tempted to drive on down the track, but he decided to think this one through. If someone had been pushed into a helicopter in the clearing, they had to have been brought there. It could, of course, have been another helicopter, but if so, why make a switch? No, the chances were that a vehicle would have been used.

Richardson got out of the cruiser and examined the track carefully. He could see one recent set of wheel marks in the dust heading toward the clearing but none coming out. The hairs on the back of his neck started to prickle. The supposed incident had happened about an hour earlier. The vehicle that had been reported as being involved in the transfer should have left—or else it was still inside. There was one other possibility.

He picked up his radio and gave his call sign. "Did our birdwatching witness drive to the clearing?"

"Negative," said the dispatcher. "His home is about two miles back, and he walked. He's there if you need him."

"I've got one set of tire tracks going in," said Richardson. "I'm going to block off the road and go in on foot. I'll call you in ten."

"Need backup?" said the dispatcher.

"No," said Richardson. "This probably doesn't amount to anything. But . . ."

He parked the cruiser across the track. Then he unclipped his shotgun. You never knew, and the mere sight of a shotgun tended to make potential assailants think twice. There was something about the sheer size of the muzzle.

He walked carefully and slowly down the track toward the clearing, examining not only the track itself but the undergrowth and woods on either side. If someone had been struggling in the car, they just might have been able to drop something out of the window. Perhaps some identification or a note. Well, it was unlikely, given the prevalence of air-conditioning combined with fully closed windows, but he had to check and now was the best time.

It was alarming how quickly the integrity of a crime scene could be compromised. Items of value that might also be clues had a tendency to vanish no matter how you tried to secure the scene. Human nature was just that—all too human. Of course, this was not yet a crime scene, but when you had a report you had to act as if the location might be. Certainly that was Richardson's way.

He held his shotgun in his right hand and used a stick to push aside the vegetation. All kinds of things that crawled and slithered and bit flourished in North Carolina—and not all were human. He smiled to himself, and then the joke lost some of its flavor as his stick revealed a rattlesnake curled up next to a rock. The snake seemed to look at him as if debating the odds, then shot into the undergrowth. It did not like shotguns either.

Richardson was used to snakes, but that kind of eyeball-to-eyeball encounter certainly got the adrenaline going. He waited until his heart had stopped pounding and then radioed in.

This time he was transferred to the lieutenant, who was becoming somewhat frustrated at how long checking out one simple call was taking. Particularly when it was almost certainly nothing.

"Hurry it up, Andy, will you?" said the lieutenant.

"Roger that, Lieutenant," said Richardson flatly.

He entered the clearing a few minutes later. If he had read the tracks right, there should have been a car there, but there was nothing. This was all getting ridiculous, he decided. They would be talking flying saucers and little green men soon. In the real world, vehicles did not drive into lonely clearings and just vanish. Life was much more mundane. Solid stayed solid and flesh stayed flesh. And visible stayed visible.

All good sensible thinking, he reflected, but he still could not see that damned automobile and there was no track out of the clearing.

He started a perimeter search. The trees were growing too close together and too irregularly for a vehicle to have been driven between them. Then he saw the break in the tree line where maybe there had been a lightning strike or storm damage. Anyway, a couple of trees were down. The vegetation had been cut away and then replaced in a crude attempt to buy time.

He pulled the cut undergrowth out of the way. It did not take too long, and then there in front of him was the trunk of a Dodge sedan. A rental, by the look of it. The hood pointed into the forest.

The trunk was locked. He tried the doors and they were open. There were no keys in the ignition, but he found the trunk release lever.

He recognized the odor immediately. It was an amalgam of blood and excrement and fear. It was the smell of violent death.

He edged up the lid of the trunk with his stick and looked in.

Staring up at him, wide-eyed mouth open in a rictus grin of fear, was the body of a young woman. Her throat had been cut and it looked as if she had bled to death there. Her clothing and the inside of the trunk itself were saturated in blood.

Richardson could imagine her lying there terrified and helpless in the confines of the trunk as her executioner stood over her, knife in hand. There were severe slashes on her hands. She had tried to defend herself. Closer examination showed blood on and around the front passenger seat. She had been hit there, he surmised, and then dumped as she was dying. The callousness was chilling.

Subdued and depressed, he called in. He could take traffic accidents except where they involved the injury or death of children.

This kind of wanton butchery shook him. He thought of Susan. It could have been she in there.

Procedure dictated that he wait for the scene-of-crime team, but he had to do something and he knew he was professional enough to do it right. He started searching the clearing slowly and thoroughly, working to an imaginary grid.

There were clear signs of the reported helicopter and of activity surrounding it. Leaves and small branches had been dislodged by the downdraft, and some branches in the center of the clearing by landing skid marks suggested that the pilot had maybe clipped the tree tops coming in. Out of practice, inexperienced, or just a hotshot? Hard to know. Richardson favored out of practice. A novice would scarcely try landing in a narrow clearing like this.

After twelve minutes of searching, he saw a glint in the sandy earth fairly near the skid marks. Whatever it was seemed practically covered. Dropped by accident or deliberately.

He bent down and scratched the earth away with his stick. It was an unusual charm bracelet made of two types of gold, by the looks of it. He hunkered down, hooked the bracelet on the stick, and brought it close. The design was abstract, but one of the charms looked like a harp. It was an expensive item and had both a clasp and a safety chain. This had not fallen by accident.

He read the inscription inside.

Richardson took an evidence bag out of his hip pocket and slipped the bracelet inside. He was thinking. The kind of gutsy person who dropped this will have tried to drop something more than once. But he had found nothing on the track, and the car's windows were, as he had expected, closed. Maybe she had been kept in the trunk with the other woman. Hell, maybe there was only one woman and the witness had been mistaken. She had struggled as she was being put on board and had been killed.

No, that did not feel right. The witness had proved out so far, so why not give him the benefit of the doubt and assume two women? That meant that the kidnap victim could have been kept either in the trunk or in the back of the car.

Either way, it meant searching the car, and that was very much against the rules.

On the other hand, in a kidnapping—and now he was fairly certain there had been one—time was crucial.

He found the telephone message slip pushed down behind the upholstery of the backseat. It was the kind of thing you would jot down to remind you what room you were in. There was no date, but the paper looked fresh.

They now had a dead woman, murdered for sure, a probable kidnapping, and some guy named Hugo was involved. The message slip was from Fayetteville.

Richardson called in again. He did not do any more searching. A kidnapping—and a helicopter being used—was going to mean federal involvement for sure.

And the feds could be more than difficult if they felt their scene of crime had been screwed up.

Sergeant Richardson did not think he had screwed up, but as with most things in life it was going to be a matter of perception.

He checked his watch and hoped that the scene-of-crime team would get their ass in gear. It was going to be dark soon.

SHELBY Jacklin, sheriff of Fayetteville, put down the phone and thought. When he had been younger he had been a great believer in immediate action. Now he liked to get the flavor of a situation before moving.

It had taken just one quick phone call to identify this "Hugo." The question now was what to do. Hugo Fitzduane might be the killer or he might be entirely innocent. But the probability was that either the dead woman or the kidnap victim was closely connected to him. And it was a statistical fact that most murders were carried out by someone you knew and most probably were close to. Like married to.

This business was going to get complicated. The body had been discovered by the state police outside his jurisdiction, but this Fitzduane was staying right in the sheriff's patch. And before long the feds would be on the scene.

They could question Fitzduane immediately or go for a search warrant first. Then they could search this Irishman's room with impunity. It was the safer route. A search warrant would not take long. Judge Rikel was a hard-liner with strong views on violent crime.

It would also be a good idea to check Fitzduane with the FBI. Sheriff Jacklin was not overly fond of the feds, but he had learned to sup with the devil if it got the job done.

 **CHAPTER EIGHT**

COUNTRY-AND-WESTERN music filled the air and a demonstration team of line dancers in yellow shirts, red kerchiefs, and white Stetsons sashayed and pivoted with drill-team precision.

Several hundred exhibitors were gathered around the poolside and the open bar was having its predictable effect. Tables covered in checked tablecloths had been set up and the barbecue team were in full action.

After a long hard day, people drank and ate and networked and relaxed. There were many more women present than were actually attending the exhibition. Wives and girlfriends who had steered clear while their menfolk played with weaponry had surfaced.

It was a festive atmosphere, and the evening had all the makings of a really good party. The parachute demonstration would be the last event that was special operations oriented, and then the focus would be on nothing more than having fun.

As agreed, Dana was keeping an eye on Kathleen. Texas was doing much the same for her team. She had considered attending the party, but that would have turned the whole thing into a social event, and she was supposed to be working.

So she stood behind the parapet on the flat roof of the right-hand accommodation block and watched the festivities below. From that location, five stories up, she had the high ground and could actually keep quite a close eye on her charges through binoculars. At full power she was visually near enough to lip-read.

Another reason she had not gone to the party was Don Shanley. It had been a perfect night, and that was the way she wanted to remember it. If they met again face-to-face it could get complicated, and she knew she would get hurt. Shanley was attracted to her, she knew, but he was a certain kind of man. He might stray if she worked hard, but his loyalties lay elsewhere and he would not change them. That she knew, and it hurt because there was something about him that had connected. Too bad. The best ones were so often married.

She checked out her surroundings afresh. The courtyard below was pool and party. To her left was the main hotel block. Directly across from her was the other accommodation wing, similar to where she was standing but two blocks lower. The fourth side of the rectangle was open. There was an access road and a car park. The free-fall parachutists, she had been told, would float in the open end and land around the pool. It should be quite spectacular.

She considered the exhibition security. At the end of the day, all weapons on display were locked up by the individual exhibitors and then kept either on the exhibition hall floor or in the exhibitors' own rooms. The corollary of that was that the organizers' security was relaxed somewhat. If the weapons were locked up there was no need for as many guards, so went the argument. And having full strength at night was expensive.

The Bastogne Inn was one location where they really should be safe. But Texas was a professional. She stayed and she watched, because you never really knew. In the final analysis, it was all a giant craps game.

Then she saw Shanley and her heart leaped.

You tried to stay in control and then your body betrayed you.

"HUGO," said Kilmara patiently. "Relax and enjoy yourself. If Kathleen has gone to the coast to spend the day sight-seeing, which is my understanding, there is no way she will be back before late this evening. She may even stay there overnight. There is a lot of driving involved. So take it easy. She is a grown woman, Dana is keeping an eye on her, and Kathleen is pregnant, which does things to your hormones and moods. She wants some space. It's normal."

Fitzduane looked at his friend. He wanted to believe him with every fiber of his being. Yet his instincts told him something was wrong, and, unfortunately, his instincts rarely let him down.

It was not a blessing. Much of the time it was a curse. Life was hassle enough without advance and imprecise warning of upcoming difficulties. However, the other side of the coin was that he was equipped with an equable temperament that also rarely let him down.

He struggled for the middle ground. The music was infectious and people were having fun. He did not want to cast around doom and gloom.

"I'd be happier if she had telephoned," he said quietly. "She almost always phones."

Kilmara looked at him sharply. Privately, he was as concerned as Fitzduane, but he could not see what they could do right now that would be of any practical advantage.

"Hugo," he said firmly. "You had a row. Kathleen wants to keep her distance for a few hours. Accept it and stop behaving like an old woman."

Fitzduane smiled. Shane was right. He was overreacting. It was time to change the subject.

He gestured at the line dancers. "You know, I've never danced or made love wearing a hat and cowboy boots."

"You don't know what you're missing," said Shanley. "Where's Maury?"

Kilmara laughed. "Maury can make it one to one with difficulty. He can't handle large gatherings. He's in his trailer working."

"And Texas is on the roof," said Fitzduane conversationally. "The beautiful blonde with the binoculars on the skyline. She's our guardian angel."

Shanley looked up and straight into Texas's eyes. "I know," he said quietly.

SHERIFF Jacklin went through the FBI report once again.

Hugo Fitzduane was indeed known to the Bureau, only no criminal record was involved. The Irishman was on the side of the good guys and he was connected. There were a series of reference numbers that could be called. Most were inside the Beltway. One was Langley. The Hill was well represented. And the man was a colonel in some counterterrorist outfit. This thing had all kinds of nasty ramifications.

"Holy shit!" he said half to himself. "I was mindful to arrest you for murder."

Mike Erdman, a sheriff's department investigator, poked his head through the door. "Sheriff," he said. "We've got the warrant to search Fitzduane's room."

The sheriff looked up. "Wait awhile. I've a hunch this thing is a mite more complicated," he said.

He thought. There was a conjunction of elements here that had ramifications way outside his normal daily concerns. This was not about drunken airborne troopers smashing up a bar or some cuckolded husband back from a foreign tour blowing the brains out of his wife or lover.

This smacked of another battlefield. Murder, a kidnapping, a helicopter, counterterrorism. The mysterious Hugo Fitzduane. A special-operations exhibition.

Connections in Washington. Too many connections in Washington. The feds—all kinds of feds. This could become downright horrible. Feds were like a social disease—intrusive and hard to shake.

He looked up at Mike Erdman. "Mike," he said. "Phone the MPs at Bragg and tell them."

"What?" said Erdman.

"Something is going down," said the sheriff.

"What?" said Erdman. "You know, Sheriff, underneath their fatigues they are cops up there. They ask questions like that. Who? What? Why? Motive? Means? Opportunity?"

Sheriff Jacklin took a flier, which was something he never did. But something screamed inside him.

"Tell them we have reason to believe there are terrorists in the area and that something big is going down."

Erdman gaped at him.

"Mike," said the sheriff. "You're a fine detective. But sometimes you're an asshole." He smiled. "Nothing personal. Now, MOVE!"

Erdman went back to his desk.

He was lifting the phone when they heard the explosion and felt the tremor.

"Bragg?" he said out loud.

Sheriff Jacklin stood in the doorway. "No," he said. "Much closer."

They did not have long to wait. The first call came in within thirty seconds.

"Sheriff?"

Jacklin raised his head. He felt unbelievably tired.

"Sheriff, they've bombed the Oak Park Shopping Center. Dozens dead. Hundreds injured. Lots of military families hit, by the looks of it."

The thought that Jacklin had considered yet suppressed in the past came through. You don't have to hit Bragg to hit Bragg. All you have to do to kill lots of soldiers and their families is to strike at the nearby shopping centers. No MPs and minimal security. Child's play for a dedicated terrorist. Child's play for any psycho.

He had thought about it and even raised it at a local-state-federal security meeting. He had been brushed aside. He had done nothing. It was hard to go up against the system. You questioned it at your peril.

There was not a serious terrorist threat in the United States of America. That was the conventional wisdom.

It was accurate in a bizarre way. It was not a threat anymore. It was happening.

FITZDUANE put his hand inside his light cotton jacket and adjusted his holster. It was idiotic having to cart around a lump of metal at a social occasion, but he had been caught short on the Hill and did not feel like making the same mistake twice.

He could hear the buzz of a light aircraft. So could others. A ripple ran through the crowd. The aircraft drew nearer and then began to circle. A wind indicator was dropped and fluttered to the surface. There was little wind that evening. It would not be a factor in the drop.

The aircraft climbed until it was about 3,000 feet. All eyes were fixed upon it, waiting for the first free-fall parachutist to emerge. They could see a small back dot and then a stream of pink smoke. The jumper had a smoke canister clipped to his boot.

Accelerating at 32 feet per second, the jumper fell through the air until he reached a terminal velocity of 120 miles an hour. At that point, wind resistance offset the tendency to accelerate. Seemingly liquid air fostered the illusion that it was providing a cushion and that you were really flying as surely as a swimmer was supported by the sea.

It was an illusion that had killed on more than a few occasions when a sky diver left pulling the D ring until too late.

The jumper hurtled toward the upturned faces below.

Suddenly there was a flash of color as the rectangular ram air parachute was pulled open by the miniature drag 'chute. At the same time, a second smoke canister on the jumper's other boot ignited.

He now presented quite a spectacle. His parachute, helmet, and jumpsuit were scarlet and he streamed pink and yellow smoke. As he came nearer, Fitzduane could see that the jumpsuit had been modified to look like a pantomime devil. The helmet had little horns and there was even a tail at the back.

Ram air parachutes were highly maneuverable, Fitzduane knew. Toggles on the left and right of the jumper allowed air to be spilled and the direction of the glide to be controlled. In some ways, ram air parachutes were more like flying wings than the traditional umbrella-shaped model.

In this case the jumper was not doing anything too exotic. Now that his 'chute was open he was merely spiraling around in large circles, trailing smoke. The plan, Fitzduane could now see, was to make the final approach over the parking lot at the back of the hotel and glide in between the two accommodation wings to land by the pool. Maybe even in the pool, if he really wanted to please the crowd, who, after over an hour's steady drinking, were in a boisterous mood.

Four more figures had emerged from the aircraft, but the focus was on the first sky diver as he commenced the last spiral ready to make his approach.

Kilmara was watching through military field glasses that gave him 10× magnification. Fitzduane was using a motor drive–equipped Nikon with a zoom lens. Boots would have loved this, he reflected. Still, since the Rangers trained on his island, his son was no stranger to spectacles such as this.

Up on the roof, Texas was doing what her security training had taught her. She was keeping her eyes moving. She glanced occasionally at the sky divers, but her main concern was the bigger picture.

The line dancers had stopped for the moment and were gazing skyward like everyone else, but the sound of music had not diminished. It had increased. The pool loudspeakers, turned up full volume, were now blasting out "The Ride of the Valkyries." It fit the mood of the exhibitors, many of whom were Vietnam veterans, since they associated it with the helicopter assault in *Apocalypse Now*, but it was so loud it was hard to hear yourself think.

It was too damn noisy for good security.

The first sky diver, still spewing smoke, was circling for the final approach. Everyone was looking toward the direction he was coming from.

Texas panned around to look in the opposite direction. More surprises! A helicopter flying low was heading straight for the center block of the hotel. Black masked figures wearing SWAT assault gear were standing on the skids to the left and right, ready to jump down.

It was a dramatic sight, and the audience below was going to love it. Just when they were looking in one direction, this mock helicopter assault would take them in the rear. She could see it now. Simulated explosions. Black-clad figures running into assault positions. The chatter of blanks from automatic weapons. Thrills for the crowd.

All of this had once thrilled her, too, when she was doing it. Now she increasingly felt she would like to do something more constructive. Like make something. A baby seemed a good place to start. She had fought against being stereotyped as a woman, but recently her hormones seemed to be telling her something.

She glanced down at Shanley. He was standing in the same group as Fitzduane and Kilmara. And Kilmara was shouting something and pointing.

At that moment, Shanley looked up at her and pointed also at the first sky diver who was coming in to land, and she saw the three men head behind a low wall as if diving for cover.

She turned again to look at the helicopter that was now almost at the hotel and she saw lights flashing underneath it. Then she half-turned back again to look down at Shanley as the long burst of heavy-caliber machine-gun fire smashed into her and blew her off the roof in a mist of blood and flesh and bone.

Her body plummeted down and smashed into the barbecue area below, scattering hot charcoal in every direction.

Shanley died a little as he watched. Then his head hit the ground hard as Fitzduane knocked him down behind cover.

"Look at his arms, Hugo!" Kilmara had shouted. "They are strapped to his sides. He's not controlling his own 'chute."

Fitzduane had snatched the binoculars. The sky diver's head lolled forward. He looked lifeless, like some full-size puppet. There was a device on his chest with wires connecting it to the toggles.

And then the import of what they had seen hit them and, grabbing Shanley and shouting at the others, they dived for cover.

The sky diver floated in for what looked like a perfect landing.

The crowd made way as he glided in, then surged forward as he touched down.

It was at that moment that the fléchette-packed bomb strapped to the radio-controlled corpse of the sky diver exploded, sending several thousands of miniature metal darts in every direction. The man's body was blasted into a fragmented pink cloud of blood and fragments of flesh and bone.

The flash of the explosion was followed by the noise of the blast. Confined and magnified within the confines of the pool area, it seemed to last for an eternity. The ground shook under them.

As the initial shock faded, there were further sounds of glass and other debris crashing to the ground in a rain of destruction.

Fitzduane was disoriented for several seconds. Then realization returned. He raised his head from behind the low wall that had saved their lives. Bodies lay strewn everywhere, and farther away from the main blast survivors were standing or slumped, dazed with shock. Many were bleeding from injuries, some superficial, some serious.

Others had been blasted into the pool. Its clear blue water was turning a murky streaked crimson made all the more sickening by the underwater lighting.

Those still alive began trying to get out of the pool, and some survivors went forward to aid them.

Fitzduane was just moving out of cover to help also when he saw the helicopter pulling away from the roof of the block where Texas had been and masked black-clad figures appearing at the parapet. For a moment he thought it might be the local SWAT team coming to help, and then he heard the chatter of automatic weapons and saw the helpers at the poolside cut down one after the other as if an invisible saw had sliced through them.

The water in the pool frothed as machine-gun fire from both the helicopter and the terrorists who lined the roof was poured down into the pool area. What had been the location for a poolside party was now a killing ground.

Fitzduane watched appalled as the gunfire reached a trio of line dancers and they jerked like marionettes as the rounds punched into them.

He ducked down. Kilmara and Shanley lay there also. Kilmara had drawn his automatic but made no move to fire back. Given the sheer weight of fire raining down upon the area, it would have been suicide.

The door into the accommodation block was only twenty feet away, but to cross that divide meant inviting death. As they watched, one of the exhibition security men made a run for it, turning around halfway to return covering fire from his pistol and then sprinting on.

A rocket hissed down from the parapet and blew the legs off the unfortunate man and his torso back into the open corridor.

"We've got to get out of here," said Kilmara. "Our friendly wall will stop rounds, but RPGs will walk right through it. All ideas welcome. I haven't got a fucking clue how to move without getting perforated. And that's a hell of an admission for a general."

Fitzduane was a great believer in the principle that any decision was better than no decision but in this case it seemed wiser to put that particular aphorism on hold. As of now they had a place out of the line of fire. Better yet, the terrorists did not seem to know they were there or a few more rockets would have come their way.

"My room is just up the corridor," said Shanley. He sounded shaky, but he was hanging in there. "I've got an M16 and a Barrett inside which I use for demonstrations. If we can get at them, we can do something. They're locked up in security boxes, of course, but I have the keys."

Fitzduane was struck by the irony of it all. Here they were surrounded by every conceivable light infantry weapon in the exhibition, but most of the weaponry had no ammunition and all was locked up. A further irony was that no one was going to react to all the shooting. The hotel was freestanding, and the fact that there was going to be some kind of special-operations demonstration had been widely announced precisely to prevent the local citizenry from getting worried. And the police had also been informed. So for the next few minutes at least they were on their own. And people were dying.

"Ammunition?" he said.

"Not a lot," admitted Shanley. "I used most of it at the range. Perhaps thirty rounds for the M16 and half that for the Barrett."

"How about your Stinger missile?" said Kilmara.

"It's a mock-up," said Shanley. "The case is real, but there is no electronics or firing mechanism."

"What's your Barrett ammo?" said Fitzduane. His life had once been saved by a marksman with a Barrett, and he had made a point of finding out everything he could about the weapon, down to visiting the plant in Tennessee. The Barrett was a large rifle ingeniously designed to make it possible for an individual soldier to fire rounds the size of a cigar without being flattened by the recoil. The benefits for certain situations were considerable. You could snipe at up to two kilometers, you could penetrate light armor, and you could fire right through a concrete wall.

"Raufoss multipurpose," said Shanley.

Fitzduane looked at Kilmara and both nodded. The Norwegian-made rounds were armor piercing with an explosive core and incendiary characteristics. They would do a very nice job on the parapet of the wall from which the fire was coming—and on whoever was behind the wall.

But there was still the problem of getting at the weapons. Also, if the black-clad terrorists were on the roof opposite, there was a reasonable chance that they had landed people on the opposite block. Carrying that thought further, some terrorists might be working their way down to the pool to finish off the job.

In other words, as they made a dive for the door to Shanley's room to get the heavier weapons they could meet terrorists coming in the other direction.

Fitzduane did not like this scenario at all. They had to move. And there had to be a way.

Doors crashed open about fifty feet away and a hotel employee emerged pushing a trolley stacked high with freshly starched laundry, apparently oblivious to the mayhem around him. The earphones of a Walkman were clamped to his ears and he pushed his heavy load with his head down, doing little dance steps from time to time.

All three men shouted warnings, but the laundryman was in another world. He advanced down the path toward where they lay. He seemed to have a charmed life. At first he was unnoticed by the terrorists, and then their fusillades missed both him and the trolley.

It was a distraction.

Shanley and Kilmara leapt for the open doorway and just made it before heavy fire raked the wall behind them.

Fitzduane aimed his automatic with care and shot the laundryman below the knee. He fell behind the safety of the low wall and stared around frantically, shocked and terrified.

"STAY DOWN!" shouted Fitzduane, and made a gesture with his arm.

The laundryman looked at him, his mouth open. He was only about thirty feet away, but there was a gap in the low wall and fire was pouring through it. The Walkman had fallen off the laundryman as he had collapsed, but the earphones were still clipped around his head. Fitzduane fired at the machine and blew it apart.

The laundryman's eyes became round saucers. Then he suddenly seemed to realize the earphones and ripped them off.

"STAY THE FUCK DOWN!" shouted Fitzduane again. "THIS ISN'T SOME WAR GAME. IT'S REAL. STAY RIGHT DOWN AND DO NOT MOVE!"

The laundryman nodded frantically and then squeezed himself up as small as he could in the angle formed by the wall and the path.

Fitzduane got ready, waited until the focus of fire had moved away for a moment, and then launched himself at the trolley. Linen flew in every direction as he threw himself flat on the top and propelled it through the open doorway into the corridor. It shot down the corridor and smashed into a mirror.

"Seven years' bad luck," said Fitzduane savagely to himself, "and I was doing so well."

He picked up a piece of mirror and used it as a crude periscope to check around the next corner.

A hooded terrorist clad in the familiar black was moving carefully up the corridor. As Fitzduane had feared, they were moving down to finish the job. But there just could not be that many of them, or they would be checking the rooms too. There should be at least one backup, but he could see no one. It was bad military practice, but this seemed like a lone scout.

The terrorist came around the corner. As he did so, Fitzduane pushed his weapon up and rammed the mirror splinter into his throat.

The man gurgled, and then blood poured through the fabric of his hood and he slumped. Fitzduane broke his neck. A dying enemy could still be a dangerous enemy.

The man was carrying the Russian version of the M16, an AK–74. It helped to explain the intensity and accuracy of the fire. The weapon was equipped with double forty-round plastic magazines on a neat device that allowed a magazine change by simply sliding the empty magazine to one side and the new one into place. It also came with an unusually effective muzzle brake, which allowed more-accurate automatic fire. The downside was that the gases were deflected to either side with a considerable risk of doing no good to your companions.

Fitzduane checked the ammunition pouches of the dead man. He had come loaded with fifteen magazines, six hundred rounds, and only three spare magazines were left in addition to the two on the rifle. That, and the sheer risk of local law enforcement being alerted eventually, suggested that the terrorists would be pulling out soon.

He lay down and rolled over once so he could check the corridor while presenting a minimum target. He knew he should have used the mirror trick again, but the sliver he had used before was deep in the terrorist's throat and he did not feel like going back to the broken mirror. He wanted to link up with Kilmara and Shanley, and quickly.

Muzzle flash blinded him and rounds sliced through the air above his head. If he had been standing or even kneeling, it would have been inconvenient. There was a backup man, and he had fired instinctively from the hip when he had seen movement. He was very fast, but his target was not where he had expected it to be.

Fitzduane fired back low, and then as his assailant buckled, he put a second burst into his head.

"KILMARA! SHANLEY!" he shouted. He could not remember where Shanley's room was, and this was no time for playing hide-and-seek.

There was an answering shout from down the corridor. Then a door opened and the long muzzle of a Barrett emerged.

Fitzduane thought through the next action. The block they were in had three stories and the one across the way had five. So if they went up on the roof they would still have the low ground. Worse still, they would be exposed.

They could head through the main body of the hotel and try and get up to the higher roof that way. That would take too long, and who knew what shit was going down in the middle.

The best solution seemed to be to fire from the second floor from the cover of a room window. They would be shooting at a diagonal and up, but since the Barrett round could travel eight miles gravity at that short range should not be much of a problem. The distance across the pool area to the parapet was less than a hundred and fifty meters.

"One floor up," said Fitzduane.

"My thoughts exactly," said Kilmara.

Shanley made to lead, but Fitzduane beckoned him to one side. The Barrett had many fine qualities, but close-in fighting going up a stairs was more the job of a lighter, short-barreled weapon. The Barrett weighed well over twenty pounds. You could drop it on someone's toe and put him out of action.

The stairs was empty. The second-floor corridor was empty.

Fitzduane kicked at a door with the flat of his foot and the room door splintered at the lock and sprang open. The room was empty. The blinds were drawn, but the glass had been blasted away by terrorist gunfire from across the pool area. The walls of the room were pockmarked with bullet holes.

He could hear a series of other crashes from the corridor as Kilmara kicked in the doors. First, he did not want any surprises, and second, they wanted to be able to move from room to room at will. It made no sense to present a static target when you could move around.

Kilmara would watch their back from the corridor while he and Shanley took on the other side. It was not something they had discussed. They had worked together for so long and trained so often that the moves came naturally.

They could hear the *whump* of rotor blades but could not see it from their position. He tried to judge the helicopter's location. It sounded as if it had landed on the roof of the main block. The terrorists were withdrawing. The parapet was still manned, but any second now they would start pulling away out of sight.

"I've only got seven rounds," said Shanley apologetically. He had remembered to put acoustic plugs in his ears, Fitzduane observed. A very good idea, given the decibel count of a .50 in a confined space.

"I'm going hot," said Shanley.

Fitzduane put his fingers to his ears and was glad he had. There was a deafening crack, and a large chunk of parapet blew away, carrying a black-hooded gunman with it.

Shanley fired again and again in a measured sequence, demolishing a long chunk of the parapet. A figure rose from the rubble, and Fitzduane snapped the AKM to his shoulder and dropped him.

The terrorist helicopter rose from behind the dome of the main block and swiveled its machine guns toward their position.

Shanley was taking aim with the Barrett. Fitzduane grabbed him and pulled him down.

A long, intense burst of fire raked along the second floor and blew every remaining window apart.

Fitzduane and Shanley crouched down below the window as the air was filled with fire. Then they could hear the helicopter pulling away. They stood up and Shanley raised the Barrett hopefully, but already it was out of sight behind the cover of the hotel and receding into the distance.

"How many rounds have you got left in that thing?" said Fitzduane.

Shanley removed the magazine. It was empty. He worked the bolt. The round was ejected. "One," he said.

Fitzduane contemplated his companion. The man was surprisingly calm for someone who had seen action for the first time. His forehead was beaded with sweat, but he was in control.

"Shanley," he said. "You are a piece of work."

Kilmara came in brushing plaster dust from his clothing and eyed the damage to the parapet across the way. It looked as if a demolition crew had been at work for a morning. "The hotel may not like you," he said.

"Don was planning to take on the helicopter with one round," said Fitzduane. "This is a man who believes in his weapon."

Kilmara was still eyeing the destruction. "One round, one helicopter! Well, by the looks of that mess it would probably be enough."

Shanley did not say anything. He could not stop it. Tears flooded from his eyes. He felt confused, tired, and terribly sad. As he looked up at the wrecked parapet he could see only Texas still alive. And then she was blasted apart and falling through this terrible red mist.

It could not have happened. It was his imagination. All of this was some elaborate war game. It was simulated. Soon everyone would get up and walk around and the music would start up again.

He looked down to the poolside below.

It was a mistake.

Her body was still there. Nothing had changed. It was not a dream. The water was now a solid, glowing, backlit crimson.

He slumped to his knees and sobbed uncontrollably.

Fitzduane reached out and rested his hand on Shanley's shoulder. He knew it helped. It had been done to him under very similar circumstances.

Kilmara looked at them and remembered. Fitzduane had been young then. They both had.

There was always a reaction. After a while it did not show, but it stayed with you.

M AURY had designed his mobile home to be as near soundproof as possible. He wanted to be able to work anywhere without interruption.

In this case, matters were made even more convenient by the fact that the Bastogne Inn, which specialized in conferences and exhibitions, had a special serviced area for mobile homes and trailers. You had to pay, of course, but you could plug in to the hotel phone system, cable TV, power and plumbing, and even utilize room service if you wanted. For Maury, it was an ideal arrangement.

He was oblivious to the terrorist attack. He was also so buried in his analysis that he had completely forgotten to pass on a message he had received. It had not struck him as particularly urgent, and then Lee Cochrane had phoned and the fax had beeped and the note got buried under a file.

After a while, the phone became a nuisance and he hit the mute button and engaged the answering machine. He needed to focus. There were aspects to this Mexican thing that did not make sense. There had to be more to it. There was an agenda he was missing, he was sure of it. But what?

He learned about the attack when Kilmara came to get him. Immediately he tried to notify Cochrane but could not get through.

Feeling decidedly shaken and, for no rational reason, guilty for not having been there, he went to help Fitzduane and Kilmara do what they could with the injured and the shell-shocked survivors. A stream of ambulances was already beginning to arrive, and medical teams were soon hard at work. The air was filled with the sound of medevac and other helicopters. Local, state, and federal law-enforcement units poured in.

The message remained forgotten.

FITZDUANE watched the ambulance doors close and the vehicle accelerate away, siren screaming and lights flashing.

That was the last of the wounded taken care of. There would now be the whole wretched business of being questioned by the bevy of law-enforcement people who had spent the last couple of hours installing themselves in strength and debating jurisdiction. Some had tried to question him earlier, but apart from giving what descriptions he could of the terrorist helicopter, he had refused to say any more until the wounded were attended to.

His motive was not entirely altruistic. He had found that giving succor to another helped ease the stress reaction that cut in after combat and the suppressed guilt that came from the taking of human life. On the conscious level he had no regret about what he had done, but his subconscious seemed to have feelings of its own. It was confusing, and all the more so because he was incredibly tired.

He slumped down on a sofa in the reception area. The rooms were all cordoned off. They were going to have to bunk down in Maury's trailer, he supposed. He looked down at his clothing. God, he was a mess!

His shirt and trousers were ripped, and caked with dried blood. His hands and forearms were streaked with dried blood also. The blood of the killers and the blood of the victims. It had been a long time since he had seen so many terrible injuries. More than sixty had been killed and perhaps two hundred wounded. Many were critical. The butcher's bill would mount up over the next few days.

Where was Kathleen?

He felt a sudden rush of concern. He checked his watch. It was after 10:00 P.M. and it was dark outside. Actually, it was a blessing that she had not been at the party, but still, he was worried. It was not in her nature to stay out of touch like this. They were not a typical couple who could wander at will. They were under terrorist threat, and there were routines and disciplines they had to stick to. One key routine was regular communication. It was a burden but it was reality, and Kathleen was conscientious. In fact, she was better than he was.

Two men with law enforcement stamped all over them were talking to a grim-faced Kilmara over by the reception counter. One slid a photograph out of a file and showed it to Kilmara. He studied it intently and shook his head. The other then slid something small and gold out of a small plastic envelope and held it in the palm of his hand.

Kilmara picked up the bracelet and read the inscription inside, then nodded. He looked across at Fitzduane, and there was both shock and sympathy in his face.

Fitzduane suddenly felt cold and sick. He tried to stand up, but for a moment his body seemed unwilling to respond. His limbs felt leaden and he seemed to have no strength.

Kilmara and the two men came over.

"Hugo," said Kilmara quietly, "just prepare yourself. This may not be as bad as it seems."

What? Fitzduane wanted to scream. *What is it? Why don't you just tell me?* At the same time he understood what Kilmara was trying to do and his whole being fought to be ready for what he was going to hear.

The photograph of the murdered woman meant nothing to him, and his hopes began to rise. She was young and blond, and her features were not remotely familiar.

Then he saw the bracelet and absolute horror swept through him. Kathleen had been kidnapped. But by whom and why?

The older of the two men spoke. "My name is Sheriff Jacklin, Colonel Fitzduane, and this here is Detective Erdman. I hate to say this, but it looks as if your wife might have been taken by the same people"—he made a gesture toward the pool—"who did all this. And as to who they are, you can rest assured we're going to find out."

Fitzduane looked at him blankly, as if he had not heard the words. Then he got to his feet unsteadily and turned away without explanation and walked toward the entrance. He felt as if he could not breathe and fresh air was the only solution. He staggered like a drunken man.

Kathleen was gone. He would never see her again. The people who had taken her killed without hesitation. They would *not* let her live. She would be a witness. She would have learned something. You always learned something, and these were people who took no chances. Kathleen would die—might already be dead—and he would have to accept it.

He could not accept it. Emotion ran through him. He held up his bloody hands. He was responsible for all this. Action and reaction and his cursed curiosity. It all went back to finding a hanging body and deciding to find out why. It was one body too many and it was on his doorstep and the victim had been so damned young. If only he had just walked on and never looked back.

"Hugo!" called Kilmara, his voice loud and sharp.

Fitzduane lowered his hands, then shook his head a couple of times as if trying to wake himself up. He had been oblivious to his surroundings, aware only of the balmy night air. He breathed in and out deeply.

The forecourt was a hive of activity. Law-enforcement vehicles came and went, and media vans with TV cameras mounted on their roofs were lined up behind the guarded perimeter. Arc lights supplemented the hotel lighting. As he watched, a helicopter touched down. Other helicopters circled above. Media again, he supposed.

Beyond the perimeter held back by barriers were many hundreds, perhaps thousands, of curious onlookers wedged five or six deep.

"Publicity is the oxygen of terrorism," someone had said. Well, these terrorists were getting plenty of oxygen. He hoped they choked on it.

Maury was standing beside Kilmara, looking rather anxious. Kilmara was reading something, and then he looked up. He appeared puzzled, and, followed by Maury, he walked toward Fitzduane.

"Maury took a phone message earlier on," he said. "It was from a woman. The switch tried your room and, finding no one there, rang Maury's trailer."

Maury shrugged apologetically. "I'm sorry, Hugo. Probably I should have delivered it earlier, but you were in and out all day and I thought you would be in again soon—and then I forgot about it."

Fitzduane read the message.

CALL ME SOONEST. R. O. IS ALIVE. YAIBO ARE IN YOUR AREA. TAKE EVERY CARE.

CHIFUNE.

The number she had given bore a Fayetteville area code.

The blood drained from Fitzduane's face.

R. O.? Reiko Oshima! It was all beginning to make horrible sense.

He told Kilmara.

The General's face turned gray. He had come up against her in Ireland. She was the most dangerous terrorist he had ever encountered. Most of the time there was no longer any rationale as to why she killed. The act was an end in itself to her.

Fitzduane called the number.

"Fitzduane-*san*," she said. The voice was the same, the formal address a barrier between them. Unbidden, the memory of her body came to him.

"I have an address," she said. "It is a Yaibo safe house. Your wife may be there. Go quickly."

"How do you know?" he said. "Chifune, how do you know?"

"I've had my people out," she said. "Now hurry, Fitzduane-*san*. There is very little time. Approach carefully but *in force*. Go quickly. They will move soon. I cannot stay."

"Oshima?" said Fitzduane. "Is she behind this?"

The phone was dead.

"Sheriff," said Fitzduane, showing Jacklin the address. "Where is this place?"

Jacklin checked the paper. "About an hour away, I guess. Maybe more. It's outside my jurisdiction."

"Sheriff," said Fitzduane. "Give me some people. I beg you. There's no time to clear this. Please."

Jacklin thought quickly. "I'll lay on a chopper. There will be a SWAT team waiting when you land." He barked into his radio.

Eight minutes later, Fitzduane and his pilot were airborne.

Fitzduane's face was wet with tears. *Dear God,* he thought. *Let us be in time.* Kathleen. Our baby.

Oshima! His heart turned to stone. *It is you, I know it.* I will find you if you're with the devil himself, and this time there will be no mistake. I *will* kill you.

He dried his cheeks and checked his weapons.

However long it takes, I *will* kill you. I swear it.

The helicopter swooped in to land in a clearing. The spot was wooded. Fitzduane had no sense of location. Jacklin had said the address sounded like a farm, which seemed to make sense.

"Colonel," said the pilot. "*Semper Fi,* sir."

Fitzduane shook his head wordlessly as a rush of emotion gripped him.

A DESERTED shack had been selected as temporary headquarters. Marked and unmarked vehicles were parked around it. They entered. The room had been cleared and now housed a bank of communications equipment on trestle tables. Maps of the area were being pinned up.

"Colonel Fitzduane?" said a man in black combat fatigues. A submachine gun hung around his neck. "Special Agent Hillgrove. FBI HRT out of Raleigh."

"The house?"

"It's about four hundred meters up ahead," said Hillgrove. "Clapboard farmhouse, kinda run-down. A barn and some other outbuildings. A rusty tractor and no animals. Two cars parked outside, but no lights on inside the farm that we can see. The drapes are closed. And that's about all we know."

"It's surrounded?" said Fitzduane.

"Yes, sir," said Hillgrove. "The state troopers have it sewn up every which way. We only got here ten minutes ago."

"My wife?"

Hillgrove's face reflected compassion and caution. According to Sheriff Jacklin, the woman had been grabbed the previous afternoon and a helicopter had been involved. That suggested that she had already been flown out of the area. Still, you could never be certain.

He shook his head. "We just don't know yet, sir. An electronic-surveillance team are moving into position now. They'll try and drill through and place a few miniature probes in position. But it will take some time. Best get some rest, sir."

Fitzduane absorbed the news. He was exhausted, he knew, and still in shock. He was not thinking clearly. There was information he should pass on to the FBI man, but he could not think what it was. He felt dizzy.

"Glass of water, sir," said Hillgrove, his voice concerned but distant. "You'd better sit down."

Fitzduane could feel his vision dimming, and there was a ringing in his ears. Someone took his arm and eased him onto a chair. He took the water with both hands and drank greedily. God, he was making all the classic errors. He was in shock, he had let himself get dehydrated, and he hadn't eaten. He was way overtired. He was personally involved.

He would have to get a grip. He closed his eyes. In the background he could hear the constant chatter of radio communications and the sound of footsteps as people walked to and fro. The floor creaked.

Hillgrove seemed to know what he was doing, Fitzduane reflected sleepily. But there is something I should tell him. He dozed.

"TAC One," said a voice in Hillgrove's earpiece.

"Roger, Five," said Hillgrove.

"We're inserting now," said Five. "Should come up on video any second."

Hillgrove had a mental picture of the surveillance team withdrawing their drill bits very slowly, careful to avoid the slightest sound, and inserting cameras and sound probes no bigger than the head of a matchstick.

He stared intently at the three video monitors. Any moment the first picture would come through. Whether there was light inside or not would make no difference except to the quality of the images. The miniature cameras had night-vision capability.

The first camera was coming on stream. The focus was slightly off and was adjusted.

"My God!" said a voice in absolute shock. "What have they done to her? What's that stuff hanging out of her? Oh my God!"

The wide-angle lens distorted the image and the picture had the greenish negative quality of night vision, so flesh tones could not be seen.

Nonetheless, the content was clear.

The naked woman's arms had been tied to the rafters and her legs spread and tied apart.

Her throat had been slashed, and her body and the floor beneath her were black with blood.

She had been gutted.

The voice was a hoarse whisper, a cry of hatred, pain, and the very depths of despair. The name was drawn out, a long sibilant sound.

"Oshimaaaaaa! Oshimaaaa!" whispered Fitzduane. "That's how she kills."

Hillgrove's mouth was dry. He swallowed. Fitzduane had woken and was staring intently at the monitor.

"Is it—do you recognize . . . ?"

Fitzduane turned to look at him. One hand made a gesture toward the monitor. "I—I don't know," he whispered. "Her face. They've cut off her face."

HILLGROVE continued the electronic surveillance for an hour. The findings were clear enough. The killers, whoever they were, were long gone.

The entry team were moving into position when Fitzduane remembered. "Don't go in," he said suddenly.

"Wait one," said Hillgrove into his mouthpiece. "What did you say, sir?" he said to Fitzduane.

"I know these people," said Fitzduane, "and they know us. As soon as they find a safe house, they prepare to move on. The house then becomes a trap. They know we will find it sooner rather than later, and they know roughly how long it will take us. The place will be mined."

"Then why the body?" said Hillgrove.

"To make us angry, to stop us thinking," said Fitzduane. "To lure us in. And it's working."

Hillgrove exhaled. He had been caught up in the immediacy of the entry routine and this distraction was disorienting. He was tempted to shut the man up or have him forcibly removed, but despite the torn, bloodstained clothing and the exhausted, haunted look on Fitzduane's face there was something about the man's bearing that made him credible. According to Sheriff Jacklin, this Irishman knew the world of terrorism, which was more than Hillgrove did.

"What do you suggest?" he said.

"Pull back and send in an ordnance disposal team. Tell them to take their time and to be very careful," said Fitzduane.

"But your—your—the victim?" said Hillgrove hesitantly. It was hard to imagine that hideous thing hanging from the rafters as living flesh and blood.

Your wife was unspoken.

"It's—it's too late for her," whispered Fitzduane. He was having trouble getting the words out. "If you could have done anything, I'd have let you go in and to hell with the risks. But she's dead, and what's the point of more people following?" There was agony in his voice.

"Who are these people?" said Hillgrove.

Fitzduane did not answer. Tears were streaming down his face.

Hillgrove hesitated.

"Tac One?" said a voice in his ear. "Ready to go."

"Pull back," said Hillgrove. "Get back fifty meters and get your heads down."

"What's—"

"DO IT!" snapped Hillgrove.

The entry team were still pulling back when two tons of homemade explosive ignited.

THE noise was persistent. Fitzduane heard it through waves of sleep. He knew he was supposed to react in some way, but something told him that he did not want to wake up. There were matters he would have to face that he did not want to have to deal with. Sleep was safer. His body screamed for more rest.

The phone went silent. The hours passed. Fitzduane slept on.

"Hugo," said a familiar voice. The tone was gentle, sympathetic. He felt a hand on his shoulder.

He tried to open his eyes, but his eyelids felt leaden. His throat was dry. He felt muzzy.

"Kathleen," he whispered. There was something important he should remember, he knew, and Kathleen was involved. "Kathleen," he said again.

"Hugo, you've got to wake up," said Kilmara.

Fitzduane struggled to open his eyes. He sat up slowly and took the proffered glass of orange juice. He drank greedily.

The room was in semidarkness, but chinks of light around the drapes suggested it was daytime.

Suddenly he remembered. A long, low cry as of physical pain escaped him. Internally, Kilmara winced. He felt helpless and inadequate in the face of such suffering.

"What time is it?" said Fitzduane.

"Nearly four in the afternoon," said Kilmara. "Don't feel bad. You did all you could before you crashed, and even then you were sedated. Grab a shower and you'll feel better. But first I've got one bit of good news. The dead woman in that house was not Kathleen."

Fitzduane felt a rush of relief followed by renewed anxiety. "Kathleen? Has she been found?"

"No," said Kilmara heavily. "It looks like she's been kidnapped, all right, but they are keeping her alive. And Chifune has turned up. The dead woman was her agent. She'll explain."

"Where is she?" said Fitzduane.

"Down the hall in my room waiting for you to wake up," said Kilmara. "Oga's with her."

Fitzduane swung his legs out of the bed and sat on the edge and rubbed his eyes. "Sergeant Oga?" he said. "Good man. What the hell is he doing here?"

"Inspector Oga now," said Kilmara. "And on the same assignment as Chifune."

"Oshima," said Fitzduane heavily, and headed into the bathroom.

"Oshima," said Kilmara to his friend's back. He had been in counterterrorism most of his life and tried to remain professionally detached. Oshima was personal. But for a Delta sniper called Al Lonsdale, Oshima would have already killed his friend. It had been damn close.

Fitzduane was in the bathroom for ten minutes. When he emerged, his distress was no longer evident. He was pale but his manner was calm.

There was coffee and toast on the table. Fitzduane poured two cups and forced himself to eat a little food.

"Where are we?" he said. "I remember that damned house and the explosion and then a whole lot more questions from the feds. Then I was given something to drink and I don't remember much more. I guess I dozed off in the helicopter."

Kilmara smiled grimly. "You didn't doze. The feds gave you enough jungle juice to knock out an elephant and then flew you back to Fayetteville. We're in a hotel about two miles from the Bastogne Inn. They want us to stick around for a few more days until they've made sense of all this."

"Who's they?" said Fitzduane.

"Just about everybody who carries a badge," said Kilmara. "Which is a whole lot of people in this part of the world."

"Do they know anything?" said Fitzduane.

"Not really," said Kilmara. "But it's early."

Fitzduane was silent.

CHIFUNE had tried to prepare herself mentally for the encounter, but when Fitzduane entered the room it was as if she had learned nothing about protecting herself from the emotional rigors of the world.

A mature woman, she felt defenseless. Her self-possession deserted her. Her heart pounded and a wave of feeling swept over her. She remembered the last time they had seen each other. It had been on the aircraft as Fitzduane was about to leave Tokyo to fly back to Ireland and Kathleen. To marry Kathleen. The man she, Chifune, had fallen in love with. Was still in love with. *It hurts, Hugo. It hurts.*

She bowed formally. Beside her, Oga bowed also.

Fitzduane returned their bows. As Chifune straightened their eyes met fleetingly, and suddenly she knew that Fitzduane had not forgotten and that she was very important to him and that this would never change. She wanted to embrace him, to console him. It was not appropriate.

"Tanabu-*san* and Oga-*san*, it is good to see you again," said Fitzduane.

Oga beamed. He had been suspicious of the *gaijin* when they had first met, but that initial reserve had evolved into high regard. His one reservation concerned Chifune. He was devoted to Tanabu-*san* and did not want to see her hurt any more.

"Fitzduane-*san*, we deeply regret we could not have done more," said Chifune, "but we believe we can help."

"Kathleen is alive," said Fitzduane flatly, "and we're going to get her back. That is one of two certainties. The other is that this time Oshima will be stopped permanently."

"Fitzduane-*san*," said Chifune cautiously, "it is not certain that Oshima has Kathleen."

"But it is probable?" said Fitzduane.

"Yes, Fitzduane-*san*, it is probable," said Chifune.

"Let's talk," said Fitzduane. "How much time do you have?"

"As long as is necessary," said Chifune. "Oga-*san* was in the Japanese airborne, you may remember, Fitzduane-*san*, and the airborne have an expression which sums up our commitment."

" 'All The Way,' " quoted Oga.

The thought came to Kilmara that Oshima seemed to have much the same motto. She would stop at nothing.

THREE hours later, Fitzduane was acutely conscious of not having had enough sleep and strongly suspected that whatever the FBI medic had pumped into him was not the kind of thing you wanted to play with too often.

Still, fatigue and headache apart, some of the helplessness he had been feeling had evaporated and he felt a course of action was beginning to come clear. It might not conform to the standards of evidence the FBI required, but he, Fitzduane, ran on instinct and it seemed to work for him.

Chifune and Oga had gone. Fitzduane and Kilmara were going over what they had heard.

"Something to bear in mind," said Kilmara, "is that Chifune's position is not easy. Her own side don't entirely trust her, or they would have told her that Oshima was still alive much earlier. Even more relevant right now is her situation in the U.S. She can't just go to the FBI and pour out her life story. She's the agent of a foreign power, and currently she's working through a Koancho network set up in the U.S. Tell the feds all about this, and they'll roll them up quicker than the NRA blocking a gun-control bill."

"The Japanese are a friendly foreign power," said Fitzduane.

"That doesn't give them carte blanche to have a network of spies in the U.S.," said Kilmara. "And remember that *friendly* covers a multitude, including quite a dose of industrial espionage, which gives the feds gas pains. So *friendly* doesn't mean let's all trust each other and share secrets. Its more like how you treat your in-laws."

"Okay," said Fitzduane. "I understand that Chifune is here to track down Yaibo and is working through her own people, but why, when she got wind of action here, didn't she contact me? She knew I was around. She'd rung home. They know her. They'd told her where I was."

Because in my opinion she's still in love with you, Hugo, and did not know how to handle an encounter, Kilmara felt like saying, but this was not quite the time for such directness.

"I guess she was going to contact you," said Kilmara, "but all this shit blew up first. Also, Chifune and Oga are emphatic they did not know what was going to happen. They thought there was going to be some kind of terrorist meeting. They did not envisage any action, let alone this kind of carnage. Hell, who would!"

"But when Kathleen was brought to the terrorist safe house, Chifune made contact," said Fitzduane. "But then Kathleen was moved before we arrived."

"This time with Chifune following," said Kilmara. "Until they boarded a helicopter and headed out to sea. End of the trail."

"And the woman killed at the safe house by the terrorists was one of Chifune's agents left behind on watch," said Fitzduane. "What a mess!"

"The good news is that Kathleen is definitely alive," said Kilmara, "and since they could easily have killed her it is reasonable to assume they intend to keep her alive for some purpose. They killed that unfortunate hitchhiker she gave a lift to without hesitation."

Fitzduane nodded. "But we don't know where Kathleen is or who is holding her. Oshima is a good guess, but here people were only one of several groups involved in the assault. Oshima herself was not seen. So Kathleen could be anywhere. Or held by anyone."

"You don't believe that, Hugo," said Kilmara.

"I guess not," said Fitzduane. "Every instinct tells me she's in Tecuno, but without proof the U.S. is going to do nothing. And even with proof, Mexico seems to be a no-go area."

"All true," said Kilmara, "but those kind of constraints never stopped us before, and this time I don't think we'll be alone. Have faith."

Fitzduane went over to the window and peered through the blinds. Night had fallen, and under the lights outside he could see sheriff's deputies and state police. Off to one side a Humvee mounting a 40mm automatic grenade launcher was parked.

"Serious security," he said.

"One of these days we are going to learn to hit them before they hit us," said Kilmara.

"If they hit us tonight, I'm going to sleep through it," said Fitzduane. "I'm going to hit the sack."

"You've one more thing to do," said Kilmara. "Talk to Dana. She'd like to apologize about losing her charge." He stood up. "I'll go get her."

According to Captain Dana Felton, Kathleen had asked her three times to leave her alone. She was fed up with all this security and needed some space. Eventually, Dana had pulled way back out of sight and then lost her client when Kathleen had switched off the agreed-upon road.

The rules of the bodyguard business were that your client's safety was more important than a client's feelings. On the other hand, when Kathleen needed her space it was an unwise person who got in her way, and she was eminently capable of losing her tail. Dana's story had the ring of truth, and in all honesty Fitzduane could not see she could have acted in any other way.

Dana came in. Kilmara stayed outside.

"I feel like shit, sir," said Dana. "I should have known better. I was trained better. I have no excuses, sir. I feel sick about Mrs. Fitzduane. Anything I—"

Fitzduane held up a hand to halt the flood. "How many people does it take to provide real security on someone, Dana?" he asked.

"It depends, sir," said Dana. "Six at least if the threat is serious. One or two if you're going through the motions. Shit, sir, I didn't mean it that way."

"I know my wife when she wants to be alone," said Fitzduane, "and I know you did what you could, Dana. None of us anticipated this level of threat. If you'd been with Kathleen when she was jumped, you'd have been killed. Simple as that. You'd be dead like Texas, and I'm damn glad you're not."

Dana took several deep breaths. There was a glint of moisture at the corner of each eye.

"I miss Texas, sir. She was a good buddy. I'd like to even the score, sir. What can I do?"

Fitzduane smiled tiredly. "Keep me safe while I work on getting Kathleen back. Can do, Captain?"

"HOOAH, SIR!" said Captain Dana Felton.

Kilmara returned after Dana left. He had a bottle of red wine and two glasses. "Better than pills," he said.

"What does *hooah* mean?" said Fitzduane.

" 'Fucking A' or similar," said Kilmara. "It's also used to indicate the right stuff. If you are an Okay guy in the airborne or rangers, you are 'hooah.' "

"What's the origin?" said Fitzduane.

"Rangers in Word War Two had completed a hazardous mission and were resting when they were asked to go back into action. 'Who, us?' they said indignantly, but back they went. And 'Who us' became 'Hooah.' "

Fitzduane suddenly felt a rush of fatigue and emotion. His voice broke. "You know, Shane, in the middle of all this shit it does sometimes strike me that there are some really good people out there. Despite everything."

Kilmara filled their glasses. "Despite everything," he said with feeling. He raised his glass. "To Kathleen. We're going to get her back. Whatever it takes."

"Whatever it takes," said Fitzduane.

In the morning they heard that the murdered woman found in the trunk of the Dodge had been officially identified as Sergeant Jenny Pullman, a parachute rigger with the 82nd Airborne who had been hitching back from the coast after seventy-two hours' compassionate leave. She was an innocent victim who had been unlucky enough to hitch a lift with the wrong person.

The wreckage of the destroyed farmhouse was sifted through item by item. The body had been blown apart and pieces had been found over a wide area.

One arm was found sufficiently intact to take fingerprints. They were identified as belonging to Akio Taro, a Japanese freelance journalist doing an assignment on Fort Bragg. Chifune's agent.

The Dodge found by the state police had been rented by Kathleen Fitzduane. The rental company recognized Kathleen's photograph and the driver's-license number checked out.

There was no longer any doubt about the identity of the kidnap victim.

They had also heard that apart from the terrorist attack on the special-forces exhibition, an explosive device concealed in a large, self-propelled floor-cleaning machine had gone off in the Oak Creek shopping mall in Fayetteville. The place was packed with shoppers at the time, including thousands of off-duty airborne soldiers and their families.

The cleaning machine was capable of washing, drying, polish application, and buffing, and contained tanks for its consumables. These tanks had been packed with more than two hundred pounds of explosive and the outer metal casing modified so that it was lined with thousands of miniature steel balls suspended in a gel. An odorless gas contained in a cylinder in the built-in storage compartment—normally used for spare buffing pads—had been released in advance.

The explosives combined with the gas to create a destructive effect considerably more powerful than the explosive on its own would have achieved. It was, in effect, a fuel air bomb.

One hundred and nineteen people died in the immediate blast, and hundreds were injured.

The American military establishment was being attacked where it was most vulnerable by an unknown enemy following an unknown agenda. In strictly military terms, the casualties were of little significance.

But internationally, the political symbolism of the actions was considerable.

 **CHAPTER NINE**

THE MEETING HAD been progressing for twenty minutes.

It had started calmly with a factual description of what had happened and the progress the various agencies were making, but the dispassionate recital of facts was beginning to give way to acrimony.

"In summary," said National Security Advisor Vernon Slade, "we have had a total of seven terrorist attacks on U.S. soil over the last six months and we appear none the wiser as to who is behind all this or why they are doing it or where they are based. Giving the resources we are deploying, that might be interpreted as a failure of leadership."

The Director of the Federal Bureau of Investigation, Webster Grant, flushed. Slade had not mentioned any names, but the implication was clear. Since the FBI had statutory authority to investigate internal terrorism, their failure to date to identify and arrest the perpetrators could be attributed to him. And he was not a Slade supporter.

"Mr. Director?" said the President. Someone might have to be sacrificed, but he did not particularly want to play Vernon's game. He liked his FBI Director and did not want to lose him.

"Mr. President," said the FBI Director, "it is not true to say that we have made no progress in our investigations, or indeed that the terrorists have had it all their own way. Frankly, the problem seems to be that we may be after more than one organization. So far we have identified several members of Yaibo, a Japanese extremist group, two Iranians, and a number of other fundamentalists with connections in Lebanon, Egypt, and Syria. We also have two bodies we cannot identify. Both seem to be from Latin America. One is definitely of Indian extraction."

"Probably Cuban," said Slade. "Fidel has not changed his spots."

"They could be Americans, Vernon," said the President heavily. "We have citizens of every race, color, and creed these days. We cannot point the finger merely because someone looks as if he could be Cuban."

General William Frampton, the Chairman of the Joint Chiefs of Staff, cleared his throat. He had a thoughtful, almost pensive face and the pouched eyes of a bloodhound. His uniform seemed the wrong attire for his scholarly demeanor. He should have been in tweeds, the President thought. On the other hand, the Medal of Honor that he wore looked more appropriate with army green. He had commanded the 82nd Airborne Division earlier on in his career, he remembered. The two incidents in Fayetteville would have hit him particularly hard. Paratroopers and their wives and girlfriends and children had been killed and injured in both.

"Mr. President," General Frampton said quietly. "I would like to know more about the motives of these people. Horrible though these incidents are, these terrorist acts have no real military impact on us at all except in media terms. I do not wish to belittle the importance of public opinion, but I would like to understand better what these people hope to achieve."

The Director of Central Intelligence had been unable to attend the meeting. He had been laid low with a virus and an ever-increasing distaste for Vernon Slade. In his place he had sent his Deputy Director of Operations, William Martin.

"Mr. President," said Martin. "Do you mind if I make a contribution here?"

The President nodded.

Martin continued. "I read a report recently by a man named Lee Cochrane. He runs the Congressional Task Force on Terrorism. He puts forward some interesting theories.

"Cochrane argues that we, in America, interpret terrorism far too simplistically. A terrorist blows up a building and we assume that the destruction of that specific building is the object of the exercise. The choice of building, in fact, is probably irrelevant. The significant element in many cases is the symbolism of the act of terror—not the specifics.

"Cochrane further states that we are evaluating acts of terror in the wrong time frame. We think in terms of immediate results. In contrast, many of the cultures we are up against are prepared to think in terms of decades or even longer. They have a strategic vision that we lack."

Georgie Falls knitted his brow.

"Let me give an example," said Martin. "I'll use Yaibo, the Japanese terrorist group, but the principles could apply to any other faction."

The President looked encouraging. General Frampton's drooping eyelids had risen a fraction. His interest was fully engaged. The hunt for these people was personal. No one was going to fuck with the 82nd and get away with it.

"Yaibo were quite successful in Japan for a while. Leaving out their long-term political aims, their acts of terror gave them influence. Corporations paid them protection money. Politicians voted in certain ways at their request. Senior government officials bent regulations or made other accommodations. All did this because they were afraid of Yaibo. So Yaibo had power and influence out of all proportion to their size. They were unable to change the Japanese political system fundamentally as their manifesto demands, but in other practical ways they were effective. Terrorism worked.

"Yaibo overreached themselves and, after losing much strength, they got forced out of Japan. They fled who knows where to lick their wounds and consolidate, but Lee Cochrane surmises that they are determined at some point to return to Japan. Accordingly, they are mounting attacks in the U.S. to raise their stock in Japan. They are saying, in effect, if we can strike with relative impunity at the most powerful nation on earth, then we are a force to be reckoned with and you people in Japan should pay attention."

"Why the U.S.?" said the FBI Director.

"Because we give them the most media bang for the buck," said Martin. "Because we don't take terrorism seriously and we are vulnerable. Because we are the big guy on the block and they are jealous. Because we are constrained for all kinds of reasons from reacting properly. Because we are a shackled giant and we put on our own shackles."

Frampton rubbed his jaw slowly. "So Yaibo, for instance, attack soft targets in the U.S. instead of hard targets in Japan to raise their stock in Japan. It all seems very indirect to me."

"That's because you're thinking like a direct gung-ho American," said Martin. "And you're forgetting that it is a small world these days. Think instead of something like three-dimensional pool. Cause and effect can be kind of complicated if you don't know how to play, but it's all connected. You bounce a ball off one side to hit another, and maybe the effect ripples on. Let me put it another way. When we invaded Grenada, we weren't just invading Grenada. When we hit Panama, that was not just about Panama. We were making a point, we were sending a message, and above all, we were showing that we were deadly serious. And only incidentally, Grenada and Panama got taken out and our people got practice for bigger and better things."

There was silence in the room. Government and politics was mostly about firefighting, about reacting. Thinking long term—"the vision thing," as President George Bush had put it—was not high on the list of priorities. It was disconcerting to think that terrorists might have a "vision thing" of their own.

"Director Martin is making good sense, Mr. President," said the Chairman of the Joint Chiefs, "and I have a feeling for the Japanese agenda. But other groups seem to be involved in this. Certainly, we have identified Moslem fundamentalists."

"Lee Cochrane," said Martin, "makes the point that these kind of indirect objectives can be layered. Each individual group pursues its own objectives, but by working together another objective or, indeed, several can also be attained. As to what that is in this case, I really don't know. But if you accept Cochrane's premise, then what has happened makes a great deal more sense. Certainly, we know that multiple elements are involved."

The president was impressed by what Martin had to say, but it was not addressing the immediate issue. American citizens had been killed and a response was called for.

"If different nationalities are involved," said the President, "then they have got to get together somewhere to organize and train. These operations have been slick. They aren't just spontaneous outbursts. These have been planned and rehearsed. So where are they coming from? Libya? Cuba? Syria? Iraq? Iran? Lebanon?"

"We have found safe houses," said the FBI Director, "but there it ends. The people we have arrested are cutouts. So far, everything we have experienced could have been planned here in the U.S. or, indeed, anywhere. There is no definite link to any one base or any one organization. There may not be any central command. We just don't know. What we are experiencing is unprecedented." He paused and took a deep breath. "I'm deeply sorry, Mr. President. We are doing the best we can."

"I understand there was a kidnapping which may be connected to the Bastogne Inn business?" said the President.

"An Irish citizen, not an American," said the National Security Advisor.

"My mother was Irish," said the President. "I would not like to have seen her kidnapped while a guest in this great country of ours—and I would remind you, sir, that one-sixth of our entire population is of Irish descent. Well over forty-two million. There is a certain electoral majesty in that, is there not, Mr. Advisor."

Vernon V. Slade had absolutely no idea how to deal with the President when he was in this mood. It was as if the ghost of every past U.S. president was at his shoulder. A man who had risen to his high office by seeking to please everybody, he was becoming increasingly decisive. It was disconcerting.

"It is a difficult case, Mr. President," said the FBI Director. "We've accounted for every legitimate helicopter flight at that time and cross-checked flight-control records. Nothing. Then we checked with the military. There was an exercise on at the time with the aircraft flying out of Pope. They were testing the integration of AWACS and JSTARS."

"And what is the bottom line, Mr. Director?" said the President.

"We have an unapproved flight going out to a tanker in international waters, Mr. President. The tanker is Liberian-registered but is actually on charter to Tecuno Gas and Oil. Its next stop was Mexico, Mr. President. We asked Governor Quintana's people, and they said they would have the vessel examined when it docked."

"And?" said the President.

"Nothing," said the FBI Director. A question hovered unspoken.

President Georgie Falls had campaigned long and hard for the North American Free Trade Agreement. It was one issue that he and Security Advisor Vernon agreed on spontaneously. Mexico might not be an American-style democracy, but it was a fast-evolving nation of 87 million people and it was not in the United States' interest to treat them as some kind of banana republic.

The sovereignty and dignity of Mexico had to be respected. It was in that spirit that he had issued National Security Executive Order FA/128 after that disastrous special-operations mission against the so-called Gulf Drug Cartel. U.S. forces were explicitly forbidden to mount any operation—covert or otherwise—that had not been pre-agreed with the Mexican government. Fundamentally, the Mexicans would have to put their own house in order. It was, after all, *their* house.

Nonetheless.

"Mr. President," said Slade. "The American people are exceedingly disturbed by our apparent inability to deal satisfactorily with these terrorists. We have to do something."

The President nodded gloomily. He did not need to be reminded of the decrease in his popularity. When he had been a TV anchor he had lived and died by his rating. He read the latest polls before he listened to his CIA-prepared daily intelligence briefing. They were not good.

"What exactly do you propose, Vernon?"

"Perhaps we don't know the terrorists' base, Mr. President," said Slade, "but we do know where some of them trained. Accordingly, I recommend military action against known fundamentalist targets. It will send a clear message and it will release much of this voter frustration. It will also demonstrate the decisiveness of this administration. Questions are being asked at present about our apparent lack of resolve."

Several of the group looked uncomfortable, while others concealed their feelings. Either way, there was a general air of embarrassment in the room. The headline above the morning's *Washington Post* editorial was fresh in their minds. "Falling Down on the Job Again" was the precursor of a piece that had not been kind.

The presidency of Georgie Falls was in deep trouble. The National Security Advisor was right. Some kind of offensive against these people was essential.

"We know where many of these people train," said the Deputy Director of the CIA. "We know the countries and we know the locations of the individual camps. We have all the intelligence we need to strike tomorrow, from satellite photographs to agents-in-place. But there are always other political considerations which cancel out these advantages. Iran, Libya, Syria, Iraq, Lebanon, for instance. All of these places actively support terrorists and actions specifically directed against the United States. And there are more countries I could name, starting with Sudan. It's a long list."

"We can't hit Iran," said the Secretary of State, "because we want the moderates to succeed and we do not want public opinion to be polarized against this country. We have already hit Libya, and it may well have cost us Pan Am 103. We're trying to bring Syria into the Middle East peace process, and progress is encouraging. As to Iraq, here we have a problem with international world opinion, and we need even them as a counterbalance to Iran."

"Which leaves Lebanon," said Vernon V. Slade. "They have got fundamentalist training camps. No one gives a fuck about Lebanon."

"It is within both Israel's and Syria's sphere of influence," said the Secretary of State, "and France, the ex–colonial power, still regards itself as a player. In contrast, Israel would be all too happy if we attacked the camps, but they will expect to be informed first. Further, the U.N. are in South Lebanon in some strength and they have forces near potential targets. There are Irish and Scandinavian troops there, among others. It is not that simple."

Whoever had thought of invading Grenada had been a positive genius, reflected President Georgie Falls. All that flexing of military muscle against an enemy who practically did not exist and a country that no one had heard of.

The debate continued acrimoniously for another forty-five minutes. Finally, the voices petered out and all heads turned toward the President.

"It is your call, Mr. President," said Vernon V. Slade.

"Give us a clear mission, Mr. President," said the Chairman of the Joint Chiefs of Staff, "and I promise you that the United States Armed Forces can do the job."

We are the most powerful nation on earth, thought the Deputy Director of the CIA, but we have rendered ourselves impotent.

"Mr. Deputy Director," said the President. "I noticed a decided reaction from you when the Mexican state of Tecuno and Governor Diego Quintana was mentioned."

"It's a complex situation, Mr. President," said Martin uncomfortably.

"That's why we have the CIA," said the President unkindly. "You are there to help us simple folks unravel the knots."

"Can of worms in this case, Mr. President," said Martin. His conversation with Kilmara was still on his mind. He decided to go for it. "Frankly, what we think and what the administration wants are at loggerheads. You want harmony with Mexico, and meanwhile some bad people based in Tecuno are fucking with us."

"You have proof?" said the President. "Clear proof that would justify an overt intervention, or at least an approach to the Mexican government?"

"No, sir," said Martin. "And unfortunately Governor Quintana is part of the Mexican government. He is secretary of the PRI."

"You think Tecuno is a haven for these people?" said the President.

"That's the way it looks," said Martin.

"Well, if we can't go in the front door," said the President, "maybe there's a window we can sneak through. Any ideas, Mr. Martin?"

"There's the Irishman called Hugo Fitzduane," said Martin. "The man whose wife was kidnapped."

"Does he have any connection with this Task Force on Terrorism?" said the President, "and that terrible business in the Farnsworth Building?"

"Yes, sir," said the Deputy Director.

"He seems to have a nose for trouble," said the President. "I take it you are suggesting we help him point it."

"Unofficially, Mr. President."

"And if he brings back proof," said the President.

"We go in and we take them out," said General Frampton. "A maximum effort."

"Just like that, General?" said the President.

"Just like that, sir," said General Frampton. "I was in Fayetteville just after the bombing. I stood in the blood.

"This is war, sir, and we've got to defend ourselves."

"WHY did we invade Haiti?" said the FBI Director as they left the meeting. "I've never quite understood."

"For the same underlying reason that terrorists are active against this country," said the Deputy Director of the CIA.

"I don't understand," said the FBI Director.

"Because we could," said William Martin. "Because they can."

BOOK II

COUNTERTERROR

 **CHAPTER TEN**

THE HUMVEE GROUND its way over the dirt road of Maryland's Aberdeen Proving Grounds.

If you wanted to test and lobby for a weapon, this was the place to be. It was far from the only place to prove out instruments of death and destruction, but it was conveniently near Washingon, D.C.

The vehicle crashed into yet another pothole, and its massive suspension took the imposition in its stride. Kilmara's back was not so tolerant. General Shane Kilmara was not overly fond of the U.S. Army's replacement for the jeep. He considered it too slow, too heavy, too noisy, too hard to maintain, and far too uncomfortable at his stage in life—but since it was on loan from the U.S. Army complete with driver, he was not complaining.

Someone with clout was backing Fitzduane's little enterprise, and all Kilmara could do was speculate a little and give thanks. Cochrane had muttered jokingly about guardian angels. Kilmara had been networking on the international special-forces circuit for a long time, and he did not think angels had anything to do with it.

"Sir, we're here," said the driver, halting the vehicle and applying the brake. She was about twenty-two, and her crisp BDUs bore sergeant's stripes and airborne insignia. Kilmara was all for having women in the armed forces if they looked like this. That was probably a sexist thought, but a man needed some variety from leathery sergeants.

"Sir, what are we looking for?"

"Dilger's Baby," said Kilmara absentmindedly.

"Sir, this is a weapons range," said the sergeant.

"I surely hope so," said Kilmara. He smiled. "Or we're in deep diddly."

He brought the field glasses up to his eyes. They had been given a map reference to drive to and not much explanation. He had been told to look, and he was looking.

He saw lots of land that looked as if things had exploded in it, on it, and over it rather too often, and not much else except armored vehicle track marks. There was not much cover. There were shell holes and the terrain undulated, but there were no bushes or trees or convenient dry stone walls to hide behind. This ground had been worked over.

Yet, if he had been informed correctly and if the crisp sergeant had navigated right, Fitzduane and Guntrack were within a few hundred meters of where he stood.

Kilmara searched by quadrant. Still nothing. He gave the binoculars to the keen-eyed young sergeant. "Look for a wedge-front tracked vehicle," he said, "probably under camouflage within, say, four hundred meters or so of here."

The sergeant made two circumferences. On the third sweep, her arm came out and pointed.

Kilmara looked where she indicated. He could just see something—maybe—but mostly it looked like more torn-up ground. He pulled out the personal radio he had been issued and pointed at the location. "Sergeant Hawkeye got you on her third iteration," he said. "I can't see a fucking thing."

"Encouraging," said Fitzduane's voice, "especially since there are five of us and we are all around you."

Small pieces of ground started to move.

Four lined up about thirty meters away, and the fifth came up close. It was not until the vehicles were less than fifty meters away that they were noticeable at all, and even then it was their movement more than shape that made them stand out from the landscape.

"Sexy," breathed Sergeant Hawkeye. "What are they, sir?"

"Think of the Three Wise Monkeys," said Kilmara, "and I'll tell you."

"See, hear, and say nothing," said Hawkeye, who had had been cleared to Level One. "Deal, sir."

Fitzduane came over. "It's a Swiss-made material," he said. "Typically Swiss. Bloody expensive, but the stuff seems to work. Basically, within a limited range, it picks up the colors of the surrounding terrain and blends. And it also cuts way down on your thermal signature. It is not general-purpose camouflage, but if you know where you're going, it will do the job."

Hawkeye was examining the Guntrack close up. "If you deploy your weapons fully, you lose some of the camouflage effect on the top, sir," she said. "You were cheating a bit."

Fitzduane smiled. "We were testing lying-up during the day, Sergeant," he said. "But you've got a point."

Kilmara was amused. "We really came to see Dilger's Baby," he said. "Surprise me."

Fitzduane pointed at what looked like a thick-walled pipe mounted on the back of a Guntrack. It had a crude, almost agricultural look, but the sight on top looked state-of-the-art. The whole thing, including the breech, was no more than seven feet long.

"You start off with the A10 Thunderbolt tank-busting aircraft," he said. "The Warthog. As you know, it's a slow-flying, rather ugly aircraft built around a huge multibarreled Gatling-type gun that fires uranium-depleted rounds the size of milk bottles that go right through armor. Ground troops love it because it can stay in the battle zone for hours. Rumor has it the USAAF aren't too keen on it because it's slow and lacks avionics and they are not too fond of CAS—close-air support—in the first place.

"The upshot is that the A10 is being phased out. That means that a load of their GAU-8A Avenger guns are becoming available."

Kilmara made a gesture. "But that's a huge weapon," he said. "It's—I don't know—twenty feet long and weighs as much as a Cadillac." He pointed at the weapon on the Guntrack. "I don't get the connection."

"Think laterally," said Fitzduane agreeably. "That's what a man called Bob Dilger did. I guess it helped that he had been behind the A10 gun program in the first place. Anyway, he had the idea of taking just *one* barrel out of the seven and a simple six-shot, clip-fed breech and making a much simpler anti-armor weapon. Now you've got Dilger's Baby. It's the size you see, it weighs under a hundred pounds without mount, and it's deadly accurate. Ballistically it is remarkable. The projectile hits 1.9 kilometers a second, and up to two kilometers the trajectory is damn near flat. Armed with a laser sight it will substantially outrange any Soviet tanks short of the very latest models. Add Shanley's thermal gizmos and night becomes day. A single shot can plow through five feet of reinforced concrete or make the Fourth of July out of armor."

Kilmara was taking a folded checklist out of his map pocket. "It has come to a pretty pass when a cheap high-speed plastic box like the Guntrack can take out heavy armor."

Fitzduane smiled. "I don't know what it is, but there is something about a tank that makes people want to shoot at it. Thanks to technology, now they can. I expect people felt much the same about armored knights and bows and arrows."

He indicated the front gunner's seat.

Kilmara climbed in. He had ridden in all three crew positions quite a few times before, but always on testing and exercises. The knowledge that they were now preparing for a combat mission was a sharp reality check.

He put on the proffered helmet and plugged in the intercom. The helmet fit. A tag tied to the chin strap had listed his name. Hugo was like that.

The Guntrack purred almost silently into life. Early models had sounded like sports cars and had emitted the same exhilarating engine growls. Good for the adrenaline and bad for the life span. Now Guntracks were very, very quiet. And even that, in Fitzduane's opinion, was too noisy. Sound tended to travel at night, and that was when special-operations people, like vampires, mostly functioned best also. The idea was not to be seen—or heard.

Ten minutes later, Kilmara had gotten the point. The Guntrack had air brakes and hydraulics. They hissed to a halt.

Kilmara was contemplative. It had been a wild ride and the targets had snapped up without warning.

From exhilaration to absolute threat in maybe a tenth of a second. Maybe less. "It's—it's different," he said.

Fitzduane looked across. It had only been minutes, but his face was strained from concentration and when he took off the helmet his hair was matted with sweat. "We practiced in Ireland amidst the rocks and rain and mud," he said. "Hard to get up serious speed. And there was not the same urgency. This terrain is hot and dry and will soon be the real thing. That adds a certain dimension. It is more like flying a fighter in World War Two. It's fast and you don't too often have a second chance. And you end up drained and exhausted and dying for a pint of beer."

"Or dead," said Kilmara exhaustedly. "Probably from a heart attack." He climbed out of the Guntrack unsteadily.

Sergeant Hawkeye was staring, fascinated. There was a pronounced delay, and then her hand snapped up in a salute. Kilmara was a general and he had reappeared. Which was something of a surprise.

The whole thing had been so incredibly fast and yet had gone on for so long. Could people really maneuver and fight this way? It was a hell of a thing to see.

She snapped her hand down and glanced discreetly at her watch. Only ten fucking minutes! Unreal!

"You're still too vulnerable from the air," said Kilmara. "You've got Stingers, and they're fine if you are static, but if you're on the move and get strafed you want something heavier than the 5.56mm Ulimaxs you've mounted that will really persuade a pilot to keep his distance if he doesn't want to fly right into a buzz saw. My suggestion is that you mount a GECAL .50 as the standoff weapon on at least one Guntrack. Use the three-barrel version and you can get off two thousand rounds a minute if you are feeling sociable."

Fitzduane's eyebrows had both risen. A GECAL .50 was a Gatling gun designed originally for aircraft use. He did not doubt its effectiveness but was far from sure it could be mounted on a Guntrack. "Surely, it would be too heavy," he said.

"Well under a hundred pounds," said Kilmara. "As to ammunition, you will have to work that out. The problem with GECALs is keeping them fed. But you have that NATO pallet on the back of each Guntrack, and we put in load-carrying capacity for a reason."

"I'll look at it," said Fitzduane. "Subject to time."

There really was not much time. He was operating on the basis of the minimum time necessary to do the job right the first time.

He had allowed three weeks. Twenty-one days to plan, assemble equipment, recruit, train, and rehearse to such a level of perfection that when they hit they would not fail.

They could not fail. It was far too long to his mind, but there was so much to be done and he knew that for the duration of the mission his head must rule his heart. Every emotional feeling made him want to throw together an ad hoc mission and go storming in by helicopter, but all his experience dictated that such an approach had a high chance of failure. That was exactly what the opposition would expect and had taken precautions against. He had to find another way, even if it took longer.

He felt he was letting Kathleen down.

It was tearing him apart.

Surprisingly little showed.

Kilmara swung back into the Humvee.

Sergeant Hawkeye looked across at him. He had expected the inquiry. Fitzduane seemed to have that effect. Women almost always did ask about him, even when it was a need-to-know operation and such a question was most decidedly out of line.

"Who was that man, sir?" she said. "The colonel? The one you called Hugo?"

"The rules say its none of your business, Sergeant," said Kilmara.

"I know, sir," said Hawkeye quietly. "But I don't often see men like that. He seemed exceptional and maybe a little sad. Is that the way it is, sir?"

"He was my pupil once and he is my friend now, and I guess that is the way it is," said Kilmara heavily. "Life has a habit of screwing up the best-laid plans."

"Amen to that," said the sergeant fervently, and Kilmara looked at her and wondered.

Then the Humvee's suspension cut in and the General had more immediate and painful concerns on his mind.

IT was late when Fitzduane and Kilmara got back from the Aberdeen Proving Grounds to the apartment in Arlington.

Fitzduane made Kilmara an Irish coffee. He took his black and straight. Kilmara sprawled with relief in one of the armchairs. Fitzduane sat on the edge of his chair nursing his coffee mug. It was near midnight.

"Still no news?" inquired Kilmara cautiously but with the privilege of an old friend.

He had delayed asking earlier. Fitzduane was wound tight as a drum but seemed to be controlling himself by shutting down unnecessary thoughts of Kathleen. He rarely mentioned her name and was focused almost coldly on the mission. Kilmara could almost feel the tension building up day by day, but he knew from experience that Fitzduane had the stamina to stay in control as long as was necessary. Eventually there would be a catharsis, an explosion of pent-up feeling.

Right now the mask of normality was down. It was almost convincing.

Fitzduane had made some calls before sitting. Since the kidnapping there had been no word of Kathleen at all. No messages, no demands for ransom, nothing.

Kathleen had vanished without trace, yet Fitzduane proceeded as if he knew with absolute certainty that she was in Mexico. He was running entirely on instinct. He was probably right, Kilmara reflected. He had seen Hugo like this on a number of occasions before, and it was uncanny how often the man's feelings had proved right.

Life should be more rational, in Kilmara's opinion, but for Fitzduane, in situations like this, intuition was rationality.

"Kathleen is in Tecuno," said Fitzduane flatly.

"Has that been confirmed?" said Kilmara. "A positive ID?"

"No," said Fitzduane slowly. "Nothing more than you know, and now the near certainty that Oshima and Yaibo are behind this. I've talked more to Chifune, and it's the only thing that makes sense. Incidentally, Chifune thought Oshima was dead also. Now it appears that some of her superiors in the Japanese intelligence community have been mounting an operation which has gone somewhat adrift. Instead of a terrorist on an invisible string leading them to her colleagues, they've got a loose cannon.

"Even worse from their point of view, it looks like Oshima is mounting operations against the U.S. from her Mexican base. Given the uncertain relations between the U.S. and Japan, this is worse than embarrassing. It's bloody serious. It might just occur to someone in the U.S. government that the Japanese are behind this in some way. They are not, she insists, but it looks bad. The Tokyo bureaucrats involved hoped the problem would just go away. Now it has escalated and Chifune has been sent over to try and resolve it discreetly."

Kilmara tried to drink his Irish coffee without giving himself a cream mustache. He more or less succeeded.

He remembered Koancho agent Chifune Tanabu vividly from Japan. Now, there was a woman of true worth, if not exactly the wife and mother type. He had the feeling that she and Fitzduane had been involved briefly, but Hugo had never said anything. He had returned and married Kathleen, the homemaker.

"Chifune knows Oshima better than anyone," he said. "What's her take on Oshima's motive in grabbing Kathleen?"

"Pure revenge," said Fitzduane. "Interestingly, Chifune thinks kidnapping Kathleen was a secondary objective, a pure target of opportunity. I tend to agree."

"So you don't think Kathleen is being held as bait," said Kilmara. "A sprat to catch a mackerel, with Hugo Fitzduane being the fish in question?"

Fitzduane shook his head. "It's possible, but I don't think so. To spring a trap she would have to be sure that I knew about the Devil's Footprint, and that would mean laying a trail. So far all the evidence is that their base is being kept under wraps. No, my gut tells me that Oshima has a different agenda and Kathleen is peripheral. If precedent is anything to go by, Oshima will play with Kathleen for months, try and break her, and eventually kill her. That's the pattern. Oshima likes having a few victims around. It's a power thing. She kidnapped a policeman in Japan and kept him chained up for two years in a cave." He did not mention what Oshima had done to her victim. When the policeman had been found he had been alive, but . . . He blocked the file picture from his mind. The only consolation was that Oshima tended to leave serious physical torture until late in the game. Her initial torture was always psychological.

"Tell me more about this Japanese agent in Tecuno," Kilmara said. "If there is someone on the inside, surely you can get confirmation on whether they've got Kathleen."

Fitzduane recounted the history of the Japanese operation as far as he knew it. Then he continued. "The good news is that thanks to Chifune's man we now know much more about the physical layout and other details of the base. The bad news is that Hori-*san*, although in place and close to Oshima, is having great difficulty in communicating. In Tokyo, he could use the phone or mail a letter or meet a contact in the subway and do a brush pass. In Tecuno, trusted by Oshima or not, the poor guy is damn close to being a prisoner. These people are paranoid. That's how they have survived so long. Informers are THE enemy, so every precaution is taken against them. Worse still, the track record shows that your nearest and dearest are most likely to betray you, so even the inner circle like Hori-*san* are not excluded."

"How has Hori gotten information out so far?" said Kilmara. "From what you say, there has been some contact?"

"I asked Chifune exactly the same question," said Fitzduane. "Apparently he has been there for about fifteen months and has gotten messages out only twice. The first time he risked the mail to a Koancho address in Mexico City. The second time, he passed a package to a Japanese service technician who was inside the perimeter servicing some electronic gear. That was a real risk, because he did not know the guy. He must have been desperate. But it worked."

"Why not use the technician again if he has access?" said Kilmara.

"It was a one-off technical problem," said Fitzduane. "Normally, all the gear in the inner compound is serviced by Quintana's people. Further, the original serviceman was posted back to Tokyo. Koancho did try and initiate a follow-up call from a planted substitute, but no dice. Insofar as is possible in that place, no one goes in and no one goes out. The word is that there is not the normal Mexican *mañana* approach to security. This place is very tight, and it was precisely for this reason that Quintana brought terrorist mercenaries in.

"Oshima's primary job is to run a tight ship, and that she seems to do. Everyone is scared shitless of her. She does not give you ten days in the cells if you fail to search a truck properly. She has you staked out in the sun with your balls cut off and ants and scorpions for company. This is not a sweet-natured woman."

Kilmara smiled and then turned serious. "There has got to be some way of making contact," he said. "Tell me something about the layout and routines."

"Tecuno is vast and the least-populated state in Mexico," said Fitzduane. "Virtually all the population live on the coastal strip or in the port city of Tecuan. Inland, it is hot, dry, arid plateau country. On average, inland is about three to five thousand feet up. You bake during the day and you freeze at night. There are few roads, because there is nowhere to go to. Mexico is railway country, but the only railway line in this case goes along the coast."

"But the oil is inland?" said Kilmara.

"Oil seems to like emerging from godforsaken spots like the Saudi desert or the North Sea," said Fitzduane, "and inland Tecuno surely qualifies. So the oil is under the central plateau, which consists mainly of rock, shale, boulders, and sand. It gets pumped up by mainly automated equipment and piped down to the coast. It is a strategic resource, so the whole inland portion of Tecuno is off-limits to visitors on the grounds of protecting the oil fields against bandits and saboteurs. Because of the sheer scale of the distances involved, the security in the area is carried out by the local militia operating from a joint army and air force base called Madoa. About eight kilometers from that is the Devil's Footprint. And the Devil's Footprint is where the terrorist base is located."

"The first thought that comes to me," said Kilmara, "is that if I was Quintana, and wanted optimum security, I would have put my terrorist base inside the airfield perimeter. So why is it located eight kliks away? Quintana isn't dumb by all accounts, so there has to be a reason. And that brings us back to the Devil's Footprint. What has it got that makes it worthwhile compromising security?"

"Their security has not been much affected—unfortunately," said Fitzduane, "though your point is valid. It would be ideal for them if the two locations were merged into one or at least side by side. However, the terrain makes that impossible. You need flat land for an airfield, and the ground between the airfield and the Devil's Footprint is anything but. So this is the best arrangement under the circumstances and there is a road between the two camps. The road encircles the two locations, so it constitutes a perimeter in itself. It is too big an area to fence off, but it is patrolled regularly by light armor and there is an armored column on standby which sometimes does a circuit as well. These people are serious."

"Let's get back to the Devil's Footprint," said Kilmara. *"El Huella del Diablo!"*

Fitzduane smiled. Kilmara had had to return to Ireland and his beloved Rangers after the Fayetteville incident, and though they talked regularly, still had missed out on much of the detail. And that frustrated him. General Kilmara was used to being on the inside track.

"The Devil's Footprint," said Fitzduane, "gets its name from resembling the footprint that might be made by a cloven hoof. It consists of two box canyons side by side and from the air looks something like a pair of horseshoe-shaped valleys. To secure each valley, all you have to do is to establish a fortified position on the high ground and fence off each open end, and that is exactly what our friends have done. The first valley holds the terrorist base and the second valley, nominally the site of a top-secret oil-extraction process—so it is full of pipes and process plant—is what they are guarding."

"And what is that?" said Kilmara.

Fitzduane spread his hands. "I don't know," he said. "Theories abound. I have heard everything from a missile site to a biological-weapons production facility. When I next see pigs flying I could even believe it to be that much-referred oil-extraction process. Personally, I don't much care. I am going down there to get Kathleen back and wipe out some people who really do not do much for the advancement of the human condition. If there is a third leg to the mission. All I can say is that I hope we can do it fast, because it is not going to be healthy to stick around."

Kilmara poured himself a mug of straight black coffee. There had been a time when both men would have mortally wounded a bottle of Irish whiskey over an evening's talking, but Fitzduane was no longer much of a drinker and his sobriety was catching. Also, there was much to think through, and a reasonably clear head helped. He stood up and stretched. "I need some air, Hugo," he said.

Fitzduane opened the sliding doors and both men stood on the balcony. Fitzduane found he was quite affected by the Iwo Jima memorial each time he saw it. It had not just become an everyday part of the view from the apartment. It touched something in him. Life was the way it was—imperfect but still precious—because some people, always a minority, were willing to risk all.

"The paradox," said Kilmara, as if reading his mind, "is that the other side have beliefs and values and dedicated people too. We have patriots and they have fanatics. They are both two sides of the same coin. The only distinction is that we think they are wrong."

Fitzduane laughed. "A rather important distinction," he said.

Kilmara grinned. "Yeah, that's my conclusion when I get philosophical, and it doesn't hurt that I believe it. Love for your fellow man is all very well and has to be the better way, but until Utopia arrives after the talking stops, there will always be a need to hold the line. And that's what people like those marines did and do."

"Fortunately for us," said Fitzduane quietly.

Fortunately for us, thought Kilmara, looking at Fitzduane. Fitzduane caught the look and smiled. "You got me into all this, Shane," he said.

Kilmara shook his head. "It was always there, Hugo. Blame your ancestors. A willingness to serve: It's something that is bred into you."

Fitzduane leaned on the railings and gazed out over Washington. "Quite a country," he said with feeling. "I love the place, the land, the energy, many of the structures, and the sense that in the U.S. anything is possible. But some pundits argue that America's day is over and that power is now gravitating inexorably toward Asia or some other axis. Think so, Shane?"

Kilmara was looking again at the Iwo Jima memorial.

"We're both Irish," he said, "and these days we are both European, but the reality is that America *is us*. We are all of a piece and we are not going to go away."

He turned to Fitzduane. "Hugo," he said firmly. "You're going to get Kathleen back. But don't get killed. Do what you have to and then get the hell out. We have enough dead heroes."

Fitzduane smiled. "Deal!" he said.

They went back inside.

FITZDUANE slept for several hours and then he woke.

It was still dark, but he could not sleep. He put on some running gear and jogged down to the Iwo Jima memorial. Somehow it seemed to bring comfort.

He was thinking of Kathleen. Was she really where he thought she was? Could he really bring her back? Were his plans the best that could be devised? Was there an alternative strategy? Should he go in with helicopters, as everyone else had recommended? Was it all as impossible as some had argued?

Endless doubts coursed through his mind. He was not just putting his own life at risk. Apart from the C130 pilots and crew, he was taking with him fourteen others. All of these people had their own relationships and dependents, and it was near certain that some would die. This was too dangerous a mission for all to get through unscathed. Life was not like that. Had he the right to get other people killed and to wreck other lives?

He walked slowly around the memorial. Such self-doubt, he knew, was futile. In the end you did your best and lived or died with the consequences. And that was all you could do. But above all, you had to try.

Dawn was coming. Could Kathleen see the sky as he could, or was she held chained and blindfolded like so many hostages? Was she alive at all?

At first he had been so horrified and angered by her kidnapping that it had taken all his self-control not to head down to Mexico and just do what he could. But that would have been futile and he knew it. The initial shock and fury had passed. Now there was just a cold anger that stayed with him every waking hour and an absolute determination to get Kathleen back.

He stood back and looked at the marines raising the flag on Mount Suribachi. He was sure it had not been quite as depicted, but he was equally sure it was close enough.

He raised his hand in a silent salute and went jogging toward Arlington Cemetery.

Behind him his shadow ran easily, ever watchful. Dana had been strangely touched by what she had seen. It was not his country, but he still seemed to care.

She had lost her partner. She was not going to lose her charge. And when the mission was mounted she was going to be damn sure she was on it. Texas had been the best of people and the closest of friends, and her killing was not going to go unpunished. She smiled as she cried. Texas had been good fun, too. Outrageous sometimes, humorous practically always.

She thought Arlington National Cemetery at dawn was the most beautiful place she had ever seen. It should be somehow sad, given all the dead and the memories they evoked, but it was not. It was magnificent.

Fitzduane ran steadily toward a tombstone not too far from the Tomb of the Unknown Soldier. Then he stopped beside the tombstone, took something out of his pocket, and placed it on the base. Next he stepped back and stood with his head bowed for a good ten minutes.

After he had left, Dana checked the headstone:

JAMES N. "NICK" ROWE
COLONEL U.S. ARMY

Then she remembered. This grave had a particular significance for special forces. The inscription closed with the stark line:

KILLED BY TERRORISTS, MANILA.

Fitzduane had left an Irish Rangers shoulder patch on the base, held in place by a small stone. The rituals of warriors before battle, Dana thought. We think we have changed, but we have not. We prepare, we draw strength from our heroes, we pay our dues, and then we fight. Ancient Roman, Norman knight, or twentieth-century special forces. Different causes, different customs, different weapons, but when it came to facing the reality of combat, common traditions.

CHAPTER ELEVEN

FITZDUANE FLEW INTO Phoenix, picked up a rented Ford Bronco, and drove north and east.

He had debated phoning rather than making the trip, but he rationalized that if he was going to ask Al to put his life on the line it was something he had better do face-to-face.

In reality, he was desperate for a change of environment. The mission was coming together, but Washington was one long reminder of Kathleen. He needed space and a chance to get some perspective.

He was heading for the newly incorporated city of Medora, population all of 5,648. It was about three hours' steady driving from Phoenix. He could have rented a light aircraft and flown the last hop, but he had mixed feelings about light aircraft he did not know, and anyway he had heard that the Medora airstrip was on top of a butte.

Since a butte, as best he could recall, was a sheer-sided mountain jutting out of the ground rather like a rocket, its top, even if flat, did not seem a terrific place to land. The pilot could miss or you could fall off the edge or something. Fitzduane preferred his airstrips on the ground, preferably very flat ground without things to bump into.

A few miles outside Phoenix, the highway climbed steadily. The rolling foothills stretched away on either side and the ground looked hard and arid. This was high desert dotted with scrub and mesquite and cacti. Some people found it harsh and forbidding. Fitzduane relished the contours of the land and the clear light and the sense of space, and found it achingly beautiful.

It was so different from his home country. Ireland's scenery was on an altogether smaller and more human scale. Here, the vistas were immense and mankind almost insignificant.

It was hard to imagine how anyone had survived in such a vast, rugged, water-starved landscape, yet this was the terrain that the Apaches had made their own and over which Geronimo had been hunted. Five thousand troops trying to find thirty men in an era before helicopters and radios and modern technology. Endless locations in the heavily contoured landscape to hide in. The difficulties and hardships overcome in the hunt were hard to comprehend.

Al Lonsdale's mother had been a full-blooded Apache. His father, the sheriff of a border town in Texas, had been of mixed English and Irish stock, and the combination had produced a striking-looking man. Al had thick black hair, a high forehead, deep-set thoughtful eyes, high cheekbones, and a strong nose and chin. He stood six feet three in his socks.

Lonsdale had followed his father's profession and spent a few years as a sheriff's deputy, but then had joined the U.S. Army in search of wider horizons. He had grown up with weapons, and hunting was a family tradition, so the transition to U.S. Army Special Forces had been smooth. But Lonsdale wanted to be the best of the best, so he volunteered for the top-secret U.S. Army counterterrorist unit, Delta, which had been set up by Colonel Charlie Beckwith on SAS lines. When he was accepted by Delta, Al Lonsdale felt he had arrived.

The Irish equivalent of Delta were the Rangers commanded by General Shane Kilmara. Master Sergeant Al Lonsdale had been on secondment to them, training on Fitzduane's island off the West of Ireland, when they had stumbled across a terrorist assassination attempt.

Superb long-range shooting by Lonsdale with a .50 Barrett at over 1,800 meters had saved the lives of both Fitzduane and his son, Boots. Subsequently, Lonsdale had fought beside Fitzduane and Chifune Tanabu on a counterterrorist action in Japan.

It was a relationship born and tempered under fire, and as a consequence, Lonsdale was a natural choice for the Mexican mission. But whether he could be persuaded to join the team was another matter. Al's leaving Delta had been unexpected. His appointment as Chief of Police of the tiny city of Medora had compounded the surprise.

Fitzduane had tabbed Al Lonsdale as hard-core military through and through. A caliber soldier. A warrior. His reasons for abandoning a promising military career for the vicissitudes of the civilian world were unknown. Still, Fitzduane had faith in Al Lonsdale. There would be reasons, and they would be good. Well, he hoped they would be good.

People were people the world over. All were a little flaky. In its way, the consistency of the human factor was kind of reassuring.

––––––

"Mrs. Zanduski," said Chief of Medora Police Al Lonsdale patiently, "what we're looking for here, ma'am, is a certain dynamic tension. Simply put, your right hand holding the firearm pushes out and is braced against your left arm pulling in. The result is—or should be—a stable weapons platform."

"I don't want a weapons platform, Chief," said five-foot-two seventy-eight-year-old Mrs. Zanduski, her outstretched hands holding the .357 Magnum with the six-inch barrel hesitantly. "I want to hit the goddamn target. I want to blow the motherfuckers away."

"There is a relationship, ma'am," said Lonsdale quietly. "You point the weapon in the right direction and the round goes more or less the same way. It's a useful principle to keep in mind."

"Don't patronize me, young man," said Mrs. Zanduski sharply. There was a flash from the weapon's muzzle and a loud boom. The metal can she had been aiming at some twenty-five yards away was blasted off the wooden plank against the wall of sandbags.

The crowd cheered and whistled and clapped. "Way to go, Granny!" could be heard. Mrs. Zanduski looked up at Chief Lonsdale triumphantly.

"Very nice, Mrs. Zanduski," said Lonsdale, "but don't you think a smaller caliber might be better?"

Mrs. Zanduski's chin jutted out. "Clint Eastwood uses a large-caliber weapon, young man, and I would point out that he is now practically a senior citizen himself."

Chief Lonsdale sighed. Life and fantasy seemed to be getting increasingly intertwined these days. "Next!" he called.

Hiram Albertsen was an eighty-two-year-old retired accountant. He was not much taller than Mrs. Clara Zanduski, and carried a bull pup High Standard Model 10B shotgun equipped with a laser sight and a Choate magazine extension.

"Where is the target, young man?" he said.

Lonsdale pointed at the next can in a row of seven. This was supposed to be a familiarization lesson. One shot each and they would focus on weapons handling and get to serious shooting later. He was already forming the view that he had underestimated the senior citizens of Medora.

Mr. Albertsen adjusted his bifocals, held his weapon at his hip, and then activated the laser sight. A red dot hovered unsteadily around the target.

BOOM! BOOM! The seven cans were near-simultaneously propelled into the air, and the plank on which they had sat reduced to matchwood. Lonsdale looked on in disbelief as slivers of wood and wood dust fluttered to the ground. The cans were shredded, most split right open.

Mr. Albertsen cackled. "That old hag's six-gun isn't worth spit."

The rivalry on all issues between Clara Zanduski and Hiram Albertsen was legendary. Rumor had it that it had started at the bridge table but had speedily spread to just about every aspect of life that could be remotely regarded as competitive. The consensus was that both were thriving on the endless confrontations.

"What in heavens are you firing, Mr. Albertsen?" said Lonsdale weakly.

Mr. Albertsen held up his weapon. The muzzle had been fitted with a duckbill diverter, which spread the steel darts in an elliptical pattern. "Loaded 'em myself, young man," he said. "Twenty fléchettes to a twelve-gauge. With the duckbill, at twenty-five meters, they'll clear everyone in a pattern twelve feet wide and five feet high. And deafen 'em, too! Hot damn!"

"Hot damn indeed!" agreed Lonsdale. This police chief business was not working out quite as he had expected. The city of Medora was two-thirds a retirement community and loved being incorporated. City politics was what kept the adrenaline of the senior citizens flowing. But for all practical purposes there was no crime. And the citizens, armed to the teeth, intended to keep it that way.

Apart from being a pawn to be argued over at weekly meetings of the city council, Medora's four-man police department had almost nothing of substance to do except traffic control during the season when hundreds of thousands of tourists streamed through on the way to the Grand Canyon. Ironically, thanks to fines resulting from traffic violations, the police department even made a profit.

Pay and benefits were good, the scenery was superb, the air was clear, and his golf handicap was coming down, but Chief of Police Al Lonsdale was bored.

It was then that he saw Colonel Hugo Fitzduane standing apart from the gun crowd, looking fit and tanned and a little thinner than he remembered. And he knew things would start to happen the way they normally did when the Irishman was around.

Fitzduane was a charming man, but he was a magnet for trouble. Al Lonsdale knew he should know better, but he was very pleased to see him. He felt a stirring in the blood, a lust for adventure, for life on the edge. A mature man should have gotten over such feelings. The Chief was glad he still had some way to go.

LONSDALE lived five miles out of town in a valley that the local Indians considered sacred. He had built his own house in an as-yet-undeveloped area, but had consulted the local medicine men before commencing construction. They had consulted the spirits and then recommended a series of purification ceremonies that lasted on and off for a month. The rituals did not come free. Lonsdale did not break ground until they were completed.

"Did the ceremonies work?" said Fitzduane.

They were sitting on the raised deck of the house. A bloodred sun was setting in the V formed by the walls of the valley. The red rock glowed as if on fire. It was not hard to see why the Indians considered the location sacred. There was a special, almost spiritual quality about the place, and it was more than beautiful. It was spectacular. It was also isolated. The nearest neighbor was more than two miles away in the next valley.

Lonsdale grinned. "Sure." Earlier on he had raised the subject of Kathleen, and Fitzduane had frozen. The look in the man's eyes had said it all. Now Lonsdale steered the conversation to safer subjects. The man was on autopilot. He could function as long as he did not think of her except when absolutely necessary.

The Chief made a gesture encompassing the house. It was a large two-story adobe dwelling surrounded by a high wall that fit near perfectly into the landscape. In terms of the basic comforts it was completely modern, but externally it would not have seemed out of place when Arizona was part of Mexico. In truth, it was more like a small fort than a house.

"The last man to try building in this valley," continued Lonsdale, "dismissed the Indians' objections as superstition and an attempt at extortion. Medicine men don't perform their ceremonies for free."

"So what happened to him?" said Fitzduane.

"He was overseeing the clearing of the site when the bulldozer cut into a nest of snakes. One moment he was standing there shouting directions, and the next he was flat on his back on the ground under a whole mess of writhing snakes. They had antitoxin, but he was way beyond that. He was dead within minutes. They say he was bitten more than fifty times and most of his face was torn off. He had no eyes by the time they were finished and his skin was black from the venom."

"Nice story," said Fitzduane dryly, looking out over the unspoiled valley, "but I doubt it will do much for the real estate market around here."

"I hope not," said Lonsdale. "I like the solitude. This really is God's country. I would surely hate to see it spoiled. Snakes are one effective way to keep the crowds down."

"I hope you keep your medicine men sweet," said Fitzduane. "And the local snakes. I would not be at all surprised to find they can be one and the same."

Lonsdale laughed. "We have an accommodation," he said.

As the sun sank, a line of shadow crept up the burning walls of the valley until eventually only the rim glowed a fiery red. Fitzduane was reminded of the contrast between molten lava as it emerged brilliant and glowing from the earth's interior, and its appearance when it faded to a dull patina as it cooled.

Then suddenly the sun was gone. There was a brief afterglow, and then that was gone too. The night skies of northern Arizona were, if anything, even more dramatic.

Fitzduane thought of his thirteenth-century Norman ancestor and the rain-sodden little Irish island he had made his own, and wondered why the man hadn't taken ship and headed west for a modest five thousand miles.

AFTER they had eaten, Fitzduane went through the plan in some detail. Lonsdale listened intently. Special operations had been his world for most of his adult life, and it was part of the special-forces tradition that a plan was rarely imposed.

The process was not so much democratic as pragmatic. Enemy fire was no respecter of rank, and the best special-forces troops were risk averse. Unnecessary-risk averse.

"Why not helicopters?" said Lonsdale. "You get in fast. You get out fast. And obstacles like perimeter fences and minefields don't mean a fucking thing. You envelop the enemy."

Fitzduane nodded. Heliborne operations were synonymous with the U.S. military, and since the Iranian fiasco, many of the traditional objections to helicopters, such as mechanical unreliability, had been overcome. Still, they were not the only way to mount a raid.

"Quintana has organized his defenses based upon two threats," he said. "An attack by the Mexican Army or some kind of helicopter-borne raid. Well, the Mexican army *could* try and invade. Based upon their strengths, that would almost certainly mean a traditional ground-based attack spearheaded by armor and supported by artillery. To counter that, Quintana has armor and artillery of his own smuggled in from Eastern Europe, and he has the terrain on his side. You can only get up to the plateau where the oil is through a small number of passes, and they are easy to defend.

"Now, the Mexicans do have some paratroops, but not any quantity and they suffer from the classic weakness of many airborne forces. They are too lightly equipped. If they drop onto the plateau, they are going to be cut to pieces by Quintana's army. Mexican airborne are not like the U.S. with their own built-in helicopter and other support—not to mention air supremacy and the might of the U.S. Air Force. These guys just don't have the firepower. Further, they don't have the expertise. Mexico has not fought a modern war."

"None of that is an argument against a heliborne raid by us," said Lonsdale. He grinned. "And we surely have the practice."

Fitzduane took note of the *us*. Reiko Oshima was unfinished business and the Chief of Police, despite his beautiful surroundings, was bored. And there was another element that would cement the deal. Lonsdale had been much taken by Chifune.

"Quintana and his people are no fools," said Fitzduane. "The other obvious threat is a helicopter assault. Indeed, that is exactly what they are expecting and have already experienced. The DEA mounted a black antinarcotic operation there about a year ago and it went horribly wrong. Quintana has invested heavily in radar and handheld missiles. There is perimeter defense around the plateau and a second line of defense at the airfield and the Devil's Footprint. You've got to remember that this kind of equipment is easy to get these days from the East, and it is not even that expensive."

Lonsdale got up to throw a log on the fire. He turned around and spoke. "You fly low and fast and, most likely, you'll get through the outer screen. That's a big perimeter they have to watch. If you are contour flying they'll lose you in the ground clutter. As to the target themselves, if you stay low, they probably won't pick you up either."

"Helicopters might work," Fitzduane admitted. "But what we are talking about is what is likely to work best. And there are a few more objections to choppers.

"First, even when the noise is suppressed, they remain noisy bloody things. Second, they are vulnerable to ground fire. A rifle can take out a helicopter. Third, they are complex mechanically and require one hell of a logistics tail. Fourth, whether or not we get in undetected, no one is going to miss the actual arrival of two or more helicopters, so when we would try and leave, we would be sitting ducks. Remember, Quintana is expecting helicopters, so that is what he has geared up for. The place is stiff with SAMs."

Lonsdale grinned ruefully. "And finally, this is not an officially sanctioned U.S. government operation whereby we can have whatever supporting fire-power we need. There will be no close-air support on call up there. Okay. I get the picture."

"The essence of what I am proposing is stealth," said Fitzduane. "We fly in real low in two C130s equipped with contour-following radar and ECM equipment. As you've said, there is a good chance we won't get picked up, but even if we are, the electronic countermeasures will scramble the radar screens for the necessary few seconds. Then the Guntracks get pulled out by LAPES at twenty feet or less. Next, the aircraft pop up to two-fifty feet and we jump. Then down they go again and head for home."

"Two hundred and fifty feet is goddamn low, Hugo," said Lonsdale. "Where I come from, five hundred feet scarcely gives you time to scratch your crotch. Any lower and you start digging holes in the ground."

Fitzduane laughed. "You're not keeping up to date, Al," he said. "Irwin has a new fast-opening combat 'chute. It will open in time and you will land as lightly as a ballerina."

Lonsdale looked dubious. "I'd hate to try this thing only to find out that the minimum jump height spec was just a copywriter getting carried away. Parachuting is like sleeping with a few snakes. Most people don't fancy it, but dangerous as it looks, it's actually quite safe until something goes wrong. Then you rarely get a second chance."

Fitzduane spoke quietly. "I jumped with the Irwin a week ago. Seven jumps in all with seven different 'chutes, each time at two-fifty. I was curious too."

"I guess the first time was the hardest, Colonel," said Lonsdale slowly. "Well, you don't look as if you bounced, so let's move on."

"We've got satellite and other intel on what happens where on the plateau," said Fitzduane. "You have got to remember it consists of hundreds of thousands of square miles of decidedly inhospitable terrain. Theoretically it is patrolled, but in practice that means that the main oil facilities and pipelines get regular attention and the balance is just ignored except for random helicopter overflights. Frankly, what else can they do? What else need they do?"

Lonsdale was lying back with his eyes closed.

He was trying to build up a mental model of Fitzduane's plan. The fact that helicopters were not being used had thrown him a little initially, but now he was getting into the swing of things. It helped that he had trained with Guntracks and the Rangers in Ireland. He had participated in low-altitude parachute extraction exercises before.

LAPES was an extraordinary technique if you were not used to it, but it worked. A cargo aircraft like the C130 throttled back to around 120 miles an hour and flew as little as six feet above the ground, almost as if landing. Then, at the designated spot, a parachute was opened and as it filled it pulled a palletized Guntrack—or other equipment—out of the rear door of the aircraft.

The parachute acted as a brake to kill the forward momentum. The effects of the short vertical drop were countered by special compressible pallets and careful packing.

It was not a barrel of laughs for humans, but for supplies and equipment it was remarkably successful.

"So," said Lonsdale, "we land inside the plateau rim far away from the outer defenses but also some distance from the terrorist bases. Better yet, we pick some godforsaken spot which is off any regularly patrolled route and has cover. We are all alone with the scorpions. We have gotten in undetected during the night. Now we lie up well camouflaged and hope some wandering peasant does not stumble on us."

"The plateau is clear of wandering peasants," said Fitzduane. "For a start, since there is neither arable land nor grazing there is no reason to be there. Second, Quintana obligingly rounded up the few remaining Indians and either killed them or trucked them down to a settlement on the coast. Whatever he is up to, he is serious about not being seen. But it will help us."

"How many people and vehicles are we using?" said Lonsdale.

"The strike team, including myself," said Fitzduane, "will consist of fifteen personnel—five three-person teams in five Guntracks."

"Why those numbers?" said Lonsdale.

"As you will remember," said Fitzduane, "a Guntrack needs a crew of three for optimum effectiveness. Driver, front gunner/navigator, and rear gunner. Regarding the number of vehicles, five is the minimum number required to allow successful completion of the mission plus some redundancy. The capacity of the C130s comes into play. It's a judgment call."

FITZDUANE woke up at dawn the following day as the morning light streamed into his bedroom. Without thinking, he reached out for Kathleen and then sat up with a start as he remembered. He lay back and closed his eyes and focused on the mission. He blotted Kathleen from his mind.

"The team," said Lonsdale over breakfast. The sun was well up, and they were eating outside. "The fighting fifteen. As of now, there is you and there is me, which is nice but makes only two."

Fitzduane was looking over the deck at the yard below. He turned back to Lonsdale. "Al," he said. "I can count eight snakes down there. And they are not babies."

"They beat hell out of a guard dog," said Lonsdale equably.

He refilled their coffee. "The team?" he repeated.

"There is substantial backing for the operation within the system," said Fitzduane, "but the number-one rule is that I can't use any serving member of the U.S. armed forces for the ground team."

"Deniability," said Lonsdale scathingly. "Shit, you would think we would have learned by now. This smacks of politics and President Georgie Falls and his abiding love of playing both ends against the middle. It's this kind of indecisiveness that makes outfits like Delta all training and no action. It's why terrorists supported by countries like Iran piss on us and get away with it."

Fitzduane was beginning to see why Master Sergeant Al Lonsdale had quit Delta.

"Think positive, Al," he said. "The positive aspect of all this is that we have near-total flexibility. We don't have a chain of command stretching through endless second-guessers to a situation room in the White House. We aren't being micromanaged. We can do what has to be done, how we want it, and when we want it."

Lonsdale shrugged. He could blow hot, but he cooled off as quickly. He smiled. "Put that way, you've got a point, but there are still a few Delta people I would give a lot for. You've got to understand, Colonel, the U.S. Army of today is the most powerful, best equipped, and best trained in the world. Sure we fuck up sometimes and use too much force or too much firepower, but most of those problems are political.

"The best of our people are not just good. They're *real* good. Too good to pass up. There's gotta be a way! And you can't mount an operation like this with amateurs."

Fitzduane drank some coffee. "I like to run in Arlington Cemetery," he said. "A man whose premises we are using at present to operate from, Grant Lamar, suggested I might like to run a bit further—to Fort Myer. There, I met a man called General Frampton."

"The Chairman of the Joint Chiefs?" said Lonsdale incredulously.

"Something like that," said Fitzduane mildly. "He said his discussion with me was entirely unofficial but he would like to introduce some men who had suddenly resigned from the U.S. Army and were in need of employment in civilian life. He said they would consider anything, even a short assignment. He added that he hoped that he could entice them to reenlist in the future."

"Who are they?" said Lonsdale. "I may know a couple of them."

Fitzduane told him.

"Fucking A!" said Lonsdale. "These are my people." He stood up and shouted. "Ya-hoo!" The sound echoed back from the walls of the valley.

"I don't think that is entirely a coincidence," said Fitzduane gently. "And please do not disturb the snakes."

Lonsdale grinned. "They don't mind the odd yell," he said. "These snakes are Arizonans. They have been listening to Indians and cowboys sounding off for the last hundreds of years."

Fitzduane looked along the deserted valley. Someday, snakes or not, it was going to be built upon from end to end. He had already noticed some Realtor's signs hammered into the brush as they drove to Al's house. It was quite a paradox. It was just too beautiful to escape unspoiled.

Lonsdale saw where he was looking and read his expression. "Yeah," he said with feeling.

He turned back to the subject. "You and I and six Delta. We're up to eight."

"Chifune Tanabu and Oga," said Fitzduane. "They've been tracking Reiko Oshima and Yaibo for quite some time, and they'd like to finish it. You remember

Chifune from Japan, Al, and you also met Oga. He's ex–Japanese airborne. Both are good shooters."

Lonsdale remembered how taken aback he had been when he had discovered that the security agent he was to work with was not just a woman but someone so slight and feminine and beautiful as Chifune. She looked too gentle to hurt a fly. Appearances in her case were totally misleading. She was a crack shot and cool as ice under fire. Quite a woman, quite a person.

"Chifune is good," he said. "Better than good. As to Oga—"

"I *know* Oga," said Fitzduane.

"Five to go," said Lonsdale.

"The British are contributing three," said Fitzduane. "SAS have a score to settle with Yaibo. Then there is a man called Shanley I ran into who I think you'd approve of. Which leaves one to go. A civilian but ex–Airborne captain, Dana Felton, wants that slot and I think maybe she's entitled. She lost a friend to these people. She's good. Then there are couple of Irish Rangers, Grady and Harty, who know the Guntrack particularly well. We have, as they say in Ireland, an elegant sufficiency. It'll be tough to make the final selection."

Lonsdale nodded. "Geronimo Grady. One hell of a driver. You know, one name on that Delta list has set me thinking," said Lonsdale.

"Who?" said Fitzduane.

"Calvin Welbourne," said Lonsdale. "Short thin black guy with a manic sense of humor and no nerves that I've ever detected. A very bright fellow. Thinks in three dimensions."

"What does Calvin do?" said Fitzduane.

Lonsdale flashed a grin. "Delta, Colonel, as you know, walks on water. Calvin goes one better."

"Hit me with it," said Fitzduane.

"He flies," said Lonsdale.

THEY started into the finer details of the mission.

Lonsdale's police radio chattered occasionally in the background. He was on duty around the clock if he was needed, but apart from that proviso, his hours were flexible. The main issue on the radio seemed to be where the two officers on duty should meet up for lunch.

The phone rang. It was Lee Cochrane calling from Washington.

"Developments, Hugo," he said, his voice sounding tired and serious. "You'd better get back here fast."

"Anything you can talk about?"

"Negative," said Cochrane firmly. Tension and fatigue could be detected in his voice. "Some serious shit is going down. So ASAP, Hugo."

"Roger that," said Fitzduane. He replaced the receiver.

Outside, on the deck, Lonsdale was standing talking intently into his radio. He finished as Fitzduane emerged into the bright sunlight.

"Come on, Hugo. Let's go!" he said.

Fitzduane looked at him. "I've got to get back to Washington," he said. "Something's happened."

"You don't have to go back to Washington for kicks," said Lonsdale savagely, buckling on his gun belt and clipping the radio to it. "The fucking bank has been robbed. I'll never get away if this is not sorted out. Are you carrying?"

Fitzduane nodded, trying to suppress a smile. "I thought nothing ever happened in Medora."

"Nothing does except when you're around, Hugo," said Lonsdale. "Come on! Let's move!" He headed down the stairs that led from the deck to the yard below.

"What are we doing?" said Fitzduane, following in Lonsdale's footsteps.

"We're going to try and cut them off," said Lonsdale, getting into his vehicle. "There are four of them in a jeep, and they are headed out of Medora this way. Lots of places to hide out in. This is big country."

"Armed?" said Fitzduane.

Lonsdale roared away, leaving a bunch of disturbed-looking snakes in his wake.

"Of course they're armed," said Lonsdale irritably. "I don't know how they rob banks in Ireland, but goddamn it, Hugo, this is the United States. Guns are the American way. The right to bear them is written into our Constitution. So far we have one dead bank guard and a teller who is not looking so good."

"What kind of firepower?" said Fitzduane.

"Assault rifles and shotguns and doubtless a few handguns," said Lonsdale. He grinned. "And they seem quite happy to use them. So if the shit hits, shoot fast and often."

"Very nice," said Fitzduane. "But don't forget to tell them that I'm a tourist."

CHAPTER TWELVE

KATHLEEN HAD NOT expected the violence. The possibility was always there, she knew, but she had rationalized that it was remote.

North Carolina was not some combat zone. Outside the high-crime areas, the United States was relatively—mostly—fairly peaceful. She was vacationing, relaxing in the warmth of the day. Her depression had passed. She had been feeling mellow and outgoing, and it was in that spirit that she had picked up the perky army sergeant who had been hitching back to Fort Bragg.

The shock of the assault had stunned her.

The hitchhiker she had picked up had been alive and chatting to this lost Japanese tourist, and a short while later she was spewing blood all over Kathleen, her throat gaping open like some obscene parody of a mouth.

Her eyes were still alive and her body was dying, and she knew and was afraid and there was nothing either of them could do. It was only a few seconds, but it seemed an endless horror. And then the light went from her eyes and her face grew slack and she was no longer a human being. And Kathleen screamed.

"My b—"

My baby! My baby!

Her words were cut off half spoken and unheard as a fist slammed into her mouth. Dazed, she was dragged from the rental, thrown to the ground facedown, and then bound and gagged in seconds. There was no time to resist or protest. She felt a needle and she was unconscious.

She had a faint recollection of the beating of rotor blades and of vibration, and then there was an increase in tempo as the helicopter took off. The flight seemed to be short. She had been thrown onto the floor and handcuffed to the metal frame of the seat. She was injected again and lost consciousness.

She woke up as someone was chaining her hands. She had thought at first that she was still on the aircraft, but then realized that the floor was different. She was now lying on rough concrete and the air was hot and dry and there was no drone of an aircraft.

Shortly afterward, she felt someone put chains on her ankles and she started to sob and was slapped in the face. She could see nothing. She was blindfolded. She could hear voices. One language, she thought, was Japanese, but she also heard Spanish.

She was sure about the Spanish. Both sexes were speaking. One voice was authoritative, a woman's. Other voices were agreeing with her orders.

She was thirsty and called for water. None came, and the hours passed. It grew cold and she started to shiver, and her thirst grew even greater. It was a nightmare, but she was awake and there was no end. She slept until she was kicked awake. Then bliss: She could taste water, a whole mouthful of water.

She held up her chained hands to grasp the plastic bottle, and just as she touched it, it was pulled away from her and there was laughter and she could feel the water pouring over her body and draining onto the floor and she pressed her face to the wet floor and licked it until her tongue bled.

Always, there was The Voice. *Oshima?* Could it be her?

She had tried to keep time by counting meals, such as they were, and sleep, but after a while she realized that her captors were deliberately varying food intervals and were also keeping her from sleeping for a natural length of time. She had an impression of weeks rather than days, but there was no certainty in this thought. She was kept blindfolded and chained, and there was no point of reference.

The blindfold was totally opaque and was taped in place, and she had not even the relief of light percolating through to tell whether it was day or night. She tried to tell by the temperature, but sometimes the heat of the day seemed to last so long that she was convinced they were heating her cell at night to further disorient her. She cried at the thought. She had almost run out of tears, but this was such a petty, malevolent act. They were leaving her nothing.

She grew thin and very weak on the minimal rice-and-water diet she was fed, but every so often, when it seemed she would faint from hunger and escape from her suffering, her food allocation would be increased for several meals. There would be refried beans and perhaps an orange, and occasionally some tinned fish. They wanted her to suffer but not to die as yet. She was being kept like an animal in a cage, a curiosity. She was far from sure there was any other purpose.

She almost got used to being kicked and slapped and beaten, but The Voice brought her to the edge of despair. Since her body was held captive, she focused on her mind, and The Voice followed her there seeking to destroy any positive thought, any remaining hope. And The Voice was without pity. Remorselessly, it focused on destroying her until nothing would be left but despair.

The Voice, to Kathleen, was the true embodiment of evil, and it never seemed to go away. She could hear it when it was not speaking. She could hear it in her troubled dreams.

The Voice would taunt her to her grave. It reminded her that no one knew where she was. Perhaps no one even cared.

She would be kept chained and blindfolded until she died. Her situation was hopeless, The Voice constantly reminded.

She would not die well, The Voice reminded her often. After her spirit was broken, then would come pain. She had pain to look forward to. Pain was her future.

After pain would come death, Kathleen thought, and she began to long for pain and the eventual release it would bring.

No, said The Voice. After pain would come recovery and then more pain. Pain would be her world for a very long time.

It would not just be pain. When it was explained what was to be done to her, the horror was too much and she fainted.

They would start with her extremities, The Voice said, and then piece by piece, limb by limb, she would be hacked apart. Over time she would be completely dismembered. After each procedure—to be carried out without anesthetic—she would receive the best possible medical treatment. All in all, her destruction could take several years.

Each body part would be sent to the *gaijin*, her lover, her husband, the Irishman Fitzduane. Kathleen herself was of no importance. She was merely an instrument of revenge. Of justice.

Kathleen was given two days on extra rations after this announcement. She was then advised that the first dismemberment would start in a week. She was to have plenty of time to contemplate the horror of her fate. For seven remaining days her body would be whole and entire, and from then on she would never know life as it had been again.

The Voice had described the body parts she would lose. Her toes and fingers, her feet and hands, her ears, her legs below the knee, her arms to the elbow, the balance of her limbs, her ears and lips and nose and eyes.

Her eyes.

She was too shocked to cry, too terrified to react in any way. She felt sanity slipping way. She could neither eat nor drink. Then she made herself eat something.

My baby! she thought. Oshima does not know. *Must not know!*

I don't know how, but Hugo will come.

———

THE law of unintended consequences.

Oshima smiled as she remembered the phrase. The black DEA mission a year earlier had been an attempt to prove there was a major drug-processing facility in Tecuno. The word on the street was unambiguous, but satellite surveillance went just so far. Proof was needed. Instead, the two helicopters had been shot down shortly after they crossed the Tecuno border, and the public outcry throughout Mexico that had resulted had contributed significantly to the issuing of President Falls's hands-off-Mexico declaration. The Yanquis were interfering with a sovereign nation. The arrogance! How dare they!

The photographs of the wreckage of the two machines and the charred bodies of the crews had been an unparalleled propaganda tool.

Irony of ironies, the abortive DEA raid had served to further protect the enormous Mexican drug-processing and -smuggling industry. And, incidentally, the activities of the state of Tecuno. Governor Diego Quintana had roared with laughter when he read out the U.S. president's National Security Executive Order FA/128. "They bind themselves," he had said. "They know and yet they can do nothing."

The official story was that all twelve members of the raiding party had been killed in the two crashes. Five bodies had been returned. The others had been kept as a bargaining tool. They would be released "over time." There were procedures to be followed. The unofficial subtext was that if the U.S. authorities behaved themselves, one body would be released every six months. Perhaps. The Iranians had shown how far you could push this particular strategy.

The administration accepted the deal. The men were dead. The mission should never have happened in the first place. Improving U.S.-Mexican relations was the priority.

The seven survivors had been given to Oshima to use as she saw fit. But above all, they must not escape. They were dead. They must stay dead.

Keeping the mercenaries at the Devil's Footprint in line had been a problem. The prisoners were used to set an example. Their deaths were spread out over the months. The first prisoner had been burned alive in a metal cage in front of the assembled garrison. The conflagration had taken place at night and had been quite spectacular. The entire cage had glowed white hot as the thing inside it screamed.

Discipline had improved dramatically.

The second prisoner had been guillotined. The French had invaded Mexico for a while, and the mercenaries had constructed a play around the execution. The entertainment value of these events was clear.

The third man had been ritually hanged, drawn, and quartered. This had proved a little more than some of even the most hardened members of the garrison could take.

The fourth man had been crushed by a tank.

The fifth man had been strapped across the muzzle of an artillery piece and a blank charge fired. The blast had showered pieces of him over the canyon wall.

The sixth man had been slowly garotted.

The seventh man was still alive.

As Oshima strode out in front of the assembled mercenaries, the naked body of her victim was strapped to crossed timbers.

The troops were hushed and expectant.

Oshima cut off his hands and feet and then disemboweled the man. It was her favorite way to kill, and she marveled at how long it could take for a human being to die when a skilled executioner was at work.

In her mind, the victim under her sword was the *gaijin* Fitzduane. She took her time, but there were practical problems when performing in front of the mercenaries. A parade could take just so long. Guards had to be relieved. There were duties to be carried out.

She would be under no such pressure when working on Kathleen. This was a woman whose agony would be endless.

CHAPTER THIRTEEN

FITZDUANE DOZED UNEASILY on the aircraft while flying back to Washington. Since Vietnam, where he had been shot down on several occasions, and from various similar experiences in war zones since, he had learned that aircraft had different ways of returning to earth, and not all of them were pleasant.

He was not overly fond of flying. If he could sleep through it, he would. This time it was not that easy. His subconscious flooded his mind with dark images and he had the terrible feeling that the mission he had embarked upon was going to get much worse before it got better.

His black mood had started with the bank raid in Medora. The burst of adrenaline that had kicked in when Lonsdale and he had roared away from Lonsdale's extraordinary home had turned into depression when they caught up with the perpetrators at an Arizona Highway Patrol roadblock a few miles outside the city limits.

With good reason, the state troopers were not taking any chances. When the bank robbers had opened fire and tried to run the roadblock, the troopers, hunkered down behind the cover of their cruisers, had returned fire with a vengeance.

The driver had taken a shotgun blast in the face in the first fusillade.

Out of control, the jeep had spun off the road and overturned. One passenger broke his neck in the crash. The two surviving robbers, already wounded, were thrown clear and as they tried to rise, were chopped down almost clinically by a trooper armed with a heavy-caliber sniper rifle.

Fitzduane and Lonsdale had come on the scene seconds later. The dead robbers had weapons in their hands or just beside them. It was a righteous shoot without question, but the rivulets of blood and the destroyed splayed bodies of what had been up till a few moments ago healthy young men caused the bile to rise in Fitzduane's throat. So this was civilization as we approached the twenty-first century. So this was how far we had come.

Fitzduane's revulsion was further increased by his own sense of guilt. It was not what he wanted—indeed, it was what he had run from when he had resigned from the army—but there had been circumstances and he had killed, and he was good at it and he would kill again.

The causes had been just, and doubtless would be just, but still there was a voice inside him saying that he was wrong and there had to be a better way. And then there were the faces of those who had died as a result of his actions, who seemed to take a little piece of his life force with them as the life flickered from their eyes.

An examination of the corpses quickly revealed that all four of the dead young men had been Mexican and had only recently crossed the border. All wore the clothes of itinerant workers. One wore sandals. One wore cheap shoes without socks.

The man who had taken the shotgun blast in his face had a gold crucifix on a thin gold chain around his neck.

The fourth man, killed by the sniper, lay on his back where he had been thrown, his hair, features, and coloring strongly Indian.

"There but for a quirk of fate go I," said Lonsdale, quietly looking at the body of the fourth man. "Ninety-odd million Mexicans rammed up against the border of the richest country in the world. What would you do if you were them?"

"Try and make Mexico work," said one of the state troopers. "They've got their own country. Some of it is poor, but some of it is rich. They've got oil. Certainly, coming up here to rob and kill isn't the answer."

"What do you do if you have and they have not?" said Fitzduane almost to himself as he gazed at the carnage. "This thing is not about the U.S. and Mexico. It's about the whole world and how you slice the pie."

"You hold the line, Hugo," said Lonsdale firmly. "You try and do what you can, but you accept the world as it is. Or you're fucked."

Fitzduane had a last terrible dream as his flight neared its end.

He could see Kathleen lying in a cell. She was blindfolded and chained and her chains were secured to a ring in the wall. Her clothing was ripped and torn. The crude concrete floor was dusty. As he watched, she traced words in the dust. Her fingertips were bleeding as if she had done this again and again. He strained to try to read what she had written. He could just see his own name, HUGO, and then another word beginning with H. He could not read the rest.

Figures came into the cell.

He could not make out their faces. They were indistinct but menacing. One carried something. It was a piece of board like a butcher's block. Kathleen's hand was placed upon it. She was struggling and screaming, but she was held firmly.

The figure of a woman came forward with a long heavy blade in her hand.

Its edge glittered unevenly as if freshly sharpened upon a stone. It was a crude instrument, a simple machete, the tool of a peasant, an elemental weapon.

Here it was an instrument of torture.

The figure of the torturer turned toward Fitzduane so that for the first time he could see her face. The features were Japanese. Once beautiful, she was now hideously scarred, but she acted as if still supremely confident of her appeal, of her sexuality, and of her power.

She was half smiling. She could see Fitzduane looking and she was pleased. This was why she was doing it. It was aimed at him. He understood.

She raised the heavy blade and brought it down into Kathleen's flesh. Fitzduane could hear the sound. Kathleen did not scream. But he could see the tears as they welled from under her blindfold and coursed through the grime on her face.

COCHRANE was in the underground conference room in the STR Virginia facility in the building they all called Son Tay.

As he had got to know the area better, Fitzduane had learned that there were a dozen or more buildings of various sizes in the complex and doubtless more elsewhere on the estate. Most of the buildings were at least partially underground, as best he could determine. They were linked by subterranean passages. Access was on a "need to know" basis. The Task Force and Fitzduane had the run of the first building they had met in and were using it as a base. As to what happened elsewhere, Fitzduane had absolutely no idea.

The whole setup reminded him forcibly of the iceberg nature of power. The average citizen rarely saw the extent of the forces that controlled and guided him or her, and such secrecy was not confined to totalitarian states. Even the United States, the most open nation on earth, kept much hidden. It was in the nature of those who truly understood power to be secretive. Even if you were an insider, there was much that was secret. No one had full access.

But Grant Lamar, in Fitzduane's opinion, had more access than most. Otherwise, none of this made sense.

Cochrane was buttoning up a crisp white shirt as Fitzduane came in. A regimental tie followed. An electric razor appeared out of a drawer. A quick combing completed the transformation. Within a couple of minutes Cochrane, his face drawn with fatigue, was transformed into a reasonable similitude of the whip-sharp chief of staff whom Fitzduane had first met.

"You caught me, Hugo," said Cochrane briskly, the anger suppressed but escaping as he talked. "Sprucing up on the run is something you learn in the House. You work long, stupidly long hours, sometimes for remarkably stupid people. Most of your work gets shit-canned, but appearances—boy, they really count. You've got to look STRAC.

"You learn to bathe in a water glass and keep your wardrobe in a drawer in your filing cabinet and fuck between votes. The legacy of the Founding Fathers. Those good ole boys set up a hell of a system. It must have been easier in the days of the Roman emperors. Then you still might be knifed in the back, but at least you didn't have to worry about the people. Frankly, democracy sucks."

Fitzduane dropped into a chair. "You look like shined-up shit, Lee," he said. "Sleep has a lot to recommend it. What's this about being knifed in the back?"

"Not your problem, Hugo," said Cochrane grimly. "You're an Irishman. This is strictly an American political matter. It is an old custom. It is called throwing out the baby with the bathwater. It is also called shitting on your friends."

Fitzduane smiled. "The U.S. has no monopoly on either slinging babies out or dumping on the undeserving. So enlighten me."

Cochrane looked straight at Fitzduane. "The Task Force on Terrorism has been a highly effective tool of the United States Congress for nearly a decade and a half. Now it is to be wrapped up. It is all part of the lesser government drive being pushed by our new Speaker. It is a good idea, but it is being implemented indiscriminately. There has never been a greater threat to this country from terrorism and our work has never been more in demand or more on the button—but the Task Force is to go. Go figure!"

Fitzduane was momentarily speechless. The entire Mexican operation was being driven through the Task Force. Kathleen! The implications were horrendous.

"What about the Tecuno mission, Lee?"

A vein throbbed in Cochrane's forehead. "I seem to recall a recent time when you weren't too keen on going to Mexico, Hugo," said Cochrane, sarcasm and anger heavy in his voice. His whole body was tense with rage. The chief of staff had a short fuse and liked to crack the whip, but Fitzduane had never seen him like this before.

He tried to defuse the situation. "Lee, you're tired and quite reasonably pissed off with what is being done to the Task Force. But maybe it is not such a good idea to take it out on me. You know exactly why I changed my mind."

"Fuck you, you damned Irishman," exploded Cochrane. "I care about this country. I fight for the United States. I fight for a cause. All you seem to care about is some damned woman. There are bigger issues, and you don't seem to give a shit about them. You're nothing but a fucking mercenary!"

Fitzduane could feel his own anger boiling up, which would accomplish precisely nothing. He fought for control. He had a tremendous desire to hit the man. He took his time answering.

"Causes are about people, Lee," he said quietly, "and you know that better than most, which is why you do what you do. And Kathleen is rather more than 'some damned woman.' Further, she is being held by people who threaten the well-being of this country. We're on the same side on this thing. So swear away at me if it will advance our cause. Better yet, get some sleep."

Cochrane slumped back into his seat. "Goddamn you, Fitzduane," he said wearily. "Why don't you lose it like a normal human being? It's fucking frustrating to talk to someone who is being calm and reasonable when all you want is to let fly. Hell man, have you no understanding? I thought all you Irish flared up at the slightest provocation."

Fitzduane smiled grimly. "I can't afford to, Lee," he said. "Too much at stake."

Cochrane rubbed his forehead. The outburst was over. He suddenly looked incredibly tired. "I'm sorry," he said.

"Let's focus," said Fitzduane.

"There is a wind-down period for the Task Force," said Cochrane. "And no one likes losers on the Hill, so our effectiveness will be cut in half. We'll be lame ducks flapping our wings and going nowhere except into somebody's cooking pot. But the mission will proceed as planned. There is more than the Task Force behind this thing now. But you know that, Hugo, don't you?"

Fitzduane nodded. "I know we've got friends," he said. "But I haven't put much time into finding out who and why. There are other priorities. But I know the Task Force is the mainspring of this thing, and I appreciate it. And I appreciate what you stand for."

Cochrane stared at the table in silence for a few moments. Then he looked up. "Enough to do something for me?" he said.

"Maybe," said Fitzduane. "But only after you get some sleep. Crisp white shirts will take you just so far."

"I want to go with you," said Cochrane.

Fitzduane's eyebrows shot up. "You're shitting me, Lee!" he said. "Look, the Hill is your battleground."

"I've spent fifteen years pushing the Task Force," said Cochrane, "and now it's going to be wiped. I want to go out in style. I'm owed that. And I can do what has to be done. I'm a trained soldier and I'm fit. I can hack it."

"This is a special-forces mission," said Fitzduane, "and the word 'special' is no accident."

"I can do it," said Cochrane stubbornly. He looked straight at Fitzduane again. "Do you want an apology?"

Fitzduane smiled. "I'll settle for you telling me why I had to get back here ASAP."

Cochrane leapt to his feet. "Shit! I was forgetting all about Jaeger."

"Who is Jaeger?" said Fitzduane.

" 'Doctor' Jaeger," said Cochrane. "Maury tracked him down. He's from Livermore."

"Livermore as in the Lawrence Livermore Laboratory where they do nuclear and other weapons research?" said Fitzduane.

"The very same," said Cochrane. "Ten thousand mad scientists all working on Doomsday. We're trying to get there before the Russians, or whoever are the bad guys these days. The word is that we're doing pretty well. The Japanese may have consumer electronics sewn up, but when Earth is blown into smithereens, the device that does it will have 'Made in the USA' stamped on it. There will probably be a subtext: 'Researched at the Lawrence Livermore Laboratories.' "

"That thought may bring a lump to your throat when you salute the flag, Lee," said Fitzduane, "but what has Dr. Jaeger of Livermore got to do with the mission?"

"You don't want to know," said Cochrane. He smiled. He looked less tired. Here was a man who thrived on action. "But you're going to have to."

"I have not said you can go," warned Fitzduane. "But you can train, and then we'll see."

"I may surprise you," said Cochrane.

"I will be surprised if you don't, Lee," said Fitzduane. "So bring on Jaeger."

"Maury will lead off," said Cochrane. "This is really his jigsaw. He is good at jigsaws, and this is one of his best. It just shows what the Task Force can do— and should continue to do."

"Everyone around here walks on water," said Fitzduane pleasantly. "In Ireland, we're more used to it descending on us from a height."

"The Task Force runs on it," said Cochrane.

THE footsteps sounded different.

Permanently blindfolded as she was, Kathleen was becoming quite proficient at recognizing sounds and building up a mental model of her surroundings. The guards, wearing boots and doubtless armed and laden down with military equipment, walked heavily and talked loudly. Doors were slammed. Jokes were made. Coarse laughter echoed from the concrete walls. Shouts were exchanged.

The Voice had a distinctive walk. There was a liquidity about her movements that suggested a lithe, supple body, but there was also arrogance. This new arrival was not her tormentor. In fact, The Voice now visited less frequently. The novelty had worn off. She was becoming bored, and had indeed said as much. Kathleen's chosen strategy of not reacting had worked. A defiant prisoner would have provided entertainment. An immobile slumped body quickly palled.

These sounds were a break from the normal pattern. The cell door was closed quietly. The footfalls sounded more like civilian shoes. She could hear a faint squeak of leather, and the soles, she thought, were made from softer rubber.

She could just detect the sound of breathing. Her visitor was close and was at her level, which meant he or she had bent down. She was being examined. She could smell soap and an aftershave, and there was no smell of stale sweat. This person was freshly groomed.

Her hand throbbed, but the pain had been her salvation. The shock of her kidnapping and the drugs and then the horror of what she was going through had temporarily driven her over the edge.

Then had come the first dismemberment.

As the machete had cut into her hand and had removed her finger, such a powerful anger had surged through her that she had suddenly realized she could win. No matter how hopeless her position looked, she could and would triumph. She was strong. Her spirit, the essence of her being, was extraordinarily strong. They might desecrate her body, but no matter what they did, she would win. As the pain coursed through her, she knew that she was going to make it. Her baby would make it.

I am strong, she said silently over and over again. I am strong and they cannot break me. They cannot break me because *I will not break.* I am strong. I am strong. I am strong. . . . My body may be weak and in pain, but *I am strong. I am strong. I am strong. . . .*

"Kathleen," said a voice. He called again. She did not react but lay slumped. My eyes might have given me away, she thought, and shown fear, but I am blindfolded so he cannot see. I can use their weapons, their devices, against them. If I show no fear, I am not afraid. I am strong. I am strong. I am strong. I will show nothing. I will give them nothing.

I am strong.

"Kathleen," called the voice yet again.

The tone was sympathetic. Warm? Perhaps. It was a trick, of course, so she would not react visibly, but in her mind she would make the most of the diversion. Truly, the mind was amazing. *Her* mind was amazing. For most of her life to date she had taken it for granted. It was just one of several assets, and since she was a beautiful woman, her looks had arguably been more important on a day-to-day basis because, quite simply, her appearance got results.

But her mind was her true friend, and it had taken all this to bring that home to her. And the power of the mind was quite staggering. She could feel the force.

A hand was stroking her cheek. The touch was tentative and lasted for only a few seconds and then was gone. Was it an illusion? She longed to be touched, to be held, to be caressed gently by Hugo.

She wanted to cry but fought back her tears. She would not show weakness. She would not move. She would not react in any way. She imagined her body in a state of suspension. It was completely immobile. It was just as well. She needed all her energy for her mind. It was a powerhouse. It was a dynamic, thrusting, vital world, and best of all, it was *her* world.

The voice called yet again.

She wished it would go away. It was distracting her and she was extremely busy. Her mind was a hive of activity. Ideas were just flooding into it. And memories, too. People, places, smells, textures, sounds; the very fabric of life. Truly, it was a wonderful world. And there was so much to do. She was never going to have enough time. The possibilities seemed endless. I never knew it was like this, she thought. There is so much here. I am so rich, so lucky, so blessed.

"Perhaps I should start by telling you my name," said the voice. "We are not being introduced under the best of circumstances, but there is much to be said for the formalities all the same. They oil the social wheels, don't you think? Anyway, my name is Edgar Rheiman. You spell that R-H-E-I-M-A-N. Silent *H*. Not an obvious spelling."

An American accent, thought Kathleen. Now, where in the United States? Not the South or California, for sure? Not New York City either. Somewhere Northern. Beyond that she was not sure. She had a good ear and had spent considerable time in the United States, but she had been born and spent most of her life in Ireland.

"Kathleen," said Rheiman. "I can guess how you must feel, but I would like if you would trust me. You see, we're both in the same boat. You're a prisoner and they are going to kill you. That's a given. Well, though I can walk around within the base, I am effectively a prisoner too. And when I have completed doing what they want, I am for the chopping block as well. That's the way these people are."

He paused. "Do you mind if I sit down?"

Kathleen remained immobile.

"I guess not," said Rheiman. His voice sounded middle-aged.

There were sounds of rustling and then a sign of satisfaction. He's in his late forties or early fifties, thought Kathleen, and he is somewhat overweight and certainly not fit. But he is intelligent, indeed very smart in his way. So who is he and what is he? What is he doing here? Why is he being nice to me?

"There are no chairs in here," said Rheiman, "not even a stool, and I'm really not built for floors. But that's Reiko Oshima for you. She is good at her job—you cannot deny that—but she is not a kindly woman. I'll bet she chopped worms up when she was a kid and pulled the wings off flies when they were still alive. Well, who knows. Certainly, she is a major league psycho right now. A very vicious woman. If they did not need me, I would be sushi. But they do need me. Lucky old me! Born in the North to die in the South. That's what the North Vietnamese used to say. Over two million killed against our fifty-eight thousand. An interesting way to win a victory. But that is fanaticism for you. Not reasonable. I guess that kind of defines Reiko Oshima. She is about as reasonable as Dracula. And she needs to spill blood to stay alive."

He leaned forward. She could feel his breath on her face.

"Mrs. Fitzduane, you are *not* in good hands. So you would be well advised to avail yourself of my friendship.

"I would like us to be very good friends."

Kathleen had a sudden urge to spit in his face. She did not move. She had learned to husband every resource. She was going to be raped. It would make no difference. They could take her body. They would not touch her mind.

I am strong.

JAEGER looked like a fading beach boy who still kept himself—mostly—in excellent condition.

The blond hair was flecked with gray but was still thick and flopped over one eye. His upper body was muscular under the light tan suit. His piercing blue eyes were well complemented by his shirt. His tie was loose and the top two buttons of his collar were unbuttoned. He peered over half-glasses. He carried his slight paunch well.

"John is a friend," Cochrane had announced. In Task Force language, Fitzduane had learned, that meant he could be trusted.

He is one of us.

Grant Lamar was sitting in one corner. The man had the ability to render himself damn near invisible. Most people when entering or exiting a room communicated with their fellow men even if it was only "Hi!" or "I'm out of here!" Lamar normally did not. He came and went without comment and seemingly without affecting the equilibrium of those present.

Maury cleared his throat and looked around. He really did not have to. He had everyone's attention.

"This is a reconnaissance photo of the terrorist base in Tecuno known as the Devil's Footprint. The valley on the left is where the actual terrorist base is located, together with a supporting garrison of about six hundred troops. The valley on the right is what we are currently concerned with. We have christened the two valleys Salvador and Dali. Salvador is the base. Dali is the big question."

He pressed the remote again and the screen filled with an aerial photo of Dali.

The illustration was marked with numbers and had been computer enhanced, and there were other signs of the photo interpreter's art.

To Fitzduane, at first glance it did not mean very much except that it bore all the signs of some kind of industrial installation. There were what looked like long pipes, and some of these were cross-linked. One was massive. There were also large containers of various types.

At a quick glance it looked just like the sort of steel-spaghetti facility the oil industry seemed to love, but if someone had told him it was for making breakfast cereal on an industrial scale, he wouldn't have argued too much.

"The Devil's Footprint installation is guarded by a battalion of Tecuno troops and an inner force of somewhere between thirty-five and fifty terrorist mercenaries, in addition to the brigade stationed at the air base only eight kilometers away. Given the strategic importance of the Tecuno oil fields, that might seem reasonable if the other major oil installations were similarly guarded. The reality is that they are not. There are token forces—ten to thirty soldiers—at other pumping stations and patrols along the pipelines, but there is nothing approaching this scale of security elsewhere. No, the evidence is clear that whatever is going on in Dali is special and warrants maximum protection.

"We showed this photograph to a number of military analysts. They could not work out what was going on but were able to point out certain features and to eliminate certain possibilities.

"The installation in the valley we have named Dali is not—on the face of it— consistent with nuclear, chemical, or biological manufacturing plants. I won't get technical, but the military assure me that, based upon known production techniques, the Dali structures do not have what it takes. However, they did add that there were some interesting structures in the valley of the kind you would not normally associate with civilian activities."

Maury activated a laser pointer. The red beam settled on a low mound that seemed almost part of the valley until you looked closely.

"Have a look at that, for example. There, say my military friends, you are talking about a reinforced observation blockhouse. It is the kind of thing you would build if you wanted to look fairly closely at a missile taking off without being fried. Plenty of protection. You will note it is built into one side of the valley and overlooks the other.

"Our military friends identified other blockhouses designed, it would appear, purely for storage. Estimates suggest they are also heavily reinforced against blast. Hardened bomb or resistant structures."

Fitzduane shook his head in some puzzlement. "So we've got what looks like an oil installation of some kind—lots of pipes, and reinforced storage facilities and a blockhouse. I don't get it. Frankly, that kind of setup seems entirely consistent with a process for extracting oil under pressure. We're talking big numbers here. The compression of whatever they are pumping into the ground must be enormous. So if something blows you are likely to need all the protection you can get. A reinforced blockhouse seems entirely reasonable under such circumstances."

Maury nodded. "Fair enough if you exclude the street cop's instincts. But, in this case, we *know* Governor Quintana and Reiko Oshima and their followers. These are not people who take these kind of precautions over an industrial process unless it can be put to practical—and normally destructive—use. These are seriously bad people."

"So?" said Fitzduane quizzically.

"The U.S. of A. has more than a passing interest in oil," said Maury. "We use a lot of the stuff, and we like to know where there is more and what people are doing with it and how we can lay our hands on it. That translates into a formidable intelligence capability. Not only can we detect where it is likely to be, but we can also monitor through various types of detection and sensor equipment where it is. We can, for instance, monitor oil flow through pipelines from remote satellite sensors. And frankly, we can do much more.

"Much of this technological capability has been focused upon Tecuno recently. We have not learned much that is new—Tecuno's oil riches are no secret—but we were interested to find out that there is *no* evidence of oil in the Devil's Footprint itself except for the stuff required to run trucks. What looks like an oil installation, but positively no oil.

"None! Nada! Zilch!"

There was a long silence in the room. Then a collective reaction of surprise. Out of sheer curiosity, Fitzduane shot a look at Lamar. Even he was displaying a faint flicker of something or other.

"No oil?" said Fitzduane helpfully.

"No oil," agreed Maury, "and no activity in most of the pipes. We can detect that kind of thing with infrared and the like. You shove oil or water down a pipe and you do things to it. It becomes hotter or cooler compared to ambient. And there is more, but I'm not technical. But those are the principles."

"So the next thing you did," said Fitzduane, "was take a computer-enhanced photo of Dali and strip out the pipes where there was no activity?"

Maury's jaw dropped. "Fuck it, Hugo, how did you know?"

Fitzduane grinned enigmatically. Back on his island, Henssen played these kinds of games routinely when doing intelligence analyses, and Fitzduane, while no expert, had become quite used to some of the procedures.

Combat was becoming more technological, and there was no choice but to keep up. Fitzduane had gotten through most of his early years with nothing much more complex than an electronic calculator and automatic exposure meters on his cameras, but his hunt for the terrorist known as the Hangman had changed all that.

The slide changed again. The new image of the valley known as Dali showed a much simpler picture. Most of the steel spaghetti had gone. There was now one dominant pipe and a host of supporting equipment. The dominant pipe ran up the side of one wall of the valley. It was made of bolted-together sections and looked rather like a massive irrigation pipe, or maybe part of a sewage scheme.

" 'The Purloined Letter,' " said Grant Lamar quietly. "It's an Edgar Allan Poe story, as I recall. Everyone was looking for the missing letter, but it was in plain sight all along. I fear our Governor Quintana is a very clever man. I just hope we are not underestimating him."

"I'm not sure this was Quintana's idea," said Maury. "There is another name to factor in. I think I'll let Dr. Jaeger take it from here. He's more familiar with the background and the technologies. John?"

Maury sat down and Jaeger ambled to his feet. His body language was disarmingly reassuring. He was more the kindly uncle than someone who worked in one of the foremost U.S. weapons laboratories.

"Interesting problems you people do have," he said agreeably. "Me, I like crossword puzzles, but the kind of things that Maury comes up with are more fun. Part detective work and part science. And I have to admit that I'm no good at crossword puzzles. But here I think I can make a contribution."

"When Patricio Nicanor was killed—in front of some of you, I gather, which must have been most unpleasant—he brought with him several items that seemed to make little sense. You may remember them: a sample of maraging steel; some concrete; a gas controller; an unfinished layout of the Devil's Footprint; and a three-and-a-half-inch computer floppy disk.

"Not exactly good reasons to die for, especially since the floppy disk proved to be blank. Nothing on it. Classic example of what happens to magnetic media when you go through a magnetic field. And we've now learned that walking through such a field is standard procedure when you either enter or leave the terrorist base. These people are serious about security. They don't want a virus being brought in or their trade secrets being brought out. Very thorough. Not foolproof, but a good precaution and enough to zap Patricio's contribution. Or so we thought!

"The concrete interested us. Normal concrete is crude stuff, because it is full of air bubbles and rather brittle, but it is cheap and malleable and you can strengthen it adequately with reinforcing rods and sheer mass. Now, when examined under an electron microscope and with the kind of technology we have at

Livermore—where atom splitting is routine business and quarks are particles we hunt, not put on our bread—this stuff was rather special.

"The air bubbles had been squeezed out and microfibers of steel and polymer had been added. The end result was a product comparable in strength to high-grade steel. Brittleness was down to a fraction of a percent of conventional concrete, and this stuff, according to our computer simulations, also had tensile strength. It was flexible. It could take shock without shattering. Remarkably strong shit indeed."

He paused to drink some water. Fitzduane's brain was in high gear. "What could you make from it, John?" he said.

"Well, I don't know the cost implications," said Jaeger cheerfully. "You know us scientists. But theoretically you could manufacture anything you could make with conventional concrete but without using reinforcing bars and with vastly less mass. Additionally, you could make near anything you could manufacture with steel and it would perform as well or better according to the grade of steel we are talking about. Now, only practical experimentation would determine the reality of this, but based on the sample we have, it looks damn good."

"So, for example, you could make a car out of this concrete?" said Cochrane.

"Sure," said Jaeger. "Your greatest difficulty would be with the molding, and there would be a slight weight penalty, but you could do it. The point is, materials are more adaptable than you would think."

Fitzduane looked at the slide and then at Jaeger. "John, I take it you don't want us to guess where you're going with this?"

Jaeger looked shocked. "Good heavens, no! It would take the enjoyment out of it. Have faith. I'm getting there."

"Crank it up, John," said Cochrane firmly.

Jaeger made an agreeable gesture. "Okay, we've covered maraging steel and super concrete. The layout of Dali is up on the screen. Now we come to the useless floppy disk. Maury had it checked by his computer people, and when we got it to Livermore we really got to work. You have never seen so much technology thrown at a floppy in your life."

"So how did it go?" said Fitzduane.

"You know computer nerds," said Jaeger. "They only think in computer terms. They were working on the premise that something had been there but had been wiped, but just maybe could be brought back. So they went through the damn thing trying to give the kiss of life to each magnetic particle. Painful process. I have never seen so much pizza and Chinese eaten to so little purpose."

"And?" said Fitzduane.

"We can be slow at times at Livermore," said Jaeger. "Personally I think it's all that MSG—but finally we got around to thinking more in terms of Doom and less in terms of computer technology. At 3:28 A.M. in the morning, one of the guys got carried away and slit the floppy open with a pizza knife. It was unusually hard to open, so he ended up smashing the thing."

Even Grant Lamar was showing involvement. "And he found?" he said.

"Buckets of blood!" chortled Jaeger.

He held up his hands in apology. "No, I jest, guys. Inside he found a liberal quantity of tomato sauce from the pizza knife, a passport-size photograph, a bunch of letters and numbers that don't mean much, and several names separated with dashes with a question mark afterwards.

"The photograph and the writing were on the inside of the case, so the floppy could still rotate. It had been meticulously done. You could see nothing from the outside. In retrospect, the only revealing feature was that the casing on that brand of floppy was only spot welded. After it was glued it appeared to be full-seam welded. Your Patricio Nicanor was a smart man and something of a craftsman."

"What were the names?" said Fitzduane.

"Edgar Rheiman . . . Edward Mann . . . George Bull?" said Jaeger. "Probably the first two names don't mean anything to you?"

Fitzduane nodded. "They don't," he said.

"But the third name?" said Jaeger.

Fitzduane looked up at the enhanced computer image and then leaned back in his chair. "I thought that was technology that was going nowhere," he said. "Nice idea but outgunned by rockets?"

"That's what most people think," said Jaeger, "insofar as they think at all. The supergun? It's the notion of a madman. Well, I can tell you, most people are absolutely wrong."

"How do you know?" said Fitzduane.

"I've built one at Livermore," said Jaeger over his half-glasses, "and though we make jokes"—he paused for a beat—"we're serious people down there. It works."

He leaned forward to emphasize the point, his face inches from Fitzduane's. "It really works. It's fucking beautiful. And the fuel source is everywhere."

Fitzduane raised an eyebrow.

"Tell me about your fuel," he said dryly.

Jaeger straightened and roared with laughter. "The raw material is everywhere. You drink it. You bathe in it, and for all I know you fuck in it."

"But split out the oxygen?" said Fitzduane.

Jaeger froze in surprise and then beamed approval. "Colonel Fitzduane, for the first time I am beginning to think you may succeed on your mission."

Fitzduane smiled. "If I get into trouble, John, I'll think of you and die laughing."

Grant Lamar leaned across to Cochrane. "Am I missing something here, Lee?" he said quietly.

"Hydrogen," said Cochrane. "One of the main components of water. Split out the oxygen and you've got a gas that goes bang. They've built a supergun that runs on hydrogen, and apparently the fucking thing works."

"How far could such a weapon go?" said Lamar. "From Mexico, that is?"

Jaeger roared with laughter. "You guys don't know the half of it."

"How far?" said Lamar in the loudest and firmest tone of voice that Fitzduane had ever heard him use.

"Washington, D.C.? NO FUCKING PROBLEM!" said Jaeger. He spread his arms wide and looked around the room. "Am I getting through, people?"

"Could be," said Fitzduane.

APART from the security lights, the camp was dark. It was 2:30 A.M. For once there was no night training, and the team members were making the most of it.

Chifune tried not to notice Fitzduane's window as she jogged past.

Darkness. A feeling of melancholy swept over her. Just once she needed to talk to Hugo alone. She knew what had happened before in Tokyo could not be repeated—and certainly not under these circumstances—but she craved some moments of intimacy with him. Though she yearned for his touch, for the feeling of his naked body under her fingers, a simple conversation would be enough. But they had to be alone. Completely alone.

A small thing to want. To need.

So far there was always someone else present. It was in the nature of the training, she knew, and in some ways the constant presence of others had made their meeting again somewhat easier, but now her heart ached.

Behind her, his heart heavy with concern, Oga looked out through the window of his hut at his charge until she vanished into the woods. Then he lay on his bunk and tried to sleep.

Tanabu-*san*, so beautiful, so strong, so competent in so many ways—and yet so vulnerable. What can I do to protect you? You must rest. Our fate will be decided in fractions of a second, and if you are tired . . .

Chifune ran on to the killing house. The basic scenario was now second nature. This time she focused on what might go wrong.

My weapon might jam.

They could be waiting for us.

My night-vision goggles are damaged or knocked off, and I am in the same darkness that they are.

I am injured.

One of my team is hit.

We break through, *but Kathleen is dead!*

Hugo is injured!

What do I do?

Again and again, Chifune activated the automatic pop-up targeting mechanism and rehearsed her moves. The silenced Calico hissed death. Spent rounds were ejected downward into the clip-on bag. No empty case tinkling on the ground. No brass to slip on. Details, details, details.

Targets sprang up again, were hit again, and scores automatically logged.

Despite the air-conditioning, the atmosphere in the killing house grew thick with fumes. She activated the extraction system and the massive fans cut in.

Her fatigues drenched in sweat, Chifune finally slumped to the ground panting. She lay there for several minutes and then walked to the showers. She missed her Japanese bath, but in addition to the showers there was a hot tub there, and that was close enough.

The shower block was empty. She had the place to herself. It would be another two hours before the camp woke.

She stripped off her clothes. She did not switch on the lights. There was just enough illumination from security lights filtering through the roof lights of the shower room, and the combination of the streaming water against her body and the near darkness was soothing. She turned off the shower. Toweling her hair while she walked, she made her way to the hot tub and slid in.

Eyes closed, she stretched out her legs.

Flesh.

A figure leaped into the air. "JUDAS PRIEST!" yelled a voice, clearly freshly wakened. "Who the hell is that?"

Chifune started to laugh.

"They say it's dangerous to fall asleep in a hot tub, Hugo," she said sweetly. "Didn't your mother ever tell you that?"

The figure slid back into the water. "My mother told me to beware of Japanese women," growled Fitzduane. There was a long pause before he spoke again. "Especially the kind a man has learned to really care about."

"Men forget," said Chifune softly.

"We make choices," said Fitzduane, "and we live with those choices, but we don't forget. We were close and we'll always be close. It doesn't end just because . . ." He left the last words unspoken.

He leaned across and kissed her on the forehead, and her arms went around him and for a moment they were locked together. Then they separated.

Chifune sat in the darkness and cried. Fitzduane put his arm around her. After a while her tears ceased and she began to talk. Mostly Fitzduane listened.

"I must go, Hugo," she said eventually, "or Oga-*san* will be out looking." She laughed. She felt a great sense of peace.

She moved toward him and kissed him once on the lips. *Our lives are intertwined,* she thought. *I will be your shadow.*

"I'm glad you're here, Chifune," said Fitzduane quietly. "It means more than I can say. When I've doubts I see you and I think 'Yes, we can do it.' I often have doubts."

"We'll get Kathleen back," said Chifune simply.

In the morning, Oga expected Chifune to look tired and to eat little, as had been her habit recently. Instead she was in sparkling form and ate like a little horse. He felt immensely relieved.

Oshima, he thought, you're going to have problems. Whatever happened last night, Tanabu-*san* is back on form.

CHAPTER FOURTEEN

IT WAS RHEIMAN'S fourth visit.

He did not seem to mind that she did not reply. He chattered away and she stayed silent and that was accepted as the natural order of things. Nonetheless, despite her inner campaign of silent resistance, Kathleen looked forward to his visits. Rheiman, whatever he had done and whatever he was, was gentle. He was considerate, and above all, he came across as a normal, warm fellow human being.

A lie? Another unpleasant twist in the psychological battle Reiko Oshima was waging to break her? Perhaps, but she thought not.

Kathleen wanted to cry with relief when Rheiman came to visit, but nothing showed. The mantra was repeated again and again.

I am strong.

It was no longer just a slogan. It was the truth. And there was a new mantra. *I know.*

I am strong and I know. Blindfolded, bound, and helpless though she was, she felt an ever-increasing strength and understanding that had previously eluded her. Motives and behavior, previously inexplicable, now made sense. It was if her mind had been out of focus in the past and the conclusions blurred. Now the focus was tight and clear and vivid.

She heard his marvelously civilian footsteps outside and then a brief interchange with the guard. They made jokes about him when his back was turned, but to his face they treated Rheiman with respect. He had no direct authority over them, she gathered, but he had clout of some sort. He was a senior figure in the scheme of things.

But what did he do? Why was he here? So far, she had no idea. He had talked a great deal, but always in generalities. It was a kind of verbal reconnaissance. As Rheiman had said, people like to chew over a new idea before swallowing it. And

Rheiman as a friend—which was what he clearly wanted to be—was certainly a novel proposition. For he was also the enemy. And *she was strong*.

She would not be seduced or flattered or won over by gentle words any more than she would give in to physical abuse. She would hold fast and she would win. Somehow. There was always a way.

Sometimes you found out too late.

The cell door opened and closed and his footsteps came closer, and then there was a new noise. She racked her brain. She was getting good at identifying sounds. She smiled. *Got you!* It was a folding chair.

Small victories, Fitzduane used to say when he was blocked by something, they're all you need to keep going.

Rheiman cleared his throat. He seemed to feel the need to announce himself before he started to speak. Once he got going there was scant trace of hesitation, but initially he always betrayed that he was not quite sure of his ground. This did not support the idea that he was part of some plan of Oshima's. It was much more as if he was following his own agenda but was not quite sure how to proceed.

A weakness! A weakness that could be exploited!

"I brought a chair, Kathleen," said Rheiman apologetically. "It's not for you, I'm afraid. They insist you stay chained to the wall. That's the way they are. But then, you know that."

Kathleen remained stony-faced.

"I saw you smile when I came in," said Rheiman. He paused and then continued almost sadly. "For me? I think not. But you have a most beautiful smile, Kathleen. It melts my heart when I see you like this. I really do want us to be friends."

Kathleen swore silently. She was almost sure that she had shown no expression when she had guessed that the sound was the chair, but her damn body was letting her down.

"I used to work for a man called George Bull," said Rheiman. "He was a genius—way ahead of his time—and I hated him. Quite a few people did. People generally don't like people who are that smart.

"I loathed Bull's guts because he was attractive to women in a way that I was not. On the scientific side, I could more than give Bull a run for his money. I'm proving it now. I am building what he only dreamed about—but my installation is way superior.

"The secret, you must know, is in the use of hydrogen as propellant. Bull, you know, used a form of gunpowder. An odd choice for such a progressive man. Apart from being technologically less efficient, it is *not* the kind of thing that you can buy by the ton without attracting unwelcome attention. Hydrogen, on the other hand, is used for activities as innocent as children's balloons, and you can make it from ordinary water."

Kathleen knew she had a decision to make. She could maintain her silent resistance or switch tactics. Rheiman was dangling information in front of her as an incentive to speak. And if she did speak she could begin to guide the conversation and perhaps learn something that would help her escape. On the other hand, if she did break her silence it could be seen as a sign of weakness.

But what counted was not so much what they thought but how she felt inside. *I am strong and I know!*

She made her decision.

"I don't—don't understand," she said slowly. Her throat was dry, and speech did not come easily.

"I'm sorry," said Rheiman. "I should have realized how you felt." She heard the sound of water pouring, and then her hands were being folded around a cup and steered gently toward her lips.

Water! It meant more than she could ever express. She was kept permanently thirsty. She felt a rush of gratitude toward Rheiman, and then her defense mechanisms cut in. *Don't be fooled, Kathleen. This is a trick. This man is the enemy. Use him. Do not weaken.*

"Feel better?" said Rheiman.

"A little," said Kathleen. Follow up an advantage. "It would be easier if I could see you, Mr. Rheiman. It's difficult to talk when you cannot see the other person."

There was silence. "I—I'm sorry," said Rheiman. "You're right, of course, but there are limits to what I can do. How they're treating you is barbaric, but you are Oshima's prisoner. She is not someone one defies lightly. Do you know who she is?"

Kathleen nodded. "I know who she is," she said with feeling. "And what she is." She looked toward where Rheiman was sitting. There was an opportunity here, a sensitivity to exploit. She would use his first name. "And you're working with her, Edgar?"

There was another long pause. "I—I . . . there are reasons, Kathleen."

"Tell me about them, Edgar," said Kathleen, her blindfolded face facing his, her voice soft. "Tell me about them."

She heard the metal frame of his chair rasp against the stone of the floor, then hurried footsteps. For long seconds there was silence as he paused by the door, and then it was opened and closed quietly.

She had pushed too hard and had alienated her one potential ally. Despair seized her, but then she fought back. She remembered a story Fitzduane had once told her.

"A man owned a valuable mule," he had said, "not just any old mule but a valuable, fine, upstanding animal with a glossy coat and clear eyes. Unfortunately, the mule would not do what it was told. To put it mildly, it was a bloody-minded beast.

"The mule owner, not unreasonably, was frustrated by this recalcitrant animal. He tried various techniques and a whole raft of different mule tamers, but to no avail. The mule remained uncooperative.

"The mule owner was a rich man, and he was determined this animal would not beat him. He put out the word, and eventually he heard of a mule tamer who never failed. The man was expensive but, so said everyone, he always succeeded. Where mules were concerned, he knew what to do and when to do it.

"The mule owner contacted the mule tamer and, after much haggling, procured his services. The man arrived and, being quite famous, a crowd assembled to see him practice his art. What would he do? How would he operate?

"The mule tamer walked around the mule. The animal tossed his head and bared his teeth and tried his various tricks. The tamer, being an experienced man, was unscathed, but it was a close-run thing. This was one mean mule.

"The tamer had brought a well-worn leather bag. It was quite a long affair, similar in a way to a modern sports bag. He carried it slung over one shoulder.

"The mule tamer opened the bag and removed a sledgehammer. He then closed the bag—he was a neat man—and, carrying the hammer, walked back towards the mule.

"The mule owner was alarmed. 'What are you doing?' he cried. 'This is one valuable mule.'

"The mule tamer did not reply. He stood directly in front of the mule as if daring it to bite him, and then, as it lunged, he swung the hammer in a mighty blow and hit the mule smack on top of his head.

"Everyone could hear the dreadful sound of the hammer hitting the mule.

"*Thunk!*

"The mule collapsed. It went straight down just like that and lay on the ground motionless. Not even a quiver.

"There was an awed group intake of breath from the crowd, and then silence.

"The owner was horrified and incredulous in about equal measure. He was too surprised to say anything at first, but then words came spluttering out. 'What—what did you do that for? I hired you to tame the animal.'

"The mule tamer looked at the rich mule owner with a clear, steady gaze. 'First,' he said, 'I had to get the mule's attention.' "

Kathleen smiled as she remembered. It was one of Fitzduane's favorite stories. Despite her chains and her thirst, she drifted into sleep content.

Rheiman had been deeply upset. But she was now convinced she had his attention.

THERE were six rooms divided by a central corridor in the killing house.

The object was to clear the house of fourteen terrorists while preserving two hostages. The location of the hostages was not known in advance.

Initial exercises were carried out with silenced 9mm Calico submachine guns firing live ammunition and using electronic targets, with each assault team member going through alone. When hit, the human-shaped targets registered the accuracy of fire by individual round on a computer and, in addition, each assault was timed, videoed from several angles, and observed by umpires. The final score was a matrix of time and accuracy. Including gaining access, all were within two and a half minutes.

At the end of five run-throughs by each team member, the top three shooters were Chifune Tanabu, Al Lonsdale, and Peter Harty of the Irish Rangers.

Fitzduane came in a politically acceptable fifth. In his opinion, he had done at least as well as he deserved, given his recent lack of regular firearms training, but his competitive nature still urged him to do better. It was not going to be easy. The standard was high.

Changing magazines or clearing stoppages took place so fast, it was scarcely possible to see the action except on slow-motion video. Neither remedial action should have been necessary given that the Calico could take a hundred-round magazine that functioned near flawlessly given the right ammunition, but Fitzduane wanted the shooters to start off working for a living. For initial training, magazine capacity was limited to thirty rounds, and two dud rounds were placed at random in each shooter's loads.

The result of years of expensive investment in the training and equipment of top-quality Western counterterrorist forces could be observed. These were people who typically shot more rounds in a week than most regular soldiers did in a couple of years—and it showed. They moved through the grim business of killing with a sureness and elegance that was stunning to watch.

Fitzduane then changed the exercise. Whereas before each shooter was using live ammunition on targets, now they would use Simmunition against their peers.

Simmunition was real ammunition that was powerful enough to cycle the weapon and allow full automatic fire but fired projectiles made of a special material that stung and left a visible red mark but were otherwise harmless.

The prospect of being hit—and being rated accordingly—caused behavior to change.

The true combat shooters started to surface. The league table changed slightly. Fitzduane moved up from fifth to second place. Chifune still remained the top shooter.

The final series of exercises involved each unit member clearing the killing house against fourteen armed occupants who were spread throughout the rooms and not dug in but engaged in normal nighttime off-duty activities. The killing house was blacked out and the attacker had the advantage of surprise, night-vision goggles, and a silenced Calico now equipped with a hundred-round magazine and a laser sight that could only be seen by the person wearing the specially filtered goggles.

Fitzduane was encouraged to find that eleven out of his little force, now fully in the rhythm, were able to make a silent entrance and kill everyone inside without being hit in under ninety seconds.

Such clinically precise killing was frightening to behold, but it gave him hope.

FITZDUANE contemplated the screen of his notebook computer.

Whom to choose? Some choices were obvious. On the margin it was not so clear-cut.

He had fourteen slots to fill in addition to himself, and nineteen people to pick from. For security and resource reasons, he did not really like training anybody who was not going on the mission, but training accidents were a fact of life and one had to be prepared.

He had originally planned on three alternates as an adequate safety margin, but then Lee Cochrane had made his case and finally Maury had volunteered. It was just as well that Dan Warner was still in Mexico, or doubtless he would have volunteered also. As it was, he was going to be faced with four unhappy people.

Why did human beings in good health volunteer so readily to get killed?

He switched focus to consider the mission training. He had been tempted to carry out the initial training in the Ranger facility on his island back in Ireland. Most of the facilities of the special-forces trade were located there, and it would have had the advantage that he was intimately familiar with the resources available.

He had rejected the Irish option with regret. There would have been logistical difficulties given the distances involved, and anyway rain-sodden Ireland was not really the right environment in which to train for Mexico, even if you had a better-than-average sense of humor.

Kilmara had quipped that if he was going to use Ireland he would need twice as many people—the extra hands to hold umbrellas for the assault team.

Fitzduane had settled in the end for operating from Lamar's Son Tay estate in Virginia—from which they could easily access the Aberdeen Proving Grounds—and then a final intensive session at the U.S. Army's National Training Center in the Mojave Desert, a particularly godforsaken part of California.

The NTC was hot and dry and dusty and generally miserable, and as close to the terrain in Tecuno as would make no difference. Also, the NTC had a resident opposing force equipped with Russian armor whose sole purpose in life was to give the U.S. Army units training there a hard time. Since they knew the terrain intimately and had the luxury of being there all the time instead of only a couple of weeks, the resident opposition were horrible people to go up against. To make matters worse, they normally won.

But you learned fast. The damn place was equipped with pop-up targets and laser simulators and concealed video cameras and all kinds of toys to monitor progress. Fitzduane could not think of a better place to hone the unit in dealing with the kind of opposition that Tecuno could muster. The concept of a heavily armed but unarmored fast attack vehicle like the Guntrack being able to combat traditional tanks was a theory. Fitzduane had never actually seen it in practice. At the NTC they would have a chance to find out. Of course, what he would do if his theories did not pan out in practice was another matter.

However the war games turned out, there was one immutable as far as Fitzduane was concerned. The mission was *not* going to be aborted.

There was a knock on the door.

As mission commander, he had a hut to himself. There was accommodation in plenty. It made Fitzduane wonder what Grant Lamar got up to from time to time. Lamar, the evidence would appear to indicate, was a man with complex interests.

He blanked the screen and checked his watch. It was near midnight. When this was all over he was going to sleep for a week. Maybe longer. One thing was certain: The military did not sleep enough.

"Come in!"

A fatigues-clad Lee Cochrane stood in the doorway. Fitzduane waved him to a chair. There was a perceptible odor of propellant and gun oil off him. The unit was training for sixteen hours a day, but Cochrane still put in two more hours in the killing house or on the range. He had not done well in the initial killing-house exercises and was grimly determined to succeed.

Cochrane found taking orders from Fitzduane difficult. He had been chief of staff for a long time and absolute ruler of his little congressional kingdom. Being another grunt in the woods was something that did not come easy. And in the background was the thought that he was *still* chief of staff.

"A beer, Lee?" said Fitzduane. Serious drinking was not encouraged, but a couple of cans at the end of a long sweaty workday—or night—could help. This looked like such a situation. Cochrane was decidedly strung out. He was just in control, but the joins were showing.

Cochrane shook his head. Fitzduane threw him a can anyway and poured himself one. A little sociability might not go amiss.

Cochrane pulled the ring of his can, took a long pull, and stared at him. "Fitzduane, you're a head case. We're camped in the woods and you're using a fucking glass."

Fitzduane picked up his glass and sipped a little beer.

"My ancestors have been fighting for some cause or other for about eight hundred years that I know of," he said, "which translates into a whole lot of camping. One thing they have learned: Any fool can be uncomfortable."

Cochrane glared at him. His eyes were bloodshot from fatigue and cordite fumes, and his face was covered with a thin sheen of sweat.

"Damn you, Fitzduane!" he said quietly.

Fitzduane felt a stirring of anger. It was too late and he was too tired to just sit there and be abused by some asshole. On the other hand, Cochrane had been fighting for a good cause for some time and had earned the right to be cut some slack.

"What's on your mind, Lee?" said Fitzduane agreeably.

Cochrane suddenly flung his head back and chugalugged his beer. He wiped his mouth with his hand. His face was flushed, and his fatigues were spotted where the froth had overflowed.

"I need to know," he said. "Am I going to be picked for the assault group? *I've got to be on it!*"

Fitzduane took his time replying. "As you well know, Lee, people are picked for assignments such as this because of their very special qualifications. It's not personal. It's a matter of whether you are right for the job."

"You haven't answered my question," said Cochrane.

"You were a good soldier, Lee," said Fitzduane, "and you've kept yourself in exceptional shape. But your military days were a long time ago and military skills atrophy without practice. Your shooting was not good for the first couple of days because you were rusty as hell. Now, because you've worked yourself to the bone, it is vastly improved, but it is still not Delta or SAS or Ranger standard. Perhaps it could be over time, but we don't have that luxury. People are going to be trying to kill us very shortly, and the difference of a fraction of a second is going to make the difference between life and death. This is serious shit, Lee. So, as matters stand, I am *not* going to pick you."

Cochrane was silent, stunned. It was one thing to expect the worst. It was another to hear it.

Eventually he looked up at Fitzduane and shrugged. "I guess I'd better pack my kit and go home. I could say shooting isn't the only thing. I could give you quite an argument. I could say I deserve to go. But I get the impression whatever I say won't make much difference."

"My comments about your shooting skills are merely an illustration, Lee," said Fitzduane. "I could move on to communications, heavy weapons, the whole enchilada. And remember one thing—you asked."

Cochrane laughed bitterly. "Never get yourself into a situation where the other party is forced to say no. Basic negotiations skills. You'd think I would have learned more on the Hill. So what now?"

Fitzduane tossed Cochrane two more cans of beer. "We get a little drunk. We sleep not quite enough. And we go back to work."

Lee looked bemused. "I thought you said you weren't picking me."

"We've got enough people to fight without fighting each other," said Fitzduane. "So shut up and drink and listen. I've got an idea."

CHAPTER FIFTEEN

KILMARA FOLLOWED THE maneuvers intently.

For the purpose of this preliminary exercise the five Guntracks were not camouflaged, which made his job a whole lot easier. Also, it was daylight. Movement during the Tecuno mission was planned to take place entirely at night under stealth conditions. No talking, no lights, camouflaged, silenced exhausts, thermal signatures minimized, radio silence, anything and everything that could make a noise muffled, slow speed to keep down dust.

A helicopter suddenly appeared flying low, and then a second behind it and to the right. A classic hunter-killer team.

Two Guntracks halted and then shot into reverse before halting again. Thick smoke filled the air and obscured them. The remaining three, also trailing thick smoke, raced in different directions before looping back to hide in the smoke. The speed of the Guntrack reactions was extraordinary.

Fitzduane watched the action through a thermal viewer while listening intently to a radio commentary coming through his earphones. The whole action, including all the resultant maneuvers, took no more than a minute.

He winced. "Best estimate by the observers, the helicopters got one of us and we got both of them. Helicopter gunships are our worst nightmare. When they come in fast and low like that, there is very little warning. On the other hand, what we are going to be up against in Tecuno is not so sophisticated and unlikely to be as well trained. And I have got to say, thermal is one hell of an edge. We can see through the smoke, and the combination of the Mag thermal sight on the Stinger makes for real fast acquisition. But we've got to do better."

"Did you factor in your .50s?" said Kilmara.

"No," said Fitzduane. "They have not come yet, so the team are working with what they've got. The GECALs are due in a couple of days. I'm kind of curious to see them in action."

"Puff the Magic Dragon, only in a heavier caliber," said Kilmara. "But the heavier round makes quite a difference. The way things are shaping up, you are going to be glad to have them. There is going to be rather more on your shopping list of objectives than you know."

Fitzduane looked him. "So this is not quite a social call, General."

Kilmara shook his head. "Not quite. Let's head back to base. Jaeger's turned up again and Lamar's been stirring the pot. They want to ask you a small favor, seeing as how you'll be in the Tecuno neighborhood."

"We're going into Tecuno very, very hard and we're coming out with Kathleen," said Fitzduane. "And we are not going to fuck around in the middle. That makes for a nice, clean, simple mission. That's a hard thing to find in these political days, but that's the way it's going to be."

"Let's go and talk," said Kilmara wearily. "Unfortunately, life is rarely simple."

KATHLEEN was taken aback at how affected she was when he returned.

The civilian footsteps, the brief exchange with the guard, the noisy opening of the cell door by the guard, and then its gentle closure by Rheiman. The sound of his breathing. He was not a fit man. The squeak of the chair frame against the concrete as he sat down.

"Edgar," she said quietly, "I'm glad you came back."

"You can tell?" he said, sounding pleased. "I—I missed you, Kathleen."

This time Kathleen said nothing. She was working on instinct, nothing more. Rheiman *had* to make a move. He had to work to earn her favor without being aware of what he was doing. Eventually, he would not care. But that would be in the future. Right now it was a matter of pulling in a little but not too hard. Keep up the tension on the line. Give him enough room to swim away a little but not get free.

She smiled. Again she was reminded of Fitzduane and the lake by the castle where they had fished. He had said the worst thing about fishing was catching the things. The peace, the lapping of the water, the beauty of the scenery, the lure of the hunt. Those were aspects he enjoyed. But he fished well like all his class. They were reared to such things. Kathleen's family had not been so privileged. Her life had not been so preordained. There were things she had to find out for herself.

"It's good to see you smile again," he said. "This time we must really talk and get to know each other. So you ask the questions. There must be a great deal you want to know, and I do so want to help."

"I don't want to upset you, Edgar," said Kathleen. "Last time you were upset, and I don't want that to happen again." She laughed slightly. "So you must warn me, Edgar, if I'm touching on difficult issues."

Rheiman breathed in as if steeling himself. "Go ahead. Ask whatever you like."

"Where am I, Edgar?"

Rheiman told her.

She tried to visualize his words and imagine a map of Mexico. Christ! She was in the middle of nowhere, and there were even rumors of trouble between Tecuno and the central government. The notion of rescue from the outside vanished. She was just too inaccessible, even if anyone did find out where she was.

She was on her own. This is where she would die unless she could change her own fate. No one else was going to help. *No one!*

She felt wave after wave of panic, but fought not to show it. *I am strong and I know!* But she did not know enough. She had to get Rheiman talking seriously. God knows, he wanted to.

"Why was I taken?" she said. "Why me? How did it happen?"

"There are eight million people in New York," said Rheiman. "You go to New York knowing no one and suddenly you meet someone on Fifth Avenue whom you were at school with. That's the way it works. I don't know why or how. I guess we're all connected in some weird way we can't comprehend as yet."

"I don't understand, Edgar," said Kathleen.

"Reiko Oshima heads up security here in the Devil's Footprint," said Rheiman. "I run the scientific side of the project. General Luis Barragan heads up the whole complex, including the nearby military base, and he reports to his cousin, Governor Diego Quintana.

"Essentially, Quintana is the dictator of a new country. Officially, Tecuno is still part of Mexico, but that is all smoke and mirrors. The reality is that Mexico City's writ stops at the Tecuno border. You're in at the beginning of Tecuno's independence, Kathleen, and it may not be the only part of Mexico to break away. Chiapas is not looking so healthy, and there are other states with notions. But Tecuno has oil, and that is buying what is needed to make the move. Weaponry, mercenaries, technology, political influence in the right places. It's all there and it's all coming together."

"Why was I kidnapped?" repeated Kathleen.

"Oshima won't speak to me, but she sleeps with General Luis Barragan and Luis and I get on fine. What I'm telling you is filtered through Luis—but he is not as savvy as Oshima, so put your own gloss on it."

"Why?" said Kathleen, just a hint of desperation in her voice.

"Governor Quintana wanted my project buttoned up real tight, and he did not think the locals were capable of doing it. Or maybe he just wanted to give them some competition. Anyway, Reiko Oshima was brought in and she, in turn, brought in quite a few of her old gang, Yaibo, and a number of other odds and sods she had picked up in the Middle East—about fifty in all. They are the Praetorian Guard of this little setup. They guard the center. And I run it.

"Reiko Oshima is a hard-core terrorist. It is no longer important why. That's history. Now she hates the world in general, and she hates Hugo Fitzduane in particular. Apparently, some years ago she had a boyfriend called the Hangman. Fitzduane tracked down the Hangman and killed him—and Reiko was down one lover. She is not the kind of person who forgets. You were involved with Fitzduane at the time, so your picture went up on her shit list. You're not at the top, but you are there."

"I'm not entirely with you," said Kathleen.

Rheiman leaned forward. Kathleen could feel his breath. She could imagine his gestures as he strove to make his point. "Reiko Oshima survives because she is an immensely capable woman who has the ability to turn on just enough people to give her the tools she needs. When I say capable, I don't mean she is just daring. That is a given. No, I am now talking about basic management skills. This woman is organized, structured, disciplined. She know logistics. She knows administration. She knows motivation.

"When I said your picture was up on her shit list, I was not using a figure of speech, Kathleen. Your actual photograph is up there for all the Yaibo trainees to target on and slobber over. In fact, that is where I first saw you. You were up there—a target.

"The next thing is that Oshima fucks the brains out of a young Yaibo recruit called Jin Endo, and he goes up to Washington on a scouting assignment, motivated to do anything to please his scar-faced lover. Oshima's ten most wanted are imprinted on his mind. And lo and behold, you are in Washington too. I guess it was just fate or you were plain unlucky. But from the time he caught sight of you, young Jin Endo was determined to get you. He wanted to prove himself. No one down here thought he would do so well, but to everyone's surprise, he did good. Real good. That, it turns out, is one very dangerous young man. He racked up quite a score when he was up north."

"Oshima was very pleased and is nursing him back to health in the only way she knows how. That means General Luis Barragan is not getting as much as he wants, so he comes and gets drunk with me. That's the trouble with this fucking place. There is nothing to do except work. Barragan's troops have TV and radio, but Oshima's people are not allowed to watch or listen. Apparently, they might get contaminated by capitalist filth. So they have to make do with propaganda sessions and a few whores. Once in, the whores are not allowed out. They don't last too long. There are some very warped people up here. A ritual execution is their substitute for the Movie of the Week."

Kathleen collected her thoughts. Fitzduane had called the world of terrorism and counterterrorism the only unending war. It only ended when all your enemies were dead. There could be lulls and truces and peace talks, but there was always some element that refused to forget and might strike back for some real or imagined causes years later. It was frightening.

"How did *you* end up here, Edgar?" she said. "This is not your world. This is no place for you."

"It is now," said Rheiman grimly. "I did something from which there was no turning back, and from that one act followed everything. I had to survive, so I did what was necessary and traded what I was good at."

"But you're a kind, gentle man," said Kathleen with as much conviction as she could muster. "How could you contemplate working with these animals?"

"I'm not so gentle," said Rheiman flatly.

Kathleen suddenly felt his hands tight around her neck. He was squeezing.

"Put your hands on mine," he said.

"E-Edgar!" she gasped, terrified.

"Do it!" he shouted. "DO IT!"

She put her hands on his. Rheiman's hands were large and strong, and she could feel scar tissue on the backs, as if they had been cut doing something physical. This was a man who worked with his brain but with his hands too. In a workshop or a laboratory? Somewhere like that.

Her neck was held tightly, but he was not increasing the pressure.

She could hear him breathing rapidly, as if under great strain. But nothing happened. This was not an attack on her. This was some memory being relived. Her fear diminished.

He took his hands away. He was very close to her, his face just above her. She felt drops on her face, a warm wet liquid like blood. He was sweating!

"That is how it started," he said unsteadily, "one simple killing with these very hands. A crime of passion, they would call it in France, and it would get a nominal jail sentence.

"Where I lived in the States, I faced execution. I ran. But it meant I could never go back. I had to find some place where there was no extradition and they could use my services.

"I drifted and ended up in Libya. And that is where I met up with Oshima. We were both on the run, so we got on well enough at first. She was interested in what I could do and brokered the deal with Luis Barragan. I would get to do what George Bull would not let me do—build a hydrogen-powered supergun. Quintana and Barragan would get a deterrent weapon which would allow them to break away from Mexico without the fear that one day the Mexican Army would turn up and rain on their parade.

"Now, I think there is more to it. The way things are going, I don't think this is being planned as a deterrent at all. I don't know about Barragan, but I think Oshima is going to use it and I think Quintana is involved."

"So stop the work, Edgar," said Kathleen. "Or delay it in some way they won't understand."

Rheiman stood up and paced the cell without speaking. He was clearly upset. Kathleen thought of saying something, but it seemed better to let whatever it was burn itself out. She had no sense that he was annoyed with her. This was some inner turmoil that only he could deal with.

God, between Reiko Oshima and Edgar Rheiman she was certainly keeping interesting company. And the smaller fry like Jin Endo sounded like no day at the beach either. Curiously, she was not afraid as she contemplated the situation. She should be in despair, but somehow she was not. A rural Irish upbringing must be a more solid foundation than she had thought.

Rheiman sat down again and leaned toward her. "Kathleen, in the past—when I worked for Bull and on other occasions—I argued and I argued and I argued for my ideas and no one would listen. Here, they are doing more than listening. They are putting up the funds and other resources to make my life's work possible. Every scientist of serious caliber has a dream they want fulfilled, and it rarely happens. Other people don't have the vision. Here, in this godforsaken spot and for the worst of motives, my vision is going to happen. I'm so close I can touch it. *I can't stop it now!*"

"And when it's done?" said Kathleen.

"Nothing will matter very much," said Rheiman calmly.

DR. John Jaeger was in the operations room at Lamar's when Fitzduane arrived.

"Dr. Death," said Fitzduane, agreeably, to the Livermore scientist. He regretted the words as soon as they passed his lips.

"I'm sorry, John," he said, "I'm getting a little frayed. That was a cheap shot."

Jaeger had been examining the STR shield. He turned as Fitzduane spoke, and smiled. "Forget it," he said. "I've been called much worse. The Lawrence Livermore Lab tends to provoke strong reactions."

"I know practically nothing about the place," confessed Fitzduane.

"Edward Teller, one of the pioneers of the nuclear program, was behind it," said Jaeger. "He reckoned that Los Alamos was not getting results fast enough and that a little competition would be healthy, competition being the American way and all. It was the early fifties and the Soviet threat was very real, so after some hard bureaucratic infighting, he had his way. The old Livermore Naval Air Station near Berkley, California, was where it all started."

"What do you do these days?" said Fitzduane.

"We're a scientific think tank," said Jaeger, "about eight thousand people strong. Roughly a third work on thermonuclear and other weapons research. The rest of us do all kinds of good stuff."

"Such as?" said Fitzduane.

Jaeger shrugged. "It's a long list," he said. "One example is a 'radar on a chip'—a miniature radar which can be used for all kinds of civilian applications from wall-stud finders to sudden infant death syndrome monitors. Another project is a 'biofilter.' It uses living microorganisms to clean up polluted groundwater. And so it goes. You must come and see us."

"And your project?" said Fitzduane.

"You'll be hearing more about that when the others come in," said Jaeger. "It's all of a piece with what is going on in Tecuno, but our motives and objectives are different. But the science is similar. Science has no loyalties."

"We have it and they have it," said Fitzduane, "and the human factor makes the difference?"

"We have it and we try and make sure they never get it," said Jaeger.

"But if they do—we take it away," said Fitzduane. "All men—countries—are equal, but some are more equal than others."

"Some we trust and some we don't—for very good reasons," said Jaeger. "There is idealism and there is personal survival. I think you know that, Hugo."

Fitzduane nodded. "Would it were otherwise," he said quietly.

DAN Warner, Deputy Chief of Staff of the Congress of the United States of America's Task Force on Terrorism, raised his right hand and made a gesture to the bartender.

Soon afterward another beer appeared on the table. That made four. Up north, he would have felt the effects. Down here, in Mexico, he had the feeling he was sweating it out faster than he could drink it in.

It was HOT! There was no air-conditioning. It was not that the machine was broken. It did not exist.

Nothing seemed to have changed in the last century, if you ignored the large color TV over one end of the bar and the jukebox. The jukebox, a collector's item beneath the dust, was playing "Down Mexico Way," which had to be half a century old.

"South of the border," Warner hummed, "down Mexico way." He de-dummed the rest. He had put on the jukebox and punched in the song as a temporary distraction from the endless speeches of Valiente Zarra. The candidate was an inspired speaker, but Warner was suffering from a serious case of overexposure.

There were 756,000 square miles of Mexico, according to Warner's guidebook, and Zarra seemed intent on covering every one. Except Tecuno, of course, where the borders had been quietly sealed, and a few other areas where even Zarra realized he was not welcome. Like Chiapas, where the terrorists had agreed to let him in—but the local landowners had not. But that still left an awful lot of real estate. This was one big country.

Lee Cochrane could be arrogant and was certainly stubborn, but he was also a patriot and a leader with a vision that was not subordinated to the short-termism that tended to pervade politics.

Assigning Warner to Zarra for the duration of the campaign was a typical outcome of that vision. Like it or not, Mexico shared a couple thousand miles of border with Uncle Sam and it was not going to go away. The two countries had to get closer. There was no other practical alternative.

Mexico's proximity also made it a prime haven for terrorists, drug runners, and other groups who did not harbor kindly thoughts toward the U.S. of A. and had not yet been awarded either their green cards or citizenship. The only way—short of direct action—to keep them in line was to have close relations with the movers and shakers in the Mexican government.

Real soon now, the head of that government was going to be Valiente Zarra. The professor was increasing his lead day by day. Even the PRI, experts in every form of election fixing and with a talent for innovation, were going to find it impossible to wish Zarra away. And the Task Force was going to have the ear of the new *Presidente* and be able to collect on a few favors, not the least of which was dealing with Governor Diego Quintana's power base.

The proposed raid into Tecuno would not put Quintana out of business, Warner considered, but it would weaken him. A weakened power broker would be easy prey for others to finish off. It would probably be done by his own party. The PRI had quite a tradition of turning on its own. The PRI was less a united party than a coalition of interests of those who wanted to hang on to power by whatever means were necessary. Some wanted to reform the PRI. Others did not. Blood had already been spilled.

The cantina was in a backwater town about eighty miles south of Guadalajara. The place had once had a silver mine, which had closed down some sixty years earlier, and right now Warner could see no economic reason for the town's existence at all. Except for a magnificent crumbling church, the cantina, and—he had been told—a whorehouse.

The reason for a location this remote was not campaigning—even Zarra drew the line somewhere, and this town was way below somewhere—but a discreet meeting with reformers in the Mexican military. The 170,000-man Mexican Army was conservative, and its officer corps schooled at the Escuela Superior de Guerra and the Colegio de Defensa Nacional even more so, but even those die-hards wanted to be on the winning side.

Tentative approaches had been made by the military to the Zarristas. Zarra had replied with promises to reform the Mexican Army along modern lines—not a hard promise to fulfill, since the existing deployment was based on a 1924 plan. The end result was an agreement that in exchange for Zarra's new military program, the Mexican Army would move "when the time was right."

It was all a little vague for Warner's liking, but the complexities of Mexican politics took a lifetime to understand, even if its fundamentals were clear enough. The end result was that if Fitzduane's force opened up Tecuno, the Mexican Army would probably go in and finish the job. If Zarra was still high in the polls and virtually certain to become the next president. And there were a few more "ifs."

The deal between Zarra and the Mexican military had not been worded with any degree of precision. It focused more on broad aspirations. To be fair, Zarra had wanted to mention Tecuno specifically as the target to enable the Mexicans to get their troops into place. It made sense in military terms, he had argued.

Warner had fought against this and had stressed the importance of keeping the assault on the Devil's Footprint a secret. *A secret!*

No one—but no one—was to know except Zarra himself.

Reluctantly, Zarra had agreed. The Mexican Army merely knew that they were likely to be called upon to take action at a time and place unspecified.

They expressed irritation but were secretly pleased. Valiente Zarra was proving to be a man who understood the realities. They had no desire to be allied with a political naïf. Certainly, the army would back him if it looked as if he was winning, but equally certainly someone—more likely several people—in the army high command would be keeping the current *el Presidente* and his party, the PRI, posted. Precise information would have got back to Quintana rather faster than shit through a goose. Such was the world of politics.

So this secret meeting between Zarra and the Mexican high command might, in fact, have taken place in Mexico City in the full hearing of the Presidential Palace or the Ministry of War and National Defense, for all the secrecy it really invoked. But such was Mexico, where going through the motions was very important. A secret meeting—even if not really secret—showed that the generals were really serious about supporting Zarra and had taken something of a risk. Accordingly, Zarra, when he became president, would now owe them. On the other hand, since the PRI and the incumbent *el Presidente* had been kept informed, they would owe the generals also.

It made Dan Warner feel right at home. It was just like Washington in high summer, but without the humidity.

But it was even HOTTER! And that was saying something.

✳ CHAPTER SIXTEEN

"You want us to WHAT?" said Fitzduane incredulously.

"Take out Governor Quintana's supergun," said Jaeger helpfully. "I think that is the military term. Hell, man, you'll be down in the Devil's Footprint anyway. A bit of this and a bit of that, and you'll be outa there with almost no time lost."

Fitzduane looked around the conference table. Lamar was there and so were Cochrane and Maury and Kilmara, but there were also some new faces. General Frampton, Chairman of the Joint Chiefs, was there unofficially, and so was William Martin of the CIA, doubtless equally unofficially.

It was a regular unofficial teddy bear's picnic, and it was beginning to look as if he was the main course. If these yo-yos had their way, he was going to end up unofficially dead.

"I thought you were watching my back," Fitzduane said to Kilmara, "keeping me free of the political shit so I could concentrate on the mission. Terrific job you're doing."

Kilmara looked uncomfortable. "The mission is getting every cooperation," he said. "But in turn, *they* would like—would appreciate—a certain quid pro quo. They help us and we help them."

Fitzduane stared at General Frampton, William Martin, and Grant Lamar. "Who are 'they'?" he said.

"I think you know, Hugo," said Lamar quietly. "We're not going to insist on it. It will be your decision. But we'd like to make the case. The fact is that we are faced with a threat to national security which, for various reasons, we cannot officially act against right now. You know the background. You know all about President Falls's Mexican policy and NSA Slade's influence. Hands off Mexico. That was serious enough when we were talking conventional terrorism. Add in an offensive capability, and we have just got to act. Your mission is jumping off in a couple of weeks. So you, Colonel, are the obvious candidate."

Fitzduane leaned forward to emphasize his point. "According to the latest intelligence, General Luis Barragan has at least two thousand troops equipped with Eastern bloc armor at Madoa airfield eight kilometers away from the base. At the Devil's Footprint itself, there are fifty hard-core terrorists and a further six hundred mercenary troops, also equipped with all kinds of nasty things and an unfriendly attitude towards good guys like us.

"Now, since you people won't send in air strikes and the kind of sizable force this mission really requires, I'm going in with a total force of fifteen personnel—not to go head-to-head with these vermin, but because I think speed and stealth are our best weapons. Anything that delays us or makes us more likely to be discovered erodes our advantages. They are slim enough. We need to hang on to what we've got."

He looked around at the group one by one. "Have I made myself clear?"

Grant Lamar nodded. General Frampton cut in before he had time to speak. "We understand the situation, Colonel Fitzduane. We would not be raising this if we had an alternative."

William Martin spoke. "Colonel Fitzduane, hear out Dr. Jaeger and then decide."

"Have you gentlemen ever heard the term 'mission creep'?" said Fitzduane. "It is something of a U.S. custom. A nice clean mission with a simple objective and a clear chain of command gets truly fucked up with so many additional requirements and idiotic restrictions that no one knows quite what they are supposed to be doing. Add micromanagement and a dose of friendly fire and you've got a recipe for a lot of people dying and your objective lost in a cacophony of sound bites."

General Frampton met Fitzduane's gaze. "Ouch!" he said grimly. He paused for a beat. "But we have learned a few things from our mistakes."

"Maybe," said Fitzduane without conviction. He glanced over at Jaeger. "Go ahead, John. I'm a reasonable man."

Jaeger laughed. "With a hard edge, Colonel. With a very hard edge."

Fitzduane smiled somewhat grimly. "It seems probable, gentlemen, that I'm going to need it."

JAEGER was well into his stride.

"George Bull was a Canadian genius who believed that a gun could do much of what a rocket can do, only more efficiently. He argued that a focused explosion contained within a barrel is inherently more efficient than something like a rocket, which dissipates much of its energy into the general neighborhood.

"So don't think of the supergun as a giant artillery piece. Think instead of it as being the equivalent of a first-stage rocket, with the projectile—the missile—

being the second stage. The supergun gives the missile an initial momentum and then, once it is partially released from the gravitational field, the missile's own small motor takes over. The significant point here is that, weight for weight, the supergun can do the same job with a fraction of the energy and at a fraction of the cost."

"Theoretically?" said Fitzduane.

"Actually," said Jaeger. "I told you I'd built a hydrogen-powered gun. Well, we didn't just screw it together. We carried out a full firing program."

There was silence in the room.

"So you've built a weapon," said Fitzduane slowly, "similar to whatever they have built in Mexico."

Jaeger shook his head. "Ours is not a weapon," he said. "Our gizmo is designed to ferry material up into space at about one-twentieth the cost of a rocket. The cost of putting materials into space is currently greater than their weight in gold, which concentrates the mind, does not overly please Congress, and ticks off the electorate. We've tested it. We've fired it, and it works. In fact, it works exceptionally well."

Fitzduane looked dubious. The interchange was giving him time to think.

"Look," continued Jaeger, "rockets were right at the time and continue to have advantages. Human beings are not too well adapted to being fired out of a gun barrel into space. But equipment, supplies, and so on are another matter. They don't care how they get up there. It is just a matter of physics, and the bottom line is that a supergun can do it much cheaper than a rocket. But not with gunpowder. That's where Bull was wrong. Gunpowder works okay, but it is expensive, slow to load, and hell to clean up. No, the way to go is hydrogen."

"And that is what you used at Livermore?" said Fitzduane. "Or is it 'use'?"

"More or less," said Jaeger. He grinned. "To both."

Fitzduane nodded. "My understanding from the media is that a supergun is too unwieldy to be a weapon. We're in the age of maneuver warfare. You can't put one of these things on the back of a Humvee and go and hide under a palm tree. And anyway, a thermal imager will see right through the leaves. Privacy is not what it was."

Jaeger looked at the CIA Deputy Director. William Martin took over. It was Jaeger's job to explain the science. The use to which the end result might be put required a different mind-set.

"What you're saying is the conventional wisdom," said Martin, "but our underlying assumption is that Quintana is an intelligent man and he must have been as aware of the limitations as we were. Yet he proceeded on the endeavor and committed very substantial resources.

"So, what is he up to? Leaving out his political motivations for the moment, why would he consider that the supergun can be made an effective weapon when others have dismissed it?

"The most significant new factor in the equation is the scientist behind Quintana's weapon. He has been identified as Dr. Edgar Rheiman, a very interesting man indeed.

"Rheiman worked for George Bull for some years and was regarded as a major talent, but they fell out over women and science. Bull was attractive to women. Rheiman was not. Rheiman fell deeply for a lab assistant called Gloria Engleman. Unfortunately, Gloria preferred Bull. She slept with Rheiman but worshiped Bull from afar. If she had kept that to herself, it would not have mattered. Unfortunately, she uttered Bull's name during an intimate moment.

"That slight preyed on Rheiman's mind. Two days later, he marched into the rather busy lab—there were eight witnesses—and, after a diatribe, blew Gloria's head off with both barrels of a twelve-gauge from a range of approximately eight inches. The defense argued it was a crime of passion. The prosecution said it showed clear premeditation. Any sane observer would have supported both viewpoints, but the upshot was that Rheiman was sent for psychiatric assessment before sentencing and escaped from the secure facility in the hospital after killing a nurse. By all accounts, he killed twice more before getting out of the country. Each time the victim looked something like Gloria: brunette, strong-featured, leggy, and in her thirties. Both were strangled."

Fitzduane's mind was focused on dredging up everything he knew on the supergun, and for the moment the CIA Deputy Director's words did not register. When they did, a cold chill ran through him. Kathleen! He was describing Kathleen.

"Perhaps more interesting than Rheiman's rather aggressive approach to women," continued Martin, "were his scientific views. He advanced three ideas of particular relevance.

"First, he argued that the use of hydrogen as a propellant was vastly preferable to traditional gunpowder. Second, he said that a hydrogen-based supergun could be used as a weapon if it focused on low-earth satellites which could be brought down on command on the enemy. Third, to offset the intrinsically unwieldy nature of an individual supergun, he advocated the construction of multiple tubes using cheap, readily available raw materials. His point was that since a supergun requires a long slow explosion, traditional gun-barrel materials would not be required. So you could offset the lack of mobility with a high rate of fire—thanks to hydrogen—and multiple installations."

"Concrete!" breathed Fitzduane as understanding hit. "The sample of special concrete brought out by Patricio Nicanor. But then, why make the first gun out of maraging steel when he could have used superhard concrete sewer pipes?"

Jaeger laughed. "His concrete is just a shade more exotic than that—but essentially you've got a point."

"Quintana has a reputation for not suffering fools gladly," said Martin. "Our assumption is that the first supergun—made out of steel—is proof of principle, and in using such a high grade of material, Rheiman is sensibly covering his ass. Concrete barrels are unproven. A split barrel on an initial test firing would be embarrassing for him. Fatally so if Quintana was present."

"Has the supergun been test-fired as yet?" said Fitzduane.

The CIA Deputy Director shook his head. "We're pretty sure not," he said. "These things make a big bang. If it had been fired we'd have picked it up on satellite. As it is, what I have said is all based upon our analysis. We could be wrong." He smiled ruefully. "It has been known to happen. We could be looking at some kind of specialized oil-extraction facility, but given the characters involved, we doubt that."

"Guilt by association?" said Fitzduane.

"Damn right," said Cochrane.

"So you want us to check it out and if it looks antisocial, blow it up," said Fitzduane. "How big is this thing?"

Martin looked at Jaeger. They were back on the scientist's territory. Jaeger looked somewhat uncomfortable.

"Big," said Jaeger. "Very big, actually."

Fitzduane leaned forward. "Trust me with your secret, John," he said. "If we are going to waste this thing it would be nice to know if we need a Swiss Army knife or a two-thousand-pound bomb."

Jaeger took a deep breath. "The supergun in the Devil's Footprint—if that is what it is—would appear to be two hundred meters long. That is about the height of a sixty-story skyscraper. It weighs, we estimate, just over twenty-one hundred tons."

Fitzduane's face rarely expressed total surprise, but this time it did. "And how the fuck are we going to destroy something that size?" he snarled. "Especially with a brigade of unfriendly troops looking on. We're not talking a weapon here. We're talking about a goddamn monument."

"It is a problem," admitted Jaeger. "But we have some of the best people at Livermore looking at it. We'll have an answer . . ."

". . . real soon now," completed Fitzduane. He got to his feet. "Unreal," he said, and left the room.

CALVIN Welbourne saluted. "Colonel," he said.

Fitzduane looked around. No one saluted on the team. Either Calvin had been out in the sun too long or some conventional green army type had sneaked in. Bad news either way. This was supposed to be a restricted area, and just because you had rank did not entitle you to access.

There was no one there. He turned back to face Calvin. He was still saluting. "Are you feeling all right, Calvin?" said Fitzduane, concerned. He did not want to lose the man.

"You put your hand up to your forehead and bring it down again, Colonel," said Calvin, "otherwise I'm stuck like this indefinitely."

Fitzduane acknowledged the salute.

He smiled. "Calvin, you're up to something. You never salute."

"This is a historic day, Colonel. I'm going to fly."

"Well, of course you are, Calvin," said Fitzduane benevolently. "I can see your wingtips sprouting as we speak."

"This way, Colonel," Calvin beckoned.

He followed Calvin.

A long U-shaped tube stood outside. Under the tube was a ruggedized wheeled suspension. If Fitzduane had been told it was a car trailer specially designed to carry something long and thin like a canoe, he would have believed it. As it was, the damn thing looked extremely unlikely to fly. There was nothing around that looked remotely like a pair of wings.

"Hop in, boss," said Calvin, climbing into the passenger seat of the Guntrack that was linked to the tube. Fitzduane climbed in beside him and Calvin took off in the aggressive style that had become normal for many mobile operations in the Guntracks. Either you were creeping along silently in stealth mode or else it was foot to floor and taking the concept of maneuver warfare all too literally.

"We've got to put a sick bag in these things," said Fitzduane as they hit a bump and Guntrack and trailer rocketed into the air and then crashed to the ground.

The ride continued, and then Calvin slewed to a halt in open space.

"The point," said Calvin, "is that the aircraft and trailer are robust. They are designed for this kind of unfriendly treatment. But would you believe me? No sir! So I had to demonstrate it. Believe me, boss, these things are tough! MilSpec is not in it. This aircraft is designed for the real world where shit happens. Bang them, bash them, shoot holes in them, and they still fly. Outstanding aircraft, wouldn't you say, sir?"

Fitzduane tried to catch his breath. "Possibly," he said, "if I could see an aircraft."

"Ah!" said Calvin. He leaped out of the vehicle and ran around behind the long trailer. The process was rather like assembling a frame tent, only faster. The entire happening took only about five minutes. At the end, there was a rigid fabric wing kept taut by stiffeners, and slung below it on poles a two-person open cockpit with a triangular suspension. A pusher propeller—which meant that the propeller was behind the occupants—provided power.

"Hop in," said Calvin.

"I don't like aircraft," said Fitzduane. "I'll jump out of them no problem, but I fly in them as little as possible. Further, Calvin, I'm far from sure this even qualifies as an aircraft. It looks like something your grandmother knitted. Jesus, the wings are scarcely tied to the superstructure. This thing is full of holes. It's a horrible device."

Calvin looked hurt. "Colonel, it works. It has a wing, something to sit in, and an engine. What more can you want?"

To stay on the ground, Fitzduane thought firmly. But then he weakened. Calvin looked depressed.

Fitzduane climbed gingerly into the pointed baby bath that passed as a cockpit. The side came up to his lower hip. If he sneezed, he was going to fall out. Why did people invent these things! He looked for a safety harness and found one with relief and clipped it on. This maniac was probably going to loop the loop. He thought about parachutes, but it was too late.

"Tally-ho!" shouted Calvin. Fitzduane flinched as the propeller cut in behind them, and seconds later they were airborne. They had needed minimal runway. It was remarkable. Up they climbed like a rocket in slow motion.

"This thing is all wing," said Calvin into the boom microphone attached to his helmet. "Phenomenal lift—but because the wing is made of fabric coated with radar-absorbent material, there is almost no radar signature."

"Speed?" said Fitzduane.

"Well, it's not exactly an F-16," admitted Calvin. "Say, eighty kliks flat out. But speed and acceleration are not the idea. This is an aerial advantage you can carry with you. Open the trailer, clunk-click, and you are airborne. Simplicity itself. Better yet, there is a miniature FLIR, and if you want to fly solo, you can carry some firepower."

"Can you silence the engine?" said Fitzduane.

"Sure," said Calvin. He flicked a switch and the decibel level dropped dramatically. "You lose some power, but if we were flying at night, we would be inaudible—and invisible—above a thousand feet."

Fitzduane was silent. This beast was terrifying, but it was interesting. It would be more interesting still if they could land in one piece.

"Let's head for the floor," he said.

"In a few minutes," said Calvin. "First, Colonel, I've just got to show you what this baby can really do." He sideslipped and then put the baby aircraft into a steep dive. Seconds later they were flying upside down.

"This is horrible," shouted Fitzduane. "And what the fuck use is it being upside down?"

There was a long pause, and then suddenly they were the right way up again. "I never thought about that," said Calvin.

CHAPTER SEVENTEEN

FITZDUANE SLOWED TO a halt, stood absolutely still, and then seemed to merge with the surrounding trees.

He had been running for an hour in full camouflaged fatigues and combat equipment, and despite the relative chill of the predawn air, he was drenched in sweat.

He wanted to wipe his face.

He remained immobile, his Calico submachine gun now ready to fire. There was a hundred-round magazine on the weapon and six more in his load-bearing vest. He was carrying a further arsenal in his belt pouches. Training so heavily loaded was not the most comfortable way to start the day, but the unit trained hard and the tone was set from the top.

People normally noticed movement itself before identifying *what* it was that was moving.

What had he seen?

There was some light in the sky, but the tree cover made visibility at ground level a somewhat inexact business. It was somewhat better in the clearing, but not much.

There was another quick movement, and Fitzduane focused in on it.

There was a tree stump in the tree line at the edge of the clearing roughly facing the entrance to his hut.

Someone was sitting on it, almost completely concealed by the surrounding trees. If he had not moved, Fitzduane would probably not, he considered, have seen him.

A threat? Unlikely. Not only were they inside the perimeter of Grant Lamar's Son Tay estate, but there was additional security around the training camp itself. Further, a potential attacker would not normally sit on a tree stump, albeit under some cover.

Still. A visual decoy was an old trick. You saw the one and forgot to consider the others.

At that moment, the figure stood up and stretched. Then it turned around to look in Fitzduane's direction.

The face was hideous, distorted, grotesque.

Then a hand came up and peeled the face away.

It was Grant Lamar, as elegantly dressed as always, the night-vision goggles dangling from his hand. He was smiling as he handed Fitzduane an envelope.

"It's a computer-enhanced enlargement courtesy of the National Security Agency," he said. "She's a beautiful woman."

Fitzduane tore open the envelope and stared at the picture. There was not enough daylight to be certain.

He ran to his hut and snapped on the light. The detail was blurred, as if slightly out of focus. Nonetheless, the likeness was unmistakable.

"Kathleen," he whispered. "Kathleen . . . Thank God."

Lamar entered the hut. For days Lamar had seen Fitzduane operate with a controlled purposefulness that betrayed little emotion and at times was almost cold in its intensity.

Now the Irishman stood there with tears streaming down his cheeks.

"Only fourteen hours old," said Lamar. "Straight from the Tecuno plateau courtesy of Aurora. Positive confirmation."

"The Devil's Footprint?" said Fitzduane.

"The Devil's Footprint," confirmed Lamar. *"Huella del Diablo."*

Fitzduane experienced such an intense feeling of joy and anger that he did not know quite whether to laugh or cry or shout or what to do.

After a couple of minutes he wiped the tears from his face. "I don't know how to thank you, Grant," he said.

"Do the deed," said Lamar. "Just do the deed."

THE .50-caliber GECALs arrived and were fitted.

The weapon operated on the Gatling principle. Each weapon had three electrically driven rotating barrels, so while one was actually firing the other two could be reloaded and have the crucial time necessary to cool down. The rate of fire could be varied from a thousand to two thousand rounds a minute.

A *single* .50 multipurpose armor-piercing explosive round—correctly placed— was capable of penetrating a light armored vehicle or downing a helicopter.

The effect of a sixty-round burst fired in less than two seconds was awesome. Conventional cover was swept away. Anything short of a main battle tank was shredded. Reinforced concrete bunkers were drilled through as if by a jackhammer.

The weapons had quite phenomenal shock value.

The greatest benefit came from the GECAL's antiaircraft capability. Reaction time was in fractions of a second. Low-flying helicopters now flew into a curtain of fire up to around 5,000 feet. Above that, the small, fast-moving Guntracks were hard enough to see, let alone hit, from the air. Further, Fitzduane had added the Shorts Starburst missile. Unlike the heat-sensitive Stinger, this was optically guided onto the target by a low-power laser beam and was immune to conventional countermeasures such as dropping flares. It required some more operator skill, but a few hours' practice resulted in a steady kill rate up to a height of 20,000 feet. They shot against small Skeets targets that were one-twentieth the size of a typical fighter aircraft.

"We're taking along a few Stingers as well, because they are compact and everyone knows them," said Fitzduane, "but the Stinger, being heat sensitive, is at its best shooting at a target after it has made a pass over you. Then it goes for the hot tail of the aircraft like a bat out of hell. Well, that is fine, but by that time you have already been strafed.

"The advantage of the Starburst, although it is slightly slower, is that you can take out an aircraft *before* it can do the business, which is very nice. I'm a great believer in fucking the enemy before he fucks you. Also, if you find out the supposed attacker is friendly after you have fired—an embarrassing discovery—you can steer the thing away with the laser and detonate it safely."

Shanley nodded. Fitzduane had brought him along officially to see if the Magnavox thermal sight used on the Stinger could be adapted to work with the Starburst as well. Thermals were great at acquiring a target. You were able to detect not just the target itself but the heat all around it. Much more to see.

The unofficial reason was to sound him out on the mission. Fitzduane moved on to that delicate matter. Shanley was coming through the training with flying colors, but he had a wife and children and he was a civilian.

"I've thought about it, Hugo," said Shanley. "I've thought about it a great deal and I've talked it over with Lydia. The long and the short of it is, I've got to go on this thing. I've briefed guys before dozens of missions in the past and always wondered why they should be putting their asses on the line for me. Now I'm getting a chance to do my bit. It's just the right thing to do. I was at Fayetteville and I've seen what these people will do if given the chance. Well, they've got to be stopped, and I intend to help do it."

"Fifteen of us are going out, and even if we are successful, it is unlikely that all of us will make it back," said Fitzduane quietly. "You could be killed or wounded or taken prisoner. A professional soldier takes his chances. Risk goes with the territory. For a civilian it is very different. Whatever you feel inside, you are under no obligation to go. We all appreciate your technical input. You've nothing to prove."

Shanley looked at Fitzduane. "It's the right thing," he said firmly. "I know it's right, and so does Lydia. We've no second thoughts. Besides, Hugo, I've never seen a better-planned mission. This is gonna work."

As he drove away, Fitzduane felt weighed down by Shanley's words. He had been on enough missions to know that you could prepare as much as you wanted but death came randomly on the battlefield.

Would he bring Shanley back home to his little family? Who the hell really knew? Faith was great, but it was not enough.

Faith and firepower and a team of the right caliber. Now you were talking.

THERE still remained the problem of the supergun.

Fitzduane had pored over intelligence information of every kind on the Devil's Footprint and amended his initial scenario to take in an assault on the weapon, but how to destroy it physically was another matter.

There was no shortage of ideas, but all foundered on the sheer size of the weapon and the time they would have to accomplish the task. Fitzduane was adamant they were not going to hang around. Once the alarm was raised, reinforcements from the Madoa air base could be there in twenty minutes or less, and there were two thousand troops who were likely to arrive with decidedly unfriendly intentions.

Acid down the barrel would work but would be dangerous to carry in sufficient quantity. Shaped charges could damage the breech but would take time to place correctly and would leave the bulk of the weapon unscathed. Using a plasma cutter would be possible but again would take far too long.

They considered seeding it with radioactivity until Lonsdale remarked that Quintana would still use the weapon and it would be just tough shit on the gun crew. Quintana was not renowned for concern about his workforce.

"What we really want to do is shake their confidence in the weapon itself," mused Maury during one bull session.

Fitzduane pricked up his ears. "Explain."

"We damage the weapon," said Maury, "the bad guys are going to think it is worth damaging—and therefore worth repairing. On the other hand, if we could do something to the installation so the weapon would not work when test-fired, then Quintana might be persuaded that he was on a loser, string up his scientists, and go back to something normal like buying a few more tanks or poisoning water supplies. There is a psychological-warfare element to counterterrorism, and we should be paying more attention to it."

Fitzduane looked at him. "Maury," he said, "you are not just a thing of beauty with a horribly devious mind. Contact Livermore and donate Jaeger your golden thought. I think you may have come up with something."

Maury looked pleased. "What?" he said.

"Let Livermore worry about the details," said Fitzduane. "That is what they are good at. You just give them the slant. I think it will appeal to Jaeger. He's got that kind of mind."

"A nice detail," said Maury. "I was checking on Livermore. The first nuke they produced in 1953 had only enough of a blast to mangle the top of the three-hundred-foot tower. The second did not do much better. Mind you, they have made up for it since then."

Fitzduane smiled. "Two failed test firings in a row would be just fine down in Tecuno. Go to it, Maury—now. We don't have much time."

FITZDUANE hit a computer key and leaned back in his chair.

The laser printer whirred quietly and a single sheet of paper emerged. The cycle was repeated until a thin sheaf lay stacked in the tray.

He stapled the sheets together and tossed the document to Kilmara.

"That's it," he said. "I've made the final selection of the team and most of the preparations are completed. War games in the National Training Center and then we go.

"Regarding the supergun, we still don't know what the fuck to do. Livermore tells me they've got a solution but they've still got a few things to do. Jaeger is going to catch up with us when we are tooling around in the Mojave Desert. He says it will save him commuting. It's a whole lot closer to Livermore."

Kilmara read carefully through the lists before looking up. "One Mexican name, I see?"

Fitzduane nodded. "Ernesto Robles of Delta, and as it happens, Mexican-born. A U.S. citizen these days. Good people. None better. As to how he feels, he lost friends in the bombing in Fayetteville. He'd like to close the account."

"By invading Mexico?" insisted Kilmara.

"He doesn't see it as invading Mexico," said Fitzduane. "This is a hostage-rescue mission which just happens to be taking place in Mexico. If we succeed, we'll be doing the Mexicans a service. I'd be happier still if we had some Mexican citizens along, but that is not politically possible. So stop shit-stirring!"

Kilmara laughed. "Just so you've thought things through," he said. He flicked through the report again. "You've assembled quite some firepower for a force only fifteen strong. Frankly, I've never seen anything like it. You can handle most anything from infantry to tanks on the ground, and now you've got good antiair defense. But you're duck soup if they corner you and bring in artillery. That's where the lack of heavy armor on the Guntracks will really show up."

Fitzduane shrugged. "We've been through enough war games at this stage to be aware of what we can do and what we can't do. This mission is based upon stealth and speed—and faith and firepower. Nothing is perfect. If we get cornered we'll need a little help from above to get us out." He smiled. "Which, I guess, brings us back to faith."

"Talk to me about the team," said Kilmara.

"Five Guntracks each with a crew of three," said Fitzduane. "Shadow One is the command Guntrack. That's myself, Steve Kent driving, and a rear gunner still to be decided. Probably Calvin Welbourne when he isn't flying.

"Shadow Two consists of Al Lonsdale, Dana Felton, and Don Shanley. Since that Fayetteville business, Al and Don have picked up where they left off to make an exceptionally smooth team, and Dana is airborne at its best. Al is the mission second in command. If I go down, he takes over."

"Al is not even a commissioned officer, let alone the most senior," said Kilmara. "Has that created any waves?"

Fitzduane shook his head. "You don't make command sergeant major in Delta by being a lightweight. Al knows what to do and when and how to do it—and it shows. The man has camouflaged blood in his veins."

"Shadow Three?" said Kilmara.

"Chifune, Chuck Freeman, and Grady," said Fitzduane. "All good shooters. Freeman is another Delta sergeant and a quiet, introspective type. He's vastly experienced and the sort of man who inspires confidence without having to say anything. Al suggested the combination. He knows Freeman of old and said if you had a couple of unorthodox types and wanted to put a team together, Freeman was the glue to use. Seems he was right."

Kilmara checked the list and looked up again. "I've got to ask," he said. "What have you done with Lee Cochrane? I have never seen a man so anxious to put himself in harm's way. I suspect he has the Stars and Stripes tattooed on his balls."

Fitzduane laughed. "Ouch!" he said, "Shane, you might retract that statement if someone showed you a mirror. After all, who is commanding the two C130s that are coming in to pick us up?"

"Hell, I wouldn't miss this if you paid me," said Kilmara.

"Lee is your 2 I/C," said Fitzduane. "You can't fly in two aircraft at once. You get shot down, he takes over. One thing I can be sure of is that Lee won't back off. If it is humanly possible, Lee Cochrane will come through—tattooed balls and all."

Kilmara beamed at him. "Hugo, you are a genius," he said, "and a diplomat."

"Only occasionally," said Fitzduane politely.

"Shadow Four?" said Kilmara.

THE venue for the latest Valiente Zarra presidential rally was a bullring.

It was not the biggest bullring in the world, but it officially held thirty thousand, and given the modest population of Gualara that seemed likely to be more than enough.

It was not.

People poured in from the surrounding countryside, and several hours before the rally was due to start, not only was the bullring full to overflowing but the immediate area around the ring was jammed and laughing, cheering crowds filled the nearby streets and squares.

There was but one topic—the imminent victory of Valiente Zarra—and despite his deep skepticism about effecting real change in the Mexican political system, Dan Warner was beginning to believe it.

The PRI were going to be overturned and Mexico was at last going to be able to realize its potential. The excitement in the air was electric. "Everywhere there was the two-syllable chant "ZAR-RA! ZAR-RA! ZAR-RA!"

THE broadcast was coming in live from Mexico.

Lee Cochrane had left the confines of the camp to watch the rally with Grant Lamar in his house.

Dan Warner was very much on Cochrane's mind. Dan liked his Washington comforts and wheeling and dealing politically in Bullfeathers, but he had accepted the Zarra assignment without any more than the normal quota of bitching, and when down in Mexico had done—was still doing—an outstanding job. With Zarra elected, there would be genuine dialog between Mexico and the United States. Protectionism would become a thing of the past. The two economies together would really go places.

Mexico would no longer be a haven for drug barons and terrorists. The country would begin to demonstrate its enormous economic potential and the United States would gain a genuinely strong ally. Such an alliance was sorely needed. China was suddenly becoming an economic and military force to be reckoned with, and Japan was showing increasing signs of being focused on its own regional objectives. As for Europe, that part of the world seemed tired and indecisive.

The camera panned around the bullring, showing endless excited brown faces and waving Zarrista banners.

There was a decided carnival atmosphere. There was going to be change, and it was going to be good change, and they were part of it. Unlike so many previous regimes throughout Mexico's bloody history, Valiente Zarra would not let them down. Here was a man who could drag Mexico from its feudal roots into the wealth and dynamism of the twenty-first century.

The Zarrista party was unstoppable. Within ten years, twenty years at the most, Mexico would enjoy the same wealth and prosperity as the United States. Countries in the Far East like Japan, Korea, Singapore, and Malaysia had done it on the back of the vast U.S. market. Why could not Mexico, so much closer, do it too? All it would take was shaking off the dead hand of the PRI and voting in a new progressive regime.

The camera zoomed in on the podium where Zarra and his immediate entourage would stand. The original plan had been for the podium to be in the bullring itself.

For security reasons, Dan Warner had been uneasy at Zarra being totally out in the open without a convenient exit, so, after his objections, the new podium had been located on the side of the arena where the band normally was located. The band were now playing from some seats normally occupied by spectators.

The slight change from their normal location had not dampened their ardor. Assisted by loudspeakers, music blasted out over the arena.

There was silence, then a single trumpet call followed by a huge shout from the crowd.

The bandstand, empty up to now, began to fill up with Zarra's inner group. Then came his immediate advisers, including Warner.

Six bodyguards followed, surrounding Zarra himself.

The party moved to the front of the bandstand and then the bodyguards moved to the sides, leaving Zarra, dressed in a white suit and shirt, in front of a bank of microphones in the center.

He was wearing a tie, but it had been loosened and his top shirt button was undone. Zarra was correctly dressed as befitted his status as a professor, but he was also informal and approachable—a man of the people.

Zarra raised his arms above his head in a salute to the crowd.

People rose to their feet as one and the air was filled with the rhythmic chants of "VIVA ZARRA! VIVA ZARRA!"

Zarra put his arms down and was about to speak. Suddenly he roared with laughter, and then, still shaking with mirth, pointed down at the bullring below.

The cameras followed the direction he was indicating.

Down below in the ring itself, seated on more comfortable chairs than the hard benches of the spectators, a group of officials and leading dignitaries from the town and the surrounding countryside had been assembled to hear Zarra from this privileged location. All were dressed in their best clothes, and officials wore sashes of office.

They were running in every direction, tripping over fallen chairs and diving headfirst over the wooden barriers at the ringside.

A clown's bull had been let loose in the ring. His horns were padded and he was festooned with streamers, but he was no joke to the people actually in his way. He could not kill or seriously wound, but he could butt and create chaos, and that he was certainly doing.

Zarra's laughter was joined by that of the crowd, and the camera picked up little vignettes of slapstick comedy as a landowner had his pants ripped off and only just made it to cover, while the bull turned and chased an unpopular mayor.

It was the best day of the campaign so far, in Dan Warner's opinion.

CHAPTER EIGHTEEN

"SHADOW FOUR," CONTINUED Fitzduane, "is a mainly British SAS team with Oga for seasoning, Bob 'Brick' Stephens and a guy called Hayden.

"In principle, I like to mix up the nationalities and make the unit rather than nationality the focus, but with the professionals on this mission, it really has not proved necessary. Also, Stephens and Hayden have worked together so long and so well, it would be a waste. They don't have to speak to each other. A gesture, a look, and they all seem to understand. They love the Guntrack. It's right in the SAS tradition. They say changing a clutch in a Guntrack compared to the Land-Rover is sheer pleasure. Minutes as opposed to hours."

"Do they know your father was a founding member of the SAS in North Africa?" said Kilmara.

"Sure," said Fitzduane with a smile, "and it doesn't hurt. On the other hand, trying to explain to the British why the Irish, while willing to fight with the British, prefer an independent country has been hard work."

"Which leaves Shadow Five," said Kilmara.

"One of our lads from the Rangers," said Fitzduane, "plus two Delta. Harty, Ernesto Robles, and Ross Gallini."

"Tell me more about Calvin Welbourne?" said Kilmara.

"Calvin flies," said Fitzduane, "in the kind of aircraft that you might expect to fall out of a Christmas cracker. It's a frightening little machine, but it works. They drag it around in a tube behind their Guntrack. I do not recommend it unless you are a masochist."

There was a pounding on the door. Fitzduane looked up at the security monitor. It was Lee Cochrane looking very agitated. He let him in.

Cochrane had been running. He was breathing more heavily than normal, but he was very fit. There was only a slight sweat.

"You alone?" he said to Fitzduane.

Fitzduane ushered him in. "Shane is here. No one else. You can speak." Cochrane sank into a chair. Fitzduane handed him a glass of water, which he drank greedily.

"It's not secret," he said. "The whole fucking world knows. They did it on television. You could see them killing him. They put a bull in the ring as a distraction, and when people were looking the other way, two of his bodyguards drew their guns and killed him. The camera came back on him as they were still firing.

"You could see the blood spewing out over that white suit. And then one of them blew off the side of his head to make sure. You could see his skull coming to pieces."

"Who was killed?" said Fitzduane, who already had a decided suspicion.

"Dan Warner and Zarra," said Cochrane. "Valiente Zarra."

He suddenly looked defeated and aged. "Dan tried to intervene. He was close and he made a grab for one of them. The Mexicans would not let him carry a piece. Dan got one of the killers' guns, but the other just stepped forward and let him have it in the back of the neck. They butchered him like some animal."

Cochrane put his head in his hands. "Oh, Jesus! We're up against some bad, bad people."

Kilmara took Fitzduane to one side. "Zarra was your reserve," he said. "If things had gone wrong in Tecuno, he could perhaps have helped you. Now you're on your own. The PRI will do nothing. Quintana has too much of a lock on them." There was a question in the statement.

"We go anyway," said Fitzduane. "But there'll be one change. We'll cut the National Training Center sessions in half and move the assault date up."

"Why?" said Kilmara.

"Quintana has killed Zarra. He'll be feeling cocky and invulnerable, and so will his people. I want to hit them while they still feel like that. Cocky makes you careless."

Kilmara shook his head. "People gravitate towards success," he said. "Quintana will now pick up support. He may even get the Mexican Army on his side. After this, he stands a good chance of making president if he wants to. Either way, he will be stronger."

"We're going to spend three days in the Mojave at the NTC," said Fitzduane, "and two days doing a final check. Then we'll go."

"You'll be on your own," said Kilmara. "You fuck up and there will be nobody to help. You'll be in the middle of nowhere in bad company. They'll cut your balls off and your skin off in strips. These are evil fucks."

"Faith and firepower are great equalizers," said Fitzduane, "and good people help, too. Believe me." He smiled grimly. "Besides, you may recall a promise. I'm getting Kathleen back. No matter what. *No matter what!*"

He walked across to Lee Cochrane. "Do you think it can be done, Lee?"

"I don't know," said Cochrane, his voice tired. "I don't know anything anymore. But we've got to try. Damn it, we've got to do something, or else they win. We can't just make speeches."

Fitzduane studied the chief of staff. "I would be honored, Lee, if you would come with us."

Cochrane looked up and his face was transformed from fatigue and sadness into a resolution that damn near glowed. "Are you sure, Hugo?"

Fitzduane smiled. "Positively," he said.

THERE was a difference in the sound of Rheiman's footsteps, thought Kathleen.

Something as simple as different shoes? She considered this carefully. No, this was more an eagerness as if he had news to impart. Good news? In his terms, probably yes. She would find out soon enough.

There was scant conversation with the guard today. This time Rheiman was in a hurry. Of course, he had missed a day. Now he wanted to make up for lost time. A by-product of the Rheiman visits was that she was now fed regularly if not well, and could monitor the passing of the days with reasonable accuracy.

She heard him sit down. He almost always sat before he spoke, curious behavior now that she thought of it. Given the friendly tone he adopted, it would have been more natural for him to call a greeting as he entered. But normally he did not.

He would enter the room, sit down, and then look at her for some while before he spoke.

As if he was contemplating a prized possession.

It was an unsettling thought.

Kathleen never spoke first. This was not a deliberate strategy but had developed naturally from her original silence. It had seemed appropriate then. It still seemed like the correct way to handle things. If someone wanted to speak to her, then they had to acknowledge her as a human being first.

In her soul, Kathleen was terrified. She lived every moment in fear so great she now regarded it as a living force. Something you could touch and feel like fire or water. Something so horrible and yet so familiar, she almost regarded it as a friend. *Fear I can trust. But nothing else.*

No one else?

Rheiman? Pleasant, warm, concerned.

Could Rheiman be trusted? Would Hugo trust him? Would Hugo Fitzduane trust him if he was chained and blindfolded and hungry and thirsty and desperate for human contact? Would he? Would he?

She could see Fitzduane as she thought. God, I love you, Hugo. *Our baby!* I wish. Oh, how I wish. Oh, how I yearn.

"Kathleen," said Rheiman in a pleased voice.

She had felt so close to Fitzduane, she could hear him. It could not just be imagination. There was a bond between them. It was not physical, but it was there nonetheless. Fitzduane was focused on her—*in her*—in some way. It was impossible, she knew—but the link was there. She wanted to cry. She could not, would not.

Tears welled unbidden and stained her cheeks.

"Good news!" said Rheiman. His voice was like an invasion. She could see nothing, feel nothing, and then there was this sound that cut through the silence like a jagged knife.

The voice of a man who sounded trustworthy—but whom she did not trust. The voice of a man who by his own admission had murdered.

"But, Kathleen, you're crying," he said, his voice suddenly concerned. "You missed me. I'm so sorry. I try and get away every day, but sometimes it is not possible. There is so much to do and we're near the first test firing. Everyone has one question: Will it work?"

"I missed you, Edgar," she said, and it was true. Good or bad, trustworthy or not, Rheiman was company. He brought news. He was her only link to the outside world.

Rheiman took her hand without speaking. He almost never touched her except for the occasional fleeting caress. This time he took her hand as a lover might, the back of his hand resting against her breast.

He moved his hand very slightly, as if accidentally, stroking her nipple through the material of the rough shirt she had been given. She could sense his mounting excitement, but then he pulled away and sat back in his seat.

She was playing a dangerous game, she knew, but there was not an alternative. Rheiman was all she had right now. Rheiman was what she had to use. If it took sex, she would use sex, whatever was required, however bizarre. If it took violence, she would use that too.

Without hesitation! Fitzduane had taught her. Violence should be a last resort, but where it was required *it must be fast and deadly and delivered with total commitment. Never hesitate. Never pull back. Do it to them before they do it to you. Or you will die.*

She shuddered.

Despair swept over her, and then as suddenly as it had hit it was quelled.

I will live. Our baby will live. Hugo will come. It seems impossible, *but he will come.*

Rheiman had been silent. The watcher playing with her. He reminded her of a cat. She was the mouse, chained and blindfolded.

It couldn't be much fun for the cat. A real mouse could still move, could try and make a break for freedom. It was hopeless, but it kept the game alive. Restricted as she was, she could do nothing. He could not even see her properly. Her eyes were still taped over.

It was as if Rheiman had been reading her mind. "Kathleen," he said. "I said I have good news. I have been negotiating with Oshima. She has agreed that your blindfold may be removed subject to certain conditions. There is something she wants you to see. And some things she does not want you to see."

Kathleen smiled faintly. "I'm not sure I understand, Edgar. What does she want me to see?"

"An execution," said Rheiman.

CHAPTER NINETEEN

IT WAS AN aspect of the operation that had given Fitzduane more concern than almost any other.

The Japanese Koancho agent was still inside the Devil's Footprint. When the assault team went they were going to be racking up the bodies. It would be dark and they would be programmed to kill without hesitation. The agent was going to be chopped liver unless he could be contacted in advance, kept out of the firing line in some way, and then pulled out with the team. A dangerous complication for an already hazardous mission.

But the man deserved a special effort. Hori-*san*'s courage and initiative were extraordinary. He had put together an intelligence operation of daring and at direct risk to his own life. Reiko Oshima was inarguably the most dangerous terrorist currently at large, and for every second of every day Hori was under her control. This was a man of special courage.

Further, he was Chifune's colleague and Fitzduane was in Chifune's debt. Hori's fate could not be left to chance.

The problem lay in balancing risks. The linchpin of the success of the mission was surprise. Sending someone into the terrorist compound in advance risked premature discovery. One slip and the operation was blown. To save Hori, was it worth it?

The situation with Kathleen was different. Her location was known and there would be no difficulty in identifying her. Hori, even though his picture had been handed out, in the split seconds available was going to appear just like another terrorist, especially if he was asleep with his face in the pillow or wearing the black balaclavas many wore at night when on guard duty both for camouflage and against the chill of the desert air.

Chifune had sworn she could get in without being discovered. A rough mock-up of the terrorist camp had been set up in an obscure corner of the National

Training Center, and six times in a row, despite the sentries' being alerted that she was coming, and despite the fact that they were outfitted with both night-vision equipment and thermal detectors, she had managed it.

But Fitzduane was still uneasy. The compromise was that she would go in only ten minutes in advance. That way, if something did go wrong, they could still go in hard and heavy and achieve their objectives.

But he did not like it. Total surprise was his objective. Anything less could compromise the mission.

The right thing would be to let Hori, brave man though he was, take his chances.

The "right thing" or "the most effective"? Who was to know? Fitzduane had thought of involving the entire unit in this particular dilemma, but had then decided otherwise. There were some issues that had to be an individual burden. You made a decision and you took the consequences.

At that stage choice did not enter into it. Nor did right or wrong.

Occasionally, Fitzduane wondered if morality or ethics or values or whatever you wanted to call such thoughts ever counted, or if they were some unreal set of notions fostered by academics who were not at the bleeding edge.

It did not help him much. He believed in Camelot.

THE air base was south of Laredo, Texas.

Fitzduane did not ask the name of the base or even inquire exactly where he was. It did not seem the protocol, it was not important, and he had other things on his mind.

Dusk was approaching. The two unmarked C130s were loaded, and now it was a matter of checking and checking and checking again. The checking was mostly pointless, but it passed the time. It was when you had nothing to do that fear started to play with your soul.

"The SAS have an expression," said Fitzduane. " 'The Seven Fucking Ps!' "

"What are they?" said Kilmara.

"Proper Planning and Preparation Prevents Piss-Poor Performance," said Fitzduane.

"That sounds more like the Fitzduane family motto," said Kilmara. He smiled. "Or maybe that is: 'Let not life be dull!' "

Fitzduane laughed. "Sometimes I'd settle for dull," he said.

General Kilmara contemplated his friend. "How is Cochrane shaping up?"

Fitzduane was thoughtful. "I can't fully read him," he said. "At first, he was trying too hard. The Eternal Soldier in the making and having a hard time taking orders. After Zarra and Dan Warner got killed and I invited him along, he changed. Now he's a team player and he has become very good indeed. God help the enemy."

"I doubt he will," said Kilmara. He took his time continuing, and when he did he was smiling. "You don't deserve it, but I think he's going to help you."

Fitzduane was about to make a cutting riposte, but there was a certain air of anticipation emanating from Kilmara. "Which particular angel has he designated for the task?" he growled.

"I told a mutual friend," said Kilmara, "that you were a little strained, a little stressed, about to do something decidedly dangerous, but I thought you could succeed with help. The friend, as unlikely an angel as I ever have seen—he is rather bulky and has a mustache and a Bernese accent you could cut with a knife—volunteered. He's commanding the second C130 instead of Cochrane. It seemed to make some sense to have someone up there watching over you. Better yet, more than one. God, as they say in Bragg, is 'Airborne.' "

"The Bear," breathed Fitzduane. He'd met the portly Swiss detective some years past in the original hunt for the terrorist known as the Hangman. Subsequently, the Bear had helped rescue Kathleen from a revenge mission carried out by terrorists led by Reiko Oshima. The Bear and Fitzduane went way back.

"The very man," said Kilmara. "I know you were reluctant to ask him on account of his domestic state in Bern, but you have to remember he is on Oshima's shit list too. He was there when you took down the Hangman and does not fancy remaining a target for a revenge mission. He'd like to get his paw in first. Also, he's a friend."

Fitzduane turned his head away. Maybe he rubbed his eyes and maybe that was just because of the dust. This part of Texas was decidedly dusty.

He checked his watch and headed for the briefing hut.

Shadow Team were gathered inside in a semicircle. Including him, the ground element was now sixteen strong.

"Final briefing," he said.

KILMARA watched Fitzduane's unit file into the briefing hut.

They seemed about as concerned as if they were going into a cafeteria for a meal but were not particularly hungry. This was a routine exercise, nothing more. Except that it was not. This was the real thing, and it was about to happen.

Unless they were exceptionally lucky, not all would make it back. There would probably be some dead. There would certainly be wounded.

The events of the next days would change lives forever. That was certain.

They would kill fellow human beings. That was certain too.

Kilmara tried to work out in his mind the impression that Fitzduane's people conveyed. They certainly were not an average team. They were older and more experienced than most, even in the context of the inner circles of the special-forces elites. They also mixed and matched the nationalities and sexes without any evidence of strain.

Either you could do the job or you couldn't. It was that simple. That apart, no one seemed to give a damn if you were man, woman, or zebra. It was all about performance. "Doing the job" did not mean getting a passing mark. It meant operating at a level of proficiency that was rare indeed in normal life.

The one weak link could be Lee Cochrane. God knows his military skills had improved over the past few days, but he was still an amateur among professionals. For an amateur he was excellent, and no one could doubt his commitment, but enthusiasm, in Kilmara's judgment, was not enough. You could train all you liked under live fire, but there was nothing like the moment when you faced the reality of "kill or be killed." Then enthusiasm did not come into it.

It was down to basics like mind-set and skills. Using night-vision equipment but otherwise in darkness, Chifune could draw, aim, and shoot a grapefruit-size target twenty meters away in less than one third of a second. She was exceptional, but others were still close to that league.

Cochrane did not come into it. At heart he was a congressional staffer—and a very good one—but he was no longer a soldier. Vietnam had been decades back. In Kilmara's opinion, he was a worry. Worse yet, he was a mistake. Kilmara knew why Fitzduane had made that particular decision but regarded it as a case of heart over head.

But sometimes Fitzduane was like that. He was the best combat leader Kilmara had ever seen, but his one weakness was that he had too much heart. Combat was about killing the enemy. A generous nature was a debatable asset on the battlefield.

"Listen up," said Fitzduane. "The operation is a go."

There was silence in the briefing room. Every unit member had been through the plan countless times, but still paid as much attention as if this was the first time.

"Operation Rapier," he said. "Three objectives. One: to release a hostage, Kathleen Fitzduane, an Irish citizen kidnapped in the United States of America. Two: to inflict maximum damage on the terrorist base known as the Devil's Foot-print, and specifically to wipe out the terrorist group known as Yaibo together with their leader Reiko Oshima. Three: to destroy the offensive capability they have been working on—the supergun.

"The assault team numbers sixteen divided into five Guntracks, with Calvin up on high—as needed—in the microlight. We are flying to the target in two special-operations-modified C130 Combat Talons. These will fly south initially over the Gulf of Mexico at four hundred feet—effectively below radar height—and then will make a dogleg at Waypoint Two and enter Mexican airspace from the sea at Waypoint Three over Tecuno. They will drop us northwest of the target. The aircraft will be contour flying at this stage and will be using RAVEN radar-suppression equipment, so we should arrive unseen at 1430 hours on Night One.

"The Guntracks will go out first using LAPES, and then the aircraft will pop up and drop us out from two-fifty feet.

"We hit the ground, we immediately mount up, form a combat wedge and head for this position about a klik away"—he tapped the map—"where there is cover we can blend into and where we will render ourselves as invisible as only we can and wait for daylight. So ends Night One.

"Daylight comes, we still wait. On this mission, as we have rehearsed again and again, the approach will be to travel and attack at night. We have thermal imagers. We have image enhancement. The night is our friend.

"During daylight, *we want to be invisible*. During daylight, *we will be invisible*. If we are going to be spotted, it is most likely to be by aircraft seeing our dust trail. By hiding up during the day under full camouflage with thermal blankets and not moving, the chances of our being spotted are minimal.

"Normally, military choppers in this part of the world fly at five thousand feet to avoid small-arms fire—at which height they will see fuck-all. The Guntrack is not a large lump of metal radiating heat like a tank. It is only about six feet wide and thirteen feet long—if you ignore the pallet at the back, which adds only a couple of feet—so the whole damn thing is small and low-slung and extremely easy to conceal, and thanks to its plastic body and engine baffling and thermal camouflage it is a rotten thermal target. Nonetheless, don't get cocky. *Be invisible!*

"Night Two, one hour after last light, one vehicle will leave to do a recce. Upon its return, using our night-vision equipment, the unit will advance one hundred and twenty kliks towards the target, averaging about twenty kliks per hour. The formation will be diamond with the command vehicle, Shadow One, in the center. Point will stay half a klik ahead. We will pause every half hour for five minutes for a listening watch.

"Make sure everything is padded, particularly the weapons mounts. Sound travels for miles at night, so travel slow and quiet.

"As before, we will lie up during the day. Night Three, again an hour after last light, a recce Guntrack will move out, and subsequently we will again advance. This time the objective will be to achieve a hundred and ten kliks.

"We will laager up several hours before Night Three at Strike Base, within forty kliks of the target, so great care will need to be taken. We will still be outside the defensive loop which surrounds the air base and the Devil's Footprint, but we will be close enough to need to be extremely cautious. As best we know, no ground patrols come that far out, but you never can be sure. We do know that helicopters do security checks over this area. So I want the unit to just osmose into the ground.

"We will arrive at Strike Base in time for a three-person recce team to be able to move on to take a long, hard look at the target. Remember, they will have forty miles cross country to cover, so they will use silenced motorbikes for thirty-five kliks or so and then foot the rest. The objective here is that recce team be in a hide overlooking the camp before dawn.

"Recce team will stay in position for twenty-four hours right through the day and into Night Four. During that time, all strongpoints and routines will be logged together with any other items of interest so that we have a complete idea of the target's routine before we attack. Sure, we have satellite photos and much other intel, but the Mark One eyeball still takes some beating. So, twenty-four hours of surveillance before we move.

"One of the recon team will stay on watch while the others return to Strike Base to brief us. The stayback will continue to log activities but won't make contact unless there is a significant change.

"We will strike during Night Five. The exact time will depend on their routine, but the provisional timing is set for 0100 hours. That is a time when all good terrorists are tucked up in bed and when even the most conscientious sentries are nodding off. We will be in position several hours in advance. I want everyone to have a chance to examine the objective in detail before the assault.

"The objective, the Devil's Footprint, as you can see on the map and have studied every which way, consists of two small dead-end valleys—box canyons— separated by a promontory. Facing the two valley entrances, from the other side of the perimeter road, you can see that the valley on the left—Salvador—contains the main camp and the valley on the right—Dali—the supergun and supporting equipment.

"Both valleys are dominated by a fortified blockhouse built on the promontory. From up there, you command all you survey. You can fire down into either valley. You can protect the rear. You dominate the road. You dominate the low hills on the far side. *That blockhouse is pivotal.* It is the high ground, literally and figuratively.

"One Guntrack is one fire team. We have five fire teams at our disposal. The plan of attack is that one team will neutralize the supergun while two teams take out the terrorists in Salvador and rescue Kathleen. The two remaining teams will, respectively, neutralize the blockhouse and cover the perimeter road at the front. And that's it. We're traveling light on this mission. There is no reserve.

"The intention is that the assault be over within twenty minutes of the initial contact. We are not there to slug it out toe-to-toe with the local militia. We go in. We do what is necessary and then we get the hell out.

"To concentrate your minds, keep remembering 'shoot and scoot.' 'Stay and pray' will get you killed. If that is not enough for you, try mathematics. There are nearly seven hundred bad guys in the Devil's Footprint and two thousand–plus more just up the road at the airfield. So do not do a Custer, people. Hit them as hard as you can and then you're outa there. You're invisible again. You're gone!

"We came in from the northwest. We're getting out southwest. All units will then meet up at the RV and then will zigzag towards the pickup point.

"At this stage, all hell will be breaking loose and the element of surprise will be gone, so the important thing will be to cover ground fast.

"The pickup point looks like another piece of desert these days, but our research through the oil records says it is hard enough to take C130s and was used as an airstrip during their exploration—but so were many other locations as they moved around, so this should not stand out. Better yet, we are planting remote-controlled radio as we go in. As we leave, they will go on air and give the impression we are heading north. And, as you know, we've a few other tricks.

"One final point: Over the past few years, the people we are going in to attack have wreaked unparalleled havoc—mainly on innocent civilians. Hundreds have been killed. Thousands have been directly affected. The quota of misery and suffering that these people have caused is incalculable. Left alone, what has happened to date will seem as nothing. You do not build a supergun with intercontinental capability unless you are serious.

"Our fundamental objective is not to warn these people or inflict a sharp rap on the knuckles or put them on probation. We're way past that stage. So our objective, reduced to elementals, is very simple.

"It is to destroy them. It is to kill as many of them as we can. The lesson must be: Terrorism is not conducive to longevity. Terrorism gets you killed. So when your finger is on the trigger, do not hesitate to fire. It is a hard paradox, but taking these people out will save lives. And that is what the counterterrorist business is all about."

Fitzduane, a faint smile on his face, looked at the group. "Well, folks, there is the mission plan. Clean, hard, and simple. Comments?"

A member of the SAS contingent, Shadow Four, raised his considerable eyebrows. Bob "Brick" Stephens, a short squarish weather-beaten sergeant in his late thirties, spoke. This was an event because Bob spoke seldom. His specialty was demolitions. Bob truly loved to blow things up.

"Fly a thousand miles, spend five days in hostile territory in plastic dodgems up against heavy armor, attack two positions defended by nearly seven hundred men with another couple of thousand just up the road, kill an inner core of fifty

Yaibo terrorists, rescue a damsel, destroy a weapon that is too big to be destroyed, and get out with half an army on air tail. Hell, Colonel, it looks like a cakewalk. Isn't there anything else you want us to do?"

"Get back in one piece, Brick," said Fitzduane politely, "if you would be so kind."

The Brick looked thoughtful and then he grinned. He had spent six months with the Australian SAS two years earlier. "No worries, boss," he said.

Fitzduane did not doubt him.

"Now to details," he said. "I know you people love details. I know you love checking on them even more." He smiled. "Again and again and again."

Outside the sun was setting. Soon it would be time. Meanwhile, there was work to do. There was always work to do when Fitzduane was around. The man knew how to push, and he never seemed to let up.

✳ CHAPTER TWENTY

KILMARA HAD ARRANGED for the Bear to act as jumpmaster on Fitzduane's C130 on the inward flight.

It was a good move. There was something vastly reassuring about the Bear's presence and about exchanging tall tales as they flew. It helped to counteract the long buffeting ride in the Combat Talon and the smell of puke in the aircraft and the suppressed terror as they hooked up and prepared to jump into the darkness.

To step from safety into space was an unnatural act, and even through Fitzduane had done it before and his brain told him it could be done, his very being cried that *two hundred and fifty feet was too low! The parachute would not open in time. Could not open in time. The pilot would misjudge the height. Something would go wrong.*

The incredible relief as the canopies blossomed—each and every one. And then the silence as the sound of the aircraft receded and they lay there, weapons loaded and ready, getting used to this new environment and listening for any sign that the DZ that was supposed to be safe and empty was occupied and dangerous and they were about to die.

As they flew in, the DZ had been scanned by sensors that could detect a snake changing its sleeping position, but still he worried. There were things you knew and there were fears that impinged regardless of the logic.

But the sensors had been right. There was nothing. Just backbreaking work as the vehicles were unpacked from their drop pallets and loaded and readied. And then more work as the pallets and 'chutes were buried. That was the toughest part, and really only possible because each Guntrack came equipped with a miniature bulldozer blade in front of it. The primary role of the blade was to enable the vehicle to dig itself in, but in this case it was used to conceal the evidence of the incursion. No ground patrol would pass by, but from the air one glimpse of a 'chute would be enough to raise the alarm. The burial process was thorough.

A final meticulous check of the DZ. Nothing could be seen.

The column moved off.

When dawn came up, it was as if Task Force Rapier had vanished into the rocky shale and packed, reddish clay of the plateau.

Nothing could be seen.

Underneath the camouflage nets, a quarter of the team manned sensor units and other passive detective equipment, while the balance ate and slept and cleaned weapons.

The heat steadily increased until by midday the whole plateau seemed in shimmering motion.

In the shade, leaning back against the side of a Guntrack, Al Lonsdale once again gave thanks to the designer of the Guntrack for building copious water tanks into each vehicle. He had been trained to survive on a couple of canteens, but dehydration got to you in the end no matter how good your endurance. Here each track carried enough water to last a couple of weeks. This was special-forces soldiering in comfort. The tanks were even muffled and baffled inside to eliminate the sound of water sloshing as they moved.

A helicopter patrol passed by in the distance, tracked by a Starburst missile team and one of the SAS on a GECAL—just in case. The pilot was flying nice and straight and was about 3,000 feet up. He was obviously an unworried man. He was also a lucky one.

"What a hellhole," said Lonsdale, wiping his face with a towel and then draping it loosely around his neck. "No people, no water, no greenery. Just sun like a flame out of hell, and snakes and scorpions and terrorists. No wonder they call it the Devil's Footprint. He must have thought he was home."

Fitzduane yawned. "You're forgetting oil," he said sleepily. "Tecuno has not got much else, but it has got oil."

"Oil and the devil seem to run together," said Lonsdale lazily. "That's my insight for the day."

Fitzduane did not reply. He was asleep.

MADOA AIR BASE, TECUNO, MEXICO

GENERAL LUIS BARRAGAN'S naked body was not responding to Reiko Oshima's ministrations.

Her tongue explored his groin and plowed little damp trails through his plentiful and already sodden pubic hair, but to no avail. The supergun might be ready to test-fire in a few days, but Barragan's personal weapon was down for maintenance.

Privately, he was of the opinion that he had more than done his duty. He had taken her twice over the last three hours and had brought her to orgasm in other ways. That really ought to be enough for any woman, but Oshima did few things in moderation.

He wondered about her upbringing. What had caused a middle-class Japanese brat like Oshima to reject her upbringing and turn to a philosophy that was little more than destruction turned into a religion? Upon reflection, he decided he did not really care. It was too hot and she was phenomenal in bed and she served her purpose. The fact that her schoolteacher had exposed himself to her when she was seven—or whatever had set her off—was of little consequence. Probably, it was as simple as a severe case of repression. All that Japanese social obligation and enforced group behavior was enough to drive anyone nuts. Though was Oshima insane? Not in a legal sense, he thought. She was rational in her way and certainly was aware of the difference between right and wrong. So it could be argued that she was not insane. But she was certainly warped. Seriously sick was another way of putting it. And obsessive.

Whatever Reiko did, she did obsessively.

An evil woman? By conventional bourgeois standards, without question. But a great lay. And in this kind of heat, what else was a man to do in the middle of the day? Apart from rest.

He did not like admitting it even to himself, but right now rest was decidedly the preferred option.

Distraction was required or Oshima was going to wear away parts of his body he was rather attached to. She had a tongue like velvet sandpaper, a penchant for marathons—and the stamina to go with it. But fortunately she had a strong sense of duty, which she exercised to excess like everything else. And General Luis Barragan was, at least nominally, her superior.

Mention work and she hopped to it. Of course, she had her own long-term agenda, but right now she had done what she had been hired to do extremely well. Security at the Devil's Footprint was as tight as one could wish. The only slipup had been Patricio Nicanor, and frankly that had been Barragan's error in the first place in hiring a Zarrista. Well, who would have expected such idiocy in his own family!

But Oshima had redeemed the Nicanor situation before any damage was done. An incredible operator. Hard to control, but worth the effort.

Oshima's relationship with Edgar Rheiman remained a worry. Both, ideally, were needed if the project was to be brought to completion, but the reality was that whereas Oshima's security talents were incredibly useful, Rheiman's scientific skills were essential.

Without Rheiman, the whole Devil's Footprint project would not have been possible, and without a weapon such as the supergun, breaking Tecuno away from Mexico would have been much more hazardous. The supergun meant they could thumb their noses at Mexico City. Tecuno would become an independent country, and from then on the possibilities were endless.

Oil profits, drug profits, money laundering, forgery, arms trading, the fast-growing area of electronic piracy, the counterfeiting of branded goods. There were so many opportunities to exploit if you ran your own country. Because who was to touch you when you were the law?

God knows the Mexican elite had proved that very point over the years. It had not done much for the population as a whole, of course, but no intelligent man really gave a fuck about the masses. There would always be a very few who ruled and prospered—and General Luis Barragan intended to stay one of them—and the rest were a resource to be used.

Idealism: nice if you were a middle-class adolescent.

The practicalities: what most people concerned themselves with.

Barragan considered himself a practical man. He was not an opportunistic strategist like his brother-in-law Diego Quintana, or a fanatic like Oshima, or a major talent with rather bad habits when it came to women like Edgar Rheiman. He was a hands-on, take-charge kind of guy who got things done. The world was run by practical men like him.

Which brought the subject back to Rheiman. Oshima had moved from tonguing him to small nips with her lips. Now the scientist was someone guaranteed to distract her. Just as well, because when she started to bite down there the omens were worrying. This was a woman who would not necessarily stop.

"Oshima-*san*," said Barragan. "There are some matters we must discuss. With regret, but time is short and there are issues to review."

Oshima lifted her head. She looked, he thought, like some animal disturbed momentarily from eating its prey. A plastic surgeon could have minimized her scars. As it was, she wore them like a badge of pride, her long black hair tied back to reveal every detail.

She was a frightening and erotic sight. Her lips were full, the skin of her face and body shiny with sweat and bodily juices. Her teeth white and sharp. Shadows reminded him of blood. Fortunately, it was an illusion. If there had been blood, it would be his. That was not a prospect he liked to contemplate.

There was a momentary hesitation, and then she rose from her end of the bed and sat cross-legged, facing him.

She was completely naked and appeared entirely unselfconscious as she sat there, her sex revealed—indeed displayed—by her posture. Her breasts were firm, the nipples prominent. She was in superb physical condition for her age. She was old enough, he realized, to be a grandmother. Hard to imagine. Had Oshima ever had children? He thought not. But then again, Oshima's past was something of a mystery and not something she talked about.

"Rheiman worries me, Reiko," he said, his manner now less formal as he saw he had her attention. "More to the point, your attitude towards him concerns me. We've less than a week to go and there is much at stake, and there you are, Reiko, still playing games with him. Or are you?"

Oshima's eyes were on him as she replied. He had rarely encountered a woman with more beautiful eyes, and Luis Barragan prided himself on knowing many women.

"Rheiman is a sick man," she said. "He killed in America and he has killed again since he came here. Six women have died in this camp alone."

"Prostitutes brought in for the men," said Barragan. "Of no consequence. They could not be returned anyway."

"At your request, I gave him—lent him—the Irishwoman," said Oshima demurely, casting her eyes downward. "What more could I do, my general?"

Barragan eyed her suspiciously. When Oshima was submissive, she was up to something. She could never let a situation alone. Always there was a subtext, a maneuver, a scheme.

"You can let him play with the damned woman for as long as it lasts," growled Barragan. "I want him content for as long as his services are required, without interference from you."

"And if she dies?" said Oshima softly. "After all, she is mine, my general, and she has a purpose to serve."

To be played with and broken and finally to be dismembered solely as an act of vengeance against this man Fitzduane. Barragan shuddered inwardly. He found it hard to imagine the level of hate this woman felt toward her enemies. Barragan had his opponents killed as any sane man in his position would do, but he did not dwell on the process. Such things were necessary, no more.

And this Irishman. What would he do? By all accounts he was resourceful, yet in truth what *could* he do? He would have no idea where his wife had been taken. The Devil's Footprint was about as remote a spot as could be imagined and was virtually a sealed environment. So how could the man find out? But if by some miracle he did manage to locate his wife and throw together some operation, he had no chance of penetrating the defenses. Using two state-of-the-art stealth helicopters, the American Drug Enforcement Administration had tried and had failed a year earlier, and Tecuno's antihelicopter precautions had been increased since then. So Oshima's opportunistic move at picking up her enemy's wife was a distraction from the main event but posed no real threat. Though perhaps it was an indication that Reiko needed to be kept under tighter control.

"If Rheiman strangles her as he has strangled the others, it will be unfortunate," said Barragan, "but there are priorities. Personally, I don't think he will for some little time. This is not some *puta*. This is a real Caucasian woman he can talk to, boast to, fuck if he wants to. The woman is helpless. She is a marvelous plaything, and not easy to replace in this part of the world. No, he won't kill her yet. So don't interfere, Reiko, or I may forget what you can do for me."

Oshima said nothing. There was the briefest flash of anger and then she bowed her head submissively. She held the position and then her head bent lower.

Seconds later, Barragan was surprised to find that his most favored appendage seemed to have recovered. He lay back to enjoy and think.

Rheiman was happy and was delivering the goods. Oshima had been pulled back from stirring up the Americans before any serious damage had been caused. Valiente Zarra had been taken out with some finesse. The PRI would get back into power as normal, and Diego Quintana could handle them and President Marinas with both hands tied behind his back.

Most important of all, the base was secure. The plateau defenses could not be breached without his knowing, and his combined forces in and around the Devil's Footprint could handle anything. Not that the Americans would ever mount such a mission. If the media was right, all President Georgie Falls's firmness of resolve went into his prick and he had no more for anything else. Clearly, his *cojones* were not up to the job.

Barragan groaned with pleasure as Oshima brought him to a peak of ecstasy. Visibly, the General's *cojones* were in better shape.

Oshima raised her head but kept it bowed. Then she reached behind and released her hair. In the shaded room, it was now nearly impossible to read her expression.

The precaution was scarcely necessary. Since she was out of arm's reach, Barragan gave her a slight squeeze with his legs in acknowledgment and fell asleep.

The flaw in Barragan's plans is very simple, reflected Oshima. He and Quintana are motivated by money and see the supergun merely as a deterrent. Leave us alone and we'll leave you alone. All we want is one small country called Tecuno.

But the flaw was that Reiko Oshima had altogether different plans and her group, Yaibo, controlled the inner security perimeter, including that of the supergun itself. An independent Tecuno was neither here nor there compared to the opportunity to inflict serious damage on the United States of America.

Such a blow would expiate some of the rage that threatened, at times, to engulf her, and the knowledge that it had been carried out by her would establish her once again as a terrorist force to be reckoned with.

She could return to Japan and followers would flow to her. The system was rotten, and ripe for the plucking.

The first projectile to be fired from the supergun was supposed to be a test. It would not be. Instead it would be a small missile of Russian origin—not hard to purchase—targeted right at that part of Washington known colloquially as the Hill.

The warhead was not nuclear. It did not need to be. It was still capable of inflicting casualties on a scale commensurate with Hiroshima.

Japanese politicians, dominated by America for half a century, would make shocked noises and go through all the right motions. But the people of Japan would support her.

They had not forgotten. They would never forget.

Reiko Oshima would never let them forget.

She uncoiled herself. General Luis Barragan snored on. He was, in his way, she reflected, not a bad man. But he paled compared to the only man she had ever really loved, the terrorist known as the Hangman. But her lover was dead, and since that time she had resolved that no one would ever get close to her. Soon Barragan would die too.

In this business it is your friends who betray you, she had been taught and she had not forgotten. The inner circle of Yaibo was regularly purged. It was a technique that worked. The terrorist leaders and dictators that survived practiced it. And Stalin, who had purged more than most, had died in his bed.

It was something of a paradox, but to survive in the world she had chosen, *you had to kill your friends.*

It was best that a death served a purpose. Barragan was right. Rheiman would have to be kept sweet for the moment—which meant Fitzduane's woman could not be touched physically. But the effect of the execution on her would be amusing. This was something she would not be used to. This would shake her up and maybe drive her into Rheiman's arms. Which would be a small revenge in its way.

The person to be executed? That was no problem. Who had served her best and most faithfully? Who had succored her after she had dragged herself from Tokyo Bay?

Hori would die. He was the man who least deserved to. It was appropriate. History had shown he was the most likely person to have betrayed her. Who else had become close?

Jin Endo had occupied her bed much recently, and her thoughts more than a little. He was young and he was devoted to her. He was a point of vulnerability. He had done well in the United States. He had served his purpose. There were always others.

Endo-*san* would die too. But perhaps not yet.

No, for the moment, Hori would die alone.

APPROACHING THE DEVIL'S FOOTPRINT, TECUNO, MEXICO

"HERE comes SkyEye," said Chuck Freeman, one of the Delta contingent, his eyes glued to image-intensifying binoculars. "Just watch that sucker land. I swear Calvin flew before he crawled."

Fitzduane smiled and raised his own night-vision binoculars in the direction that Chuck was indicating. He was just in time to see Calvin make one of his famed landings.

The aviator took full advantage of the airfoil qualities of the dihedral wing and the very low stall speed of the microlight, and did not so much land as drop the tiny aircraft gently onto the ground at the last minute after a gentle glide with all the power switched off.

With forward momentum virtually canceled by air resistance when still airborne, the microlight rolled for only a few yards before coming to a halt.

Fitzduane had been worried about the feasibility of finding suitable landing and takeoff surfaces in the rough terrain, but he need not have. Calvin could take off and land almost anywhere.

The decision to bring the microlight had turned out to be a fortunate one. Their maps and satellite photographs were inadequate for the finer details of the terrain, and on several occasions so far aerial reconnaissance had enabled them to steer around obstacles.

Guntracks could handle most surfaces, but gullies, ravines, and wadis could pose problems. Of course, even near-vertical surfaces could be handled with the right winch technique—and every vehicle mounted a built-in winch with a forty-nine-meter cable—but winching vehicles up and down was notoriously time-consuming, and surplus time was a commodity that Team Rapier did not possess.

Fitzduane and Freeman helped Calvin pack up the microlight and slide it into its travel tube.

"The recce team is on the way back, Colonel," said Calvin. "They should be here in about twenty minutes."

He was wearing black flame-resistant Nomex overalls, black body armor, and a black helmet, so he might have looked a little like Batman except for the black goose-down parka he wore over the top.

It was cold in the desert plateau at night, and even colder when you were flying in an open cockpit, so Calvin—whose unclothed build was slight—when fully bundled and padded out, looked more like the exceptionally rotund Penguin. Add in the night-vision goggles and he looked even more horrific.

Fitzduane thought he was probably scaring hell out of the local vultures. There did not seem to be any more friendly bird life in the area. Vultures set the tone.

Since Calvin had come recommended by people he trusted, and the mission had been put together in a hurry, Fitzduane had not looked at his file at first. Special forces were NCO heavy and everyone seemed to call Calvin by his first name, so he had assumed the man was a sergeant. Though he looked far too young, it turned out Calvin was a major. It was not important. What counted was not your rank but how you did your job, and in that context the aviator was a formidable asset.

Minutes later, the recce team were detected over a kilometer away by the mast-mounted FLIR on Fitzduane's Guntrack.

Weapons were trained on them until they were identified. Soon they entered the perimeter of the concealed camp. It was good navigation in this rocky waste-land, but although they were using traditional methods—it did not come easy to put all your faith in technology—they were also equipped with GPS, or global positioning sets, which determined one's position by picking up prepositioned navigation-satellite signals.

Fitzduane gave the recce team a few minutes to eat and drink and then called a briefing. He used the flattopped rear engine compartment of his Guntrack as a map board.

The layout of the camp was now augmented by the observations of the recce team over twenty-four hours. The team reported in detail. All the electronic intelligence in the world could not substitute for hands-on human intelligence. These people had felt the texture of the enemy position. They had been close enough to reach out and nearly touch the very people they had come to kill. But first they had looked and learned.

The assault plan remained intact. There were changes of detail to be accommodated, but that was normal. Fitzduane summarized.

"As we all better know by now—or we are in deep shit—the target, the Devil's Footprint, consists of two box canyons divided by a spur of land. Salvador, the valley on the left as you face in, contains the people. Dali, the valley on the right, contains the supergun and support buildings. Because the supergun is going to be so fucking noisy when it fires, Dali is empty at night except for the guards, and there are not many of them because the emphasis is on perimeter security.

"We're going to be in position by 2200 hours. At 0100 hours, having had three hours to eyeball the target and fine-tune our understanding of the opposition, we're going to attack.

"The assaults will be silent and simultaneous. Shadow Four will infiltrate Dali and do what has to be done on the supergun. Shadow Two will take out the blockhouse on the central spur. Shadow Three and Shadow Five will enter Salvador, hit the Yaibo barracks, extract Kathleen, and kill all Yaibo members, including—if we are so lucky—Reiko Oshima. Shadow One, my track, will run interference from the other side of the perimeter road and will coordinate. Calvin will fly topside and advise us of any approaching hassle. We go in and out in twenty minutes—no more! So no stopping for a shower, a shit, and a shave. We are not tourists, people.

"Now to the detail."

The briefing continued. The twenty-four-hour reconnaissance, as well as confirming intelligence they already possessed, had added detail that could only be gathered by close observation.

The two valleys had separate generator systems. The main camp generator in Salvador was particularly noisy and prone to brownouts and breakdowns. It had cut out twice while the recce team was in position, and each time a bored soldier had left the guardhouse at the main gate and after ten minutes or so had restored it to life. There had been no reaction from elsewhere in the camp when the lights had died. It was clear that this was a routine occurrence.

In contrast, the generator in Dali, while still noisy, was quieter and manifestly more reliable. There, illuminating the maze of pipes that included the supergun, the security lights burned bright and even. Even more to the point, it had been ascertained that the double fence that circled the camp from the main gate at the front to the rim of the valley at the back was electrified on the inside perimeter. It would have been convenient if this had been powered by the faulty generator in the main camp, Salvador, but unfortunately that was not so.

"That's the bad news," continued Fitzduane. "However, by the standards of this landscape, the ground beneath the fence is soft—well, vulnerable—in places, and the recce team have already probed an entry point on the rim. Al's team, Shadow Two, will go in from there. A regular jeep patrol goes by every fifteen minutes, but that apart, it will be just good old-fashioned burrowing. Healthy exercise, I'm told."

The team of Shadow Two looked appropriately thrilled. In fact, their digging had been extensively rehearsed and their Guntrack was equipped with a variety of powered tools to cope with various contingencies. The fastest was a compressed-air powered auger that was portable and virtually silent. Other equipment was hydraulically based and derived from devices used by rescue teams and police SWAT teams to prize apart obstacles. Such specialized tools could peel armor plate back in seconds as if it were aluminum foil.

There had been concern about motion sensors or beams, even though the notes on Patricio Nicanor's plan had stated they were not being used. The reconnaissance using sensors had shown he was right. A high-technology fence of such dimensions would have been expensive and difficult to maintain in such a location. Further, motion sensors would have been hard to coordinate with the jeep patrols and vulnerable to being set off by wild animals. Still, two fences, the inner one electrified, separated by a patrolled strip and overlooked by a blockhouse, were not insignificant.

"In sum," continued Fitzduane, "while Shadow Two is infiltrating from behind to take out the blockhouse on the high ground, three other teams are going to enter by the front gates. After all, what are gates for?

"In Salvador, the valley containing the mercenary garrison and the terrorists, the sentries will be taken out with silenced weapons, and two teams, six people, Chifune's Shadow Three and Peter Harty's Shadow Five, will enter on foot and head immediately for the Yaibo barracks building. You will shut off the generator silently so it looks like a normal breakdown. You will also destroy the radio room, which is on the first floor of the main building. Then, again using silenced weapons, you will kill—I repeat kill—all Yaibo inside and anyone else you encounter except for the hostage. In the ensuing darkness, all of you will exfiltrate with the hostage and rejoin your vehicles, which will be concealed in the scrub and rocks on the other side of the perimeter road. In all, I expect you to be in the camp for no more than five to seven minutes—ten at the outside.

"At precisely the same time as Salvador is being entered and the blockhouse being neutralized, Brick's team, Shadow Four, will enter Dali, the supergun valley. In this case, they will bring in their Guntrack when the internal opposition has been neutralized. Here, apart from mercenaries at the entrance, you will have to deal with four Yaibo guarding the supergun control bunker. That done, you can tame the supergun and check out what kind of warheads they have in store. No matter what you find, I expect you to be inside for no more than fifteen minutes.

"All of this adds up to three synchronized assaults taking out respectively the terrorists, the supergun, and the blockhouse that commands the two valleys. The watchwords are stealth, speed, and silence.

"Although you know the enemy dispositions full well, I am going to repeat that we are not just up against around fifty Yaibo terrorists. On the left-hand side of the main camp, Salvador, as you enter—that is the side opposite the Yaibo barracks—there is tented accommodation for over six hundred Tecuno mercenary soldiers, and just to make life more interesting there are normally half a dozen tanks laagered up in the middle, and there is a helicopter pad. In short, tiptoes might be a good idea. These guys are classified as special forces themselves, and though they may not be the best in the world, even six hundred idiots can spray a lot of lead around, and they have other unfriendly toys like heavy mortars and rocket launchers.

"To further encourage discretion, I would remind you that the twin valleys, Salvador and Dali, that make up the Devil's Footprint are bordered by a perimeter road that also circles the Madoa military airfield only eight kilometers away. Convoys of armor patrol that perimeter road. Finally, I should mention that the Madoa airfield, apart from being the base for two thousand more troops, boasts MiG-23s and armed helicopters. So be discreet folks. Keep the decibels down.

"The mercenaries—the battalion in the Devil's Footprint and the brigade in the air base—are not on the menu unless we have no alternative. But if the shit does hit the fan, *I want very serious destruction*.

"These people are not our friends. They threaten our countries. They threaten our values. They have already killed many hundreds of our people. So do not pull back. I can promise you, this is no time to be nice. They won't kiss you back. And I intend to go home no matter who or what is in the way. Fundamentally, like Lee here, I'm a carpet slippers type."

There was laughter, and Steve Kent slapped Cochrane on the back. The incident was a small thing, but Lee at last felt part of the team. It was a strange feeling, as if a circuit had been closed. He no longer had to prove anything. He just had to perform better than he would ever have thought possible. By himself it could not be done. With these people—*his people*—he would do it. Unit pride? It was more than that. It was an understanding; something very deep and very strong. It was a higher level of commitment. Beyond words.

It was a crazy feeling. It was probable that he was about to die. But he was happy.

Fitzduane had joined in the laughter. Now he turned serious and held a hand up for silence. "I have to talk about a sad event, the death of a very brave man. It behooves us to pay attention. What we are about to witness could be any one of us. This is the face of our enemy. It says everything that needs to be said.

"The quality of our intelligence on the target has a great deal to do with Koancho, the Japanese security service, and their agent in place, Hori-*san*. Recently you memorized his photograph so that you would not kill him in error. The intention had been that Chifune would go in in advance to remove her colleague from the line of fire. Now, I regret to say, it is academic. Yesterday the recce team witnessed this."

A ruggedized television monitor had been set up to show the videos of the target made by the reconnaissance team. So far they had viewed the routine functioning of the camp both in context and in close-up. Now the high-power telephoto lens of the miniaturized surveillance camera was focused on the Yaibo compound in the Salvador valley. It was wired off from the general camp area.

It looked at first as if some game was being played.

There were two teams of roughly fifteen people, each side pulling at opposite ends of a rope as if it were a tug-of-war.

But there was someone in the middle. And his hands and feet were bound and the rope was looped in a slipknot around his neck.

He was being executed.

The camera zoomed in, and they could see the man's face in close-up as his face and body contorted and he was slowly—very slowly—strangled to death.

Fitzduane froze the image. "I don't thing we need to see any more. The whole thing took over fifteen minutes and ended with his decapitation by rope. That is Yaibo in action. They have a tradition of purges. Why? Who knows?"

He looked at Chifune. Her face was expressionless, but he could feel a great grief. There was no anger. Instead there was a feeling of enormous strength, of resolution.

Hori-*san* had died, but his torch had been passed. His sense of purpose would live on. Those who had killed him would pay for their crime. It was a matter of justice, and it was certain.

"I am deeply sorry, Chifune," said Fitzduane. "Sorry for what has happened and sorry to have to show the manner of his death."

Chifune lifted her eyes, and there were tears in them. "It was necessary," she said. "We all have to understand. To know."

There was silence in the group.

Chifune looked back to the frozen image. Her face was pale. "It makes me ashamed to be Japanese," she said quietly. "Why do we produce people who could do such things? What are we doing that is so wrong?"

"Nothing to be ashamed of, Chifune," said Calvin. "The man who died was Japanese too. Every nation has good and bad. That's just the way of it."

Chifune raised her hand and gently placed two fingers on the monitor screen on the frozen scene of the dying man's face. It was at once a gesture of affection and farewell.

Fitzduane switched off the video and the screen went blank and there was silence for a little time. It seemed appropriate. No one had met the man who had died, but he had been a colleague. He deserved respect.

The group dispersed, but Calvin remained behind.

He cleared his throat. "I'd like to change the aviation plan. I've been thinking, and I can do more than fly top cover."

Fitzduane looked at him. It was a relief to be able to focus on a technical problem, and Calvin was normally worth listening to. "A little late in the day, Calvin, don't you think?"

Calvin reminded him in a way of U.S. General Billy Mitchell. Mitchell had pioneered the use of airpower in warfare in the 1920s, against stubborn opposition, with such enthusiasm that he had been court-martialed for his pains before the merit of his thinking had been vindicated.

Calvin had the same zeal when it came to pushing the airborne role in special-forces operations. He was not just a competent aviator. He had a definite vision of how air assets might be used, and he and Fitzduane had talked at length on the subject.

Calvin nodded. "I should have spoken earlier, but I wanted to get the hang of the terrain first. Now I'm sure I can do it, and it won't change the ground-assault plan."

"Do what?" said Fitzduane.

"Hit Madoa airfield," said Calvin. "When we bug out after the assault, the greatest threat is going to come from the air, and in particular from helicopter gunships. They are the ones that can hunt us down and counter the Guntracks' speed and agility. Sure, I know we've got air defenses, but I think it makes more sense to take them out on the ground."

Fitzduane thought for a moment. The microlight was a tiny machine and up to now it had been positioned only for observation. But maybe that was blinkered thinking.

"When would you propose doing this, Calvin? There is a balance here between alerting the enemy flyboys and making the hit. Throwing stones at a wasps' nest is not a good idea."

Calvin smiled. "I'd suggest striking after the ground attack on the Devil's Footprint," he said. "That way Madoa air base won't alert the target before we are in, and at the same time when the target calls them they'll be too busy with their own world of woe to respond."

"Do you really think you can do that much damage from the SkyEye?" said Fitzduane. "You don't have much of a payload left after the FLIR."

"It's a two-seater even with the FLIR," said Calvin. "That means I have up to about two hundred pounds to play with. That's ten RAW projectiles, an Ultimax, and a forty-millimeter pump-action grenade launcher—with room to spare. That is serious grief from the sky, and the sat photos show aircraft parked out in the open. They have no hardened bunkers. No need, they think. There is supposed to be no threat around here. Only the devil walks in these parts, and he's a friend."

Fitzduane smiled. "Very droll, Calvin."

He considered the proposition and then called in the others for discussion. Since Calvin's arrival, the team had become rather attached to their eye in the sky and were not sure they wanted it put at risk. On the other hand, armed helicopters were not a pleasant prospect.

Fitzduane made the decision. If Calvin was in position over the airstrip when the ground attack went in, he should be back in time for the exfiltration. His little machine could go at over a mile a minute when the sound suppressor was not switched on.

"Go for it, Calvin," he said, and explained. Calvin nodded.

Final preparations were made, and for the first time miniature headsets were worn. Radio silence disciplines had been absolute so far and would continue until the assault. But Fitzduane had weighed the options. The advantages of instant communication between team members during the actual assault outweighed the risks of the signals being overheard. In addition, the transmissions were encrypted. An eavesdropper would hear something that would sound like static.

There was a last equipment check. Watches were synchronized. It was a moonless night, but the sky was cloudless and a canopy of stars ensured just enough light to make the passive night-vision goggles fully effective. It would not have mattered if the darkness had been absolute. Shanley's company's thermal driving aids had become second nature.

Calvin, again dressed like the Penguin, took off.

Fitzduane made a hand signal, which was passed on from Guntrack to Guntrack. The column moved off toward the target.

In a few hours, thought Shanley, I am going to have to kill another human being. I don't care what they have done. I cannot be judge, jury, and executioner. The others can do it. They are professionals. Even Lee Cochrane served in Vietnam. I cannot do it. In Fayetteville, it was self-defense and I did not have time to think.

Here I have plenty of time to think, and I know I cannot do this. I have never served.

If I can, if my body does not betray me, I will try to do everything that is required of me—but I will not kill. I cannot. Let the others take life.

I have not served.

Guilt and fear ran raw through him. He had thought it would be like the endless training. The careful preparation, the long periods of waiting, the excitement of the impending assault, the adrenaline rush, and then action.

This was superficially just like that in many ways. The same people, the same equipment, the same feel of the Guntrack's suspension as it leveled the appalling terrain. But inwardly, inside his very being, he felt entirely different.

The certainty was gone. It was as if the skills that had given him so much confidence had evaporated and every last defense stripped away. Now there was nothing but terror and overwhelming self-doubt.

I have abandoned my family for nothing. I cannot do this thing. I will let down my comrades. I will die here in Mexico to no purpose.

Why me? Why now?

I am afraid beyond the very meaning of fear.

THE DEVIL'S FOOTPRINT

T H E guard on the main gate of the Devil's Footprint valley known as "Salvador" looked at his watch.

Time seemed to have slowed its tempo. It was an occupational hazard on guard duty and especially so in this mind-numbingly dull part of the world. Nothing ever happened. The main defenses were on the perimeter of the plateau hundreds of kilometers away, and the immediate area was deserted. It was scarcely surprising. Who, in their right mind, would want to live in this hellhole?

He had come on duty at midnight, only an hour ago if he was to believe the evidence of his watch, but it seemed an eternity, a particularly cold eternity. The Devil's Footprint was not only 3,800 feet up on the plateau, but it was in the foothills of the Tecuno mountains and every foot of additional height seemed to make a difference for the worse. The high desert at night was cold enough. Throw in some altitude and it was downright uncomfortable. In his opinion, the location was well named. It was fit only for the devil.

It was too cold at night and too hot during the day, and the ground was harsh and arid and stony and brutal on boots, and there were far too many things around that bit, like flies and scorpions and snakes and lizards. Frankly, why the base was located here was beyond him. Still, no one had asked him his opinion or seemed likely to. As a mercenary, he got paid but not consulted.

"Hey, Ahmed," he called.

Ahmed grunted. He was sitting in the turret of the T55 tank that blocked the camp entrance at night. He was marginally more comfortable than his colleague, since he had a woolly hat his wife had knitted him on his head and was well bundled up and gaining some benefit from a small oil heater inside the tank; but his main distraction came from the pornographic Japanese comic book he was looking at.

Manga, they called such things. He had traded a stack from one of the Yaibo fanatics in exchange for hash.

"Ahmed," repeated the gate guard. Ahmed raised his head from the comic book, and as he did so pieces of his skull seemed to detach themselves from his head. They could be seen like bloody snow reflecting in the gate floodlights, except that they flew sideways. And there was no snow.

The guard's mouth dropped open and then he, too, crumpled. His body twitched as it lay on the ground and a further burst tore into it.

Black-clad figures ran forward, and a split second later the Yaibo guard on the inner perimeter lay lifeless on his back.

Two black figures entered the guardroom where six off-duty guards were sleeping. It took seven seconds.

The entire group were now at the base of the Yaibo barracks. An orange light glowed in one window where the duty radio operator sat; otherwise the place was in darkness.

There was a hand signal and a faint click as the power supply to the building was severed. Seconds later, the radio operator came out swearing under his breath. He had been practically asleep. He had assumed it was that fucking generator again, but then he saw that the perimeter lights were on, and anyway he could hear the bloody thing thumping. It must be a main fuse.

He started to turn just as his mouth and nose were clamped and his head pulled back. His own momentum helped to do the work of the blade. Dead, his heart was still pumping as he was lowered to the ground. The only sound was a slight gurgle.

The assault group split into two three-person teams and entered the two floors simultaneously.

FITZDUANE was positioned on the reverse slope of a low ridge facing the entrance to the main camp.

The two temporarily abandoned vehicles of the assault group were concealed nearby. To retrieve them the crews would have to cross the perimeter road. During the day, when it was well traveled, that would be risky, but this time of night there should be no problem.

Fitzduane watched the assault teams go in with mixed feelings.

A special-forces assault bestrode a fine line between recklessness and audacity, and being forced to let other people spearhead the action while he remained in reserve did not please him. On the other hand, the people he had selected were younger and better qualified for the particular tasks involved, and a commander's job was to look at the woods, not get lost in the trees. Still, no matter how he rationalized, waiting outside was difficult.

He rotated the FLIR, but so far nothing untoward could be seen. The viewing head of the high-magnification night/day vision device was extended over the rim of the hill. He felt like a submariner looking through his periscope. Steve Kent, his driver, sat beside him. Lee Cochrane, his rear gunner who had checked out surprisingly well with the GECAL, was fifteen yards away, lying in a dip of the rim, monitoring the road.

Fitzduane missed his eye in the sky.

Calvin would warn him of any vehicles approaching from the north, but he would not be able to see any southern arrivals while away at the airfield. Still, life was a compromise. Armed helicopters were *the* most lethal short-term threat, and if he could neutralize them the exfiltration would be a whole lot safer. There were no other helicopters based within range.

He focused the FLIR on the Yaibo barracks. There was one light burning on the first floor. That would be the radio room.

He watched as the light went out. Inside that building, according to his information, Kathleen lay. In seconds she would be free or perhaps dead. He knew she had been maltreated and abused and was kept blindfolded and chained—but had it been even more serious? Could she walk? Was she still sane? Had she been tortured? Had she been raped? *The baby! How was the baby? Could it have survived?*

He wanted to put his arms around Kathleen and hug her as he had so many times in the past, but he could do nothing but watch and wait.

NEAR THE DEVIL'S FOOTPRINT,
TECUNO, MEXICO

CALVIN allowed himself plenty of time and traveled slowly and in optimum stealth mode to Madoa airfield.

On a moonless light like this and a thousand feet up the SkyEye was almost impossible to detect visually, but the engine could conceivably be heard unless the "super trap" silencer was used.

The super trap—fitted also to the Guntracks—was highly effective, but though it increased torque, it decreased performance. The system could be varied by the operator, but fully invoked, the price for being nearly silent was a top speed dropped from over eighty to around thirty miles an hour.

The air was cold and clear against his face, and with the engine noise almost completely suppressed, he felt like some giant bird of prey as he flew over the nearly deserted landscape beneath him.

The northern end of the perimeter road was dark. There were no truck lights. He peered through his FLIR and examined the lozenge-shaped ribbon of the road more closely. There was still nothing to be seen. Team Rapier was safe from the north. As for the south, that would have to be the boss's problem, because Calvin could see the lights of the airfield show up ahead. It was clear they were not anticipating any enemy action. There were lights at the main gate and in the barracks and around the maintenance hangars. The runway was dark.

Six MiG-23 jets stood parked in sandbagged emplacements, and nearby another four helicopters were similarly lined up.

Calvin circled the airfield at a discreet distance, studying every detail through his FLIR. He had practiced until he could fire an aimed RAW projectile every ten seconds. Close examination showed half a dozen heavy-machine-gun positions around the base. They might not be designed for antiaircraft work, but they could still make life very unpleasant for him if he was detected.

"Don't be either a hero or a perfectionist, Calvin," Fitzduane had said. "How can you lobby the cause of special-forces air if you're a permanent part of the Tecuno landscape? Do what you can in a single pass and then get the fuck out AFAFP—As Fast As Fucking Possible."

Calvin smiled to himself as he prepared to attack. He would confine himself to the aircraft parked outside. Anything under repair in the maintenance hangar was unlikely to be flyable in time to pose a threat anyway.

Unfortunately, he did not see the small passenger helicopter parked inside one of the hangars for no more serious reason than it was having its windscreen cleaned. It was used by Reiko Oshima, and it was at Madoa airfield because Oshima was spending that particular night with General Louis Barragan.

Unaware of either's presence, Calvin prepared to attack.

THE DEVIL'S FOOTPRINT, TECUNO, MEXICO

CHIFUNE entered the second floor of the Yaibo barracks, the layout imprinted on her mind.

Toilets, four stalls. Thirty-six-bed barracks area with passage down the center. Two rooms at end either side of the corridor. Kathleen on the right. Oshima sometimes—she moved around—on the left.

Chifune was designated right and Chuck Freeman was assigned left, with Grady acting as backup. Nothing was said. This was a prearranged routine practiced so many times it was an instinctive reflex.

The floor was dark, but through her PNV goggles she could see. There were no colors except shades of green fading to black and the red dot of her laser gun sight, which was invisible except to those wearing the goggles and the appropriate filter.

A figure rose from a bed and stumbled sleepily toward the toilets. Outside the stalls, as he fumbled for a light switch, Chifune shot him twice in the back of the head and caught the body and lowered it to the ground. Black liquid ran out of his skull. She checked the other stalls. All were empty.

Thirty of the beds were still occupied.

Chifune fired, and a split second later Chuck Freeman opened up. The weapons made almost no noise, and the ejected brass fell downward into cloth bags so there was not even the sound of empty cases rattling on the floor.

Bodies whipped as rounds tore into them, and blood blackened the bedclothes and sheets and leaked onto the floor and spread in a great pool.

The attackers advanced, firing steadily in aimed three-round bursts, and Grady followed up with head shots.

One terrorist rose up and screamed and reached for his weapon, but died as Chifune fired a longer burst and five 10mm armor-piercing slugs cut through his torso.

At the end of the room, a Yaibo member got his weapon up and cocked it, then slammed back and slid along the corridor as Grady spotted him and took him out with a head shot and a burst to the throat.

A pair of lovers sharing the same bed half rose in alarm as the man in the next bed shuddered and fell back, and then Freeman's rounds found them and they collapsed in each other's arms.

A Yaibo woman seized a sword and ran down the central aisle toward her executioners until three streams of Calico rounds converged and cut her nearly in half.

She fell forward and her weapon cut into the toe of Freeman's boot before falling from her lifeless hands.

One young Yaibo member—he was older but he looked no more than sixteen—held up his hands in a vain effort to surrender. The movement attracted Grady's attention and a burst took him in the face.

A terrorist rolled off his bed and, crawling frantically, emerged between Chifune and Freeman. Neither could fire without hitting the other. Grady was blocked by Freeman.

The terrorist scrabbled to cock his automatic rifle. As he did so, Freeman drew his fighting knife with his left hand and stabbed the man in the throat.

In less than thirty seconds, thirty-one members of Yaibo lay dead or dying and the air was thick with the smells of slaughter. All the bodies were checked quickly, and where there was any sign of life at all, it was terminated.

The assault team moved on. There was no emotion. This was what they had trained to do. Reaction would come later.

The door of Oshima's room was flung open. It was empty.

THE BLOCKHOUSE ABOVE THE DEVIL'S
FOOTPRINT, TECUNO, MEXICO

SHANLEY watched through filtered PNV goggles as Al Lonsdale emerged on the inside of the electrified fence.

Despite their equipment and hindered by the requirement for absolute silence, tunneling under it had proved to be harder and to take longer than expected. What had appeared like sandy ground had degenerated into rock, and they had been forced to hunt for another location.

Seconds later, Dana Felton emerged and Shanley passed through the Clucas pole in sections. The Clucas had been designed for Britain's SBS—Special Boat Service—marine commando unit as a way of covertly climbing onto ships from an assault boat below. It consisted of a central shaft of light, strong alloy with short steps protruding on either side. It could be up to fifty-four feet long and was much faster to climb than a rope ladder.

Shanley could see headlights. He sank back to the ground, and Al and Dana did the same. A minute later the guard jeep with its crew of four and mounting a heavy machine gun passed by, headlights blazing and occupants chatting away.

They are bored out of their minds and the lights and the fence give an illusion of security, thought Shanley. The form and the substance—the split between the two was a curious paradox in the military world. People still only went through the motions, even when their very lives were at stake. It was the "It can't happen to me" syndrome, and it was the friend of special forces the world over.

Al Lonsdale and Dana rose from the ground and, making every use of the terrain and keeping to the shadows, moved towards the reinforced concrete observation post that commanded the two valleys below. Even with his night-vision equipment and knowing they were there, Shanley found it very hard to follow them. Mostly there was more the faintest impression of movement than a hard image.

When they came to the base of the post, they vanished.

They will now be moving around to the base on the other side, thought Shanley. Seconds later, three clicks and then one sounded in his earpiece.

Keeping well under cover, he picked up a lamp and pointed it at the observation post and shouted in Japanese. It was not a language he spoke, but he had parrot-learned a few phrases. Seconds later, a searchlight swung in his direction and he ducked right down as the beam moved toward him.

"What's up? What did you see?" said the startled second guard on the blockhouse roof. He spoke in Spanish. Numb with boredom and the chill of the night, he had two blankets wrapped around him and had been almost asleep when his companion had cried out.

"I saw a headlight," said the first guard, "and then someone shouted in Japanese. It sounds like the yo-yos are playing games out there." Relations between the Japanese Yaibo terrorists and the mainly Mexican mercenary force were not cordial.

"Well, fuck 'em," said his companion. "They should know better. Give them a burst and teach them to behave. It'll liven things up."

The first guard swung the 12.7mm heavy machine gun around. It was sorely tempting, but Yaibo were supposed to be their allies, and shooting up a group who had got lost on some exercise would not look like such fun in the light of day. He decided to play it safe and call the guardhouse.

He was reaching for the telephone as the burst from Al Lonsdale's silenced Calico struck him in the back. The 10mm armor-piercing rounds plowed effortlessly through his Russian-made flak jacket.

His companion fell at the same time Dana fired. Seconds later, the two members of Shadow Two had descended into the floor below where eight other members of the duty section lay sleeping.

It did not take long. They checked the bodies, switched the current off the electric fence, and ascended to the roof again.

Shanley watched with growing concern as the lights of the duty jeep came closer. The jeep, in the normal scheme of things, was not due back for another fifteen minutes, so he could only assume that the blockhouse had called them up to investigate the mysterious light. Bloody hell, it was an obvious move with hindsight, but actually not one they had anticipated. There was always something staring you in the face that you missed. As Brick had once remarked, life was a monument to mankind's fuckups.

"The blockhouse is secure," said Al Lonsdale's voice in his earpiece. This was technically correct and though on the open net primarily for Fitzduane's benefit, Shanley meanwhile had a jeepload of Mexican mercenaries bearing down on him.

What to do? It had to be done virtually silently. A shout would not attract attention in either of the camps below, but unsilenced gunshots were another matter.

He would have to take out the four before they could respond. This was what he had trained for. It could be done.

"Take them out"—kill them.

Kill four perfect strangers. Take the lives of four human beings as peremptorily as one might swat a fly.

He broke out in a sweat.

I cannot kill. I will not kill. Let the others take life.

He had known this moment would come, and yet he had no idea how he would respond. It was not an issue you could resolve in a vacuum. This was not a theoretical debate. This was not an exercise. Albeit for reasons he considered valid, this was the slaughter of sentient human beings. It was immoral. It was wrong. It was something he could not do—would not do.

The guard jeep slewed to a halt.

It was the other side of the double fence and past him by about ten meters. At the most they were fifteen meters away from his position and looking away from him.

Two dismounted from the jeep and went to look more closely. The driver and the machine gunner remained in position.

Shanley, faced with the immediate reality, no longer rationalized.

Reflex took over and basic survival instinct took over—and something more. A determination not to let his people down. They were not perfect. Some he did not even like.

Not important. They were a team. There was a shared purpose, shared loyalties, shared experiences. They were *his* people. Better yet, even those he did not warm to were his comrades. They were his friends.

He fired four quick, silent bursts and then a further burst at the machine gunner who was still alive. Black blood fountained from the man's throat as the second burst hit him, and he fell over the pintle mount, his arms seeming to reach out toward the wire.

"Blockhouse power off," said a voice in his ear. "The wire is tame."

Shanley cut his way through the fences and drove the Guntrack toward the blockhouse.

Al Lonsdale had watched the entire exchange through high-powered vision equipment. He reached down a helping hand as Shanley climbed the Clucas pole. "Welcome aboard," he said.

Dana smiled at Shanley as he stepped on the OP roof. It was a quiet smile, but it said all that was needed. Shanley thought he was going to be sick, but then things seemed to come into focus and he looked at Al Lonsdale and nodded. "Yeah," he said. "No problems."

"I should hope not," said Lonsdale with a slight smile.

Then they all heard the same transmission. It came from Brick Stephens, who was on road watch.

"More guests at the party, boss," said Stephens, his voice quiet but clear, his remark directed specifically at Fitzduane. "Tanks, APCs and trucked troops on the perimeter road heading north towards us. ETA five to ten minutes. They are moving fairly fast. The sound was blanketed by the hill, but you'll be able to hear them now."

Shadow Two, the strongpoint commanding the two valleys below them now secure, looked south at the new arrivals. A quick estimate suggested a battalion-size force.

No matter how you looked at it, it was not a visit from the tooth fairy.

THE BARRACKS, THE DEVIL'S FOOTPRINT, TECUNO, MEXICO

RHEIMAN made sure the small window was covered and then lit the six candles he had brought. He liked to look at her by candlelight, and he had made the occasions into something of a ritual.

It was his eighth visit, she thought. Her mental makeup, she was discovering, was tougher than she would ever have believed.

Rheiman had undressed her after his last visit, and as her soiled clothing was removed she had expected the inevitable to follow. There was not much she could do to resist. A chained victim was every rapist's dream. But he had not raped her. Instead, he washed her and tended to her cuts and bruises and gave her water and extra food and vitamin pills and antibiotics. He was saving her life.

The Voice and the other terrorists thought he was screwing her every time he visited, but all he actually wanted to do was undress her and look at her by candle-light and talk.

And his talk was not sexual. He talked of his creation and the destruction it would wreak and the fame it would bring. He talked of the missile it would carry and the lethal nerve agent it would carry. He digressed into technicalities and explained at length why hydrogen was a superior propellant to anything Bull had ever thought up.

It came to Kathleen with some force that her plight was of little significance in the scheme of things. The carnage that Rheiman's warped mind threatened to let loose must be stopped.

He talked on, and Kathleen encouraged him. He held her hand.

CHIFUNE prepared to enter Kathleen's door.

Freeman turned the handle and flung it open. There seemed to be candles everywhere, and she could see a naked figure chained to the wall.

"FRIENDS, KATHLEEN!" she shouted.

Kathleen! It did not look like her at first. The contrast between the beautiful full-bodied woman she had met in Ireland and this abused figure was truly shocking.

Bile rose in her throat.

She took in another figure, a European in desert khakis, and was within a tenth of a second of shooting him when Kathleen screamed.

"NO! NO! DON'T KILL HIM. WE NEED HIM."

Chifune grunted, and smashed Rheiman against the wall.

She spun him around and tied his wrists with plasticuffs. She had a great desire to put a burst through his head, but she heard Kathleen's plea, and if she, who had been through all this, wanted the bastard kept alive there had to be a good reason.

There had better be, or she would kill him where he stood.

Freeman removed the hostage's blindfold, then took bolt cutters from a belt pouch and cut through the chains. Kathleen! It was definitely her. She was crying and gesturing toward the man in khaki. "You mustn't kill him. We need him. He knows."

Freeman wrapped her clothes around her and then a bulletproof vest. "Hugo is outside," he said. "We're taking you home." He indicated Rheiman. "What about this fuck? Friend or enemy?"

Kathleen looked at him, her hands rubbing her eyes. "He's one of them," she said, "but we *must* take him. He knows too much."

"Roger that," said Freeman. He picked her up and slung her over his shoulder. He was used to exercising with a hundred-and-fifty-pound pack. She felt disturbingly light.

"Shadow One," said Chifune. "Yaibo barracks clear and we have Kathleen. She's okay. We have a prisoner. Leaving now."

"Roger that, Shadow Two," said Fitzduane. He felt light-headed with relief at the news, but fought to keep his mind focused. "Move it fucking fast. We have visitors coming up the perimeter road from the southern. ETA less than five minutes."

A prisoner? There were to be *no* prisoners. Chifune knew that as well as anyone, so there had to be a reason.

"Shadow Four," said the Brick. He was inside the supergun bunker working on the firing mechanism, aided by Hayden, while Sergeant Oga kept watch outside. The shattered bodies of the Yaibo guards lay where they had fallen. The work was demanding. "We are in, but we need minimum seven to ten minutes more—I repeat, seven to ten."

Fitzduane made a quick assessment.

He currently had four teams inside the camps. Two had neutralized the Yaibo barracks and looked like they would get out in time, but the remaining two units would be cut off when the approaching column arrived.

It would occupy the road end to end, from the main camp to way beyond the supergun valley. It was dark, and he considered having them infiltrate the column, but that would mean leaving the Guntracks, and they still had to make the pickup point forty kilometers away. The logic was simple and the outcome would be bloody, but there was very little choice.

The lights flickered as the generator in the main camp coughed and then died again. Suddenly it was dark. Chifune and the five other members of her assault group ran for the main gates and then across the perimeter road to their waiting Guntracks.

"I'm going to thin out the approaching column," said Fitzduane. "Heavy shit for the next ten minutes and then we all bug out for the emergency RV. Acknowledge."

The four teams acknowledged in numerical order.

"Go! Go! Go!" said Fitzduane. "Calvin, where the fuck are you?"

There was no reply.

Fitzduane's Shadow One shot forward toward the approaching column. The Guntrack was maneuvering through the low hills beside the perimeter road, traveling a roughly parallel route.

In a little over a minute they would be side by side, separated by little more than a hundred meters but traveling in opposite directions. It was, Fitzduane reflected briefly as he roared toward the T55 tank that headed the column, almost a modern version of medieval jousting, except that only one side knew he had an enemy to deal with. The Guntracks had not been detected.

This was not a joust. It was war. It was the business of killing. Fair play did not come into it.

Fitzduane spoke into his microphone on the internal net, and Steve Kent slewed to a halt and crept into a firing position shielded by a rocky outcrop.

Lee Cochrane readied the .50 GECAL heavy machine gun.

Fitzduane brought his RAW up to the point of aim.

A T55 tank looked disconcertingly formidable to rifle-equipped infantry and was strongly armored at the front, but it was vulnerable at the side and at the rear engine compartment. And Shadow One would be firing down, which would help. Tanks were thinly armored at the top. It was a matter of keeping the weight down. Maximum armor everywhere had the same effect as on a knight of old. The end result was unwieldy and virtually too heavy to move.

The T55 ground tank passed them, treads squealing in protest. This was a tank that had been six months on routine patrols and needed tender loving care from the maintenance shop. It did not get it. A split second after the RAW smashed into its engine compartment it ignited, flames jetting into the darkness.

Fitzduane fitted another RAW and fired at the next vehicle, an armored personnel carrier. The vehicle exploded.

Troop-laden trucks following the two lead vehicles braked to avoid crashing into the burning wrecks, and several crashed into each other. Soldiers poured out of the backs of the trucks, and it was into this chaos that the rotating-barreled .50 GECAL began to fire.

Seconds afterward, Shadow Four leapfrogged Fitzduane and headed down to the end of the column, guns blazing and extending the slaughter. Shortly afterward, the Brick aimed his Dilger's Baby at the vehicle bringing up the rear.

There was an earsplitting crack and a tongue of flame, and the uranium-depleted projectile smashed through the side of the tank and ignited the ammunition inside. The whole tank blew and the turret sailed into the air and turned, landing upside down.

"Reverse! Move fifty," said Fitzduane, and Steve Kent shot Shadow One backward and moved to a fresh firing position fifty meters away.

And so it continued. Fire and movement. Shoot and maneuver. And using night-vision equipment under cover of darkness so that the Guntracks were almost never seen.

Take every advantage.

The engagement was brutal, and it took little time before most of the vehicles in the convoy were ablaze. Cochrane raked the carnage one more time and the two vehicles sped away to the rendezvous point. The survivors were convinced they had been hit by at least a battalion-size force.

AL Lonsdale's team high in the blockhouse and commanding both valleys and the perimeter road below entered the fray.

When the order came to shoot up the main camp, he sent Dana down to the Guntrack while he and Shanley stayed on the blockhouse roof to use the weapons available. Team Rapier had massive firepower, but ammunition was limited and it made sense to use what the other side was kind enough to provide. They appeared to have been generous. Apart from the 12.7mm heavy machine gun, there was an 82mm mortar and substantial stocks of ammunition.

Dana maneuvered the Guntrack into firing position and then went back to man the 40mm grenade launcher. Below them they could see sudden frantic action as the tented lines heard the sound of the perimeter guard column being shot up. A klaxon sounded. Tank crew ran toward their vehicles. Weapons teams sped toward mortar pits. Other troops spilled out of their tents while officers shouted and tried to impose some order.

Al Lonsdale's first mortar bomb exploded in the middle of the tented lines at almost the same time Dana and Shanley opened fire.

Armored personnel carriers ignited and their crews ran from them into the maelstrom as the 40mm grenades cut through their thin armor. Dana was firing a cocktail of armor-piercing, high explosive, and fléchettes in three-round bursts at a cyclical rate 350 rounds a minute.

In the confined space of the camp, the destruction was appalling. Each single high-explosive grenade had a kill radius of five meters. It was intensified by the green tracer from Shanley's heavy machine gun.

Further firepower came from Guntracks firing from the low hills opposite the main entrance outside the camp. RAW projectiles were followed by streams of armor-piercing Ultimax fire and the earsplitting crack of Dilger's Baby.

The tank guarding the main entrance gate burst into flame. Another T55 had its track blown off and spun slowly round in circles until a depleted uranium shell blew its turret off. The colonel commanding the armored battalion tried to make a run for his armored command vehicle but was eviscerated by a Dilger round as he was climbing in. The APC ignited and commander and vehicle burned together.

Laser sights, night-vision equipment, and high-magnification optics not only had vastly increased the first hit probability of Team Rapier's weapons but also, at such close ranges, made the business of killing disturbingly personal.

Through the viewfinders of the weapons sights the enemy looked close enough to touch, and the expressions of individual soldiers could be seen as high-velocity metal and explosives tore through them and blew them apart.

In the intensity of the action, the sights of such horrors made no impression on the outnumbered assault force. It was a matter of brute survival, and such images were repressed as fast as they were seen.

The killing continued with savage precision.

CHAPTER TWENTY-ONE

REIKO OSHIMA LAY on her back, her knees drawn up and spread apart and her hands grasping the metal bed-head of the military-issue bed.

Her forehead was beaded with sweat and her loins were sticky with sexual fluids. General Luis Barragan's principal attraction, as far as she was concerned, was a combination of his endurance and imagination, and he had already been working on her for several hours. A few moments ago, just as she had been about to come yet again, he had withdrawn from her and now stood gazing out of the window at the night sky. There was a flash of flame as he lit a cigarette, and as he turned to look at her she could see that his organ was still hard and erect.

She wanted to hit him, to inflict pain, but she was helpless, her wrists bound to the metal frame. He smiled at her, a flash of white teeth, and then he came nearer, the red tip of the cigarette glowing in the darkened room. Her eyes fixed on the red tip and she followed it as it approached her lower body.

She clenched her teeth in anticipation of the sharp pain and the sudden jolting burst of intense sexual pleasure that would follow, and then Luis would enter her again and pound in and out of her and finish what he had started. And then it would commence again, but always with a subtle variation. Or perhaps he would be the victim next time around. That was a pleasing prospect.

There was a flash in the sky and a thunderous explosion, and the window shattered and she could hear bursts of machine-gun fire. She pulled in reflex at her bonds, but it was useless.

"Cut me loose, you fool," she shouted at Barragan as she switched her gaze from the window to her lover.

He seemed frozen with shock. The cigarette fell from his hand and he took a couple of uncertain steps toward her and then collapsed on her body, crimson pouring from his severed jugular, the shard of glass still protruding.

She lay there screaming in rage and frustration and disgust as Barragan's life-blood gushed over her and soaked into the bed. Then she noticed that the shard of glass was near her right wrist and she moved the leather thong against it.

It took several minutes, but gradually she worked herself free.

Outside on the airfield, every single weapons emplacement seemed to be in action, but to what purpose it was far from clear. Tracer crisscrossed the sky in wild abandon, and on the ground explosion followed explosion.

She threw on some clothes over her blood-soaked body, grabbed her AK-47, and ran outside to see if she could make sense of what was going on. They were under attack obviously, but whether from the air or from the ground she could not tell.

The scene that greeted her was total chaos. She ran toward her helicopter. Around her, an ammunition dump was exploding and the flames from a fuel bowser licked at the sky, but her helicopter seemed untouched. Better still, her pilot was already at the controls.

She jumped in, and seconds later they were airborne.

ABOVE MADOA AIR BASE, TECUNO, MEXICO

CALVIN banked the microlight steeply to the left as a stream of green tracer arced toward him.

There was bedlam below. None of the fire seemed to be aimed, but so much lead was being thrown up there was a reasonable chance he would be hit by accident unless he got out fast. He dived to fifty feet and accelerated to maximum speed.

A mortar pit below started to fire as he flashed over. In their haste they had misjudged the range, and the heavy teardrop-shaped bombs instead of landing outside the airfield among the imagined attackers were landing inside it among the defending troops as they crouched in their trenches and blazed away into the darkness.

The little aircraft lurched as he crossed the perimeter, and he had to lean to the right to keep his balance. The miniature machine was hit, fuck it, but he did not take the time to check the damage. Instead he concentrated on the decidedly hairy business of flying down a long twisting wadi at ground-hugging height. The dry riverbed was pointing northwest, so it was in the wrong direction, but it took him away from the action and another chance encounter with an unfriendly projectile.

He slowed down, activated the sound suppressor, and climbed.

A quick glance told him that one of his supporting struts had been severed.

Unless he made some emergency repairs fairly soon, the wing might go on flying, but the fuselage that contained him would part company from the airfoil and head straight for the ground. This was not a prospect that attracted him. To maximize his weapons load under the tight weight constraint, he had opted not to wear a parachute.

He put in an abortive radio call to Fitzduane, but either he was out of range or things had gone badly wrong for the ground-based members of Team Rapier. Suddenly he felt very alone, and as the adrenaline rush wore off, the reaction hit and he felt tendrils of fear.

He decided that he just did not have time to feel afraid.

He activated the FLIR and looked for a reasonably friendly patch of ground to land on. The bottom of the wadi was a mass of loose boulders and larger rocks, so he focused on the perimeter.

Three minutes later, he was on the ground.

In the distance he could see that the fireworks display at the airfield was still continuing and he wondered how much damage he had done. He had certainly gotten their attention, but the key issue was the extent to which the helicopters and the MiGs had been damaged.

He started to get out of his tiny cockpit to repair the damaged struts, and it was only then that he noticed he had been hit.

The whole front of his duvet jacket had been torn away, and under it the ceramic plate body armor insert that protected his vital organs was exposed. The heavy round had hit him on the diagonal and cut through the outer layers of Kevlar as effortlessly as if they were paper, but had then been deflected by the ceramic plate.

He had damn nearly left the insert plates behind but had rethought after Fitzduane's caution.

Calvin sat down on a rock and for nearly two minutes shook like a leaf. The spasm ended when he heaved violently and threw up.

He felt weak but able to function again, and went back to work.

OUTSIDE THE DEVIL'S FOOTPRINT,
TECUNO, MEXICO

FITZDUANE tried to look at his watch, then swore as Steve threw the Guntrack into reverse and shot backward for thirty meters.

A tank shell impacted in the hill just behind the spot they had just vacated and showered them with debris.

"Shoot and scoot" was the tactic, but as the battle progressed and the enemy began to learn the rules, it made sense for there to be more emphasis on "scoot." It was then that the driver's battle skills really came into play. There was not time for him to merely respond to the vehicle commander's instruction. He had to read the battleground and follow his intuition.

Cochrane turned the .50 GECAL on the tank and hosed for a weakness away from the glacis at the front. Individually, the armor-piercing rounds would not penetrate a tank's frontal armor, but at sixty rounds a second against the less protected areas, hit after hit pounded its way through.

His periscopes blinded, and the tank's commander—fighting from his open cupola to try to see what was going on—was obliterated. Shortly after, there was penetration under the turret ring by explosive-filled multipurpose .50 rounds and the stored shells blew up.

It was time, in Fitzduane's opinion, to get the fuck out. Belting across this brutal terrain in a Guntrack with a repressed Formula One racing driver like Steve Kent at the wheel was dangerous enough in itself without hostiles shooting at you.

"Shadow One, this is Shadow Four," said the Brick. "Mission successful. We are loaded up and ready to come out."

"Roger that," said Fitzduane. "Shadow Two—where the fuck are you?" The plan was that Lonsdale's unit, Shadow Two, having infiltrated through the wire on the rim, would hold the blockhouse until the Brick had done his thing in the valley below. Then both would leave together.

There was an access road from the blockhouse on high to the supergun valley. They would then cross the perimeter road with the other three Guntracks, who had already made the trip, providing cover.

The plan had not included an armored column approaching from the south and a major firefight in progress. Still, life was rarely perfect, and as of now, the column was stalled and in decidedly bad shape, though it still had fangs.

Shadow Two was barreling down the access road to the valley floor with Shanley at the wheel when Fitzduane's check call came in. In Al Lonsdale's view they had stayed perhaps a minute or two too long on the rim, but the domination of the battlefield they had enjoyed from that position linked to all that ammunition had been hard to resist.

"Shadow Two to Shadow One," said Lonsdale over the open net. "We're sixty seconds behind Shadow Four. We'll make the break together."

"Roger that," said Fitzduane.

"Affirmative," said the Brick from Shadow Four. "We'll break in about forty-five seconds."

"Make smoke! Make smoke!" said Fitzduane.

All three Guntracks beyond the perimeter road and already under cover now fired their smoke dischargers, and within seconds a thick blanket of black smoke blocked the view of the supergun valley entrance from the column.

The smoke contained particulates that obscured infrared-vision equipment as well as normal vision, but this was overkill since none of the T55 tanks or armored personnel carriers was so equipped. However, the survivors of the mechanized column, already shattered by the intensity of the unexpected assault, panicked when the thick black smoke rolled over them.

The high-tech particulates made the smoke different from normal and tended to make the eyes itch, although it was otherwise harmless. There were immediate cries of "NERVE GAS! CHEMICAL WEAPONS!" and any semblance of discipline that remained with the unit vanished. To a man, they turned and fled.

It looked as if Shadow Two and Shadow Four would have a clear run across the perimeter road into the cover beyond, and then a helicopter gunship loomed out of the darkness in a reconnaissance pass before vanishing again.

"Rat shit!" said Kent, and moved their position fifty meters.

"If all they're going to do is look at us, I won't complain," said Fitzduane.

He put out an air threat warning on the net, but as he spoke into the boom microphone his thoughts were of Calvin. He reached for a Stinger.

The damn thing did not feel right.

The missile was full of holes. Well, better it than him.

But there was still the matter of the fucking helicopter. Green tracer began to wink down at them, and if memory served it also carried rockets and bombs.

Calvin, my son, where are you?

GUNFIRE damage to the SkyEye was a predictable hazard, so the microlight was equipped with a spares kit.

The damaged struts were splinted together with Kevlar tape, and within five minutes Calvin was airborne again. The repair would hold, he thought, provided he could avoid violent maneuvers, but anyway it was the best he could do.

He climbed to 2,000 feet and headed back to the Devil's Footprint and Team Rapier. Fitzduane had stipulated a maximum twenty-minute action before exfiltration, and at full speed Calvin would arrive to provide top cover just as they were withdrawing.

His route took him to one side of the air base, but he was high enough to keep out of harm's way and attracted no fire. He tried the FLIR to see if he could get some reading on damage to the helicopters, but although the magnification was more than adequate, all he could see from this angle were the sandbag revetments and flames from half a dozen fires. He had done considerable damage, he was sure, but the scale was hard to estimate.

Suddenly, he noticed a small helicopter take off. He throttled back and watched it circle as if waiting for something. Thirty seconds later, a much larger helicopter could be seen. The first helicopter had not disturbed him unduly, since it was a militarized version of a civilian Bell and carried, as far as he could see, no heavy weapons. However, the sight of the second helicopter made his heart sink.

It was a Russian-built Mil Mi-4 Hound fitted with a DShK 12.7mm heavy machine gun in the gondola, four sets of rocket pods, and four five-hundred-kilo bombs. Russian helicopters, like their ships, always seemed to carry a horrendous amount of firepower. Creature comfort was always a secondary issue.

The two helicopters formed up and headed for the Devil's Footprint.

Calvin followed, furious at himself for not having risked a second pass and maybe then having destroyed all the helicopters. Steadily, the two enemy machines pulled away from him. They were a good thirty miles an hour faster and would reach the camp a couple of minutes before he could.

He spoke into his radio as he came within range to warn Fitzduane, but there was no response. The radio was dead.

He looked at his remaining stock of weaponry. He still had four RAW projectiles and three hundred-round Ultimax magazines left. He had never heard of a microlight attacking a heavily armed helicopter gunship, but right now he had no better ideas.

He flew on, alone and ill-equipped for the task, but determined. The fear he had felt earlier had completely vanished.

He kept the two enemy helicopters in sight with the FLIR, and ahead of them he could see the smoke, flames, muzzle flashes, and tracer that marked Team Rapier's bloody little war.

As her helicopter powered toward the Yaibo base in the Devil's Footprint, Reiko Oshima finished speaking to the air base and then tried to make some sense of what was going on.

The base commander reported that one other helicopter gunship could be airborne shortly but the remaining two had been totally destroyed, as had four out of the six MiGs. He had been near apoplectic with rage. No one had expected a raid this far from the Tecuno border. They were supposed to be safe.

He blamed it on the Mexican armed forces. Oshima was not so sure. The commander had reported that the damaged helicopters and jets had been riddled by some new type of weapon. Several of the aircraft had looked intact until you got up close; then it could be seen that they had been riddled with thousands of small holes as if fired upon by some giant shotgun.

Special weapons, to Oshima, suggested special counterterrorist forces, and her mind turned immediately to who might be involved. Given the distances to get to this isolated spot, the logistics problems were immense, and that suggested the Americans or the Israelis.

Both had many reasons to want Yaibo out of existence. Delta, in particular, harbored a grudge. She had blown up a civilian plane with 340 passengers on board three years earlier to kill an eight-man Delta team who happened to be on board returning from the Middle East.

U.S. or Israeli special forces suggested air involvement. She turned her mind to how they operated and where they might operate from. This was a raid on the lines of Entebbe. How had that been carried out?

She pulled out a map. Air involvement imposed its own parameters. You could parachute in, but how would you get out? There had been no mention of helicopters, U.S. Special Forces' favorite toys.

Curious. The intensity of firepower suggested more than infantry. What could a special-forces aircraft carry? Tanks? No, they were too heavy for this kind of mission. Heavily armed jeeps? Yes, it would be something like that. She started looking at routes and possible landing fields.

Oshima had survived for as long as she had because she was very quick and very smart and she studied the ways of her enemies.

THE pilot of the helicopter gunship had been trained by Russians who had fought in Afghanistan.

They taught him well, and they had warned him in particular about the threat of handheld SAMs, surface-to-air missiles. The arrival of the U.S.-made Stingers had not eliminated Russian use of helicopters, but it had forced them to fly high and to adopt new tactics. Unfortunately, most of these tactics required the involvement of several gunships, and he was on his own. Oshima's little Bell was not worth shit in terms of firepower and was totally unarmored.

He decided to climb to 5,000 feet and prep the area outside the two camps with his 12.7mm. The camps were obviously the target, and that gave him a clear idea of the general area where the enemy must be. Unfortunately, he had no night-vision equipment, but he was still able to orient himself by the road below and by the burning wrecks of tanks and armored cars.

In his low recce maneuver he thought he had detected some movement in the suspect area below, but he had no idea what he had seen.

He had just been able to make out some vague black shapes, and then they were gone. They were in the right place for hostiles, but it was hard to be sure. Their tracer would have helped, but they did not appear to be using it. Other gun flashes were too brief to really help adequately.

At 5,000 feet he leveled off and opened fire with the 12.7mm and salvos of rockets. The 12.7mm could be seen vanishing into the black smoke, and seconds later there were brief bursts of flame as the rockets plowed into the ground. He wasn't sure he was hitting anything, but at least he would be distracting any enemy force and taking some of the pressure off the camps.

"Get lower! Get lower!" shrieked Oshima over the radio into his ear.

He could just make out her machine. The lunatic was circling around to one side of him but several thousand feet beneath. He couldn't see it, but he knew damn well she would have the side door open and be firing into the maelstrom with her personal weapon.

She would have a Stinger up her arse if she did not watch it—which would be no loss to the world.

He finished his firing pass and circled for another. This time he would drop a couple of bombs. As he circled he noticed a small black shape to one side. It looked like some giant bird.

A vulture? Did vultures fly at night? He wished he had night-vision equipment. Flying the Mi-4 at night without it was really fucking Stone Age and no way to fight a civilized war.

The black shape came closer, and suddenly he realized what he was seeing. He'd never seen one in the flesh, but he'd read about them in aviation magazines.

So this was a microlight. Really it was little more than a cloth wing with a fuselage hanging underneath suspended by wires. He could see the pilot bundled up underneath.

The microlight looked too light and small to carry weapons, but it was not up there in the middle of the night for pleasure. It was some sort of reconnaissance vehicle.

He banked the helicopter and moved into a better firing position.

Fuck! The damn thing was not where he'd left it. He turned and lost height and scanned the sky. The microlight was small, but it should show up against the sky. Starlight had its uses.

He had just found it when the RAW projectile fired by Calvin hit the outer casing of his Shvetsov ASH-82v 1,700-horsepower engine and blew it right out of its mountings and through the fuselage where he sat.

The helicopter broke into flaming fragments and rained down on the remains of the main camp below. Four of the larger fragments were five-hundred-kilo bombs. The entire bowl of the valley erupted in a series of violent explosions, lighting up the surrounding hills with searing white flashes. A moment later the main ammunition store and refueling depot blew up.

Shadow Three and Shadow Five roared across the perimeter road and into the hills on the other side.

"Elegant," said Steve Kent, a broad grin on his face. "Fucking outrageously elegant. The Regiment could not have done any better."

"High praise from SAS," said Fitzduane. He keyed his transmit button. "Shadow One to all. Who got the Mi-4? I didn't see a Stinger, so maybe Calvin's up there, but I can't see shit from here. We're in a world of smoke."

Four negatives came back.

"Head for the RV," said Fitzduane. "Shadow One will follow ASAP. Wait fifteen and head for the pickup."

"Roger that," came four times over the radio, and then they were alone.

"Steve," said Fitzduane, "take us back out of the smoke a couple of hundred meters and cut the engine. According to my vibes, Calvin's somewhere near, and we are not going to see him in this smog."

The Guntrack did not move. Fitzduane turned toward Steve. He was slumped back in his seat, the front of his combat smock drenched in blood. Most of his head was missing.

Fitzduane felt suddenly overwhelmingly tired. He put his hand on the dead man's, which still gripped the steering wheel, and clasped it for a moment. Then he turned to Cochrane, who was searching the surrounding terrain with his GECAL.

"Lee," he said. "I need a hand. Steve's bought it."

Cochrane looked shocked for a moment, then jumped down and helped Fitzduane remove Steve from behind the steering wheel and into a body bag. The body was then strapped to the rear engine compartment. It was a contingency they did not like to dwell upon, but they had come prepared for it and the exercise had been rehearsed. No bodies were to be left behind. The enemy were not to be given even that much satisfaction.

Fitzduane slid into Steve's seat. It was still slippery with blood.

He drove out of the smoke to some dead ground where they could assess the situation with the FLIR and still stay concealed.

In his bones he knew that Calvin was around there somewhere.

It was unthinkable to leave him behind—but there was only minutes to look for him.

A very shaken Reiko Oshima circled the main camp.

It was a scene out of hell lit by dozens of fires, large and small. Destroyed tanks and armored vehicles still poured black smoke, and some were still actively burning. There were sudden flashes and explosions as ammunition was ignited by the extreme heat. Green tracer fired spontaneously.

The neat lines of tents and wooden huts of the mercenary guard battalion had completely vanished, and everywhere she looked there were bodies. She tried to count them, but there were hundreds. Most were still. A few moved in a vain attempt to attract assistance.

She ordered the pilot to circle the observation post on the rim. As they approached there was an enormous explosion and the small Alouette helicopter was caught in the blast and thrown up and to one side. For a few long seconds she thought they were going to crash, and then the pilot regained control.

He looked at her briefly, mutely pleading. Sweat beaded his forehead and he looked quite terrified. She could see that he wanted to ask permission to return to the airfield, but he was even more terrified of her. She grunted. It was just as well. No weak man was going to break when Oshima was in command.

She was beginning to get a rough idea of what had happened. Given the isolated location and the large guard force, the twin valleys of the Devil's Footprint had looked exceptionally secure. However, with the benefit of hindsight it was easy to see that once the attacking force had seized the observation post and the high ground, both valleys were vulnerable.

Still, who could have expected such heavy firepower to be deployed against them and for it to be deployed with such speed and ferocity? The defending force, apart from substantial manpower, had heavy armor and other weapons at its disposal. It should have been able to put up some kind of resistance and to buy time until relief arrived.

No, this was not just a conventional commando raid against them by soldiers on foot. This was some new kind of warfare, faster and more deadly than anything she had either experienced or heard of before.

"Pilot, I want you to land behind the Yaibo barracks," she said, pointing.

The pilot looked at her, ashen. He tried to speak, but his mouth had gone dry. He licked his lips and tried again. "Oshima-*san*," he croaked, "that is insane. You can see for yourself the camp is a death trap."

Oshima drew her 9mm Makarov pistol and placed the tip of the barrel against the pilot's scrotum.

"Listen, you fuckhead," she snarled. "If you don't do what I tell you, I'm going to shoot this decoration off. Whatever it contains, it certainly isn't balls."

The pilot started shaking. But he landed.

Amid the destruction and the carnage, the Yaibo barracks was still miraculously intact. Oshima felt a surge of pride as she approached. Though the perimeter guards had been vanquished, the force she had trained was made of tougher stuff. There might be casualties, but most would have survived, she was sure of it.

Two minutes after she entered the building, over the background sounds of conflagration and the moaning of the wounded and the sharp crack of exploding ammunition, the pilot heard the most terrible bloodcurdling scream. It was piercingly loud and it rose to a crescendo before it fell, and then this dreadful cadence was repeated again and again.

It was the most awful sound he had ever heard in his life.

Five minutes later, Oshima staggered out the door and then collapsed. The pilot went to help her, and as he lifted her to her feet he saw with horror that her clothing was completely saturated in blood.

She clawed at him and he pushed her away in panic, but she clung on to him and would not let go. Her fingernails ripped his face, and he could feel his flesh tearing.

"They're all dead!" she screamed. "Everyone! Everyone! Everyone! Everyone! They're all dead!

"There's nothing but blood! BLOOD! BLOOD! BLOOD! BLOOD!"

The words hammered out of her. Her spittle showered his face. He wanted to retch. At first he had thought Oshima was experiencing some kind of a breakdown, but then he realized that what he was witnessing was nothing of the sort.

It was an uncontrollable rage.

OUTSIDE THE DEVIL'S FOOTPRINT, TECUNO, MEXICO

SEVEN minutes had passed.

Fitzduane was methodically searching the terrain around them with the FLIR, but there was no sign of Calvin. Behind him, Cochrane was doing much the same thing with his night vision-equipment.

Three mercenary soldiers ran out of the black smoke that had now settled over the perimeter road and stopped in shock as, at the last minute, they saw the menacing black wedge shape that was Shadow One.

In their initial panic as the road column was shot up, they had dropped their weapons. Most were *campesinos*—young men, peasants, wanting no more than to go home and be with their families.

They stared at the Guntrack, frozen with fear, uncertain what to do.

Let them live, said Fitzduane's heart. They are the enemy, but they can do us no harm.

Kill them, his mind said. They have seen us and they just might say something that could help the opposition, and *I owe it to my people to see they are given every chance.*

I have no choice.

He fired the pump-action grenade launcher that was kept clipped beside the driver's seat and the three soldiers shot backward as a swarm of hundreds of miniature fléchette darts ripped them asunder.

He felt nauseated.

A laser beam cut through the darkness and settled on him. He could imagine the enemy gunner registering his aim and he knew, at that precise moment, that he was going to die. He thought of Boots and he felt a great sadness that he would never see his young son grow. He thought of . . .

The laser flicked out and then on again, and there was an irregular rhythm to the beam. Then the beam slowly rose to the vertical and cut into the night sky pointing at the stars.

Morse code: "C-A-L-V-I-N."

The exhilaration that follows despair gripped him. He gunned the engine and drove toward the source of the light. He'd been an idiot. The light was the type that only Team Rapier could see through special filters. This was not the enemy.

A skirmishing line of enemy troops showed up ahead of them just beyond the light source. Through his night vision goggles, Fitzduane could see they were armed and purposeful and that this was a different problem to the three he had just killed.

He accelerated and turned slightly to the left so that he would break ground above the light source and have a clear shot at the enemy.

The mercenaries had no night-vision goggles, but they heard the rapidly approaching engine noise and opened fire. Flashes could be seen in the darkness, and there was the zip and crack of rounds passing over and around the Guntrack.

An aiming laser flashed out from Cochrane's GECAL and a moment later the weapon began to fire. Fitzduane halted the Guntrack and emptied the magazine of his grenade launcher. In just five seconds, the area occupied by the mercenary patrol was hit by more than a thousand metal projectiles. Their firing ceased.

The friendly laser flashed on again. Fitzduane zigzagged down the hill toward it and at last Calvin could be seen. He lay there on his back tied to the wing with carabineers, but there was no sign of the fuselage.

Fitzduane leaped out while Ross kept watch, cut the aviator free, then bundled him into the front gunner's seat, gave him a headset, and plugged him into the intercom.

The entire exercise took no more than forty-five seconds. Calvin was bruised and had a broken ankle and was in some pain, but otherwise he seemed in reasonable condition. Fitzduane felt an overwhelming sense of relief. He contemplated giving the aviator morphine but decided against it.

The grim fact was that someone might need it more urgently later. The shooting was not necessarily over. They had to exfiltrate successfully, and that, in special-forces operations such as this, was always the hardest part. The element of surprise was gone and now they were the hunted.

He talked to Calvin as he drove to distract him from the pain. "You went up with an engine, Calvin," he said as he sped through the night toward the RV point, "but came down without one. What gives?"

Calvin forced a laugh.

"After I got the helicopter gunship with the RAW, I got chased by a much smaller machine. It wasn't armed as such, but someone inside it had a weapon and went after me as if it was personal.

"Well, I maneuvered every which way and my whole machine started coming apart. The struts had already been damaged over the airfield and jury-rigged, and these kind of gymnastics were just too much. The fuselage and engine decided to go their own way, and I had no parachute. And I was a couple of thousand feet up. In addition, AK-47 rounds were pinging off the engine. It was a little hairy."

Fitzduane could imagine the reality behind the dry account. "So what did you do, Calvin?" he said. "Wake up?"

"I went back in aviation history a bit," said Calvin through clenched teeth as the Guntrack hit a rough patch. "The chopper was shooting at the fuselage for the obvious reason that that is where the pilot sits."

"So?" said Fitzduane encouragingly.

"Flex flying all started with the wing alone," said Calvin. "Suspending a fuselage for the pilot to sit in and to hold an engine came much later. Well, that being the case, the solution was obvious."

"Not to me, it isn't," said Fitzduane. Wearing PNV goggles, his world endless shades of green, he was driving over the appalling terrain as fast as the terrain would allow, and his concentration—to put it mildly—was not entirely on Calvin's story.

"I clipped my harness to the wing and then cut free the fuselage and engine," said Calvin. "The helicopter followed the fuselage down and blew it apart as it fell, and I just flew the wing down like a hang glider. It worked fine. I didn't need a parachute. I don't know why I was worried."

Fitzduane nearly choked with laughter and reaction.

"Fucking A!" said Cochrane.

Fitzduane recovered and then started to laugh again, and the Guntrack slithered and bucked and jumped and raced across the shale and gravel toward the RV, and up in the sky their salvation flew toward them.

Unfortunately, it was short one critical aircraft.

CHAPTER TWENTY-TWO

REIKO OSHIMA STOOD in the shower for three minutes and washed General Luis Barragan's blood off her body. It disgusted her. It was a symbol of their failure.

Her outburst had left her drained and tired, but the water was soothing and she could feel her resolution returning.

Her strength of will was one of her strongest assets, and now she focused on what should be done immediately. Recriminations would have to wait. There was a score to settle now, and she was fairly sure she knew how.

She hastily toweled her long black hair to an acceptably damp state and put it up in a bun. Then she dressed in fresh desert camouflage fatigues tucked into combat boots and donned full combat webbing. Finally she tied in place the ritual *hachimaki*—the headband—worn by Yaibo and strapped a *katana* to her back.

She paused as she finished and looked in the mirror and was pleased with what she saw. She had regained her poise and her command quality. She was once again a force to be respected and feared. The brief time lost taking the shower and dressing had been worth it.

She looked at her watch. It read 0209. It seemed an age but was actually only just over an hour since Luis had bled to death on top of her. She shuddered.

There was a banging on the door. "Oshima-*san*," said a panting voice. "Please come to the operations room immediately. Governor Quintana is calling and wants a full situation report."

There was bedlam in the operations room as she walked in. A dozen different people were talking at the top of their voices and gesticulating wildly, and there seemed to be no one person capable of restoring order.

She went through the large operations room to the adjoining radio room, but left the door open. The radio operator looked distinctly relieved as she arrived, and handed her a headset. She put on the headset and evicted the operator from the room with a single gesture, and this time closed the door.

"Governor," she said respectfully. "This is Oshima-*san*."

"Oshima," said Quintana, the strain evident in his voice, "what is happening? I hear we have been attacked, but I have received a dozen different contradictory reports."

Oshima took a deep breath.

"Out with it, woman," said Quintana. "I need to know."

Reiko Oshima gave him a situation report, appalled as she spoke at the sheer scale of the destruction. It had seemed bad enough at the time. In its totality, it was very much worse. But in one fundamental way, they had been exceptionally lucky.

The supergun was unscathed. True, one installation holding explosive and experimental chemical warheads had been completely destroyed, but the charge placed in the all-important bunker that controlled the hydrogen feed had, by some miracle, failed to go off. Evidently, the attackers had been disturbed. Oshima speculated that it must have been the arrival of the armored column from the south. And there was also the fact that the gun itself was virtually indestructible.

Quintana was normally a hard man to read, especially over the radio, but this time his relief was evident. There were plenty more terrorists, hostages, tanks, and mercenary soldiers in the world, but his future was tied to the supergun. If it had been destroyed, his future would have been painful and short. He had made too many enemies over the decades.

Oshima decided now was the time to make her move. She was the bringer of good news, and with a bit of luck, now she could reap her reward.

"Governor Quintana," she said. "The attack was ground based, and I think I know where they are going. Give me the forces I require and I'll destroy them for you."

"Explain," said Quintana. This was the first positive suggestion anyone had made to him since the attack. He considered the angles. Oshima's theory made some sense.

If armed jeeps were being used, they could be trying to escape by land to the border, but an air pickup was an option. And in that case, a deserted airstrip built by the oil people at Arkono was a reasonable possibility. Certainly, it was worth a shot, and putting Oshima in charge was justified by the special circumstances. He smiled to himself. Certainly, she had the balls for the job.

Three minutes later, a task force of twenty armed vehicles that was camped to the northwest of Arkono was roused and dispatched to block the valley that led to the airstrip, and Oshima was headed there by helicopter to take personal charge.

Quintana terminated the radio conference severely shaken but in a better mood.

The supergun was safe; and as for Oshima, if she was successful he would reap the credit, and if she failed she would make an excellent scapegoat.

"Say again, Eagle Leader," said Fitzduane.

He had arrived at the RV point and immediately called up the C130 flight that was coming to pick them up. No air cavalry and there would need to be a distinct reappraisal. It was one hell of a long way to home.

"Eagle flight on course on schedule for PUP," replied Kilmara, "but we have no Dragon. I repeat, we have no Dragon. ETA as original."

"Affirmative that there is no Dragon," said Fitzduane. "Eagle's welcome nonetheless. We've got big hearts and we're homesick. Over and out."

" 'Luck to you, Team Rapier," said Kilmara. "See you soon. Over and out."

Fitzduane peeled off the headset. The five camouflaged Guntracks were laagered in a rough semicircle, weapons pointing outward. It appeared all vehicles had made it so far. Only the microlight had been destroyed. There was now only twenty-five kliks to go, but it would be the most dangerous time, and the news he had just received was seriously disturbing.

He had looked at a great number of escape plans, from the obvious to the most exotic. All of the conventional options meant long land journeys and imposed serious logistical difficulties. Would they be detected given the extra time on the ground? Would the vehicles stand up? Could they carry enough fuel? Would there be enough water?

In the end he had opted for a simple solution—to be picked up by air the very same night as the raid. In essence, pull out before the opposition had time to rally themselves.

The downside was that an air pickup imposed certain obvious practical limitations. The aircraft needed a place to land, and in such grim terrain there were only so many options.

Second, a pickup was an attention-getter. Guntracks were small, quiet, and unobtrusive. Compared to them, C130 Combat Talons were big noisy beasts and their landing in the middle of nowhere would certainly attract attention if there was anyone around.

Fitzduane had studied satellite photographs for weeks prior to setting forth on the operation and there had never been any sign of activity either on, or adjacent to, the abandoned airstrip. This was reassuring, but he had been around long enough to know that the world is unpredictable and that fate likes its little games.

Accordingly, as a hedge against the downside, he had arranged for a U.S. Special Forces C130 Spectre gunship to cover the final withdrawal and deal with any interference. The Spectre combined heavy firepower with the most sophisticated night-vision targeting equipment, so it should have evened things up a little.

But unfortunately the gunship was not going to be there.

He would find out why afterward—mechanical failure or whatever—but right now it did not matter. The Spectre was code-named Dragon and the message had been clear.

There would be no Dragon covering their withdrawal. No problem if the coast was clear. Serious rat shit if it was not.

He called a final briefing. One man per gunship remained on sentry duty peering through night-vision equipment into the darkness. The rest gathered around.

"Casualty report?" he said. "I'll get the ball rolling. Shadow One has lost Steve. The microlight is out of the game and Calvin has a broken ankle."

Each Guntrack reported in turn. There were no other fatalities, but Chuck Freeman in Shadow Three had a piece of shrapnel in his shoulder and Peter Hayden had been seriously injured when Shadow Four had received a near miss from a T55 tank round. His Guntrack was also in bad shape. The track had been damaged and would last only a few kilometers at best.

"People," said Fitzduane, "if I can borrow some of Al's language—you done good."

There were smiles from the group, but little was said. They were all incredibly tired from the fear, tension, and exhilaration of the assault and the exfiltration, and they were under no illusions as to what might lie ahead. The unexpected guard convoy on the perimeter road from the south had been one major surprise, and there would be others. They conserved their energies and paid close attention. Fitzduane knew what he was doing.

"We're going to strip and abandon Shadow Four here," he said, "and double up where necessary. All rear pallets will be left. Ammunition and supplies will be redistributed. Fuel tanks will be topped up. The emphasis will be on speed and maneuverability. We could have a clear run, but we won't know until we are in close. We have lost our aerial recon and we are not going to have a Spectre gunship up top. So it's up to us. We should be airborne in well under an hour, but we've got to keep moving."

There was a brief silence. Fitzduane looked at each person in the dim red glow of the map light. He could not really see expressions, but full body language was sufficient. The team was in good shape, all things considered. Certainly, there was evidence of fatigue and some doubts and uncertainties, but overall he felt fortunate. These were good people.

"One extra thing," he said. "We're down to four Guntracks and we're going to need a tail-end Charlie. If everything goes sweet, they'll be the last people on board. If the shit hits the fan, Charlie stays behind or no one will get away." He pointed at the map. "I don't need to tell you why."

There was no argument. They had all participated in the discussions about the abandoned airstrip and they all knew the rationale and the problems. The negative side of the pickup point was that access to it from the north meant going through a two-mile-long valley that they had christened the Funnel; and there was no time to go around it.

Further, if the enemy got on the hills of the Funnel no aircraft was going to make it away. That meant, if opposition surfaced, holding the high ground until the two rescuing aircraft were safely airborne. That job could have been carried out by the Spectre, but now there was no alternative.

Fitzduane was right. But it was a crock. The Guntrack doing tail-end Charlie was not going to have much of a future.

"I will do Charlie," said Fitzduane. "Just so you know, that's not negotiable—but I'll need two extra crew and I'm moving to a track with a Dilger."

"I will be one," said a firm voice, "and just so you know, that's not negotiable either."

There was laughter. Fitzduane smiled and held out his hand to Lee Cochrane. "Lee, you're one persistent son of a bitch," he said.

There was a low murmur of voices and hand gestures as everyone else tried to volunteer and yet keep their voices way down. Sound traveled at night in the desert.

"SAS have more than paid their dues," said Fitzduane, referring to the injured Peter Hayden and the dead Steve Kent from that unit, "and I represent the Irish Rangers."

"Which leaves Delta," said the Delta contingent, including Calvin, virtually in unison.

"And since I was in at the beginning," said Al Lonsdale, "it just seems appropriate."

Fitzduane nodded. "Now let's do it, people. We go in ten minutes."

The team dispersed and went to complete the final preparations. Fitzduane walked across to Shadow Three, where Kathleen lay sedated and wrapped in a sleeping bag against the night cold. He put his arms around her and held her close. Then he kissed her and hugged her again.

"Half from me and half from Boots," he said. "We missed you, little love. But now you're back and you're safe."

"I knew you'd come, Hugo," said Kathleen sleepily. "*I knew you'd come*—and you have. I love you, Hugo. I never stopped thinking about you. And it made it all right, you know. Truly. It was terrible, but it was all right. I was strong. I was . . ."

Fitzduane tried to smile. It was difficult, because he was crying. *All right!* Jesus Christ! Kathleen looked terrible and he did not want to think what she had been through. *The baby?* It would be too much to hope for. He did not ask.

He hugged her again and held her. "I love you, Kathleen," he said over and over again. She was already asleep; the drugs had won out.

Chifune was guarding Shadow Three. He took her hand briefly between his, and she smiled.

"All the way," she said. And there were tears in her eyes.

"Always," said Fitzduane. "Always . . ."

They looked at each other. There was no need to speak. They had never been closer.

"Let's go," said Fitzduane.

The convoy of four Guntracks moved out. Their next destination was the pickup point—and airborne to home.

TECUNO, MEXICO

GOVERNOR Diego Quintana's mercenaries were mainly Mexican but included soldiers from many nations.

Major Khalifa Sherrif's country of birth was Libya. Major Sherrif was not without military talent, but his map-reading skills were minimal. He could get lost crossing the street, which was why currently he was within striking distance of the Arkono airstrip instead of a hundred kilometers to the west as his original orders dictated.

Normally he could rely on his adjutant to keep him more or less on course, but a shotgun blast from one recalcitrant peasant had put paid to that convenient solution and had also fucked up Major Sherrif's one and only map of this dreadful area.

He had been fast asleep when the new orders came in, and he did not take kindly to being roused so abruptly. His mood took a sharp turn for the worse when he heard that he was to prepare for action and that he was to hand over command to the Japanese woman called Reiko Oshima.

THAT WOMAN! It was unbelievable. Women had their place in his particular world, but so did camels and goats, and he could not have been more upset if one of those species had been nominated.

He frothed and he cursed and he scratched his unshaven chin, and he itched everywhere from the sand and dust and crawly things he did not even want to think about, and he only calmed down slightly when his ever-reliable sergeant brought him hot sweet tea.

A Mi-4 Hound helicopter beat its way through the darkness and landed to the side of the armored column in a haze of dust. He sipped his tea again as he waited for this Amazon to emerge and found that he was now sipping grit.

Two minutes later, he found that his command tank and his bloodstained map had been commandeered and he had been packed into the back of an APC like a common private.

With Reiko Oshima in the lead tank, the column headed at full speed for the Funnel, the narrowing valley that led to the airstrip. The Hound had already taken off again to scout the terrain.

The column was able to make excellent time. All vehicles and the helicopter were equipped with active infrared searchlights that projected a beam that was invisible to the naked eye but showed up as illumination to anyone wearing the right goggles. It was an effective enough technique unless your opponent had infrared-detection capability, in which case it was like driving along with full headlights on. You could see where you were going, but then everyone could see you—and from a considerable distance away.

Twenty minutes later, when the column was within just a few kilometers of the Funnel, a radio message came in from the helicopter that a cloud of dust heading at high speed toward the old airstrip had been sighted.

Reiko Oshima felt a surge of optimism and passed the order to prepare for action to her new command. The enemy, whoever they were, had every reason to believe that, in the middle of this vast empty space, no one would ever think of one long-abandoned airstrip among dozens built by the oilmen more than a decade ago.

Unfortunately for them, Reiko Oshima had scouted Arkono airstrip as a possible base for Yaibo only a year back and she knew the strip and the surrounding terrain intimately. She was also, she considered, getting to know her enemy.

The Arkono strip was not an obvious choice, but it would do—which made it a strong possibility. Other units were fanning out to cover other locations.

THE black silhouette of the Funnel showed up in the distance, and Fitzduane thought of Calvin and how nice it would be to be able to check the valley and its environs from the air before entering their confines.

For all they knew, the valley now contained hostiles waiting to shoot them up. It was a near-perfect choke point. Nearly a kilometer wide on the way in, it narrowed to less than a hundred meters as it approached the airstrip. The Funnel was well named.

He banished wishful thinking and focused entirely on the task at hand. He had a feeling he was missing some obvious move or precaution. He checked his watch and ran through the plan of the final stages of the exfiltration and the various contingencies and options. There was something there, he was sure of it, but what?

He switched to the Team Rapier radio net and pressed the transmit button. There was now less than twenty minutes to go before the pickup time, and they had reached the stage when speed was more important than running silent. "Rapier Team, this is Shadow One. Deactivate super traps and increase to sixty."

The diamond-shaped fighting group of four Guntracks surged ahead as the sound-suppression units were deactivated. The increased speed would be hell for the wounded, but the alternatives would be a great deal worse.

There was a sudden flash from the sky as the Mi-4 Hound turned on its infrared searchlight and swooped to try to see what this mysterious enemy consisted of. Reports had suggested armed jeeps, but no one seemed quite sure, and the armored column desperately needed more intelligence.

"Bomburst!" said Fitzduane, and instantly the four vehicles spread in four directions. "Shadow One will take it."

Heavy machine-gun fire arched up at the helicopter from three Guntracks while Shadow One halted and Al Lonsdale aimed a Starburst surface-to-air missile.

Green tracer and rocket fire from the helicopter plowed into the ground around the fleeing Guntracks, but the small black vehicles were extremely hard to hit. They were very fast and changed direction constantly, and clouds of smoke and dust confused the issue.

The helicopter's infrared searchlight showed up in Lonsdale's night-vision goggles like an arrow pointing toward a target.

Seconds later the searchlight vanished as machine-gun fire from the ground blew it apart, but he could still see the big machine through the Starburst's six-power sights.

Shoulder-launched surface-to-air missiles were not foolproof, and the pilot knew that the Stinger, to give the example he was most familiar with, could be outmaneuvered under some circumstances and that its range was limited. However, in this case the Mi-4 Hound's pilot was more scared of the known threat of Reiko Oshima than of the unknown; and he had been ordered to find out what they were up against or not come back. And he was also up against a missile that did not need a heat source to make a hit. The Starburst was optically guided by a low-power laser beam.

He did his duty. He had just finished describing one of the strange black tracked vehicles that he had caught in his infrared searchlight for a brief moment when the missile's proximity fuse ignited near the fuselage and slammed a shower of tungsten cubes into the fuel tank and rotor blades.

A fireball blossomed in the sky.

That bloody woman! the pilot thought before his world exploded.

"RE-FORM," said Fitzduane urgently. "Loose Deuce. Move! Move! Move!"

The four Guntracks of Team Rapier re-formed in two teams of two, with one Guntrack on the right set back to its partner. It was a formation that would have been familiar to fighter pilots. The vehicle in front covered threats to the front. The Guntrack set back covered threats to the rear.

They had lost time in the encounter with the helicopter. They had now increased speed to a hundred kilometers an hour. Across the rough shale and rock of the ground, this was a grueling speed even with air suspension. Weapons accuracy was affected. It was difficult—almost impossible—to use some of the advanced vision equipment because of the vibration. The engine noise had risen to a crescendo, and regularly the vehicles left the ground and hurtled through the air as they hit an undulation or a fissure.

For the wounded, it was agony. Fitzduane knew this and remembered what it had been like for him and the pain and the sense of helplessness, and he hated what he was doing.

Through his night-vision goggles, he could see a glow ahead of him but to the left. His brain tired, he thought at first it might be the dawn and he was surprised because it seemed too early, and then he realized what he was seeing.

The glow was moving, and it must be coming from a column of vehicles heading for the entrance to the funnel.

They were in a race, and the enemy column, although almost certainly slower, was sufficiently ahead of them for it to get there first.

He felt sick and then, for a brief moment, blindly angry, and then there were things to do and very little time for emotion.

"Shadow One to Eagle Leader," he said.

"Come in, Shadow One," said Kilmara. The sound quality was good. They were close.

Fitzduane could almost see the two Hercules C130 Combat Talons in their matte-black camouflage hurtling at contour-following height over the harsh terrain. The pilot and copilot and navigator would be wearing night-vision goggles and faces would be tired and strained from the long flight. There would be the steady throb and whine of turboprops. There would be the jolts and shocks that came from flying so close to the ground you were virtually in ground effect.

"Eagle Flight, what is your firepower status?" said Fitzduane.

"Both aircraft configured for Guntrack evacuation, so weapons load minimized," said Kilmara.

Fitzduane felt a sinking feeling and then realized that "minimized" was a relative term in special-forces aviation. These people felt nervous if they did not have some serious firepower up their sleeve.

"Both aircraft have two GECAL fifties for ground suppression and other toys for the air," continued Kilmara, "but they do not have gunship status and are tasked for evac. I do not want to risk the evac, but state your thinking."

"We will only be evacuating three—I repeat THREE—Guntracks," said Fitzduane. "Shadow One will be staying on ground as tail-end Charlie. Accordingly, only one aircraft will need to land. Suggest second EAGLE adopt a ground suppression role. We have heavy company from the east."

"Wait one, Shadow One," said Kilmara. He switched to the second Combat Talon and talked to the Bear. In less than a minute he was back to Fitzduane.

"Eagle Leader will land to evac," Kilmara said, "and Eagle Friend will carry out ground suppression. He can handle up to armored personnel carriers, but tanks could be a problem. Eagle Friend awaits your instructions. Please advise how crew of Shadow One plans to evac. I presume Skyhook."

"Affirmative on Skyhook," said Fitzduane. "But we will need maneuvering space. There are people down here who do not have our best interests at heart."

"Understood, Shadow One," said Eagle Friend. "We await your call." It was the Bear's voice.

Fitzduane looked at the approaching glow. He could now see a shitload of tanks and APCs. Worryingly, they were ignoring Team Rapier's convoy of Guntracks and were still heading hell-for-leather toward the Funnel. Someone too damn smart was in command.

Once the valley was blocked, the hostiles could pick off the Guntracks at their leisure.

REIKO Oshima felt excited as she rarely had before as her armored column thundered toward the Funnel.

There was the roar of the tank engine and the smell of oil and the wind against her face and the exhilaration of speed, and she felt, for the first time since this fracas had started, that she was going to end up on the winning side.

The helicopter pilot had delivered. She now knew that she was dealing with some kind of high-speed tracked vehicle and that there were four in the dust clouds off to the right.

They were obviously the advance guard. Given the scale of the damage that had been inflicted so far, it was clear that a larger force was involved, and she estimated that there were probably a further twenty or so following behind. Allowing four people to a vehicle crew—she thought commander, gunner, loader and driver per tank—that suggested an overall enemy force of about a hundred. That seemed to make sense. It also suggested that they would leave their vehicles behind when they evacuated or else that deserted strip at Arkono was going to be a busy little place for a while.

The important thing was that she had called it right. She had guessed the enemy's intentions and now she was beating this hostile force to the punch. The enemy tracks were faster, that was sure, but her force was ahead and was going to get there first.

And then there would be a killing ground. Retribution.

FITZDUANE knew that this would be the last time that Team Rapier would be together, and for a brief moment he felt unaccountably sad and tired but also immensely proud.

There were few things more satisfying than to command a combat unit at its peak, and the people of Team Rapier had been the best, the very best. And now it was almost over, this courageous, audacious adventure, and he felt regret.

The moment passed. The immediate pressed on him.

"Shadow One to all," he said on the unit net, "Shadow Three will remain with me and fight the hostile column to a halt. Shadows Two and Five will head on through the Funnel and will evac. Shadow Three will join if possible.

"Move! Move! Move!"

Cochrane brought Shadow One to a halt and lowered the rear air springs, while Al Lonsdale loaded a six-round clip into the Dilger and aligned the laser sight. After the noise and buffeting of the high-speed advance, to be still and silent on this vast undulating space seemed strange.

Off to the right, Shadow Three advanced toward the column, firing on the move with its .50 GECAL. Its job was to draw fire while Fitzduane's vehicle killed tanks. Only the Dilger could do that with certainty at this range.

The two other Guntracks sped into the distance. Both vehicles were overloaded and carrying wounded and really in no condition to fight unless there was no other option. Shadow Two carried Chifune, Geronimo Grady, and Dana Felton as crew, together with the wounded Chuck Freeman and the drugged Kathleen and Steve Kent's body. Shadow Five carried Oga, Brick Stephens, and Ross Gallini, with Ernesto Robles and Calvin injured.

Al Lonsdale's night-vision equipment pierced the darkness and aligned the Dilger on the lead tank.

He fired.

A tongue of flame jetted from the muzzle and the whole Guntrack rocked with the recoil.

Two seconds later he fired again, and then kept on firing until he had exhausted a second clip. *The* second clip.

Twelve rounds. The Dilger was now out of ammunition.

"Move! Move! Move!" said Fitzduane, and Cochrane started raising the air springs and roared away. The springs completed their adjustment on the move.

Two seconds after they had left their firing location, tank shells plowed into the evacuated space, and rock and shale fountained into the air.

THERE was a crack and Oshima's tank, roaring forward at full speed, suddenly lurched to the left, lost forward momentum, and started rotating on its own axis.

The driver's hatch opened and he leaned over the right side of the tank, then looked up at Reiko Oshima. "We've been hit. The track's gone and we're a sitting target. We'd better get out."

Oshima drew her pistol and shot him in the head, then pointed the gun at the gunner. "Does the gun still work?"

He nodded.

"Well, then stay here and fight the tank or you'll join that coward."

The loader slammed in an HE round and the gunner rotated the turret and fired. Oshima could see the flash of the impact explosion in the distance.

The infrared searchlight shattered as machine-gun rounds hit it. A further burst spanged off the armor.

Oshima hauled herself out of the turret and looked for a replacement tank. She was appalled at what she saw. The powerful column of nineteen armored vehicles that had followed her was now strewn with flaming and exploding vehicles, and as she watched, there was a row of small explosions in the ground as if a machine gun was being hosed onto target and then an armored personnel carrier in the direct line of fire blew up.

Burning figures ran into the darkness and collapsed, and the air was rent with screams.

A hundred meters away, a T55 fired its main gun and then reversed. She ran after it, waving.

An armored personnel carrier was spraying the darkness with its heavy machine gun. The gunner could see nothing because his infrared searchlight had been shot out, but he fired steadily until the ammunition box ran out. Incoming machine-gun fire caught him as he was attempting a barrel change and blew out his throat.

A black shape shot out of the darkness and there was an enormous explosion from the armored carrier, and a huge hole appeared in its side as if it had been hit by an artillery shell.

Two tanks maneuvering in opposite directions collided, then the commander's hatches opened and the two commanders started swearing at each other.

An explosive grenade hit one commander and blew his torso into pieces, showering the second man with blood and body parts. He dropped back into his cupola, banged the hatch shut, and reversed rapidly.

The air seemed to be full of flying metal. Oshima had never seen anything like it. This was not conventional machine-gun and cannon fire but some other, much more lethal, system.

Now she was beginning to understand how her base, with all its armor and security, had been overcome so quickly.

A tank roared past her, tracks churning, and she fell back terrified. The stars were fading. It would be dawn soon.

She heard the heavy throb of an armored personnel carrier and looked up. The vehicle stopped and the commander looked down.

Somehow he looked familiar. A red map light illuminated his face from below. That was ironic. The face was that of Major Khalifa Sherrif, the "hero" who could not navigate. Life, she thought, was a joke; a sick joke. It was a pity she had not understood this sooner.

The Major looked away and shouted a command.

The Major's armored personnel carrier accelerated, leaving Oshima alone in the desert.

THE evacuating Guntracks roared through the Funnel and on to the airstrip.

Behind them there was the sound and fury of the firefight, and each person's thoughts were with the rear guard as they battled.

Ten minutes later, Shadow Three disengaged on Fitzduane's instructions and joined the two other Guntracks. Less than a minute later, alerted by radio, Kilmara's C130 Combat Talon swooped in and taxied to a halt, the ramp already almost down.

Immediately, the three Guntracks drove on board and the Combat Talon, with the ramp still open, took off and headed out of Tecuno-controlled airspace at contour-following height, electronic-warfare systems fully operational. Tecuno wavebands were a mass of activity, and they could hear jet fighters being vectored into the search area. Timing was critical. They would have more than eighty minutes' exposure before the fighter threat would be over.

Kilmara hated the abrupt departure with Fitzduane and the crew of Shadow One still on the ground, but every second spent in the area increased the chance of detection and his first priority was the safety of the aircraft and crew and passengers.

It was now up to the guts and ingenuity of Fitzduane and his remaining team on the ground, the flying skills of Eagle Friend, and a quite extraordinary device known as Skyhook or the Fulton Rescue System.

And there were also the moves of the enemy to consider.

Shadow One had been located, and the noose would be tightening by the second.

FITZDUANE felt dazed and disoriented, and he could not see and he felt rising panic.

He fought for control. Where was he? What had happened? He put his hand to his face. It felt wet and sticky. Shit! He was bleeding from a gash in his forehead. He staggered to his feet and splashed some water from his belt water-bottle on his face and washed the blood from his eyes.

He could see! The relief was intense. He could feel the rush of fear receding and self-confidence reestablishing itself.

Shadow One lay on its side about twenty yards away. One track was missing and there was a huge hole in the rear engine compartment through which diesel was leaking. They had been hit but they had been lucky. Or had they? It was then that he noticed Lee Cochrane. He was bent over Al Lonsdale, who lay motionless on the ground.

Fitzduane began to remember what had happened. They had chewed up the advancing armored column with some success thanks to Dilger's Baby, night-vision equipment, and some seriously aggressive tactics. Then they had disengaged. Shadow Three had headed on to the airstrip and Shadow One had made it to the Funnel.

He recalled the Guntrack roaring down the Funnel to where it narrowed, and then suddenly everything had gone blank.

Ahead of him, he suddenly saw a Combat Talon climb into the night sky and then recede into the distance.

The sight was like a physical blow, and again there was that feeling of fear.

He went over to Cochrane. "How is he?" he said, looking at Lonsdale.

"Concussed, I think," said Cochrane. "I can't find any external wound." He held up something. "Here are your NVGs. They got ripped off when you screwed up your landing, Hugo."

Fitzduane started to raise his eyebrows in surprise, but they seemed to be stuck in place. Cochrane was in his element. This was a man who had found himself.

The goggles still worked. Fitzduane started to feel generally more optimistic. Half the Tecuno army might be on their tail, but at least he could find his way around and, truth to tell, their thermal viewers and passive night vision had given them an incredible edge over the opposition, so it was nice to hang on to some of the equipment. There was still some serious work to do.

He looked down the valley. In the distance, roughly halfway down the valley, he could see vehicles burning. Cochrane saw his look and grinned.

"The hostiles chased us into the Funnel," said Cochrane, "but I had a go with the .50 Barrett after we got hit. It seems ridiculous that a rifle can take out an armored vehicle like a BMP-1, but there is the proof. An average of three rounds each at nearly a kilometer, and up they went. Thin armor, vulnerable fuel tanks, and armor-piercing incendiary make a lethal combination. Anyway, they pulled back and now seem to be regrouping. I guess they figure time is on their side. They put up some flares a few minutes ago, so they know our track is out. And where are we going on foot? There is nothing but nothing in every direction."

Fitzduane decided to ignore that last rather disconcerting remark and focus on the shooting. "Just so you know, Lee," he said. "Running a private war—just because Al and I were unconscious—is greedy."

Cochrane laughed out loud.

"Back to business," said Fitzduane. "Any contact with Eagle Friend?"

"Affirmative," said Cochrane.

He tapped the personal radio every member of the team carried for emergencies. It was low power and strictly line of sight, but it combined voice capability with a locator beam. "He's doing a run in any minute. He's contour flying to avoid SAMs, so voice contact is intermittent."

The Combat Talon was using the surrounding mountain range to shield it from SAMs—surface-to-air missiles—as it approached. The Talon had some useful offensive firepower, but its main defense lay in being extraordinarily hard to detect. Its electronic warfare black boxes made it effectively invisible to most radar. Nonetheless, line-of-sight triple-A—antiaircraft artillery—and SAMs could be a serious threat when it could be seen with the naked eye, so Talon pilots worked hard to remain invisible. In this context, a few mountains between them and hostiles were highly approved of.

Fitzduane unclipped an Ultimax from its mount and fitted a fresh hundred-round magazine. A pump-action grenade launcher went over his shoulder and more ammunition went into a rucksack. Then he joined Adachi in carrying Al Lonsdale into a natural rock emplacement in the foothills.

It was a far-from-perfect location because there was no overhead cover, but there was nothing better immediately around and their plans depended on their moving up rather than out in the next few minutes. That meant they needed access to the sky.

Parachute flares exploded in the sky and the valley was lit up with white light. Backed up by field glasses, it was an old-fashioned solution for dealing with the visibility problem but effective enough nonetheless.

The wrecked Guntrack could clearly be seen. Fitzduane doubted that the Tecuno mercenaries could see them crouched down behind the rocks in camouflage with blackened faces, but common sense dictated their rough location.

There was a moaning sound and a salvo of mortar shells bracketed the wrecked vehicle, and blast after blast hurled metal splinters into the surrounding rocks. Half a dozen heavy machine guns joined in.

The parachute flares died out but the barrage continued, and Fitzduane knew it would only be a matter of time. They seemed to be up against some serious opposition, and the way the assault was being conducted suggested that the hostiles had recovered from their confusion.

He prayed that someone up high would come to their assistance very soon, or they would be up there themselves checking out their new wings.

It was a prospect Fitzduane was willing to postpone. He decided he would try the direct approach.

"Eagle Friend," he said quietly and deliberately into his radio, "we have heavy incoming here, so hear me well. This is no time for subtlety. Knock off your coffee break and be kind enough to seriously fuck the bad guys. Do you copy?"

"Loud and clear, Hugo," said the Bear, and there was a roar of engines as the Combat Talon popped up and tracked the valley, its two six-barrel .50-caliber GECALs blazing.

Eight thousand rounds a minute—armor-piercing, high explosive, and tracer—into the broad end of the valley occupied by the mercenary task force.

Devastation. Slaughter. A scale of destruction it was hard to comprehend.

Explosion after explosion rent the air as armored vehicles blew up. The incoming mortar and APC rounds ceased.

Fitzduane and Cochrane peered between two rocks at the holocaust.

"Unbelievable," said Fitzduane in an awed voice.

A parachute opened above them, and seconds later a bulky package hit the ground. Fitzduane grinned at Cochrane. "It's been easy up to now," he said.

MAJOR Khalifa Sherrif might have been a truly terrible map reader, but militarily he was moderately competent.

Under fire, he normally had a reasonable idea of what to do if it was only how to keep his own valuable body out of harm's way. Nonetheless, fighting Indian peasants in Tecuno armed with only shotguns, the odd AK-47 assault rifle, and RPG-7 rocket launchers had not prepared him for this kind of combat.

Rifles that could take out armored personnel carriers at well over a kilometer and aircraft guns that could put a round in every square metro of land in a valley-wide swath were new to him—and quite terrifying.

He thought about the situation. Another column had shown up from the south and he had deployed them around the airstrip. Part of the enemy force had already left—he had seen the Combat Talon taking off in the distance—but at least the remainder were now surrounded somewhere in the narrow end of the funnel and the airstrip had been rendered unusable.

The enemy, whoever they were, but certainly commandos of some kind, were trapped. They had no way out. And by morning the forces around them would be overwhelming. Infantry and armor was converging on the Funnel from every direction.

It was going to work out. The post of military aide to Governor Quintana that he had been after would be his. The minor detail that his armored column had been shot to pieces by the enemy would be glossed over, and anyway there was a useful technique called creative accounting. No one was really going to come out here to the battlefield to take a look.

He switched to consideration of immediate tactics. Sending in armor was for the birds. The burning wrecks of T55s and armored fighting vehicles dotting the valley floor were blunt proof of that.

No, the best tactic overall was to wait the enemy out and let the sun do its work tomorrow. There was no water in the Funnel, so it would only be a matter of time.

He considered this option. It certainly made most sense militarily. Still, the politics of the situation also had to be factored in. Surrounding—without doing anything more—did not have a heroic ring, and soldiers were supposed to fight.

He had one platoon of hard cases he used for chasing Indians in the hills. A small group used to this kind of terrain might just do the trick where armor had failed.

He sent them in and watched them as they disappeared into the darkness. In his report, he would lead them, of course. Fortunately, in real life he had more sense and whistled up his sergeant for a cup of tea.

THE Bear watched the loadmaster get his end of the Fulton Rescue System ready and tried to get his mind around what was about to happen.

It had been explained to him in some detail during the long flight in, but frankly it was hard to grasp.

It was not that it was complicated. It was more that it was quite loopy. It also was unnatural, decidedly only for the insane, and certainly the most terrifying way of boarding an aircraft that he had ever heard of. Bar none. In his considered opinion, it belonged only in cartoons. He could imagine Bugs Bunny having a high old time with it and Woody Woodpecker chortling with glee. But it was decidedly not for humans.

He thought about the procedure again and shuddered. It made throwing yourself out of an aircraft door with a backpack full of nylon tied together with string appear positively safe.

But if they were to get Fitzduane and his people out of terminal trouble, it was the only way.

The intercom crackled. "We're going in," said the pilot.

The GECAL crews readied their weapons.

And then the firing started.

FITZDUANE and Cochrane put on the still-unconscious Lonsdale's suit and then scrambled into their own.

A webbing harness was built into each suit, and that in turn was attached to a line. The line looked disturbingly fragile. It looked scarcely strong enough to support one person, let alone three.

The bulkiest element of the package was a cylinder of helium. Fitzduane connected the helium as indicated and turned on the valve, and with surprising speed an airship-shaped balloon begin to appear. It was bigger than he had expected and he wondered why, then realized that it had the weight of five hundred feet of line to support.

He released the balloon and it ascended speedily, the line unraveling as it climbed until the umbilical was taut, trembling only slightly as the wind blew at the miniature airship up above.

"Eagle Friend," he said into his radio. "We're ready as we'll ever be—but I feel scared shitless. It'll never work."

"It had better," said Cochrane, who was surveying the approach through binoculars. "The hostiles are learning. There is a platoon-sized group working its way up, and they'll be in range in a couple of minutes."

He raised the Barrett. He was not as good as Al Lonsdale, but he was close. Conventional rifle range and the Barrett's range were two different orders of magnitude.

He aimed and fired rapidly.

The advancing unit's point man, platoon sergeant, and radio operator lay dead on the ground when he had finished, and rest of the platoon had scurried for cover. Several were wounded by rock splinters gouged out by the massive multipurpose rounds.

There was a roar of aircraft engines and gunfire as Eagle Friend flew down the valley yet again and hosed the surviving mercenary troops.

Major Khalifa Sherrif was waiting with a SAM operator for exactly this development and held his position. Only his head was not under cover, and that seemed a reasonable risk. He wanted to see the kill. The aircraft was flying at just under 500 feet, he estimated, and was keeping surprisingly steady. The trooper would get a lock. They were going to get the aircraft.

The missile leaped from the launcher and soared toward the Combat Talon.

Bright orange fireballs drew glowing streaks in the sky as the Talon fired its antimissile flares.

The heat-seeking SAM, faced with an excess of choice, twisted and turned and plowed into the far side of the valley.

FITZDUANE and Cochrane—Lonsdale, still unconscious, held up between them—looked at each other as the huge aircraft approached.

Two eight-foot arms attached to its nose were now extended in an open V to snare the thin line attached to the balloon. The balloon could be detected in the darkness by night-vision goggles, but there was also a strobe light flashing away at the top, shielded from the ground but in the line of sight of the pilot.

The aircraft was going to snare the thin line at something like 125 knots—156 miles an hour—and Fitzduane did not want to think about what was going to happen next. Whatever he had been told in training, he imagined a horrendous jerk and horrible pain and his body being cut in half by the shock. And anyway, he did not like heights.

"Is this really a good idea?" he said to Cochrane.

"NO!" said Lee Cochrane, the chief of staff of the Congressional Task Force on Terrorism, whose enthusiasm for Washington and all its intrigues had suddenly been revived. I should be on the Hill, he thought. What the hell am I doing here! This stuff is dangerous!

It was a vain thought and ventured upon somewhat late in the day. The engine roar was magnified by the confines of the valley. It was going to happen.

It was happening—and it was unbelievable!

Suddenly, it was directly over them and all they could hear was this terrible throbbing roar and then they were airborne—whipped up into the air with less shock than a parachute opening—and the ground was receding and they were climbing higher and they were through the narrow end of the Funnel and over the abandoned airstrip and they were going higher and higher as the aircraft climbed to avoid mountains ahead and the slipstream whipped at them and it was much colder and Fitzduane realized the reason for the bulky suits.

Skyhook worked.

Instinct suggested that they should have been jerked half to death or sliced into segments by the sudden pull of the line, but the reality was that initially they were pulled up rather than forward, and only slowly—relatively speaking—brought up to the speed of the roaring aircraft. Though hard to grasp by the uninitiated, it was a matter of simple geometry.

Quietly and consistently, Skyhook had worked for nearly fifty years, from the North Pole to Southeast Asia, ever since Robert Edison Fulton had invented it and tested it at his home in Connecticut.

The front of the line was secured by the retrieval mechanism in the nose of the aircraft, and the balance of the line now stretched under the fuselage and for several hundred feet behind.

They were being towed like water skiers, except that the medium that was supporting them was air. Soon they would be winched in.

Al Lonsdale, braced between Fitzduane and Cochrane, groaned as the flow of chill air revived him. Still disoriented, he opened his eyes and all he could see was an impression of the ground rushing below at impossible speeds as he flew through the night air.

Shock and disbelief hit him.

Holy shit! Everything his mother had said was true. He had died and gone to heaven and now he was an angel and he could fly! It was terrifying and it was incredible and it was unbelievably exciting. Well, who would have guessed!

He could see a light up ahead, and slowly they approached it. It was strange. Somehow it all looked familiar. And then there was the engine noise. How many hours had he spent listening to that noise on the way to or from a mission?

His feet touched the ramp and he was pulled in by the winch crew and the ramp was raised.

He looked around, and beside him he could see Fitzduane and Cochrane, and they were grinning with relief and clapping each other on the back and the crew were smiling and there were the familiar smells of the cargo bay of a Lockheed Hercules C130 Combat Talon.

He felt confused. He had enjoyed being an angel, albeit surprised that some of his more exotic physical peccadilloes had not counted against him. For instance, there had been those two . . .

He glared at Fitzduane.

"Boss, this isn't Heaven," he said indignantly.

Fitzduane gave the Bear a high five and then turned to Al.

"Well," he said tiredly, but with a smile playing about his lips, "it will do for me."

BOOK 3

THE DEVILS

CHAPTER TWENTY-THREE

SHE WAS SLEEPING.

The blinds and drapes were drawn and only a dim sidelight illuminated the hospital room. He could see a drip feeding into her arm, and she was connected to a monitor. For a moment, despite what he had been told, he felt a spasm of dread.

Who knows what they did to her when she was a captive.

I can still lose her.

He closed the door gently and the hospital noises were muted. Carefully, he lifted a chair from the corner and placed it close to one side facing the bed so that that he could look at her and be there for her when she awoke. He longed to touch her and hold her, but for now sleep was what she needed most.

He could hear her breathing, and the sound was deep and regular and so reassuringly familiar. Emotion welled up in him and quiet tears coursed down his cheeks. *My wife. Kathleen. I have never seen you look more beautiful. I have never loved you more.*

She was thin and malnourished. Her face was pale and scratched, and there were bruises around her neck and throat. Her hair looked as if it had been hacked off. There were more bruises on her arms, and as his gaze took in her bandaged hand where her finger had been severed, anger and horror and pity gripped him and left him shaken.

But you are back, my love. We found you and we brought you back and every last effort was worth it.

Images of the carnage in the Devil's Footprint flashed through his mind. The guards outside the main camp, struck down without warning. Bodies spasming and falling in the sleeping area as rounds cut into them. Armored vehicles exploding and the screams of burning men.

So many dead. So high a price. But there were some situations where you had to fight. Evil was not some abstract notion. It existed, and you fought it without compromise until that battle was won. And you kept on fighting because the war, as such, never ended. Conflicting values. Those who wanted to build against those who were determined to destroy. It was the human condition. Reasonable people tended to rest up and drop their guard after a major struggle, but peace was an illusion. At best there was a lull in the fighting.

But while there was a lull you made the most of it. You loved and nurtured and regained your strength. And a few, a very few, kept watch. They did not rest. They stayed alert. Ordinary people with human strengths and failings who put their lives on the line to buy time for their fellows. People like Lee Cochrane and Maury and Warner. Men like Al Lonsdale. Women like Chifune. Unsung and unacknowledged except occasionally in time of open war. But mostly not just unrecognized, but unwanted.

The paradox of peace. The very people who made it possible were an unpleasant reminder of the alternative. They were starved of resources. Often they were shunned. Until the next time.

He dozed, his thoughts a fatigue-induced jumble. Great happiness and fear intermingled. Then one image began to dominate.

Oshima! She was still alive!

Fitzduane gave a start and rubbed his eyes. His unshaven chin itched, and the sand of Tecuno was still on his hair and skin and in his clothes.

The thought occurred to him that he had not slept in a bed for about a week. Catnapping on the web seating of a C130 went just so far. No wonder the gremlins were crowding his mind. Twelve hours' decent sleep in a proper bed followed by a long hot tub would restore his sense of proportion.

Kathleen was back. She was here with him. She was alive and soon she would be well, and that what was what counted.

Fitzduane gazed at his wife, and without conscious thought his hand reached out and stroked her fingers and then her eyes opened.

For a moment, her eyes were those of a stranger. Terror and suffering kept in check only by force of will stared out at him, and nothing else so conveyed the horror of what she had gone through than that split second when he seemed to be able to look into her mind.

Then relief and joy came into her eyes. She stretched out her arms, then stopped and looked with wonder at her bandaged wrists. "No chains," she whispered. "No chains. They hurt so."

Fitzduane lay beside her and took her in his arms. "Never again, my love," he said quietly.

Her fingers touched his cheek. "You're all bristly, Hugo," she said sleepily. Her eyes were closed again. Soon her breathing was relaxed and regular.

A feeling of contentment and happiness so complete that he wanted to cry out—except he was too tired and certainly did not want to wake Kathleen—swept over him.

Memories of the mission were banished from his mind. Kathleen was safe in his arms, and that was what mattered.

Even better, Romeo y Julietta had survived the ordeal. The medical staff had warned Fitzduane not to have his hopes set high, but the examination had revealed that Kathleen, despite her ordeal, was still healthily pregnant. The doctor had given away the secret. Romeo y Julietta would be a girl. No penis could be detected.

"Sounds reasonable," Fitzduane had remarked gravely.

RHEIMAN shuffled into the interrogation room and blinked in the harsh fluorescent light.

His right handcuff was removed and then locked to an eyebolt in the interrogation table. The table itself was secured to the floor. A large mirror took up much of one wall. One-way glass, he knew with certainty, and behind it a select audience. An audience he had to win over if he was to live.

Two men faced him. Not policemen, he thought. The street left its mark after a while; a certain look about the eyes. These people had Langley written all over them. Different pressures, different body language. Though again you never quite knew. The CIA was only one player in the intelligence community these days. Anyway, these were intelligence types, possibly with military backgrounds.

"Cigarette?" said the younger man. He had closely cropped blond hair and wore a tan suit.

Rheiman shook his head. "I don't smoke," he said. "I guess you know that."

The older man smiled. "There's a lot of good shit to smoke in Tecuno," he said, " and not a whole lot else to do. Or so I hear."

"I'm Olsen," said the younger man. He indicated his companion. "And this is Mr. Steele."

Steele consulted the screen of his notebook computer. "The convenient thing about you, Edgar," he said, " is that we don't have to charge you with anything. You've already been tried and sentenced. You're a fugitive from justice. All we've got to do is ship you back home and they're going to strap you in the chair and pull the switch. No new trial needed. Just the formality of an execution."

"A messy business," said Olsen. "Or so they say. And *slow*. Of course, I've never seen an actual execution. Yours will be the first, Edgar. For that I'm going to get a front seat. I'm told that you literally cook to death."

"You're a multiple murderer and a rapist, Edgar," said Steele, "and worse than that, you're a traitor. Personally, I think the chair is too good for you."

Rheiman shook his head. "I'll serve time," he said, "but I won't be executed. The governor remits every sentence where I come from." He smiled. "Good liberal values."

Steele looked across at Olsen and sighed. "You know, Edgar, you may have a point. And, frankly, that does not make me happy."

"Worse still, Mr. Steele," said Olsen, "Edgar may appeal and argue that he wasn't legally deported from Mexico and then he will probably have to be freed."

"Not a pretty picture," said Steele.

"But then again," said Olsen, "if Edgar was not legally deported, then he is not legally here in the United States."

"Which opens a whole host of possibilities," said Steele. He reached inside his jacket and removed an automatic pistol. Seconds later he screwed on a compact silencer.

Rheiman felt ill. He knew they must be bluffing. Yet it was true. He had not been legally deported. No one knew where he was. He did not know where he was. He could still be in Mexico. This could be a test. He remembered Kathleen and then pain, confusion, and nothing. This was probably one of Oshima's games, a test of loyalty. She did things like this. "Probing defenses," she called it. Well, they would not push it too far. He was essential to the project.

"Who are you people?" said Rheiman.

Steele smiled.

"None of your fucking business," said Olsen.

"What do you want?" said Rheiman.

There was a *phtt!* sound as Steele fired at Rheiman's left hand.

Blood spurted as Rheiman's thumb and half his palm were blown away. He looked at Steel in horror. "What do you want?" he whispered.

"Nothing really," said Steele cheerfully.

"We're going to kill you," said Olsen. "Though since you're not here, Edgar, you can't die."

"A consoling thought, Edgar," said Steele. He raised his pistol again and fired.

Rheiman's eyes were closed. He felt the muzzle flash burn into him. Nothing more. He opened his eyes.

"Just to set the tone," said Olsen. "But you're still alive, Edgar."

"What do you want do know?" he breathed.

"The truth, the whole truth, and nothing but the truth, Edgar," said Steele.

"Or we'll blow your fucking head off," said Olsen. "And enjoy it."

"Frankly, we'd prefer it, Edgar," said Steele.

"Who are you?" said Rheiman faintly. "I'll tell you everything, but who—who are you?"

"The government calls us in when they really—*but really*—mean it," said Olsen. "When pushed to the wall, governments are not very nice. Think of us as the end of the line. We're kind of like morticians. We bury shits like you."

"Not everyone knows that, Edgar," said Steele, "but you're a scientist, a curious type, and you were determined to find out."

"So now you know, Edgar," said Olsen. "So the thing is: What are you going to tell us?"

VERNON Slade, National Security Advisor to the President of the United States of America, sat silent, momentarily stunned at what he had heard.

"But Mexico . . ." he said weakly, "there is a great deal at stake there. Mexico is our neighbor. Our policy is to let Mexico sort out its own problems and eventually they will become truly democratic. We can't intervene in the internal affairs of a friendly nation."

"Mr. Slade," said the Chairman of the Joint Chiefs of Staff, "*eventually* is not the problem. It is the here and now we have got to worry about. As we speak, a terrorist weapon of mass destruction is pointed at this country. Perhaps even more to the point, it is aimed at this city by people we know are ruthless enough and irrational enough to act. They will use this weapon. They have attacked this country already. Consider the congressional killings and the Fayetteville massacre."

"And sooner rather than later, Mr. Slade," said William E. Martin. "And you should know that it is our assessment that the Mexican government will cooperate in this venture. They don't want Tecuno seceding any more than we do. The trick is to ask them to ask us to help sort out a little internal problem."

"And if they agree?" said the National Security Advisor.

"The 82nd Airborne goes into the Devil's Footprint, the base on the plateau," said General Frampton, "and the Mexican Army handles the mopping up." He was silent.

"The terrorist base is a strong position," said Slade, "and this man Fitzduane's assault has already alerted them. We will take casualties."

"Without the Task Force on Terrorism and Fitzduane, we would not know we had a problem," said William Martin. He remembered he was in Washington and corrected himself. "We would not know the *extent* of the problem."

The slip reassured National Security Advisor Slade. If the Deputy Director of Operations was sufficiently concerned to let his guard down that much, then there really and truly was a problem. Washington, D.C., was on the firing line. He, Vernon Slade, was in actual physical danger. The thought gave him a strange, not unpleasant feeling.

290 /// VICTOR O'REILLY

"Are you absolutely sure of this supergun's capability?" said Slade. "Can this turncoat Rheiman's information be relied upon?"

"Mr. Rheiman's information is accurate," said William E. Martin grimly. "He had every motivation to tell the truth, and unfortunately what he said checks out."

The National Security Advisor looked intently at the Chairman of the Joint Chiefs. "General Frampton, if the President authorizes this mission are you absolutely certain the 82nd Airborne will succeed?"

General Frampton smiled grimly. "Hooah, sir," he said.

The National Security Advisor looked puzzled. "I don't understand, General. What does—*hooah* mean?"

General Frampton told him.

There was silence in the room. "Sometimes we forget," said the National Security Advisor, "what we ask of our young men."

"Shall I alert the 82nd?" said the Chairman of the Joint Chiefs of Staff.

"Yes," said the National Security Advisor.

"Will you recommend the mission, sir?" said William E. Martin.

"Hooah," said the National Security Advisor.

IN shocked silence, Governor Diego Quintana drove around the box canyon that had housed the main camp of the Devil's Footprint.

His examination was detailed and took over two hours. At its conclusion, he was pale and a vein could be seen pulsing in his forehead. He tried to hide his feelings, but the tremor in his voice was perceptible. Quintana was terrified, and his fear fed a vicious anger.

His twelve-man bodyguard looked on uneasily. When the Governor was in this kind of mood, he could lash out at anyone. The Japanese woman was the obvious target, but you never quite knew.

"Over a battalion of troops, armor, most of your group, Oshima, and who knows how many fortifications and other emplacements—all destroyed as if they were defenseless. It's incredible. Who were they? How did they do it? I don't understand. We have radar all around the plateau. It spotted that DEA helicopter raid last year. Why no warning this time? And on top of the losses here, the damage to the Madoa airfield has been considerable. It's a disaster."

Oshima had been as affected as Quintana initially. But what was done was done was done. Now she was focused on what action to take in the future. Losses were just a cost of doing business. There was always more human raw material to be recruited and molded. There was no shortage of weapons if you knew where to look. The important thing was to buy time. That was the irreplaceable element.

"General Barragan planned our defenses against conventional ground attack or helicopters," said Oshima. "His precautions would normally have been more than adequate, but this was a land attack using some sort of new-technology vehicles—evidently with stealth characteristics. They caught us completely by surprise. But even so, they were not entirely successful. They got the woman, but the weapon and the warheads are unscathed. Charges were placed around the breech of the supergun, but we were able to remove them in time."

Quintana brightened momentarily, but then he remembered that Rheiman had been killed. The fire that had swept the camp after the helicopter crash had burned the block that housed Rheiman and his team to the ground. Quite a few of the scientists had struggled to safety, but evidently Edgar Rheiman had not made it. He was one of a dozen blackened bodies found in the wreckage. It was impossible to tell who was who. He had been a revolting man in many ways, but useful. He'd be hard to replace.

"The supergun has never been tested," he said, "and the chief designer is dead."

"Rheiman was a scumbag, but he was good at what he did," said Oshima. "He left behind a good team and a weapon ready for firing. We have his notes and plans. It won't be hard to build more tubes."

Quintana gave a command, and the group mounted their vehicles and headed into the valley that housed the supergun complex. Here the destruction was minimal, and he could feel his spirits rise.

The weapon was immense. It soared toward the sky, a symbol of his power, a monument to his achievement. Most men would have laughed at Rheiman and his dreams, but he, Governor Diego Quintana, had the necessary vision. And here was the proof.

"I can see their problem," he said. "How could any small raiding party destroy anything so big in twenty minutes or so? And, of course, the warheads were untouched."

"I don't think they knew about them," said Oshima. "I think this was first and foremost a hostage-rescue mission, and I believe I know who was behind it."

"The Irishman?" said Quintana.

"Fitzduane," Oshima spat out. Her eyes blazed and she swore violently in Japanese. *"Yotsu-ashi no yabajin!"*

Quintana looked at Oshima. She had proved invaluable in whipping his forces into shape, but she was a hard person to control.

Impossible, it could be argued.

Her terrorist attacks across the border were part of their original deal but had attracted more attention than he would have liked. God knows, he loathed the

Nortamericanos, but they were strong and should not be directly provoked. It was a balance. There were ways of doing such things. This raid was proof that this balance was no longer being maintained.

Reiko Oshima had outlived her usefulness. Fitzduane's savage assault was proof.

But a dead Oshima-*san* could well make a suitable peace offering. As he had learned in the drug business, every so often it was good politics to toss the Americans someone they were after. They got publicity and kept their budgets safe. The dealers had the pressure taken off. Meanwhile, business life went on as normal. Smoke and mirrors. Life was mostly about illusion.

Quintana stroked his mustache.

That beautiful hair, that perfect face scarred so horribly, yet still so compelling. That aura of menace mixed with unbridled sexuality. He had never slept with her, and now there really was not the time. Barragan had enjoyed her and that was as close as he was likely to get, though he had had descriptions of how she was and what she would do. Of how she tasted and smelled and sounded. Of every intimate perversion.

His brother-in-law had been obsessed by her. *She will do anything, Diego! Anything!*

A woman who would do anything was nice, but Quintana was not short of women who would do whatever he required. And a leader had to control his desires. There had to be an example of discipline.

Oshima's eyes had gone dead. She seemed to have withdrawn into herself. She was still physically present but was behaving as if she were utterly alone. It was almost as if she was praying.

Quintana smiled. The thought of Oshima praying was a quaint nation. But she was a strange woman. There she stood in her stained combat clothing with a gun on her hip and that damned Japanese sword strapped to her back like some Fury from Hell. And her posture was that of a nun praying in front of some relic. Her head was now bowed as if in submission.

"Tomas," he said.

"*Jefe?*" said Tomas, stepping forward. He was a head taller than the others in the bodyguard and had been with Quintana longer than most. He was loyal, and he killed without comment or scruple. He was armed with an automatic rifle and wore a razor-sharp machete at his waist.

"Kill her," said Quintana.

Tomas looked at Oshima almost as if seeking her approval.

She raised her head and looked directly into Quintana's eyes. The vacant look had gone. It was as if she was recharged with energy. Her eyes blazed, and in them there was knowledge and amusement.

"You would kill me, *jefe*?" she said mockingly. "I do what you ask, I train and discipline your men, and you order my death. Is that just?"

"Kill her *now*, Tomas," said Quintana.

"I train men well, Diego," said Oshima. She nodded at Tomas, and Diego Quintana, Governor of Tecuno, felt himself being grabbed and forced to his knees.

Oshima's sword hissed from her scabbard and, impacting on Quintana's skull, sliced on down until the Governor was cut completely in two.

The one bodyguard reeled back drenched in blood, as if caught by a power hose. He stood there openmouthed, holding half a body, as if he did not quite believe what had happened.

Oshima flicked her *katana* clean and slid it back into its home with one neat, continuous movement. Quintana was already forgotten.

Rheiman's legacy was not. The Devil's Footprint was now in her hands and the supergun was going to be put to some immediate good use. It was trained on Washington, D.C., and it was loaded.

Once fired, the Americans could do nothing to stop the missile. They had no antimissile defense. The famed Patriot was designed to shoot down aircraft. It might manage the occasional Scud, but a small ballistic missile such as that from the supergun was unstoppable.

The U.S. defense budget came to more than $250 billion a year, but against ballistic missiles the United States of America was defenseless.

By popular demand, Fitzduane had been sitting at the head of the table, but as the evening wore on the orderly layout of the celebration dinner degenerated roughly in proportion to the increase in alcohol consumed and the noise level.

Everyone had settled in for a long night. Figuring he was likely to need all the support he could get, he had reversed his chair and was leaning on the back, watching Maury doing Russian dancing on the tabletop.

All things considered, Maury was doing a creditable job, but it would have helped if the table had been cleared first. As his ungainly legs shot out to the ever-increasing tempo of the hand-clapping, bottles, glasses, and other accoutrements flew in every direction.

It was chaos. It was a terrific party. Even Grant Lamar was letting his guard down. He had discarded his jacket and his tie was loose and his hair was disheveled. For the first time, Fitzduane saw not the Washington insider but the younger man who more than two decades earlier had penetrated deep into North Vietnamese lines to rescue American prisoners at Son Tay. Lamar had been there. *He understood.*

Al Lonsdale stood up, swaying slightly, a freshly opened bottle of beer frothing in his hand. He chugalugged half of it and then pointed at Maury. "Jesus, Maury, you're wrecking the place. We've got to clear the table first."

He seized the linen tablecloth and was soon joined by Cochrane and the others. "One-two-three, PULL!"

Maury leaped up off the table as the command cut in and grabbed for the ornate central light fixture.

Lonsdale and his cronies, faced with no resistance, crashed backward to land in a tangle of arms and legs and tablecloth against the wall.

Maury shouted something triumphant in Russian at having escaped the fate that had been planned for him.

And then the light fixture gave way.

FITZDUANE awoke slowly.

He had the sense it was afternoon—whatever afternoon was—but the effort of looking at his watch was not something he felt he should rush into. Besides, he could not see.

It was rather nice not being able to see. If he could ignore someone bashing his head with a baseball bat and the feeling he had swallowed rat poison, it was pleasantly peaceful.

He remembered you had to do something if you wanted to see, but exactly what that involved was proving elusive.

Eyes! Eyes came into it. He was sure of it.

He thought about eyes for a while. He had some, he was sure, but how you activated them was another matter. Perhaps there was a switch.

Well, it all seemed like too much effort. The world could go on without him. He slept again.

THE noise was vile, horrendous, horrible. It screamed at him, slicing though his safe, warm igloo of sleep like some manic snowplow.

"Uuuagh!" he groaned.

"What the fuck!" said a hoarse voice that seemed to emanate from somewhere in the neighborhood.

The banging came next.

Thump! Thump! Thump! Fitzduane was reminded of sheltering in some bunker while incoming artillery zeroed in. Only, this was much worse. *Much, much worse!*

"I'm going to shoot them," said the hoarse voice. "Where's my gun? Has anyone seen my gun? Where the fuck am I, anyway?"

There were bangs and crashes and then the sound of falling. Fitzduane decided he had better do something. He pushed his eyelids up and a vague blur appeared. He moved his watch close to his eyes. It did not help. The watch face seemed to have taken up swimming. He shook it a bit, but it still would not cooperate. It was about as static and well-defined as a pulsating jellyfish.

His hand touched a vase. There were flowers in it. He put his fingers into the neck of the vase and they came back wet.

He removed the flowers and poured the water over his upturned face. Paradise! It felt marvelous.

The thumping started again. He had not been aware it had stopped.

There was light coming from somewhere. He shuffled toward it, one hand feeling the wall, and stopped when he encountered a tensioned cord.

The cord did something, he was sure of it. Good or bad, he did not know. Either way, it was coming in handy to hang on to.

He swayed, and pulled on the cord to steady himself.

Light flooded the room. The Iwo Jima memorial floated toward him.

Hurriedly, he closed the drapes. Muffled shouting was now alternating with the banging noise. He headed toward the door, silently praying they would not use the bell again. Another blast would surely kill him.

"I can't find my gun," said a voice.

Fitzduane's eyes swiveled slowly and grittily toward the noise. The process seemed to take an effort akin to sailors hauling up the anchor of a ship-of-the-line with a creaking windlass.

Lonsdale lay on a collapsed coffee table in his underwear and cowboy boots. His eyes were closed and his hands were flailing in slow motion.

Various other bodies lay littered around the room. Vague memories of the previous night's shenanigans came back to him.

He felt like smiling, but his facial muscles did not seem able to respond.

A party to die for. It seemed quite possible he'd succeed.

He leaned against the door and fumbled for the latch. There was a large drawing pinned to the back of the door. It had been done with a black felt pen on the back of one of the restaurant's giant menus.

The sketch showed the devil with his arms up, dancing as a circle of raiders fired at his feet. The body of each raider was loosely sketched, but the heads had been drawn with some care and each could be identified. Fitzduane himself, Lonsdale, Cochrane, Chifune, Oga. They were all there. The drawing had been signed: Grant Lamar.

The slogan was simple: "The Devil Raiders."

Memories suddenly came flooding back. The Devil's Footprint. They had done it. They had really done it. They had done the impossible and had lived to tell the tale. Except Steve. Poor bastard.

He realized then that he had never expected to live. The odds had been too great. The planning too rushed. It had to be tried, but he had expected to die.

But they had done it—IT WAS OVER!

He opened the door. Kilmara stood outside in uniform, looking unusually pressed and polished and sharp.

But he was as nothing compared to the paragon beside him. Polished jump boots with a shine so bright that Fitzduane felt he should have screwed up his eyes—except that they were screwed up already. A uniform that clearly had been intimidated into discarding even the smallest crease. A row of medals that was a one-man insult to the peace movement. A face that needed only bronzing to look instantly at home on a war memorial.

A maroon paratrooper's beret. The All-American divisional patch of the 82nd Airborne.

"What's up, Doc?" said Fitzduane.

"God, you look horrible," said Kilmara. "May we come in? This corridor is losing its charm. We've been here so long, we're taking root."

Fitzduane scratched his head. His hand came away full of wet petals and some kind of perforated metal gadget. He blinked and waved his visitors in.

Kilmara gazed around at the mélange of bodies. Accompanied by the war memorial, he walked through to the kitchen, found Fitzduane a seat, and closed the door.

"This is Colonel Zachariah Carlson," he said. "He's flown in from Fort Bragg. I'll let him speak for himself."

The one-man war machine was looking slightly uncertain. He had heard about Hugo Fitzduane and his extraordinary mission, but this bedraggled, unshaven figure pulling pieces of greenery out of his hair did not quite fit the hero picture.

Still, orders were orders.

Carlson cleared his throat. "Colonel Fitzduane," he said. "The National Command Authority has ordered the 82nd Airborne Division to take out the terrorist base at the location known as the Devil's Footprint in Tecuno, Mexico."

Fitzduane's eyebrows rose slowly. "I could have sworn we did that," he said in a puzzled voice.

"You did a great job, Colonel," said Carlson. "But Rheiman—that prisoner you brought back—talked, and it seems there are weapons of mass destruction down there which pose an immediate threat to the United States. The bottom line is that the President has ordered us in."

Fitzduane shrugged. "Nice of you to tell me, Zach. Best of luck. Sorry about the mess. We had an end-of-mission party last night. I think there's still some booze around . . ." He opened a cupboard door and a floor mop fell out. ". . . somewhere."

Carlson looked uncomfortable. "The thing is, Colonel, we're mounting this operation in seventy-two hours."

"Very nice," said Fitzduane. His voice was muffled. He was looking in another closet.

Kilmara looked at Carlson. "Try subtlety, Zachariah."

Carlson closed the closet door and sat Fitzduane down gently but firmly. "Colonel Fitzduane, we need your specialist knowledge. We'd like you and maybe one of your people to jump into the Devil's Footprint with us."

Fitzduane's eyes rose another half-inch. His face tilted until he was looking at the Airborne colonel towering above him. "Who? Us?" he said weakly.

"Airborne, sir," said Carlson.

Fitzduane's eyes rolled. His gaze switched to Kilmara. "Shane," he said. "Sit the fuck down here beside me. I'm too hungover to get up—but I'm going to strangle you. And enjoy it."

"All the way, sir," said Carlson.

H E lay down beside her and she snuggled up to him. He put his arms around her and held her. Sleep and food were already making a difference. Another couple of weeks at most and she would be able to travel. She could travel now if she had to, but rest and medical care were advised.

"They've asked me to go back," said Fitzduane. He explained.

Kathleen was silent for some time. "I would have said no," she said eventually, "but now I've seen it. I know how they are. I know what Oshima is capable of. If she isn't stopped . . . There's no real limit."

She'll come after us again, thought Fitzduane.

"What are the 82nd Airborne like?" said Kathleen.

"I don't know them close up," said Fitzduane, "but the word is they're good people. I guess I'll find out. They like jumping out of aircraft."

"Will they look after you, Hugo?" said Kathleen.

"We'll look after each other," said Fitzduane.

"Yes, you will," said Kathleen slowly. "That's part of the attraction, isn't it? You and Kilmara and the others. You kill, but you care. Soldiering as a caring profession. A strange concept. If one of you calls, the others come and help *and no one questions*. I think it's crazy—but it's magnificent."

"I won't go, my love, unless you agree," said Fitzduane.

"But you think you should?" said Kathleen.

"Oshima," said Fitzduane.

"Oshima!" agreed Kathleen grimly.

"You're not to worry about me," said Fitzduane simply. "—Okay."

Kathleen forced a small smile. *Oshima,* she thought again. God, how I hate you.

"I'm going to finish it," said Fitzduane. He kissed her long and slow. Her arms came up and held him. He could feel her fingers digging into him, and then she pulled back and looked at him.

"And then you're coming back to make more babies," said Kathleen, trying to smile.

"If I can find a good-looking woman who'll have me," said Fitzduane.

"Could happen," said Kathleen. There were tears in her eyes. "Now, go."

Fitzduane kissed his wife again.

"I'm not going to worry," said Kathleen, "so don't you worry about me. Make the most of it. Enjoy. You'll be changing diapers soon."

"I like babies," said Fitzduane. "And mostly they like me."

He blew her a final kiss and closed the door. Outside in the corridor, he felt tears coming to his eyes. He went into the rest room and washed his face.

When he emerged, his step was firm.

Oshima!

CHAPTER TWENTY-FOUR

FITZDUANE EMERGED FROM the shower with the strong feeling that he was associating with a subculture whose values the original Sir Hugo Fitzduane—he of the thirteenth century whose invasion of Ireland had started the cycle—would readily have identified with.

"They all run?" he said incredulously. "Hell, man, there's fifteen thousand of them. Some of them have to be couch potatoes. It's against human nature for the entire population of the equivalent of a small Irish city to go running every morning. I mean *I* run, Al, and *you* run—and we have our reasons—but a complete community rising up and putting in five miles before breakfast is downright kinky."

Lonsdale grinned. "Scout's honor," he said. "Every morning they close off Ardennes and, from the commanding general to the lowliest trooper, they all pound the pavement. Even after an EDRE."

"What is an EDRE?" said Fitzduane.

"Emergency deployment readiness exercise," said Lonsdale. "That's what the 82nd is all about. They're a kind of strategic fire brigade. Give them eighteen hours' notice, and they are wheels up to just about anywhere."

"In the world?" said Fitzduane.

"If an aircraft can fly over it, they can get to it," said Lonsdale. " 'Force projection,' they call it."

"A subtle turn of phrase," said Fitzduane.

"Fucking the bad guys from a height," said Lonsdale. "If I may be so bold as to translate."

"Ah!" said Fitzduane.

IT was hot in the SCIF and getting hotter, but though the 82nd had a budget of $65 million for running expenses, apparently that did not run to an effective air-conditioning system for the top-security divisional operations center.

Most present had stripped down to T-shirts. Given the useful minority of out-standingly healthy young women troopers present, Fitzduane's respect for Airborne tactics was rising. But then again, he reminded himself, he was a married man and never happier to be so. He thought of Kathleen, safe again, and smiled. He had been walking on air these past few days. A little cold reality would not go amiss.

The Airborne assault on Oshima's base looked quite likely to provide it. His previous mission had been a twenty-minute raid with all the advantages of surprise on their side. This was a military problem of a different order of magnitude. The entire terrorist base complex now known generically as the Devil's Footprint was to be seized, held, searched, and destroyed—before being turned over to Mexican federal troops. And this time there was every sign that the terrorists were prepared and waiting.

Taped-together satellite photographs covered the floor. The only way you could study the overall picture properly was by taking your boots off and walking across the imagery in your socks. You hunkered down with a magnifying glass for the small stuff. The detail was superb. Faces could not be easily recognized, but you could look at an individual's load-bearing equipment and see whether he had grenades clipped to his belt or not.

As he looked at the planning staff crawling around the floor, Fitzduane, who suffered from an irreverent cast of mind, had a surreal flash of a bunch of infants in a day-care center. He suppressed the thought. The Airborne took themselves seriously, as well they might, given what they were expected to do. Jumping out of aircraft into the darkness and a hail of enemy fire required a certain mind-set. And getting to the ground in one piece was only the start of the exercise. You then had to deal with mines and weapons emplacements and a dug-in enemy who wanted you permanently dead. Airborne assault was a deadly serious business.

Fitzduane's military specialty was special-forces warfare, where heavy weaponry was normally nonexistent and the ethos was to be as sneaky as possible. To do anything head-on was considered bad form. He had to rethink his approach when considering the 82nd's way of war. It was not that it was wrong. But it surely was different.

Lieutenant Colonel Zachariah Carlson looked up from perusing the satellite extravaganza. He looked less like a war memorial in his T-shirt and socks. And they had moved onto first-name terms, which got over the potential problem of Al Lonsdale's lack of commissioned rank.

"How do you want to play this, Zach?" said Fitzduane.

"We're on a countdown," said Carlson. He checked his watch. "If hell freezes over, we hit the Devil's Footprint in sixty-three hours and eighteen minutes.

You've been there already. You've fought these people. Anything you can contribute which will make our task easier will be appreciated."

Fitzduane looked down at the satellite photographs again. He did not like what he saw. Madoa airfield had been significantly reinforced, and there were mobile armored columns on the perimeter. In the Devil's Footprint itself the main camp had been thoroughly destroyed, but the supergun valley appeared untouched. The blockhouse had been reoccupied and surrounded by extra defenses. Troops were dug in along the rim. Whoever was now in command knew just what they were doing and had the drive and energy to see it was done. What had been accomplished in such a short time was incredible.

Oshima! he thought to himself. He had hoped against hope that she had been killed in the original assault. Looking at the hornet's nest that had been created since the attack, he knew he had been wrong.

"Let's get out of this sweatbox, Zach," he said, "and you can give me the tencent version of how the 82nd operates these days. I grew up on World War Two stories where paratroops were always dropped in the wrong place and used guts instead of firepower to do the job."

Carlson smiled. "Well, some things have changed," he said, "but when you get right down to it LGOPS are still the secret."

"Enlighten me," said Fitzduane.

Al Lonsdale grinned. "LGOPS—Little Groups Of Paratroopers," he said.

"And that's it?" said Fitzduane.

"Airborne, sir!" said Carlson seriously. The reply cracked out.

Fitzduane nodded slowly.

OSHIMA had planned the takeover of the Devil's Footprint over many months.

From the beginning she had known that Diego Quintana would turn on her. In the end, she was surprised that he had acted so clumsily. Signaling his intentions as if he alone were the determinant of the outcome.

In truth, some of Quintana's complacency was justified. Oshima knew that directly superseding Quintana's rule over all of Tecuno state would not have been possible. Leaving out her terrorist background, she was Japanese, a woman, and not from Tecuno—three strikes against her. Accordingly, she had initially planned to work through her lover, Luis Barragan. That was a promising plan, but even before Barragan's untimely death it had been fairly certain it was not going to work. She held Barragan in sexual thrall, but even so, he remained loyal to Quintana.

Rejecting the option of working through Barragan and making a play for the whole state, it came to her that taking over only the plateau and the Devil's Footprint was the obvious alternative.

It was all that was necessary. She did not want to hold territory permanently. She wanted to inflict as much damage on America as possible and return to Japan in triumph.

There were many who remembered the unforgivable insults of Hiroshima and Nagasaki. Her achievements would not go unheralded. Yaibo would rise again. New recruits would flock to her. The myth of America's invulnerability would be punctured.

After killing Quintana, Oshima had worked furiously to consolidate her position. The steel supergun was aimed at Washington and ready to fire, but that would alert the Americans and provoke an immediate counterstrike. No, what was really required was a multiple-strike capability. Then the Americans would think twice before replying. With Washington hit and New York the next target, the American options would be seriously diminished. Destroying a terrorist base when the price was serious damage to your principal financial and commercial center was the kind of trade-off the American population would not accept.

So Oshima held her fire while her people worked frantically to erect two more of the special concrete weapons. The pipes had been cast months ago and the breeches constructed. Rheiman had said the concrete guns would work and though she had despised the man, she had the utmost faith in his technical ability.

To be able to hit the capital of the United States of America and for the U.S. president to be unable to respond was a prospect that justified every risk. Now all she needed was time. The new weapons would take several more days to install fully.

Then, for all practical purposes, the Devil's Footprint would be invulnerable.

CARLSON, back in full uniform, drove Fitzduane and Lonsdale the short distance over to First Brigade Headquarters. The building was an unpretentious two-story rectangular block with a basement. A short flight of steps led up to the main entrance.

Set into the floor as they entered was the slogan "The Devil's in Baggy Pants."

Fitzduane stopped for a closer look. "We got the name in World War Two," said Carlson. "So our target is well named."

"It seems they're all over the place," said Fitzduane. They turned left and followed Carlson down a corridor to a corner office, which ran out of floor space after a desk, a couple of stuffed chairs, and a mound of combat equipment had been squeezed in.

Carlson removed a Kevlar helmet from one of the armchairs and propped it on top of a filing cabinet. "What are?" he said.

"Devils," said Fitzduane and Lonsdale in unison.

A trooper brought in Cokes. Carlson took a slug, then sat back. He opened his mouth to speak and then paused.

"I feel a little stupid trying to explain Airborne doctrine to two guys who've been there," he said eventually. "Hell, you people jumped in there only a few days ago."

"So we did," said Fitzduane. He sounded almost surprised. "But shoot and scoot is not the same as . . ."

"Jump and thump," said Lonsdale helpfully.

"Quite so," said Fitzduane. "So assume we know nothing."

"Or close to nothing," said Lonsdale. "Give or take a few details."

Carlson shrugged. "The first thing to understand is that modern airborne assault techniques have evolved a great deal.

"In the early days of the airborne half a century ago, paratroopers jumped and fought pretty much with what they carried. They had probably landed in the wrong place and were widely scattered. They had no close-air support, lousy communications, limited firepower, and no armor or artillery. They were light troops and their capabilities were limited. Even so, airborne training seemed to produce a particularly high caliber of combat soldier. The record speaks for itself. Paratroopers get the job done.

"An airborne assault today is a whole different ball game. It is force projection carrying with it lethal firepower of a vastly greater order of magnitude.

"The foundation is good intelligence. Today when we go in, thanks to satellite reconnaissance and other capability—including advance teams on the ground—we normally know everything we need to know about the enemy right down to his shoe size. Accurate and comprehensive intel is the rock on which we build.

"Next phase is to get together with the air force and try and make sure that every identified threat is neutralized before we show up. We're not trying to give the bad guys a fair fight. If they are all dead before we jump, that is just fine by us. The idea is to identify every defensive position, every radar, every enemy soldier with a missile, every form of opposition—and take out the lot of them before we go in. So every target is listed in advance and then allocated. Stealth fighters start the whole thing. Then, layer by layer, other elements in the package cut in and peel the defenses away. F16s follow the Stealth boys. A10s follow the F16s. Mostly smart weapons are used, so what we see is what we hit.

"We don't just kill the enemy. We blind him. Wild Weasels take out his radar.

ECM-equipped aircraft and helicopters blanket the electronic spectrum and shut down his communications.

"Our window of maximum vulnerability is really just before we jump. Aircraft dropping paratroopers can't jink around. They've got to fly slow and steady. For that couple of minutes we are sitting ducks for triple A or some hotshot with a handheld missile.

"The good news is that A10s and C130 Spectre gunships act as our guardian angels during that window. The A10s can take out anything heavy. The gunships can deliver pinpoint fire. From three thousand feet they can see and kill anything that moves. Higher up, JSTARS and AWACS watch the ground and air. Way low down, if we plan it right, Kiowa Warrior helicopter gunships hover out of sight. They have mast-mounted sights and high-magnification devices. They are the Airborne commander's eyes. And they have teeth too. If the air force is otherwise occupied, the Kiowas have Hellfire missiles, rockets, and heavy machine guns."

As Carlson spoke, Fitzduane was translating his words into a mental model and then relating it to the realities of combat. Everything the Airborne colonel was saying hung together, and yet the chances of something going seriously wrong were considerable.

Intelligence was never perfect. You could see a great deal from the air, but so much of modern weaponry was small and powerful. If the defenders knew what they were doing, a handheld missile was not left on permanent display for all to see. It was brought out at the last moment. It was moved around. Positions were camouflaged. Vision equipment could see through darkness, smoke, and haze, but not into a concrete bunker. Equipment broke down. And there was always the human factor. People missed things, they got confused, they fucked up. Particularly they fucked up under pressure. And people trying to kill you was serious pressure. You could ameliorate it with training and the right disciplines, but it was always there.

"What do you hate most?" said Fitzduane.

"Before we land, anything that can shoot down a troop-carrying aircraft makes us unhappy," said Carlson. "Paratroopers hate to die before they've had a chance to fight.

"Once we've landed, we get pissed off by armor, artillery, and mines in roughly that order. And then there is the NBC area. None of that is a barrel of laughs."

NBC: nuclear, biological, chemical. A terrifying amount of misery summed up by three letters, reflected Fitzduane.

Carlson smiled. "But, hey, it's an imperfect world. And we lov-v-v-e to jump." He caught Fitzduane's look. "Well, to land, anyway," he added.

Fitzduane looked at Lonsdale. He was getting some ideas. "Can we contribute?"

Lonsdale pursed his lips. "Probably," he said. Regardless of rank, you got $112 a month while on airborne status. You could earn more in tips in one night in many bars.

But the money was not really the point.

THEY were back in the SCIF.

Its full name was the Sensitive Compartmented Information Facility, a title that required excessive energy just to think about pronouncing.

Fitzduane was becoming to seriously hate the divisional plans and operations facility. Grateful nations tended to erect monuments in memory of their warriors. In the case of the 82nd Airborne, he was of the opinion that bronze statues could be usefully bypassed in favor of an air-conditioned ventilation system and deodorizer that really worked. The place was getting like the Saudi Desert crossed with the humidity of Vietnam. The atmosphere was thick enough to slice and dice. The planning staff were not going to need to acclimatize when they arrived in some tropical hellhole. The climatic conditions of the Devil's Footprint were going to be light relief.

Meanwhile, faces were shiny with sweat, clothing looked as if it had been run through a sauna, and tempers were getting frayed. Files and papers adhered to hands as if coated with thinned-out treacle. Fingers lifted from computer keyboards sounded as if they were being detached from the suckers of overfriendly octopi.

"I'll buy you an air conditioner," muttered Fitzduane. "A very large air conditioner with a Coke machine and ice-cold showers built in."

"The U.S. Army doesn't work that way," said Lonsdale. *"You work with what you've got.* A hundred and twenty years ago, the U.S. cavalry had single-shot carbines and the Indians had repeating rifles. Work that one out."

"If I was Custer," said Fitzduane, "I would feel pretty bloody upset."

BEADS of sweat formed up on Carlson's brow, slid in globule formation down his nose, waited until over the drop zone, and then went *splat!* onto the remains of a giant cheeseburger shipped over from the Airborne PX.

"Gentlemen," he said formally. "The 82nd Airborne Division is deeply grateful for your help, but now I must ask you to leave. ASAP, sirs."

Fitzduane blinked. It was an effort, because his eyelids were weighed down with sweat. He thought of wiping them with a corner of his T-shirt, but there wasn't a dry corner left. He poked under the cheeseburger, but someone else had already grabbed the napkin.

He blinked again. "Zachariah," he said, "you guys asked us to come down here. All we've done so far is help target the opposition. There is still the minor matter of what the fuck we all do when we hit the ground. Do we join hands and sing?"

Carlson looked uncomfortable. "Need to know, sir," he said. "Standard security precaution. You've gotta understand that the actual planning process is classified."

Fitzduane stood up. "We've been to the Devil's Footprint. We've tangoed and we've come back alive, and you are standing here telling me that you're throwing us out. Am I reading you right, Zachariah?"

"Orders, sir," said Carlson uncomfortably. "You must understand, Hugo, that this is a military operation, and as far as the U.S. Army is concerned, you people are civilians. Valued citizens, but whatever you have done in the past . . ."

". . . we don't need to know," said Fitzduane grimly.

"Airborne!" said Carlson.

Fitzduane eyed Carlson. In the short time he had known the man he had been impressed. The man was not just well-trained. He was bright, innovative, and thorough. But how could someone of this caliber put up with such manifest bullshit? Fitzduane figured that in this humidity no one was likely to notice the steam coming out of this ears. He counted to ten and added another decade and felt his mood calming slightly.

"My worry is that the left hand doesn't know what the right hand is doing," he said, "let alone all the fingers and toes."

FITZDUANE and Lonsdale headed back to First Brigade, made some calls, and got kitted out while they were waiting for some action. If they were going to jump in with the 82nd they were going to look like they belonged. Around them everyone moved just that bit faster. There was electricity in the air. The Airborne were going into action.

Fitzduane abandoned his Calico submachine gun with regret, but Lonsdale was adamant.

"You've spent too long on small unit actions where you know all your team, Hugo," he said. "There are going to be a shitload of aggressive young troopers on this one, and if you don't look right, they'll waste you on reflex. So wear your Kevlar, carry your M16, and don't complain."

He stood back and eyed Fitzduane. From his jump boots to body language, the Irishman looked completely at home in his U.S. Army combat fatigues and equipment, but there was one thing not quite right.

Fitzduane wore his hair cropped short but *en brosse*. It was trim but not quite the Airborne white sidewalls with a half-inch thatched oval on top. A sort of reversed tonsure.

"Who'll know when I'm wearing a helmet?" said Fitzduane.

"Trust me," said Lonsdale. "It'll be appreciated.

Within minutes of emerging from the PX barbershop, Fitzduane knew Lonsdale had been right. It was a gesture toward the Airborne way, and this was Airborne territory. It was a token of acceptance and, as such, was noted.

Fitzduane eyed his new hairstyle in a small mirror in Carlson's office. It occurred to him that judging by the tapestries he had seen, his Norman ancestors had cropped their hair in a not dissimilar style. The barbershop floor had cheered him. He was agreeably surprised he still had that much hair to lose.

"Hugo?"

Fitzduane turned.

Carlson stood in the door. He looked at Fitzduane's newly cropped head and nodded approvingly. "Good news and bad news," he said. "Full security clearance has come through."

"And?" said Fitzduane.

"Back to the SCIF," said Carlson. "A Dr. Jaeger from Livermore is joining us. The CG is sitting in."

"CG?" said Fitzduane.

"Commanding General of the 82nd," said Carlson. "General Mike Gannon. He's a two-star and climbing. A real good man, sir. Airborne from way back."

"Is he commanding the mission?" said Fitzduane.

"This is the Airborne, Hugo," said Carlson. "General Gannon will be the first man to jump."

FITZDUANE had once met a U.S. Marine general who looked more like a rather gentle schoolteacher than a hard-charging combat veteran of considerable distinction.

Physically, General Gannon was similarly cast against type. But for all his slight frame, quiet voice, and courteous Southern manner, the General was a force to be reckoned with. The mantle of command authority sat easily on his shoulders. He greeted Fitzduane and Lonsdale warmly.

They were standing around a large planning table bearing a scale mock-up of the terrorist positions. If anything, the temperature and humidity in the SCIF were even more unbearable. Gannon sweated with everyone else but made no other acknowledgment of the fact. His camouflage fatigue jacket remained in place, fully buttoned.

To Fitzduane, the sight of the three-dimensional models was somehow much more evocative than the satellite imagery. There, in miniature, were the places where they had fought over so intensely only days earlier. They had wreaked havoc on their raid and had departed, never expecting to see the Devil's Footprint again. Now it was back as if to haunt them.

This time, Fitzduane vowed, we're going to finish the job. Given the package the air force were putting together combined with the ferocity of an airborne assault, it seemed a reasonable proposition in the abstract. When the details were evaluated, it was not so easy.

"The 82nd Airborne Division regards taking down defended airfields as something of a house specialty," said Gannon. "We have the skills to do the job, and it's something we are trained and equipped to do. But the Devil's Footprint complex poses particular problems. Madoa airfield and the twin valleys of the Devil's Footprint are eight kilometers apart, and both are heavily defended locations. The core difficulty is the supergun. Intelligence reports obtained from Colonel Fitzduane's prisoner, the man Rheiman, suggest that the weapon is primed and ready to fire.

"No matter how sudden our assault, how can we be sure that the supergun won't be fired before we break through? Would not a special-forces raid on the supergun itself be a more effective approach—to be followed by the 82nd when the weapon is fully secured? Does it even matter if the gun is fired? What damage can a projectile from such a weapon do? Gentlemen, I need answers."

Fitzduane was struck once again about the paradox of intelligence. Operatives were so obsessed with secrecy and classifying information as it flowed in that surprisingly often the very people who could make best use of the intelligence were never informed. *General Gannon doesn't know!* he thought! This is going to be like Son Tay all over again unless we watch it.

"General," he said, "the situation has changed. We had the advantage of surprise when going in. Now the Devil's Footprint has been reinforced. There is no way you can guarantee getting in before the supergun is fired. And I don't care who you use. Delta, the SAS, whoever. All it takes to fire that weapon is the push of a button. One finger, one split second, and the will to do the job."

Gannon nodded slowly.

"But the point is," said Fitzduane, "that firing the supergun should not matter. In fact, that's what we want them to do."

Gannon spoke quietly to an aide and a file was passed to him. The General read at the place indicated and then looked up at Fitzduane. "My information, Colonel Fitzduane, is that the weapon is targeted on the White House," he said, "and indeed could reach anywhere in this country." He smiled slightly. "Leaving out the matter of the average American voter's political persuasion, how could a strike on the very essence of this country's system of government *not* be significant?"

"The supergun has been sabotaged," said Fitzduane.

"It won't work?" said Gannon.

"It'll work," said Fitzduane, "but not quite as intended."

GANNON listened to Fitzduane and Jaeger for a further ten minutes, saying little. He had been through engineering school at the Virginia Military Institute more years ago than he cared to think about, so the science involved was relatively familiar. In essence, it all hung on the bravery of a man named Patricio Nicanor. He had provided the key when he had smuggled out a gas controller. The man had paid a high price for his courage.

"How do you know they won't find what you have done?" he asked. "Or maybe swap out the controller as part of routine maintenance?"

"We placed delayed charges around the breech of the weapon," said Fitzduane, "to give the impression that this was our main effort. So they would have no reason to suspect the controller. Nonetheless, we also penetrated their stores and swapped out the spares."

"But no guarantees?" said Gannon.

Fitzduane shook his head. "If we'd known about the supergun's missiles, we might have done things differently," he said.

"Dr. Jaeger?" said Gannon.

"According to this man Rheiman," said Jaeger, "Governor Quintana went on a shopping trip in Eastern Europe. The supergun gave him a delivery system. Next he wanted something to shoot. He was looking for nuclear capability. He settled for an item called Xyclax Gamma 18. It's a binary nerve agent. The two components are relatively harmless in themselves, but once mixed, a single drop—smaller than that from a perfume atomizer—is fatal.

"The really unpleasant thing about the stuff is that it is not a military weapon. It doesn't kill instantly or within a few hours. It can take several days to kill you, and meanwhile you're in more agony than you can imagine. Every aspect of your body malfunctions. You bleed spontaneously from every orifice. Your lungs fill with pus. Your joints and nerves feel like they're being held in flames. It's a nightmare way to die, but it's not a military weapon because you can remain combat effective for several hours after you're hit with it.

"The stuff was developed for use in Afghanistan. Bombs and rockets weren't doing the job, especially after the Stingers made low flying unhealthy. The idea of Xyclax Gamma 18 was that you would drop in from a high-flying aircraft, airburst it at a thousand feet or so, and it would render a whole area uninhabitable. Lots of nerve agents kill you. What makes this variety so lethal is its dispersion capability and its shelf life. Xyclax Gamma 18 remains toxic for years."

"Was it used?" said Gannon.

"Apparently," said Jaeger, "but not for long. Under lab conditions with positive air pressure and everyone in special suits, it was safe enough. When they tried it in the field, they discovered that the dispersion capability was all too effective. Dispersion depends largely on particle size. The smaller the nerve agent particle, the larger the area you can cover. In this case, the particles were so small the Russians found the material went right through the standard Soviet NBC suit. A bunch of dying Afghans was followed by some serious Spetnatz casualties as they moved up to see what had happened. There was talk of getting new suits and trying it a second time, but then Gorbachev and *glasnost* came along. Xyclax Gamma 18 was quietly forgotten about until private enterprise hit and the enterprise manager realized that he had a product with real market value."

Gannon looked somber. "Will our suits work?" he said.

Jaeger shook his head. "Standard army NBC suits may help, but not for long. You need the kind of gear they have in Fort Dietrich for this, and it's not the kind of clothing you can fight in."

It struck Gannon that this was the kind of mission that should best be left to the air force alone. His paratroops were trained to fight a real human enemy. To have his young men jumping into some lethal mist was a thought that revolted him.

Carlson had been thinking the same thoughts. But then again, he was a soldier, and surely the National Command Authority had considered all these questions. Or had they? Unchecked, politicians had a habit of committing the military without really thinking through all the implications.

Fitzduane broke the mood. "Binary?" he said. "If I was Quintana and had a mercenary force of debatable caliber, I'd store the components separately if I wanted to sleep nights. Otherwise, a bottle of tequila too many, and the Devil's Hangover wouldn't come into it."

Jaeger smiled. "Quoting Rheiman," he said, "even Oshima is scared stiff of the stuff. They tested a sample before it was shipped in, so they saw what it could do. They keep the secondary in a deep bunker in the supergun valley and the primary in the command complex of Madoa airfield. No chance of mixing them up or some entrepreneur staging a coup. The one exception to that may well be the supergun. If that is being held ready to fire, then we think it's likely—certainly possible—to have both primary and secondary loaded."

"Why wouldn't they load one of the components at the last minute?" said Gannon. "That would seem safer."

"It's possible," said Jaeger, "but loading the supergun is not like inserting a shotgun round. This is a big weapon. Charging it takes hours. So if they want to keep it as a deterrent ready to roll, it *will* be loaded."

"It wasn't loaded when we were there," said Fitzduane slowly. Then he looked across at the latest satellite pictures. The Devil's Footprint seemed to be getting stronger by the hour. Oshima was driving her people. She expected to be attacked. She was bright enough to know she could not win against a full assault. So what would she do? "But I concur with Dr. Jaeger."

"If a single missile charged with Xyclax Gamma 18 airbursts over Washington, D.C.," said General Gannon, "what kind of effect would that have?"

"So much would depend on weather conditions," said Jaeger. "Rheiman says they were promised between fifteen thousand and seventy-five thousand fatalities. And decontaminating the area could take years. Of course, if it airbursts undetected over a major water supply, given that the effects are not immediate, hundreds of thousands, if not millions, could die.

"The fatalities could exceed those of a significant nuclear detonation."

THE meeting concluded.

General Gannon caught Fitzduane's eye and indicated that he would like to talk to him alone.

They left the SCIF and headed out of the division headquarters. The flag-lowering ceremony was just starting, and they stood at attention while it was completed. Then they walked on.

Dusk was falling. Fort Bragg was still a hive of activity. It would stay that way until the C130s were wheels up from Pope Air Base. Then there would just be the waiting. Sons, lovers, friends, and husbands would be gone. The post would feel empty. There would be no certainty all would return.

"Colonel Fitzduane, I understand you are not a regular soldier," said Gannon. "It's a pity. You seem well suited to the calling of arms. You seem . . . to understand"—he smiled—"perhaps too well."

Fitzduane laughed. "I'm not too good at following orders," he said, "or making the compromises you have to make. I find it hard to salute a man I don't respect merely because he has rank. I find it hard to do one thing because my masters require it when my common sense tells me to do something else. I am not overly fond of large structures. I can admire—greatly admire—a unit such as the 82nd Airborne, but I cannot suspend my sense critique."

Gannon eyed Fitzduane contemplatively. Then he laughed. "What am I going to do with you, Colonel Fitzduane? The 82nd is—well—the 82nd, and we have our own ways of doing things. We will evolve, but I doubt we will change. As to you, I'm told you have seen more of combat in more countries than all the Joint Chiefs put together, so I will allow you your sense critique. But what to do?"

"Let me work with Colonel Carlson until the planning is completed," said Fitzduane. "Then give me a small unit when we jump. Troopers who have initiative. A leader who has some dash."

"You're describing most of my men," said Gannon. He was silent, but then a smile crossed his lips.

"But one unit in particular comes to mind?" said Fitzduane.

Gannon grinned. "The Scout Platoon attached to First Brigade," he said. "You may have met your match, Colonel. Under Lieutenant Brock, they're the nearest thing to a private army the 82nd has."

"What do they normally do, General?" said Fitzduane. "*Scout* covers a multitude."

"They do anything," said Gannon. "They scout, they snipe, they kill armor, they play with mines, they HALO. They even have their own pair of tanks and work with their own helicopters. They're terrifying young men."

He looked straight at Fitzduane. "You'll wonder why I tolerate them."

"Every unit needs a few mavericks, General," said Fitzduane.

"Indeed," said Gannon. He gave a signal and his Humvee rumbled up. He got in. "I guess one more won't hurt."

Fitzduane breathed the cool air of the evening and then headed back to the SCIF.

Carlson was studying the satellite imagery intently. He looked up. "The General fire you?"

"He said he needs every swinging dick he can get, Zachariah," said Fitzduane, "seeing as how they all go limp in this sweat lodge."

"He likes your haircut," said Carlson. He tapped the satellite photo. "Listen up," he said. "Fuck the armor. I've been counting their earthmoving equipment."

"And?" said Fitzduane.

"They've got too goddamned much of it," said Carlson. "I think there's more to Madoa Air Base than we can see. Someone with a mole mentality has been screwing around with the environment."

"So what we see isn't all we're going to get?" said Fitzduane.

"That's what I figure," said Carlson. "Unless the base commander just likes collecting tracked iron."

"Infrared?" said Fitzduane.

Carlson nodded. "That'll show if earth has been disturbed. But what if they've built *under* existing structures?"

"If they've got a bunker complex underneath," said Fitzduane, "why haven't

they kept their bulldozers out of sight as well? Answer: because who would suspect some innocent earthmoving equipment and . . ."

". . . something else is in the space," said Carlson. "But what? There are plenty
of track imprints, but they could be bulldozers. God, I hate surprises when I'm
dangling from the risers. It's bad enough jumping out of an aircraft with your
face painted green and black without some steel behemoth emerging from below
ground and blowing your shit away. That kind of thing can depress you."

"What if we turned all this surprise stuff around?" said Fitzduane. "We don't
sneak up. We announce ourselves. We show ours and encourage them to show
theirs."

"A blast of trumpets before we attack?" said Carlson. "With something more
substantial hidden away."

"It worked pretty well in Jericho," said Fitzduane.

"Let's get the Air Force in on this," said Carlson. "They have things that
moles do not like. And they're Devious—with a capital *D*. Or so they say in
the Pentagon."

"What are the Army?" said Fitzduane.

"The Navy are Defiant," said Carlson. "They can afford to be when they're
out at sea snug in their carrier groups."

"The Army?"

"The Army are Dumb," said Carlson. "We're too honest, and that's why the
other services get so much of the pie. But in this situation we need Devious—and
maybe a few dozen penetrator bombs."

Six hours later, the shape of the plan had been established and now it was
down to the planning staff to hammer out the endless details. No one in the 82nd
seemed to need sleep.

Fitzduane headed away to get some rest. If General Gannon was right, he was
going to need it before he met First Brigade's Scout Platoon.

When Carlson had heard that Fitzduane was jumping in with the Scouts, he
had smiled. "The Devil's Footprint is going to be the least of your worries, Hugo.
These people are crazy. Good—outstandingly good—but absolutely wacko."

GENERAL Gannon toured the post, checking on every aspect of the division's
preparations. In any military operation every facet was interdependent, but never
more so than in the 82nd.

The Airborne picked up their entire house and flew. If you forgot something
you could not radio supply and request that they send it up the line. You brought
everything—but everything—with you or you did without. Sure, you could get

resupplied with essentials from the air, but by the time that resource cut in the really critical time was normally over. The essence of airborne assault was speed and shock value—sudden overwhelming force appearing from nowhere anywhere on earth.

Global force projection.

Force was the key. When the Airborne jumped, the time for compromise was over. It was down to elementals. You killed them before they killed you. You smashed into the enemy. You destroyed them. You did not hesitate. When attacking a heavily defended airfield—a substantial piece of real estate—the normal takedown time was two hours.

Two hours of focused carnage.

Ironically, many people—even in the military—thought of the 82nd as a light division, incapable of delivering a real punch. It had indeed been true half a century earlier. Now the destructive power of the 82nd was awesome. True, it lacked the heavy armor of a mechanized division or the stupendous firepower of a modern MLRS-equipped artillery brigade, but that was more than compensated for by the way it worked with airpower. Air support was the 82nd's heavy armor and artillery.

But even without airpower the 82nd was no longer a light division. Potent 105mm howitzers and heavy mortars gave artillery cover within fifteen minutes of the division's hitting the ground. The Stinger-equipped Avenger missile system secured the air. TOWS, Dragons, and AT4s provided potent antiarmor and antibunker capability.

The removal of the 82nd's indigenous Apache helicopters had been a controversial decision, but the Kiowas had picked up the slack with a vengeance. They were small and hard to detect and easier to airship and maintain, and though they could not carry the same payload as the Apache, they did carry the lethal Hellfire missile system. Further, by ripping out the two rear seats and stuffing the bay helicopters with electronics, the Kiowas now had outstanding sighting systems and night-vision capability. So the switch had worked to the 82nd's advantage. In fact, the controversy had been something of a storm in a teacup. On a combat mission, Apaches could always be attached to the 82nd if required.

The development in the 82nd's combat effectiveness that had pleased Gannon, an old infantryman, most was night-vision capability. Traditionally, the cost of night-vision equipment had made selective issue to squad leaders and special forces the norm. Now every single trooper in the 82nd had advanced third-generation goggles with him as he went into battle. Teamed up with laser aiming devices with beams visible only to those wearing the goggles, the effect on small-arms accuracy had exceeded expectations. Everyone knew about the Air Force's smart bombs. An Airborne trooper's firepower now approached the same level of accuracy. What a trooper saw he could—and did—hit.

Lethal young men, reflected Gannon, which was the way it should be. There were not many of them to hold the line, and the threats in today's world were legion.

The names of operations were normally chosen at the highest levels, with a weather eye on the public relations impact. In this case, because the elimination of the Devil's Footprint was a personal matter for the 82nd after the Fayetteville bombings, General Gannon had been asked to choose his own name.

Gannon was a man who studied his craft in the belief that the core lessons of combat were timeless. He had named the mission OPERATION CARTHAGE. The Carthaginians had invaded Italy and had caused the Romans serious grief on their home territory. In return, the Romans had crossed to Africa, defeated the Carthaginians utterly, and had razed Carthage to the ground.

It had all happened more than two thousand years ago, but to Gannon the parallels were clear.

LIEUTENANT Luke Brock filled six empty quart-size Coke bottles with water and hung them from target frames.

This was not the kind of exercise the range officer would approve of, but Brock was more concerned with the combat effectiveness of his unit than range safety. In his opinion, the general unwillingness of U.S. forces to train under live fire was criminal. The do-gooder liberals who had pushed the safety-first approach through did not seem to understand that lives lost in training accidents were more than compensated for in combat. They also missed the simple truth that a soldier's life, by definition, could not be risk-free. This current notion of aiming for zero-casualty combat and compromising on the mission struck Brock as being the value system of traitorous assholes who did not give a fuck about the United States. Where would the nation have been if Washington had ordered his troops to go home in case they might get too cold!

The fact that the 82nd Airborne had to compromise on training because of the red cockaded woodpecker produced in him something akin to a killing frenzy. He thought of the damn bird every time he had to go on a mission. It seemed to evoke the right throat-cutting mental attitude.

He lay down between two target frames. Zalinski and Gallo were equally positioned. Zalinski was the spotter on this one, and Gallo the shooter. Gallo did not really need a spotter, since he worked out where the enemy sniper was, through some kind of Zen-based telepathy, but even the best sniper needed a partner to back him up. Accuracy was great, but God loved firepower too. Gallo had an M24. Zalinski had a customized SAW with a two-hundred-round box attached.

Brock spoke into his radio. "Counting down."

Ten seconds later, the first Coke bottle blew apart, spattering Brock with water. The enemy sniper would continue firing and moving every thirty seconds until all the bottles were destroyed or he was detected by Zalinski and Gallo. The enemy was between five and seven hundred meters away in brush and wearing a gillie suit, so spotting him was no easy task.

Gallo had his eyes closed and was lying on his back. It was a disconcerting habit for a sniper trying to track down a hostile, but it seemed to work for him.

Brock checked his watch. Five seconds more to go. Gallo normally seemed to sense the location of his man after the third or fourth shot, but he had been getting better recently. Some brain-enhancing herb he was taking. It helped to compensate for being with a woman, he said. Sex drained his powers and positively fucked with his concentration. On the other hand, without it, he went moody.

The second bottle exploded, this time showering Zalinski.

A split second later, Gallo rolled over onto his stomach and fired the laser attached to his sniper rifle. Green smoke spewed up from the brush. A direct hit.

Brock contemplated his star sniper. Gallo was looking remarkably pleased with himself. Zalinski was soaked.

"Gallo, you tricky fuck, you could have fired earlier," said Brock.

"The vibes weren't right," said Gallo.

THE Humvee passed the Delta compound and headed on toward Sicily Drop Zone. Delta was so classified that it was referred to as "the place that doesn't officially exist," but its unofficial presence bordered with chain-link fencing topped with razor wire was substantial. Aircraft coming in over Bragg to carry out drops used Delta's distinctive red roofs to verify their positions. One covered a killing house where CQB—close quarters battle techniques, developed initially by the SAS—were refined into an art.

"Homesick?" said Fitzduane.

Lonsdale was driving. He took his right hand off the wheel and gave a cross between a salute and a wave as he passed by. "It's a fraternity," he said. "You never quite leave. On the other hand, I could never quite go back. I'm too old for some of the bullshit."

Both men were wearing 82nd Airborne combat fatigues and their faces were camouflaged with green and black cream. It was the prescribed uniform west of Fort Bragg's Gruber Road. For much of the time it was not, strictly speaking, necessary, but it evoked the right mind-set. Combat to the Airborne was not a remote possibility. It could happen at any time. It made sense to be physically, mentally, and materially prepared. Besides, if you weren't cammied up the MPs stopped you, which was a pain.

"They say if you can make it in Bragg," said Lonsdale, "you can make it anywhere in the U.S. Army. The men mostly love it. Wives and girlfriends hate the place. With one of the three brigades always on eighteen-hour standby and EDREs being called whenever you least expect, your domestic life does not get much of a look in. There are more ways of being hurt than being killed or wounded. You can end up being turned on by a pair of watermelons."

Fitzduane smiled. They'd been looking for the Scout Platoon for the last hour. They'd been to the range but found only some empty Coke bottles and a sputtering range officer. The latest word was that Lieutenant Brock and his private army had headed off to Sicily DZ to do something with tanks. If Fitzduane had heard it right, a C130 was going to drop a couple on top of them. Strange people, the Scouts.

"Cochrane called from the Hill," he said. "He sounded—how shall I put it ... ?"

"Jealous," said Lonsdale. "What did you say?"

"I told him the President needed him, Congress needed him, and there was more important work to do on counterterrorism in the nation's capital than down here," said Fitzduane.

"True enough," said Lonsdale. "On the other hand, he'd be a good man to have with us. If memory serves, we'd both be sushi without him."

Fitzduane was silent. It would have been nice to have gone back with the whole team, but the 82nd had wanted advisers rather than an army. They had pointed out that they already had an army. Fitzduane as mission commander and one other was all they would wear. The team had drawn lots for the extra place.

"Well, this is one Lee will just have to miss," said Fitzduane.

The trees thinned out and then the vast open space that was Sicily DZ lay ahead. The earth was red, not unlike the soil in Lonsdale's valley in Arizona.

A solitary C130 was making its approach. As they watched, something substantial emerged from its rear, followed by an item of similar size. Seconds later, three large parachutes opened, checking the rapid descent of the first item. Almost immediately, the parachutes on the second parcel blossomed.

"Where they land Scout Platoon should be," said Fitzduane. "More or less."

Lonsdale headed the Humvee toward the descending tanks. There was no sign of Scout Platoon.

There was something surreal about seeing tanks floating through the air. They were strapped to thick, corrugated pallets. Packing material was wedged into vulnerable areas like the tracks.

The tanks seemed close enough to touch.

Lonsdale was staring out them too.

"For fuck's sake, we're underneath the bloody things," yelled Fitzduane. "This is ridiculous."

Lonsdale jammed on the brakes and then shot backward. Compared to a Guntrack, the speed was glacial. The tanks were now close enough to read the packing instructions. Lonsdale was doubled over with laughter.

The tanks impacted ten meters away, compressing their corrugated cushioning flat and raising clouds of red dust. The second machine seemed to bounce and then fell over on its side. It was even closer.

"YOU!" screamed a voice in Fitzduane's ear. "YOU WITH THE DEATH WISH! Get out of that vehicle and go right that Sheridan. ASAP, TROOPER!"

Fitzduane hopped to it. The area was suddenly full of running troopers. Within seconds, the tank was righted and the straps and packaging were being removed. He decided he'd let the experts get on with the next phase.

"FUCKHEAD!" screamed the voice. "WHO TOLD YOU TO STOP? MOVE, MOVE, MOVE!"

Fitzduane turned around. A short, stocky figure with an almost Mongolian cast to his black and green features was standing inches from him. Red dust clung to his fatigues and webbing, but his badges of rank and name tag could just be read. He was the closest thing to a demented dervish that Fitzduane had ever seen in uniform. Which was some statement around Bragg.

"Lieutenant Brock," said Fitzduane.

Brock stepped back and took a hard look at Fitzduane. The stranger's uniform bore neither a name tag nor badges of rank. On the other hand, the man was manifestly not some nineteen-year-old trooper.

"You're screwing up my exercise," said Brock. "Who the fuck are you?"

Fitzduane looked at him.

"I'd hate us to get off on the wrong foot, Lieutenant."

"Sir," added Brock.

Fitzduane told him.

"Hooah, sir," said Brock. A smile creased his features. "You've been there before, the CG said."

"In—and OUT!" said Lonsdale. "The second bit, Lieutenant, is the secret."

Fitzduane indicated the two tanks. "Tell me about your pets," he said.

Brock positively glowed. "Pets! Outstanding, sir. Where would like me to begin?"

JAEGER woke up sweating.

The motel-room furnishings looked unfamiliar. According to his watch it was work time, and a raised curtain revealed definite daylight. Blue skies. Sun. All the trappings.

Why had he been asleep in the middle of a perfectly normal, useful day? Was he drugged or drinking? Had he forgotten the work ethic he'd grown up with? Was a woman involved? What was he doing in Fayetteville?

He drank a glass of water and lay back with his eyes closed.

In his mind's eye he could see the immense steel barrel of the supergun in the Devil's Footprint spurt an endless tongue of flame and send its deadly projectile toward his country. Washington, D.C.? New York? Cleveland? Los Angeles? What did it matter? All that was important was that a population center was targeted.

The weapon would be fired. Fitzduane was sure of it. As he understood the workings of Oshima's mind rather better, Jaeger himself was certain of it.

OPERATION CARTHAGE might bring it forward a few hours, a day, a week, but either way the supergun was going to be used.

The assault troops, no matter what they did, could not stop it.

If it worked, thousands of people would die. Probably tens of thousands. Possibly a great deal more. And that would just be the immediate effect. The greater impact would be on America's credibility.

Jaeger swung his legs off the bed and put his head between his knees. The dizziness passed. He began to remember the SCIF and the heat and the mission and Lieutenant Colonel Carlson dripping with sweat, keeping his eye on the ball. And Fitzduane and Lonsdale going back for a second time. *Back to the science of it all,* his brain told him. Forget all this emotion. Focus on the scientific facts and the physical reactions that must result.

Hydrogen was the propellant being used by Rheiman's supergun in the Devil's Footprint. Hydrogen alone was too volatile and would explode too fast, so it was blended with helium. The mixing of the two gases was controlled and monitored electronically.

Remove the original controller mechanism and substitute a replacement that would read out correctly but actually allow a mainly hydrogen mix into the barrel. And what would you get?

One hell of an explosion.

Strong enough to burst a barrel made of maraging steel?

That's what the computer simulation said would happen. But computer simulation was far from foolproof. That's why you did field trials. Real life had a habit of being quirky.

Replacing the controller mechanism had seemed like a good idea when the main objective was merely to disrupt the testing program. Now Xyclax Gamma 18 had raised the stakes beyond Jaeger's ability to handle the situation. The issue was not just would the barrel burst when fired. The question then was what would happen to the nerve agent. It *should* be incinerated. The one saving grace of the stuff was that it was volatile. It could be spread by the force of the explosion throughout the entire area. Two whole brigades of the 82nd Airborne would die. NBC suits would make no difference.

Even if it all worked out this time, from his research at Livermore, Jaeger knew better than most what other threats were in the pipeline. The millennium was approaching, and the level of threat from weapons of mass destruction was terrifying.

Jaeger rose to his feet and walked wearily into the shower. He'd had five hours' sleep in the last two days, and it did not look as if he was going to get any more until OPERATION CARTHAGE was over.

There was something he had forgotten, he was sure of it.

Several of his fellow scientists at Livermore had suggested flying a smart bomb down the meter-wide muzzle of the supergun, and Jaeger was beginning to wish he had recommended that option. It was a small target to hit, but it was certainly technically possible, especially if the aperture was lased by a ground-based special-forces team. But even that option could have needed several strikes to be absolutely sure of success. And an initial miss could precipitate the firing of the supergun in retaliation, even if a whole wing of F16s were racked up to do the job. Nothing was certain in combat except that whatever plans you made in advance would get fucked by circumstances.

No, the double advantage of the sabotaged controller option was that if it worked, it would prevent the weapon being fired successfully at all, and would undermine the credibility of the weapon.

Cochrane's task force was right. The damn things were too easy to make. The illusion had to be created that the supergun technology was inherently flawed.

What had he forgotten?

OSHIMA studied the blueprint of the supergun intently.

She had no particular scientific bent, but the good thing about the supergun itself was that, once you understood the principles, it was not really that complicated.

Rheiman had called it a giant peashooter. Put a dried pea on the table and try to try and blow it across the room and you would have a hard time moving it more than a few feet. Place it in a peashooter, give a good puff, and you could "dent a windowpane."

The real complexity lay in the supergun's projectile. But that was beyond her capabilities to worry about, so she had wiped it from her mind and focused on the gun. The weapon had been sabotaged, but unsuccessfully. That could have meant Fitzduane's raiders had not come prepared—a strong possibility, given that rescuing his woman was clearly the main object of the mission. But it could also mean that the explosive charges were a diversion.

But a diversion from what? What else had the raiders been up to?

Oshima transferred her gaze to Salerno. Rheiman had been brilliant, but erratic and lazy. He had compensated by hiring a hardworking support team. Dr. Salerno had been his second in command and had taken over Rheiman's role as project manager without missing a beat.

People were rarely indispensable, Oshima reflected.

"Salerno," she said, "I know these people. You have seen the damage they inflicted elsewhere. Why has Dr. Rheiman's weapon escaped unscathed? What have we missed?"

Salerno was terrified of Oshima, but within his area of expertise he felt confident.

"They had only fifteen to twenty minutes," he said. "They did what they could in that time, but the weapon is so large and strong it is extremely difficult to damage. The charges they placed were standard military demolitions. I really do not think, Commander, that they came prepared."

Oshima looked back at the blueprint. "The barrel," she said. "Could they have weakened it in some way?"

"We put a man down the barrel with ultrasonic equipment," said Salerno. "We have examined every millimeter of the structure *twice,* and all of it is within tolerance."

"Within tolerance?" said Oshima.

"No manufacture is perfect," said Salerno carefully. "There are flaws and imperfections in every product, but the important factor to ascertain is the scale of such problems. In this case, we have nothing to worry about. In a layperson's terms, the barrel is fine. The same judgment applies to the rest of the weapon."

"The breech, the firing mechanism, the gas lines?" said Oshima.

"All have been examined in great detail," said Salerno.

"I wonder why they didn't blow the hydrogen?" said Oshima.

"As you know, Commander," said Salerno, "the main hydrogen tanks are kept in a series of underground bunkers separate from the weapon. Either they did not know they were there or they had no time. Anyway, they would have had to blow all the hydrogen tanks to seriously affect us, and that was beyond their capabilities. Even if they had achieved all that, we have our own hydrogen-generation plant under Madoa airfield."

Oshima drew her automatic and pointed it directly at Salerno's face. "Dr. Salerno, I want you to imagine your life depends on your answer," she said softly.

She smiled and pulled back the hammer. "Because it does."

Salerno's mouth felt completely dry.

"Imagine you have only twenty minutes to accomplish your mission but that you know everything there is to know about this technology. Now, where is this weapon most vulnerable? What would you do?"

Salerno thought. His mind ran through the blueprints and electronic schematics. Suddenly, he knew. But if he admitted he had not checked the gas controller, what would this woman do?

Oshima saw the flicker in Salerno's eyes. So he had forgotten something. It was always the same with experts. Long on theory. Short on practicalities.

"Talk to me, Dr. Salerno," she said.

✳ CHAPTER TWENTY-FIVE

"THE AIR FORCE is open for business. MOUNT UP!"

Lines of paratroopers waddled toward waiting C130s. Laden with parachute, reserve, rucksack, weapon, ammunition, and specialist equipment—everything from explosives to spare batteries to AT4s—the troopers moved with the grace and dynamism of sumo wrestlers on a chain gang.

The Airborne were renowned for dash and élan, but that was after they hit the ground. Loading up was a torturous process. Flight time was not much of an improvement.

No aircraft was better loved by the Airborne than the C130, but the hard truth was that by the time sixty-four fully equipped troopers were sandwiched in, even moving a sick bag up and down required collaborative effort. There was no walking up and down the aisles. There was no aisle space left in which to perambulate. Paratroopers sat knee to knee in two double rows facing each other, with all the intervening space jammed with their equipment. If you had an itch, or a weak bladder, you were well advised to attend to your needs beforehand. The only way you could move from one end of the aircraft to the other was by behaving rather like a monkey moving around a cage, with the web mesh that supported the seating acting as the bars. A monkey in jump boots.

Fitzduane was of the opinion that the powers that be knew what they were doing. The crush was so great that as time wore on jumping out of the aircraft became an increasingly attractive option.

The ramp was half raised but not closed. There were few windows in the rear of the C130, and the air and just the sight of the sky provided a welcome respite.

The four turboprop engines fired up and clouds of red dust obscured the open aperture. The aircraft vibrated. The background noise level rose to something above pleasant but below intolerable. You could talk, but only by banging your coveralls together. The jumpmasters and safeties wore headphones and were plugged in to the flight intercom system.

Fitzduane had been custom-fitted between Lieutenant Colonel Zachariah Carlson and Lonsdale. Across him sat Brock. Scout Platoon occupied the adjoining space. The unit looked quite menacing enough to carry out the mission on their own.

Carlson leaned toward Fitzduane. "We were just like this, waiting for takeoff before the Haiti mission," he said, "when there was a banging on the door and we found one of the sergeant majors outside. He'd been on leave, but just couldn't bear to miss the action. He drove right to Green Ramp in civilian clothes. No weapon, no helmet, no parachute even."

Fitzduane wasn't paying full attention. If his eyes did not deceive him, a head had appeared above the top of the half-open ramp.

He blinked. The head had vanished. He was imagining things. The aircraft started to taxi.

He focused on Carlson. "What did you do with the guy?" he said. "Throw him out to test the wind?"

Carlson smiled. "Hell no. We kitted him out with bits and pieces. Anyone with that kind of Airborne spirit deserves to jump."

Fitzduane blinked again. This time there was no mistake. The head had reappeared above the ramp, and as he watched, the figure slid down into the aircraft in a cloud of red North Carolina dust. The C130 was picking up speed.

Sixty-four helmeted green and black faces stared at the intruder. He was wearing a suit and tie that, once given a good vacuuming, would have passed muster on the Hill when Congress was in session.

"Glad you know the form," said Fitzduane to Carlson.

"What the fuck!" said Brock.

"WHERE DO I SIT?" shouted Cochrane.

Fitzduane grinned evilly.

"Friend of yours?" said Carlson.

Fitzduane shook his head. "Pass the word to that yo-yo that it's going to be a long fucking flight."

Cochrane caught his eye and waved. "Hi, Hugo!" he shouted.

Sixty-four helmeted green and black faces stared at Fitzduane.

"What the fuck!" said Brock.

WITH some difficulty and the cooperation of his entire row, who all leaned to give him space, Fitzduane wrapped a two-inch-wide strip of white tape around Cochrane's left arm.

The chief of staff had been scavenging and negotiating for some considerable time and now looked more like a paratrooper. He had a helmet and uniform and his face was green. Even the shoes had gone, though the boots were zip-up flight issue.

His roster of equipment was nearly complete—but not quite.

"What's the tape for?" said Cochrane.

"Identifies you as belonging to First Brigade," said Fitzduane, "and may stop you getting shot. Maybe I should take it back."

Cochrane ignored the comment. "What do I need to know? Keep it very simple. Brief me like you were using big print—and I was a politician. No big words."

"When we hit the ground, we're going after Oshima," said Fitzduane.

"How do you know where she'll be?" said Cochrane.

"There's a command bunker under Madoa airfield," said Fitzduane. "Rheiman was persuaded to draw a map. In the event of an attack, apparently that's where she'll be."

"If she isn't?" said Cochrane.

"I'll be profoundly irritated," said Fitzduane.

"Anything else?" said Cochrane.

"Roll when you hit the ground," said Fitzduane. "But first, remember to borrow a parachute."

Cochrane sat very still. "Aaaah!" he said slowly. "And I was doing so well."

Brock's eyes rolled upward. He shook his head. "What the fuck!" he said.

"You forget to tell him the challenge and countersign," said Carlson.

Fitzduane nodded. "*Happiness*," he said, "is the challenge."

"What's the countersign?" said Cochrane.

"*Dead woodpecker*," said Brock. He pumped his arm.

"HOOAH, SIR!" said Scout Platoon in unison.

Cochrane leaned toward Fitzduane. "Are they always like this?" he said.

"Pretty much," said Fitzduane.

The two jumpmasters, one for each door, faced down their respective double rows of troopers. Their legs were spread, the knees slightly bent, and their arms were ready at their sides as if to draw.

The posture was straight out of Dodge City. Straight gunslinger. And just as compelling.

The tension ratcheted up. The eyes of every trooper were focused on their respective jumpmasters. Fitzduane could feel the adrenaline start to pump. Hands flashed up palms outward, opening and closing twice.

"TWENTY MINUTES!" roared the jumpmasters, voices and hand movements in perfect harmony.

"TWENTY MINUTES!" responded the combined voices of sixty-four paratroopers.

"THEY'VE secured Arkono, sir," said Colonel Dave Palmer, the divisional executive officer. "No opposition. The strip was abandoned. The Kiowas are being landed as we speak."

General Mike Gannon nodded. He was a great believer in the 82nd's Kiowa Warrior helicopters, but they had neither the range nor the air-to-air refueling capability to make the journey on their own. That meant flying them in C130s and landing them close enough to the target area to be unloaded and on station when the division went in.

The nearest airstrip of adequate size was Arkono—the same strip that Fitzduane's group had used for their escape. There had been a decided possibility that Arkono would be occupied this time, but a pathfinder team had shown it still to be deserted.

The terrorists were consolidating their manpower. The Devil's Footprint complex was going to be a hard nut to crack. Gannon had no doubt but that the 82nd would triumph, but the question of casualties was foremost in his mind.

An airborne assault accelerated the entire combat cycle. You could win your objective faster, but the price could be terrible. In the past, parachute assaults had cost as high as fifty percent casualties.

The figure should be nothing like that this time, *if* Carlson and his team had planned everything correctly.

But the wild card was the supergun.

THE faintest hint of a smile on his lips, Lieutenant Colonel Zachariah Carlson sat with his eyes closed as if meditating.

Slap a saffron robe on him and give him a begging bowl, and he would do well as a Buddhist monk, Fitzduane reflected. He already damn near had the shaven head.

An aura of calm exuded from the paratrooper. Internally he was probably using "What the fuck am I doing here?" as a mantra, but externally he looked as if he had just had sex—and it had been *good*—and Nirvana was just coming up over the horizon.

No worries. Positive vibrations.

His example seemed to be infectious. Although the tension had definitely increased in the aircraft since the jumpmasters' initial warning call, there were few external signs of fear. Of course, packed that tightly together, you could not really do much to show what was churning away inside.

You couldn't prowl up and down. You couldn't shuffle your feet. You could not even shake with fear without alerting your entire row.

You certainly could not run away. All you could do was sweat, and laden with equipment and packed together as you were, you were doing that anyway.

You were committed.

In minutes you would be doing what you had been trained to do. You would be jumping into a hot zone where several thousand hostiles would be doing their best to kill you.

Unless you killed them first. Which was beginning to seem like an increasingly good idea. In fact, the only option.

Acceptance of that decision had a definite calming effect. Instead of focusing on what might happen, you zeroed in on *what had to be done* and the tools you had to do the job.

Mission focus. The best antidote to fear. Combat-proven since the first cave dweller had sallied out to kill something large and unfriendly for supper.

Carlson's brain was racing. The assault plan was the product of the entire divisional planning team and had been signed off on by the CG and more than a few layers above his pay grade. Nonetheless the core strategy was his and, rather more than he cared to admit, Fitzduane's.

The airborne had half a century's experience in parachute assaults, so how in hell had he allowed this stranger to so influence their thinking?

Conventional wisdom dictated that they should assault Madoa airfield and the heavily reinforced supergun valley simultaneously. Instead, the entire focus was on the airfield and the supergun was being left to destroy itself—with a little follow-up help from the air force.

But what about the troops dug in around the supergun valley's perimeter? Even if the supergun did blow, what was to stop the perimeter troops from attacking the airborne from the rear as they battled to secure the airfield? There were only eight kilometers to cross, and the terrorists had artillery, mortars, and armor.

Fitzduane had argued that the supergun explosion would be devastating and that any survivors of the perimeter forces could be handled by air or mopped up afterward. The clincher was that friendly forces should be kept out of the area until the supergun was destroyed or they would be duck soup too.

It had seemed to make sense, but now Carlson was wondering. Well-dug-in troops have an incredible ability to survive blast. How violent can one conventional explosion be? Anyway, even if the sabotage works, how do we know that the terrorists will fire the weapon?

I know Oshima, Fitzduane had said with absolute certainty. *She won't fire immediately. She will keep her options open for as long as she can—but as soon as she knows the full scale of the assault and realizes that she cannot hold, then she will fire. Sooner rather than later.*

And then? Carlson had queried.

If the supergun blows, she will do three things, Fitzduane had said. She will fight a furious delaying action for as long as possible; if she has the expertise she may try to mine or activate any nerve agents stored off the command bunker in some way that will buy her time; and she will try to escape.

How can you be so sure? Carlson had argued.

She learned much of her trade under the terrorist known as the Hangman, Fitzduane had said. Her subsequent record proved that she learned well. As sure as it rains in the West of Ireland—both when you expect it and when you don't— Oshima will have an escape route planned.

The Devil's Footprint complex is hundreds of kilometers from anywhere, Carlson had said. Oshima's command bunker in Madoa is going to have two brigades of the 82nd Airborne Division descend around it and blow it to shit. The airfield itself is surrounded by a belt of mines up to half a kilometer deep. There will be so much aerial reconnaissance an AWACS will have to make sure no one bumps into each other. So how?

That's for her to know and us to find out, Fitzduane had said.

How do we do that? Carson had asked.

You lie back and soak in a nice deep hot bath with your eyes closed and think a lot, said Fitzduane.

Carson smiled to himself at the memory, but the anxiety did not go away.

"TEN MINUTES!" shouted the jumpmasters, hands opening and closing twice, energy and urgency radiating from them like some kind of psychic transfusion.

"TEN MINUTES!" roared back the planeload of paratroopers.

Carlson's mind snapped clear of doubt and uncertainty. Repining was useless. It was going to happen.

"SHIT!" said Cochrane. "I nearly forgot."

Fitzduane was thinking about the ground disturbance the infra red satellite photographs had shown up. On the face of it an extensive tunnel network had been constructed under the airfield by the relatively fast technique of evacuating the earth, constructing a deep trench, roofing it over, and then covering it in.

But Oshima must have known that surveillance would show up the disturbed ground, and it was not like her to limit her work to something so obvious.

So what else had she done? What had she constructed that would not show? How many of the tunnels she had constructed were decoys? Had she constructed other tunnels by purely underground digging that would not show up on film? The giveaway would be the extracted earth, but that could be intermingled in the earth extracted from the trenches.

Detectable tunnels near the surface. Hidden tunnels much deeper down. But deep digging would be much harder, and this was a rocky plateau. Where could you dig? How would you dig? How fast could you dig? They had seen an excess of bulldozers and surface-digging equipment, but had they seen any tunneling equipment? What were your options?

What he had really needed were the detailed geological reports. The whole area had originally been surveyed when exploring for oil.

"I've got the reports," said Cochrane. "Maury dug them up."

Fitzduane glared at him. "You've spent too long on the Hill, Lee, briefing congressmen just before they vote. It's supposed to be done differently when people are shooting at you."

Cochrane tried to shrug. It wasn't possible.

"What am I supposed to do with them?" snarled Fitzduane. "Read them on the way down?"

"Airborne!" said Brock. "Cool suggestion, sir!"

"FIVE MINUTES!" roared the jumpmasters. Five fingers came up.

"FIVE MINUTES!" came the response.

"GET READY!"

"GET READY!"

"OUTBOARD PERSONNEL, STAND UP!"

"OUTBOARD PERSONNEL, STAND UP!"

"INBOARD PERSONNEL, STAND UP!"

"INBOARD PERSONNEL, STAND UP!"

"HOOK UP!"

"HOOK UP!"

"CHECK STATIC LINE!"

"CHECK STATIC LINE!"

"CHECK EQUIPMENT!"

"CHECK EQUIPMENT!"

"I can't get to them anyway," said Cochrane. "They're in the small of my back under all this gear. God, I feel like an Egyptian mummy."

"You should live so long, sir," said Brock.

The side doors were slid open. The sound of the engines suddenly increased and was combined with the rush of air and the noise of the slipstream.

"THREE MINUTES!" shouted the jumpmasters.

"THREE MINUTES!" blasted back the paratroopers.

"STAND BY!"

"STAND BY!"

A row of holes appeared toward the tail of the aircraft.

Seconds later there was a flash of tracer and the helmet of one of the air force loadmasters seemed to explode.

Blood showered from his neck over a nearby safety officer as he collapsed. The aircraft bucked and rolled as antiaircraft fire exploded nearby.

"Guess we'd better get down there," said Brock quietly, "and refocus the fucks."

The jumping light was red. As they watched, it turned green.

"GO! GO! GO! GO! GO! GO! GO! GO! GO!"

Two open doors. A paratrooper in just under a second jumped out of each door, the rhythm alternating.

The last two to jump were the two jumpmasters.

In thirty-six seconds, the sixty-four troopers were gone and the C130 was headed to Arkono to refuel and wait to extract the dead and wounded.

The surviving air force loadmaster secured the doors, then slumped on a bench in shock. He had seen quite enough through the open doors to make him glad he had joined the air force rather than the infantry. The 82nd were jumping into a maelstrom.

THE command bunker was made up of a linked series of insulated steel spheres supported by hydraulic shock absorbers similar to the kind used by high-rise buildings in Japan to make them earthquake resistant. Above the bunker there were layers of armor plate, reinforced concrete, packed earth, and yet more concrete to a height of fifty feet.

For all practical purposes, they were invulnerable to conventional bombing. There were rumors of rocket-assisted penetrator bombs in development, but as far as anyone seemed to know they were just rumors. Certainly, they were immune to virtually all existing bombs in general use.

The bombing had started without warning. Radar screens showed nothing. Oshima had been making a personal inspection of the radar facility when the attack started, and she could see the screens for herself when she felt the shock of the first impact.

There was absolutely *nothing* on the radar—not even a hint or a shadow.

Artillery? Was the Mexican Army making a move at last? Chiapas was relatively quiet, so maybe they thought now was the time to make a move.

Yet someone would have warned them. True, Quintana was dead, but they still had plenty of informants in place. Someone would have told them if the

Mexicans were planning anything. Anyway, could the Mexicans have penetrated the plateau in strength without being detected?

Impossible.

The bunker rocked again and then again. The lights flickered and went off. Seconds later, emergency power cut in and then the reserve generator started up and full light was restored.

"Bombing, Commander. Heavy bombing," said Jin Endo, one of the few remaining Yaibo members still left alive. The few others were unfortunately not of the first rank. But, despite his youth, Jin Endo was special. He was intelligent, he was quick, and he had proved himself. Above all, he was loyal. Jin Endo would be useful.

Colonel Carranza had been General Barragan's second in command. His loyalty was based on nothing more than the stark reality that he had no place to go.

He would fight if it came to that. But this was Mexico. The Americans might conceivably bomb Tecuno if requested by the Mexican government, but they would never send in ground troops. Vietnam, Lebanon, Somalia, and the U.S. media had seen to that. Casualties were not politically acceptable.

"She's right," said Carranza grimly. "Those are bombs, and no radar warning means Stealth fighters—which means the Americans."

"Activate the monitors," said Oshima.

The command bunker exercised its command-and-control function through a network of deeply buried landlines and video monitors. The most important link was to the supergun valley. Oshima could fire the weapon from the command bunker. It was a simple matter of inserting two keys and flicking a small switch. Quintana used to be the primary key holder, but he no longer featured in the firing solution. Both keys were now around Oshima's neck.

The bank of a dozen monitors came on stream. They were on permanently during daylight hours, but in darkness they were activated only as needed to preserve the batteries on their night-vision equipment. The terrorist troops did not have night-vision devices except in key points, but a limited number of the long-lens monitor cameras were equipped with them.

As Oshima watched, one of the heavily fortified perimeter positions erupted in a massive yellow and pink blast. She could see bodies and weapon parts sail skyward and rain down. Blast followed blast with such frequency that one shock ran into another and the vibrations of the bunker on its hydraulic mounts were continuous. With each explosion, the destruction mounted.

"Do a perimeter scan," said Oshima.

The monitors followed a preset pattern. Portion after portion of the external perimeter was illuminated, but she could see nothing. If there was going to be an external attack, there would be some sign at this stage, even if it was only incoming artillery fire.

"Bring up the Devil's Footprint," said Oshima, "and let me speak to the supergun commander."

The link with the Devil's Footprint was by fiber-optic cable, with multiple redundancy built in. The images came up immediately.

As she looked, Oshima felt a surge of exhilaration. The supergun valley was not being attacked. Somehow, she suspected, the Americans must know what she had and they were afraid to act directly against the weapon in case they set it off. They were strong, incredibly strong, but they were vulnerable.

"Commander, look," said Carranza. "Look at the radar."

The screens had been blank. Now, suddenly, the radar silhouettes of dozens of approaching aircraft could be seen. The speeds were slow. These were not fighter bombers. These were transport planes. Even for transports they were flying slowly.

"Paratroops," breathed Carranza. "Incredible! Lightly armed paratroops. What a target! We'll slaughter them in the air and we'll slaughter them on the ground. When they jump, their air cover will have to cease and then we'll get them. Thank God for General Barragan's foresight."

Most of Madoa airfield's eighty-nine fixed weapons positions had been either destroyed or badly damaged. However, that was of limited significance. The positions were lightly manned and were primarily decoys.

The real defenses were buried. They included a heavily armored mechanized force and a hand surface-to-air held missile unit. The SAMs had been trained to regard their main enemy as the helicopter, but lumbering C130s traveling at much the same speed would be an even easier target.

"Shall I give the order, Commander?" said Carranza to Oshima.

Oshima waited until the lead aircraft were within visual range and showing up on the monitors. Carranza had been right. The bombing had virtually stopped. Another few seconds.

Suddenly she could see black dots falling from the aircraft and then parachutes opening.

"Now!" she said.

Carranza spoke into his microphone. From bunkers and tunnels all over the airfield, aircraft-killing teams erupted and took up position in prepared fighting holes.

TWENTY thousand feet up, an air force C141 command-and-control aircraft circled and monitored the unfolding battle below.

Inside the spacious cargo bay of the aircraft, slide-in communications modules housed a combined services team. Data was being fed in from AWACS and JSTARS aircraft and from a host of other sources, including Special Forces A-teams that were monitoring a chain of lookout posts around the perimeter.

The closest monitoring was being carried out by a Delta unit who were actually inside the terrorist base. They had HAHOed into the center of Madoa Air Base under cover of the opening assault fires and were now concealed on the roof of the main hangar and in the control tower.

They had assailed the control tower expecting it to be fully manned, but in fact it was empty. The occupants had had little to do since most of their air assets were destroyed in the microlight raid, and as soon as the first bombs had dropped they had headed for a bunker. Delta had the control tower to themselves.

It commanded a perfect view of the terrorist air base, and even with its windows blown in by the blasts of the initial bombing, it was an ideal observation point.

Delta troopers concealed on the hangar roof four hundred meters away regarded their colleagues in the tower with some envy. They did not know much about the bird life on the Tecuno plateau, but whatever there was had seemed to produce copiously and to regard the roof as its dumping ground.

The soldiers were lying in years of accumulated bird shit. It made the going hazardous and the smell vile. It might have been funny, except that the second man to land on the roof had slipped on the mess and broken his neck. Lifeless, he had been unable to stop himself and his body had slid over the edge to hang several feet below the parapet. He had been hauled back by his parachute harness without being seen and now lay in a gully temporarily out of sight and mind.

Colonel Dave Palmer, the 82nd's divisional executive officer, was the senior military man in the C141, and he regarded the unfolding developments with a blend of concern, fascination, and frustration. If military logic had had anything to do with it, the Commanding General would have been in the command-and-control aircraft. It was the location with the best overview and communications— in fact, it could be argued; far and away the best position from which to direct the battle.

However, there were some situations where immediate military logic did not come into it and overall unit pride was considered more important. In the 82nd officers led from the front, and that meant that General Mike Gannon jumped at the head of his troops.

Palmer sweated as he watched the terrorist base transform itself. Within five minutes of the cessation of the bombing, dozens of new fighting positions had appeared as top cover was pulled away, and there looked to be several hundred smaller fighting holes.

For the moment, his focus was entirely on antiaircraft defenses, particularly SAMs and heavy machine guns. Data flowed in, and after it was plotted and assigned a targeting number, the mission was passed to a killing team.

Palmer was soon convinced that virtually all the hidden antiaircraft defenses had now been plotted, but the final test was about to come. Any missiles or gun positions still hidden were certain to be revealed when the attacking aircraft were actually overhead. Far below him he watched the first flight approach the airfield. The radar showed them flying low, straight, and level, as they had to do to effect an accurate drop.

The approach to a drop zone was always the most dangerous part of an airborne operation. For those brief few minutes, the aircraft were exposed and vulnerable and the paratroopers inside—laden with the tools of killing though they were—were entirely helpless.

As he watched, missiles streaked up from the airfield and first one and then another and then most of the first flight were hit. Explosions lit up the sky and pieces of flaming aircraft cascaded toward the ground.

He felt ill as he watched. In his mind he was hooked up, ready to jump. He could see the jump light switch from red to green and feel the slap of the jumpmaster on his shoulder. "GO!"

He shook his head and looked across to his air force opposite number.

"Now?" said the colonel.

"Now," said Palmer.

A single phrase went out to the prepositioned air assets. Two aircraft had been assigned to each air defense position, and there were further aircraft in reserve to pick up any slack. Kiowa Warriors hovered hidden behind rocks or in folds in the ground, only their mast sights protruding.

"ACTIVATE BARRACUDA! ACTIVATE BARRACUDA!"

"THE radar screens have gone blank again," said Carranza. "I don't understand it. A moment ago we could see the aircraft coming in two by two like cattle into a slaughterhouse—and now there is nothing."

"We are being jammed, sir," said one of the operators at the console.

"Then why didn't they jam earlier?" said Carranza. "Why allow us to see their aircraft as they approach and then jam us after most of them have been destroyed? It makes no sense."

Oshima was looking at the monitor bank. The cameras overlooking the supergun valley showed total normality. Elsewhere, the airfield flickered with dozens of fires from falling aircraft debris. As she looked, she could see her troops moving out from their fighting positions to examine the wreckage and round up any paratroopers left alive.

Oddly enough, she could not see any parachutes on the ground, and there certainly should have been some there by now. Were they set on fire by falling debris? Had they fallen outside the perimeter? Well, it was an oddity but of no major concern. It was probably more to do with the cameras. They gave a good overall picture of the airfield, but they were no substitute for direct vision.

Carranza had been listening to reports from the units on the surface. Initial reports were vastly encouraging and confirmed what the monitors had shown. The antiaircraft crews had enjoyed major success. Nine out of the initial dozen aircraft had been totally destroyed in a couple of minutes.

Carranza tried to remember how many paratroops fit into a C130. Something like sixty, he thought. The total destroyed equated to the best part of a battalion.

His, Carranza's, troops were beating the Americans! With all their might and technology, they could bleed too.

All the monitors except those showing the supergun flickered and then went dull.

The communications operator's face went gray as a further report came in. "Major Carranza," he said. "We have a report from Captain Alonzo. He'd like to speak to you."

Carranza took the phone. "Major," said Alonzo's familiar voice. He was one of the best battalion commanders. Imaginative and cool under pressure. He never flapped.

"Major," said Alonzo dully. "The aircraft that we destroyed . . ."

"Yes," said Carranza. "A magnificent job. Absolutely magnificent."

There was a pause at the end of the phone. Alonzo was breathing heavily, as if he had been running or was completely stressed out. Either way, it was out of character. Alonzo was calm to the point of deliberateness.

"Yes, Captain," said Carranza impatiently. "What is it?"

"Major, they're drones," said Alonzo. "They're all RPVs."

Carranza's hand holding the phone fell to his side.

"What?" said Oshima impatiently.

Carranza whipped the phone back up to his ear. "Captain, GET BACK UNDER COVER NOW! NOW!"

"CARRANZA!" shouted Oshima. "WHAT IS GOING ON?"

"We've been tricked," said Carranza. "Those aircraft were decoys. Remotely piloted vehicles. Models."

"The radar picture?" said Oshima incredulously.

"We saw what they wanted us to see," said Carranza. "They've been playing with us."

The module suddenly shook, and this time the explosions were virtually continuous. Oshima tried the phones. All were silent except for the supergun. Everywhere else was shut down. The shaking continued. The bombardment seemed without end.

COLONEL Dave Palmer checked the targeting display.

Combat at this level was goddamn clinical. You identified targets, selected the best tool to handle the job in much the same manner as choosing a golf club for a tricky shot, and then passed the chosen the details.

The flight leaders muttered, "Roger that, Big Daddy," and that was that.

Minutes—sometimes seconds—later, men died. Some quickly. Some slowly and horribly. The scale of the destruction was vast, the human impact impossible to truly comprehend.

But this was the reality of war. This was what he trained for and this was what he was good at. From 20,000 feet, he could not see the blood or hear the screams. So why was it so much worse at this remove?

"Coffee, sir?" said an air force crewman.

Palmer shook his head. To be sipping coffee while Mike Gannon was slugging it out on the ground seemed wrong.

"Take some," said his air force colleague. The man was looking at him with concern. Palmer nodded and took it.

"The fast movers are out," said a chief at a monitor. "The count is good. One F16 hit, but the pilot reckons he can make it to Arkono. SAMs and triple-A pretty much wiped. The Airborne are going in. Spectres and A10s are working the margins. The Kiowas say the Fourth of July is like nothing compared to what's going on down there. It's a field of fires, sirs."

And the division is jumping right into the middle, thought Palmer. All the goddamn way. Which is the way it should be. But why am I up here out of harm's way when friends are fighting and dying?

Targeting was approached as methodically as possible, but it was an imperfect world.

Palmer had switched his focus to enemy armor deployment when the only heavy missile battery the Barracuda strikes had missed got a lock on the lumbering C141 and blew its left wing off at the root.

With fire spreading throughout the fuselage, the doomed aircraft spiraled erratically toward the ground below.

Desperately, Palmer scrabbled for his 'chute. There wasn't time to put it on. He broke out of the module and ran for a side door.

It was open. The rear air crew had already jumped.

Holding on to his parachute pack for dear life, he threw out into the safety of nothing.

Where was the D ring? He could not find it.

Above, at 23,000 feet, the reserve command-and-control aircraft had taken over. You built redundancy into airborne missions.

The new airborne command was fully operational before Palmer hit the ground.

CHAPTER TWENTY-SIX

FITZDUANE LET HIS rucksack drop away on its line as he flared in.

The ruck would hit first and he would land lighter, but that was not going to be much use if he landed smack in front of a terrorist bunker.

It was not an academic thought. He was used to the more maneuverable rectangular ram air 'chute, and the circular T15 the airborne used was markedly less responsive.

He had remembered too late and now was going to pay the penalty. What a fucking stupid, unprofessional error.

He hit hard and then skidded onto his back. Pain shot through his body and then he smashed into something soft and yielding. Without question, it was the worst landing he had made in he hated to think how many jumps. He was lying on—or half in—an eviscerated body. Whose side it belonged to it was impossible to tell.

Flame stabbed over his head and turned into green tracer. The noise was deafening.

With horror he realized he was lying directly under the firing aperture of the bunker. The only good news was that the gun crew inside had been temporarily blinded by his parachute wrapping itself around the emplacement.

There was a surge of flame as the heavy machine gun fired again through the folds of fabric and his parachute ignited.

Fitzduane rolled to one side, turning over again and again, and as he did so an AT4 rocket flamed out of the darkness and hit the bunker just below the aperture. The structure exploded.

Figures stumbled out of a trench at the back of the bunker. Silhouetted against the sudden flame of an A10 missile strike on the perimeter, he could see the curved magazines of AK-47s.

There were six terrorists in the group. Two seemed dazed, but the others carried themselves as if they would like to find out who had blown up their home.

Fitzduane's M16 was still in its padded jump case. He was of the opinion that this might be a great idea to avoid unnecessary damage while training, but as a combat technique he thought it sucked. He was going to die because some bean counter objected to wear and tear on the weaponry. If he got back, he was going to find whoever ordered this idiot shit and do something unfriendly to them.

He pulled a Willie Pete from his map pocket, pulled the pin, hoped the fuse had been set correctly, and waited three long seconds.

The terrorists heard the sound of the pin being removed, but identifying a single sound when the world was blowing up around you was not easy. In the background Fitzduane could see the breath of a dragon as an A10 blasted uranium-depleted shells at a terrorist tank.

The tank exploded as Fitzduane threw the grenade.

As the missile left his fingers he drew his pistol and fired twice at one terrorist who had been turning toward him. The rounds hit the man in the face and snapped his head back just as the phosphorus grenade exploded.

Two terrorists were left standing as the white smoke eddied around them. Both were burning, one screaming terribly.

Fitzduane fired again, double-tapping head shots.

Both figures slumped.

A smell of still-burning flesh wafted toward him. The phosphorus burned at 5,000 degrees Fahrenheit and was nearly impossible to put out.

He cut his M16 out of its case with his fighting knife and jacked in a round. The A10s and C130 Spectre gunships were pounding the perimeter, but unless requested the center belonged to the airborne.

Despite the background of flashes, it struck him that the place was damn dark, and then he remembered the night-vision goggles on a cord around his neck under his shirt. He pulled them out and clipped them on his Kevlar.

His heart gave a sudden start.

Half a dozen infrared-detectable laser beams were focused on his torso. That they had not fired already was encouraging, but the thought that six charged-up paratroops had him in their sights was a little chilling.

"Dead woodpecker," he croaked.

"Fuck 'em all, Colonel," said Brock cheerfully.

His shape detached itself from the ground, moved forward, and then went down again.

I'm up, I'm seen, I'm down. You took longer, and if your enemy was remotely competent you died. *And God will miss you.* Only the glint tape on his helmet—detectable solely with the night vision goggles and the air force's equipment—gave away his position. Brock was one mean mover, and judging by how little

Fitzduane could see of his platoon as he looked around, he had trained his men equally well.

"Situation?" said Fitzduane. Carlson had remarked that no matter how much you prepared, command during the first thirty minutes of a large-scale drop was at best all about managing chaos. Even in a tight insertion, heavy equipment ended up in the wrong place and units got horribly mixed up. Enemy fire and other hostile action compounded the confusion.

An airborne assault initially tended to be a controlled mess. Resolving that mess was less up to the commanders than to the initiative of little groups of paratroopers. In the opinion of the airborne's critics, it was a horrible way to run a war and alarmingly untidy.

The only thing that could be said in its favor was that it worked.

"I've rounded up most of the platoon," said Brock. "Two are still missing, but they know the objective. Sorvino caught one from that emplacement." He made a gesture toward the smoldering ruins of the heavy-machine-gun position. "He's dead."

"Cochrane?" said Fitzduane.

"We've got him," said Brock.

"Give me the rest of it," said Fitzduane.

"The air force have well and truly worked over the heavy hostile positions," said Brock, "but there are a lot of bad guys out there spread out in small groups and moving around through linked spider holes and tunnels. That means you don't know where they are going to pop up. If their shooting was a little better we'd have to earn our pay, but as it is they tend to fire high and don't live long enough to adjust. But we're taking some casualties. There is just too much hot metal flying around. It will get easier when our heavy stuff cuts in. It will get a whole lot worse if a reserve starts to throw at us. It's their armor that worries me. They're supposed to have it, but I don't see it. So where is the stuff? It's a fucking shell game."

The RT operator called Brock and he took the proffered microphone.

Around their position Fitzduane could hear and see the volume of fire emanating from the 82nd rapidly increasing as units and impromptu fire teams got their bearings. Targets were being identified and M60s were laying down bases of fire. Maneuver units were methodically clearing out their designated sectors with SAWs, rifle fire, and grenades. Bunkers were being taken out with AT4s and the smaller LAWs.

On a terrain model or a map, Madoa airfield encased in its perimeter defenses had seemed a neat, manageable size.

On the ground, it was brought home to Fitzduane just how large any full-size airfield really was. Two brigades of the 82nd had dropped onto the place, and now, from his ground-hugging position, the area looked surprisingly empty. True, competing tracers sliced the air and there were constant flashes and explosions over a background of machine-gun and rifle fire, but there almost no people to be seen.

They were surrounded by thousands of troops trying to kill each other, but from his position they were invisible. It was disconcerting. Fitzduane was used to special-operations missions where your own group was so small virtually your entire focus could be on the enemy.

In this situation, managing your own team was almost an end in itself. It was a whole new layer of worry, and it brought home just what conventional command in combat was all about. There was a paradox in the situation. Special operations were intrinsically much more difficult—but also they were easier. Your training was better, funded, your equipment was normally better and your focus was tighter. Your main area of responsibility was destroying the enemy. It made life simpler.

Debris fountained fifty meters away, and the blast made Fitzduane hug the ground.

Four further explosions were even closer, but the line of impacts as the mortar bombs were walked in passed in front of them.

"Eighty-two-millimeter," said Brock. "Ten to one they're moving the damn things around. Counterbattery takes care of that shit, but that's not going to be a player until we've cleared the airfield. The CB is like . . . delicate."

Fitzduane smiled despite their decidedly hairy situation. Dirt was still clumping down on his Kevlar. A minor adjustment to the mortar's aiming mechanism and the Scout Platoon would have to be raked up before being body-bagged.

The counterbattery radar was the one and only item that the Airborne did not parachute in. It could track an incoming round in flight and direct return fire before the enemy shell had even landed, but it was sensitive equipment and needed to be flown in. That could not be done until a safe landing zone was cleared and the physical obstacles were removed. Barriers of heavy rocks had been erected across the runway, interspersed with mines. It was all in a night's work to the paratroopers who dropped in with bulldozers and combat engineers, but it took time.

Brock was listening intently, a single earpiece pressed to his right ear. "Affirmative, Viper One."

A Hellfire missile streaked diagonally across their line of sight and impacted about eight hundred meters away.

A flash lit up the sky, followed by a series of others as the mortar bombs blew.

Seconds later, pink flame spat at the ground as a C130 Spectre gunship hosed the area with its 20mm Gatling.

"Straight in the balls, Viper One," said Brock to the Kiowa Warrior pilot.

Two Kiowas, a pair of Sheridan tanks, and air had been tasked to support Fitzduane's mission, which gave his small unit the unusual luxury of being able to call in their own fire support. Normally they would have had to go through channels. The heavier the weapon, the higher the clearance required.

It all made a great deal of organizational sense, unless you were a lowly trooper eating dirt as your buddies died around you and you were helpless to respond.

Scout Platoon were certainly not helpless. Oshima, it was considered, as they had sat sweating in the confines of the SCIF, was worth some very special attention.

Fitzduane did not want Oshima. It had all gone way past that point. She had spilled far too much blood. He did not want a prisoner. He was going to kill her. When this was over, one or other of them was going to be dead. Dead beyond any doubt.

He wanted her head. Literally.

"TROOPER! Where the fuck your is your rifle?" said Divisional Command Sergeant Major Webster to a Kevlared figure unfortunate enough to cross his path.

"I'm the padre, Sergeant Major," said the figure. "They don't trust me with one." He was carrying a small bag.

"A little early for spiritual guidance, sir," said Webster. "But the thing is, can you drive a bulldozer?"

"No problem," said the padre. "What do want me to do?"

"Clear the crap off the runway, Padre," said Webster, "but watch the fucking mines. We don't have many bulldozers."

"Hooah," said the padre. It was nice to know where you stood in the pecking order.

He hopped up on the combat bulldozer. The unit spat black smoke and rumbled into action. There were flashes in front of him as combat engineers started to blow the mines. The runway stretched out ahead of him. What did you need to put down a C130? Two thousand to three thousand feet, he recalled.

"ALL THE WAY, PADRE!" shouted Webster, pointing down the runway.

The padre grinned and gunned the heavy machine forward. The Lord hadn't been a paratrooper, but in his opinion, he should have been.

The steering wheel felt sticky and the instruments were splashed with something. His seat was wet, and the dampness was soaking into his fatigues. The padre suddenly realized that he was looking at and sitting in his predecessor's blood.

CARRANZA knew they could not stay in the command bunker if they were going to do any good.

He was getting reports in by landline from all over the airfield. Paratroops had landed in strength, but so far they appeared lightly armed. Further, the bombing had eased off. By now most of the aircraft would be out of ordnance and fuel. That was the weakness of fast movers for close-air support. They had almost no loiter time.

Now, before the enemy troops got organized, was the time to act. For the next twenty minutes or so there was a strike opportunity ready to be used. Now was the time to use the armored reserve.

Forty T53 tanks together with supporting infantry in armored personnel carriers were ready in the underground cavern hollowed out under the main hangar, the control tower, and the surrounding marshaling area.

So far, by some miracle, neither the hangar nor the control tower had been hit. Probably the hangar was considered of no military significance since the runway was blocked, and as for the control tower, his one thought was that the Americans were keeping that intact because they would want to make use of it after they had secured the airfield.

Whatever the reasons, it did not matter. All that counted was that the reserve was intact and—properly deployed—it could win the day.

Paratroops had a mystique, but they were not supermen. In essence, once you stripped away the maroon berets and parachute wings and jump boots, they were nothing more than underequipped infantry. Look at what had happened at Arnhem despite all the weight of allied airpower. Armor had destroyed them.

Look at what had happened at Dien Bien Phu in Vietnam. The French had been arrogant and had counted on their artillery and airpower to save them. But in the end the underdog had triumphed and the surviving French were marched into captivity.

Carranza was a keen student of military history, but his memory was selective and the memories that supported his thesis came from a different time.

But he was correct on one point.

The Airborne were particularly vulnerable after they landed and before their heavy firepower was fully unpacked and into action. But vulnerable did not mean helpless. And some heavy units were not just fast at getting into action. They were *very* fast.

He was entirely wrong in his assessment of the air. He knew nothing at all about the Kiowa Warriors.

"Major Carranza," said Oshima.

"Commander?" said Carranza.

"I would like you to lead the counterattack," said Oshima.

"Personally?" said Carranza.

"They need your leadership," said Oshima.

You're sentencing me to die, thought Carranza. *We may well triumph, but I will be killed.* It was less a feeling than a certainty.

It was odd. He did not feel anything except a certain impatience.

Oshima watched Carranza leave the command bunker. Twenty feet up, his armored reaction force sat waiting. Facing them was a ramp leading to a hydraulically controlled bombproof door similar to those installed on missile silos.

The armored door opened up directly into the hangar. For maximum shock power, the armored force could assemble a dozen tanks or more before attacking.

Individually, tanks could be picked off one by one, but en masse they were an armored fist that few soldiers could withstand.

A rifle was useless against a tank. If you stood your ground, you were crushed. AT4s and LAWs could destroy armor, but these were close-range weapons whose backblasts gave away their firing positions when used. A wedge of tanks advancing with guns blazing was every infantryman's nightmare.

GENERAL Mike Gannon watched radio aerials sprout. The news of Dave Palmer's death had just come in from the air force, and he was momentarily stunned.

Divisional HQ occupied a pair of two-thousand-pound-bomb craters. The area was already covered over with camouflage netting and sweating paratroopers were further reinforcing the position with sandbagged top cover. It was not so much that generals deserved special protection, but more the basic fact that the radios had to be kept safe.

Without radio communications, the 82nd would be shorn of most of its effective striking power. Air, artillery, antitank, his own armor, and his maneuver battalions all needed to be coordinated. The Kiowa Warriors and the Spectre gunships were his windows onto the evolving battle. Certainly all concerned knew their individual roles, but in an airborne operation things changed at speed.

First Brigade were netted in and progressing well. Second Brigade had called for artillery support. They were up against a network of bunkers defended by minefields. The air force had made two runs but then had run out of ordnance. The Spectre gunships were otherwise engaged. The A10s were around, but for some technical reason they could not be contacted.

Under heavy fire, troopers were clearing paths through the minefields by advancing on their stomachs and poking with fiberglass rods. God knows how they had the guts to do it. It was not like they could take their time. During an airborne assault this intricate and highly dangerous job was performed at speed. It had to be done that way. You had to get through. Failure was not an option.

The strike momentum had to be kept up.

The artillery was still not in action. One battery had landed in a minefield, and the gunners rushing to unpack their pieces had taken casualties as they moved in. Another battery had been hit by a mortar strike.

Gannon missed Palmer. Dave was the best executive officer he had ever had, and combined they made a near-perfect team. Gannon was a fighting general at his absolute best when leading men. Palmer was the imperturbable organization man who kept the structure together and the information flowing. The thought that he'd just been blown out of the sky and was now . . . gone, was sickening.

Gone! What more could you say? You were supposed to be safe 20,000 feet up, but that was an illusion. Nowhere was safe during an airborne assault.

There was a boom as a 105mm howitzer went off and then another. The camouflage netting fluttered as the shock waves spread.

The noise jolted Gannon back into action. Despite all the shit that had been thrown at them, the gunners were back on the firing line. He looked at his watch. They had been on the ground only twenty-two minutes. The opposition was heavier than he had expected. The air force had worked right through the targeting board, but the terrorists were dug more effectively than had been believed. And the intelligence on mines had been inadequate.

You could prepare as much as you liked, but when it came right down to it every battle had to be *fought*. There was no easy way.

Gannon suddenly thought of the supergun. If Livermore was wrong, no matter what the 82nd accomplished, a whole lot of his young men were going to die.

The operations board was coming up with the division's assets. The Kiowa Warriors, electronic countermeasures, artillery, mortars, his TOW missiles mounted on Humvees, the Sheridan tanks, the heavy machine guns. All were now unpacked and operational.

Twenty-seven minutes in. Not good enough. They could always do better. But not bad.

Gannon studied the big operations map. The wild card mission was the one commanded by Fitzduane. He was heading across to the hangar to link up with a Delta team, and together they were going to try and flush Oshima out of her bunker.

In Gannon's professional opinion, it was a fool's mission, since penetrating a series of armored doors to a location sixty feet underground was tantamount to suicide.

Nevertheless, the game in this case was certainly worth the candle. Gannon had studied Oshima's file and had walked through the bloodstained wreckage in Fayetteville. Oshima was the nearest thing to pure evil that so far in his life he had ever encountered.

Fitzduane, Al Lonsdale, that Washington fellow Cochrane, and then Brock's little army. They were good people and did not deserve to die. But then, neither had Dave Palmer.

"General?" said Carlson, who was standing in as exec. "We've a report from the Delta observer team on the hangar roof. Armor, sir, and lots of it. Twenty T53s, and they're still coming out of the ground like dragon's teeth."

"Colonel Fitzduane?" said Gannon.

"Raising him now, sir," said Carlson. "But he'll know soon enough. They're heading right for him."

Fitzduane's minder, thought Gannon. Lieutenant Brock. The Louisiana Training Center. OPFOR had attacked in force and caught Brock in a situation just like this.

Using pre-positioned AT4s, Brock had fought one of the best infantry rearguard actions against armor that Gannon had ever seen. Kill a couple of tanks, make smoke, and fall back in the confusion. Next time they advanced, hit them from a different angle. Shoot and scoot ground-pounder style.

But the enemy had been weaker than this, and technically Brock had still been killed, though he had certainly proved that the right infantry tactics could cause unsupported armor serious grief.

You could harass and you could damage, but in the final analysis pure firepower tended to tilt the scales.

And this was no training exercise.

"Tell Colonel Fitzduane's team to let the enemy armor right through," he said, "and make smoke behind them." He tapped at the airport layout. "We'll let Second Brigade block them, and we'll hit them from the flanks with TOWs and the Sheridans. Sheepdog tactics. I want that hostile force to have only one way out, and that's into their own minefield. Give the Second Brigade all the artillery support we've got. Let the Kiowas loose. Get the air force in on the act, but tell them to be damn careful. Gunships only until we can sort out who is where."

"Airborne, sir," said Carlson.

Gannon had heard the 82nd referred to as no more than a speed bump when up against massed enemy armor. He had taken the remark ill.

If his division was a mere obstacle, it was a speed bump with real killing teeth.

FITZDUANE hugged the ground as Carranza's armor rumbled past.

Stabs of flame and the deafening crack of their cannon punctuated the chattering of their coaxial machine guns.

The detritus of a bomb-blasted air defense position gave some visual cover.

Bodies and pieces of bodies completed the picture. A severed leg lay six inches in front of his eyes. He considered that he was learning more about the violent disassembly of the human form on this mission than he really wanted to know.

An armored thrust from beneath the ground. They had expected something—some kind of counterpunch—and had prepared a reserve, but the scale was disconcerting.

They had planned to bomb using penetrator weapons, which could deal with deeply buried bunkers up to forty feet or so, but had restricted their use after further consideration when the consequences of setting off the nerve agent had been considered. True, the two elements of the binary gas were stored separately, according to Rheiman, but who knew what changes Oshima had made in the last couple of days.

It had been a rational decision to forgo the penetrator bombs, but as the massed wedge of tanks had punched out of the hangar toward them, Fitzduane had second thoughts. Mere flesh and blood seemed woefully inadequate to counter this massed steel killing machine.

He wished like hell the airborne had Guntracks.

He had an enormous urge to flee very fast.

The armored wedge included vehicle-mounted guided-missile teams. Unless taken out, they would keep the Spectre gunships out of the way. Countering Oshima's surprise was going to be down to the infantry.

Brock was gritting his teeth with frustration. The Scouts were correctly positioned to take the armor from the flanks and rear, but he was under direct orders to do nothing. There was also the reality that they were down to only a handful of AT4s. Still, his two Sheridans were positioned off to the right, and they could have really stirred the pot.

Fitzduane put his Kevlar next to Brock's. The noise of engines, the squeal and rumble of tracks, and the constant gunfire made normal speech impossible. He bellowed, and Brock could just hear.

Fitzduane repeated his orders.

"WHERE THE ARMOR CAME UP, WE CAN GET DOWN!" he bawled. "IF THEY CAN GET TANKS UP, WE CAN GET TANKS DOWN! AS SOON AS THE FUCKS ARE PAST, GET YOUR PET SHERIDANS AND LET'S DO IT. TELL THEM TO USE THE SIDE DOOR!"

Brock nodded and held out his hand for the RT. It was slapped into his hand. "WHAT ABOUT OUT TWO KIOWAS?" he shouted.

Fitzduane contemplated the vast hangar. It seemed big enough. "WHY NOT!" he said.

The noise of roaring engines diminished as the last enemy armored vehicle squealed by. Fitzduane had counted forty-seven vehicles in all. He revised his total downward as two of the missile carriers exploded. Lased by Delta from the hangar roof, he conjectured accurately. Still not his war for the moment.

A row of 120mm mortar shells from division burst behind the advancing enemy armor, providing smoke cover for Fitzduane's strike force.

The Scouts poured automatic-weapons fire and 40mm grenades into the hangar. Muzzle flashes identified the opposition.

Laser beams flashed out and painted their targets, to be followed split seconds later by bursts of aimed fire.

The two Kiowas moved up and, hovering only a few feet off the ground, let loose ripple-fired antipersonnel rockets.

The terrorists inside the hangar consisted mainly of mechanics and logistics personnel who had been concentrating on helping the armor attack. They had given almost no thought to defending the hangar itself.

Many were cut down in the Scout's initial fusillade of fire. The Kiowas Hydra rockets killed most of the remainder.

The thirteen survivors ran and died as two Sheridan tanks burst through the side wall with machine guns blazing.

Scouts leapfrogged forward and secured the hangar. As they did so, Delta troopers rappelled down from the roof and reinforced the Fitzduane's little army.

As he shook hands with the first one and smelled the bird droppings, Brock sniffed and made a face. "What the fuck?" he said. "We'll gas 'em out."

Ten seconds later, the shaped charge blew and the huge armored door that concealed the ramp in the floor fell away. The Sheridans fired into the cavern below and were joined by the two Kiowas, who were now firing their rockets from inside the hangar. A second shaped charge went off and blew open the steel grille covering a ventilation shaft. Powerful antipersonnel demolition charges were dropped down and exploded with such force that the whole floor shook.

While the Sheridans and half the Scouts roared down the ramp, Fitzduane, Lonsdale, Cochrane, and the balance of the command lowered themselves into the darkness.

THE padre pushed another blade of rubble off the runway and then paused to wipe his forehead. He was streaming with sweat.

Driving a bulldozer was harder than it looked. Civilian vehicles might have air-conditioned cabs and soft seats, but the Airborne's equipment was strictly military specification and designed for ruggedness rather than comfort. Civilian 'dozers did not get dropped.

Rounds spanged off his armored front, and he crouched down in his seat as he raised the blade slightly, gunned the engine and reversed.

Doubtless it was consoling for the engine, having the massive protection of the blade in the front, but it was also a reminder that he, the human factor, was sitting up top exposed to the elements and a not inconsiderable amount of incoming fire.

The sky was crisscrossed with tracer, the solid flames of gunship fire, and the visual chaos of exploding missiles, artillery shells, mortar bombs, and other weaponry. Everywhere he looked through his night-vision goggles, he could see targets being painted with the troopers' laser beams, and he knew that the quick flash of a beam was being accompanied by bursts of aimed fire. Targets were being sought out and neutralized one by one.

He was conscious of the fact that his pastoral duties were now being created by that fire and he should probably hand over to someone else and go and provide succor to the wounded, but finding someone to delegate to was no small problem. Also, he was well aware that no matter how helpful a padre's words might be to a wounded trooper, the practical benefit of getting in reinforcements and being able to fly out the wounded could be even more appreciated.

The airstrip was nearly clear, and as best he could see the engineers clearing the mines were finished. He throttled up and headed toward a pile of cement-filled fifty-five-gallon drums. The stench of diesel fumes filled the air and mixed with the odors of sweat, fear, blood, and explosive fumes that now pervaded the battlefield.

Someone ran toward him and shouted. They were pointing toward the oil drums. The noise of the bulldozer drowned the shouter's voice, but it was clear he was indicating the obstructions still to be cleared.

The padre waived an acknowledgment and trundled on.

"MINES!" screamed the engineer behind him. "MINES! WE HAVEN'T CLEARED THERE YET! STOP, YOU FUCKING IDIOT!"

The padre sped across the airstrip and then slowed down as he approached the drums. He lowered the blade and began moving forward. Suddenly he was struck violently on his right side and propelled off the bulldozer onto the runway. He hit the ground hard and painfully, and as he shook himself he became aware that there was a heavy weight on his back.

He began to struggle, and the weight on his back moved. Seconds later, the weight was gone altogether and he rolled over. In front of him, a paratrooper was getting to his feet. It might have been a normal parachute landing fall recovery, except that this trooper had his arms through his straps as if he had jumped without putting on the 'chute properly. He seemed to have descended just holding on to the thing.

The trooper, Colonel Dave Palmer, put out his hand. "Sorry about that, Padre. Left in a hurry."

"Judas Priest, Dave!" said the padre. "You're supposed to wear that bloody thing." He struggled to his feet.

Driverless, the bulldozer was still trundling along with the pile of concrete-filled oil drums rolling in front of it.

"My bulldozer!" cried the padre.

There was a vivid flash as the antitank mine blew and the entire bulldozer seemed to rise in the air and fly for several yards before exploding. A further mine was set off, and then one explosion followed another.

The blast blew the remaining obstacles clear of the paved strip.

"Interesting way to clear a runway, Padre," said Palmer.

"The Lord helped," said the padre hoarsely.

CARRANZA'S tank force hit the perimeter of Second Brigade's firing line and veered away to the right as a barrage of TOWs, Hellfire missiles, AT4s and Sheridan tank fire plowed into it.

The volume of fire was bad enough. The accuracy was horrifying. All around him tanks were blowing up, men were on fire, and his command was dying.

Within twenty-three seconds, Carranza had lost two-thirds of his force and was driving desperately away from the wall of death that faced him. He tried to grapple with what he was up against. *Paratroopers were lightly armed troops.* This was firepower of a different order of magnitude.

A further six tanks exploded behind him. He caught a quick glimpse of a Sheridan tank in the distance. The American tank was aluminum and virtually obsolete, he had been told. He had not taken in that it was fast, light, carried the biggest gun of any tank in general use, and had been upgraded with long-range optics and night-vision equipment.

His one thought was now to get away. He did not care where he was going or what he would do when he got there. He just wanted to flee.

Shells burst around his tank and one wall glowed red when a fragment hit.

Carranza was bruised and bleeding from being bounced around the metal box.

Beside him his gunner had abandoned any attempt to load and fire the main gun. His face was gray with desperation and the foreknowledge of certain death. The driver slewed the tank from side to side in the hope that the jinking would causes incoming fire to miss. It was making Carranza sick.

The tank drove right through the perimeter defenses and into the minefield beyond.

The mines were laid according to Soviet doctrine, in a massive belt three hundred meters deep. The first two mines had been carelessly laid and did not explode. Carranza's tank hit the third mine after thirty-two meters. The force of the mine was so great, it blew the entire tank into the air.

The tank was still in the air when it was hit nearly simultaneously by a Hellfire missile and the 152mm shell from a Sheridan. The combined blast blew all the mines in a two-hundred-meter radius and could be seen with clarity from the command-and-control aircraft 20,000 feet up.

Carranza and his entire crew were vaporized

FITZDUANE fired two rounds from his M16 into the torso of a terrorist in the weapons pit and rammed the barrel into the face of the second man. The terrorist went down and Fitzduane thrust his fighting knife into his throat and wiped it on the dead man's fatigues.

He reloaded and checked his pouches. Ammunition was getting low.

Getting through the hangar had been easy. In contrast, the cavernous bunker below seemed to be defended by some kind of palace guard. They had blown the Sheridans as they came down the ramp, and since then it had been basic infantry slogging as the Scouts and Delta cleaned out a series of interlocking defensive positions.

"Why the fuck didn't I bring a Barrett?" said Lonsdale.

The heavy rifle would have punched through the armor plate of the weapons pits.

The M60 rounds made shallow dents. The M16 rounds just bounced off. They were out of 40mm grenades. They had fired the last of the AT4s. They were out of nearly everything.

"Why the fuck didn't I stay in Washington?" said Cochrane.

"We'd have missed you," said Fitzduane absentmindedly. He was focused on a steel door beyond the next terrorist emplacement. It was only about twenty meters way, but the space between was a killing zone. The terrorists had a medium machine gun and clearly had not even heard a whisper of the phrase "fire discipline." Their fire was nearly continuous, and the air was thick with the smell of cordite.

"But not a lot," said Lonsdale caustically.

"Even if they don't hit us," said Cochrane, "they're going to pollute us to death. The air quality in this place sucks."

"It could get a shitload worse," said Lonsdale.

Fitzduane was silent. If Rheiman's hand-drawn map was to be trusted, beyond that metal door was a hatchway that lead down two flights of metal stairs to the command bunker. Straight ahead was a nerve-agent store. Behind them, at the other end of the cavern, was the second nerve-gas store. If nothing had been moved, the unit had already secured the Xyclax Gamma 18. One component alone was useless.

Of course, Oshima did not have to have moved all the components together. She could have had just one cylinder transported. According to what he had been told, one matched pair of Xyclax Gamma 18 cylinders properly distributed would be enough to take out the entire airfield, let alone the cavern.

"Brock," he called.

"Yo!" said Brock.

"We need a couple of grenades up here," said Fitzduane. "Get someone to check the lockers in the Sheridan that didn't blow."

"Hot damn!" said Brock. "Neat thinking. Those guys are squirrels."

Two minutes later, the weighed end of a length of parachute cord fell beside Fitzduane. Brock was across to the left and behind a support pillar. He couldn't get any closer and keep breathing.

The terrorist machine gun and three AK-47s spat flame as they saw the cord and tried to cut it with fire. Ricochets zinged along the cavern. The concrete floor of the cavern spewed fragments as rounds bit into it around the line of the cord.

Fitzduane saw the edge of the cord fray. If he pulled too fast it could break. If he pulled too slowly the contents of the pouch at the end could go up.

Thinking of what was inside, it was an easy decision.

He pulled hard. The cord broke, but enough momentum had already been transferred to the pouch. It slid into home base.

Fitzduane opened the pouch and looked at Brock. There were three grenades inside. "What the fuck!" he mouthed.

Brock shrugged. "Go for it!" he shouted.

Fitzduane handed grenades to Lonsdale and Cochrane. They looked at him.

"All together," said Fitzduane. "FOUR, THREE, TWO . . ."

The three grenades arced through the air. Two landed inside the gun emplacement.

Four terrorists erupted from their position, guns blazing. Concentrated fire from Scout Platoon cut them to pieces. Smoke from the three signaling grenades filled the air.

Choking, Fitzduane dashed forward.

The steel door had represented a possible escape for its guardians. It was unlocked. He pulled the heavy lever and the door swung open.

He hugged the left side of the door frame. Green, purple, and yellow smoke was making the place untenable. If anyone was on the other side, they would fire into the smoke. Probably.

Or maybe if they were smart and professional, they would wait and try to pick out some kind of a human shape. But it would not really be savvy to wait. Any attacker clever enough to get this far would throw in stun grenades.

If anyone was inside, they should be firing by now.

"On your right," said Lonsdale from the right side of the door frame.

"Ready," said Cochrane's voice from behind Lonsdale.

"GO!" snapped Fitzduane.

Rows of cylinders behind a double steel grid faced them. A door on the right wall led down to the command bunker. It was closed and of the same size and mass as the kind of construction used in bank vaults.

The room itself was empty.

They examined the door. It was not just locked. It was secured as if part of the structure. There was not a hint of how it might be opened. The entire locking mechanism must be located on the other side.

"You say the magic word and this substantial chunk of real estate swings open," said Lonsdale. "You go down two flights of metal stairs. You are faced with another blast door and you knock politely. It, too, swings open and there is Oshima, a smile on her face and her arms open in welcome." He paused. "Or then again, maybe not. Either way, I don't think a foot in the right place is going to achieve much. This fucking thing is *built*."

Close examination showed that the problem did not end with the door. The whole wall seemed to be of similar strength, and the joins were so finely machined there was no place to pack explosive.

"We can huff and puff," said Cochrane, "or we can go and get a cup of coffee while the combat engineers make with the plastic. This is safe blowing. This isn't a job for clean-living amateurs."

Fitzduane rubbed his chin. Oshima had learned much of her trade from the Hangman. The Hangman always had an escape route, and a few surprises for unwelcome visitors.

He switched his gaze to the cylinders of nerve agent. How many should there be?

"We hold here," he said.

TWENTY feet below Fitzduane, Oshima's hand was poised above the firing button. The two keys were already in position and had been turned. The firing release code had been entered. The supergun was fully charged with hydrogen and helium and ready to fire.

She hesitated. If only she had more time. One missile would accomplish so little compared with what could be done. Now when she fired, the attacking paratroops would certainly assault the supergun valley and there would be no time to reload.

This would be one single gesture of hate, not the orchestrated campaign she would have liked.

Could Carranza's force make the difference? Possibly but unlikely.

Never wait until the last minute, the Hangman had said. Society is corrupt. People are venal. You will always be presented with other opportunities. They will hand you the very weapons you need to destroy them. In their avariciousness and ignorance they arm their very enemies.

Strike without pity and disappear. Prepare your escape route in advance, and when they think they have you, *hurt them.*

The confusion will aid your escape. When they are close and think they have you they get careless. They always do. You bait the trap and they will enter it and be destroyed. But don't be greedy. Don't stay and watch. *Never wait until the last minute.*

Jin Endo would be coming with her and five others. Enough to fight a rear-guard action if needed. Enough to distract and confuse, yet a small enough group to evade detection.

Six others in the command bunker would not be leaving. They had served their purpose. If left unharmed they might have attempted to interfere with the nerve-gas mechanism. Their throats had been cut as they sat in front of their consoles, and the air was thick with the smell of their blood.

The two cylinders sat linked to the dispersion unit. A timer was attached, ready to be activated. When their attackers broke in, the entire command bunker would be flooded with nerve agent, and with luck it would spread throughout the complex and to the attacking troops beyond.

But she would have to be well away by then. So really there was no good reason to wait.

Oshima mentally counted down, preparing herself for the shaft of flame as the huge weapon hurled its projectile toward Washington, D.C. In her mind she could see the path of the missile as it shot out of the supergun barrel, climbed up into the stratosphere, and then curved gracefully down toward its target below. How long would it take? A few minutes, no more.

As the missile neared its destination, a pressure-controlled mechanism would activate the two cylinders of gas. They would blend and become a liquid horror. The dispersion unit would cut in and the air over the capital of the most powerful nation in the world would fill with a vast cloud of nerve gas.

Invisibly the deadly miasma would float toward the ground.

It would be hours before the Americans would realize they had been hit, and by then it would be too late. Everywhere people would start dying. They would die at work, they would die at home. Senators and congressmen would collapse as they spoke. Lobbyists would spit blood as they advanced their causes. Policemen would die as they patrolled the streets. Prisoners would puke their guts out as they lay behind bars.

Across the Potomac, the military in the Pentagon would be hit and would be powerless to respond.

In Arlington and Rosslyn and a score of suburbs, citizens would drink the contaminated water and be affected. Ice cubes would kill. The touch of a hand or the gentlest of kisses would kill. The air itself, the very grass you walked on, the ventilator in your automobile. All would kill.

The cameras concealed throughout the supergun valley had audio pickups as well as visual. Oshima wanted to savor ever detail. She heard the klaxon sound and saw the gun crew put on ear protectors and scurry for cover in the firing bunker.

The supergun was a truly massive weapon, and as Oshima looked at the monitors, she was entranced by the sheer destructive potential of such power. And you could make one of these things out of microfiber-reinforced concrete. The implications were exhilarating.

The countdown in Spanish commenced. Through the relay she could hear the loudspeaker booming out over the now-deserted valley.

The countdown reached the final sequence. "Five—Four—Three—Two—One—FIRE!"

The last word was issued in a triumphant shout and then repeated by Oshima. "FIRE! FIRE! FIRE! FIRE!"

There was the expected thunderclap of explosions, but the sight Oshima actually witnessed strained her credulity.

The entire supergun, all 656 feet and 21,000 tons of it, blew apart in a rippling roaring thundering inferno of flame and destruction that was the most powerful explosion that Oshima had ever seen.

The structures in the valley were swept away as if by some devil's breath.

The glass-fronted bunker containing the terrorist firing team—set across the divide of the valley—was hit by the blast wave and shattered as vast lumps of flying matter smashed into it.

For the next few seconds, the sky rained pieces of the supergun and a thick cloud of dust and debris stained the sky.

And then there was a dreadful silence.

"Fitzduane-*san*!" hissed Oshima, the hate thick in her voice.

❋ CHAPTER TWENTY-SEVEN

DR. JOHN JAEGER stepped out of the Blackhawk helicopter and, holding his hat on his head, ran through the dust storm created by the downdraft of its rotors. Beyond the fog of sand, the harsh sun of the Tecuno plateau cut in and he slipped on his sunglasses with relief.

Madoa airfield was well and truly under the control of the 82nd Airborne. Around him paratroopers were methodically scouring every inch of the air base, while up above armed helicopters and gunships kept watch. Above them again there would a combat air patrol.

It was over. But then again, you never quite knew.

Security was tight. A C130 making its approach fired flares to distract any straggler with a handheld missile foolish enough to try anything, then dropped in like a stone in the stomach-wrenching maneuver known as a combat assault landing. Jaeger had experienced the procedure when he and his team were flown in, and suddenly he had realized why the Airborne preferred to jump.

He found Fitzduane near what might have been some kind of barracks building. It was hard to tell after the air force had worked it over, but a cargo parachute had been erected like a giant tent to give some shade. Inside, the filtered light was curiously peaceful.

The Irishman was lying back in a large wooden tub watching a yellow plastic duck bob up and down in the water in front of him. He had a glass of red wine in one hand.

Various other camouflaged figures sat in makeshift chairs in the general vicinity. He recognized Lonsdale and Cochrane, and there was a stocky lieutenant who looked as if he could life weights with his little finger. His eyes were closed. Farther back, other paratroopers were asleep.

"The tub was Oshima's, they tell me," said Fitzduane. "Damn near the only thing that wasn't blown to hell and back."

Jaeger collapsed with some relief into what passed for a deck chair and accepted a glass of wine. "The duck?" he said.

"The duck belongs to my son," said Fitzduane. "I gave it to him, but he loaned it to me. Sort of a good-luck charm. To bathe without one is uncivilized—though not everyone knows that."

Jaeger drank his wine. The atmosphere was pleasantly relaxing. It was like sitting on the porch after you'd done everything that had to be done and now you could just swap yarns and listen to the crickets before falling asleep. Only, there weren't any crickets. Instead there were the snores of sleeping paratroopers and crawling things that were mostly lizards but were occasionally scorpions.

"So it worked," he said. "I was having a nightmare about the whole thing, but it really worked like we hoped. We've just checked the Devil's Footprint and the area all around. Not a trace of nerve agent. Nothing. And the gun is shredded. It really bloody worked."

Fitzduane looked at him. "Hoped?" he said incredulously. "Tell me you were certain it would work, or I'll have Brock shoot you."

"When you put it like that—I was certain," said Jaeger. "We fuck up on nukes now and then at Livermore, but when it comes to hydrogen superguns we're aces."

"I'm going to shoot him," said Brock sleepily. "He didn't say positively."

"But what about Oshima?" said Jaeger. "Where's Oshima?"

"Good question," said Fitzduane.

"Well, if she's inside the command bunker, she's dead," said Jaeger. "And so would you lot have been if you'd blown that door."

There was silence. No one particularly wanted to be reminded of how close they had come to blasting their way into a slow and messy death. After Madoa Air Base had been secured, the command bunker had been drilled by a chemical-warfare team and found to contain lethal quantities of Xyclax Gamma 18 under positive pressure. Opening the door would have caused the nerve agent to flood out into the subterranean complex and possibly to spread throughout the airfield itself.

The decision had been taken to seal off the bunker rather than break in, while the chemical-warfare team figured out a way to decontaminate it safely. The problem was not straightforward. The nerve gas was volatile and so would ignite, but if the bunker contained explosives in addition to the gas, the combination could be akin to exploding a rather large bomb. True, it was sixty feet underground, but the extensive subterranean evacuations meant that there was no guarantee the effects of an explosion would be contained.

Jaeger was confident that the problem was solvable, but meanwhile it meant that no one had actually physically searched the bunker. Special suits and equipment were being flown in. In the back of his mind was the thought that some

41,000 tons of chemical agent were lying around the former Soviet Union. This was a problem that was not going to go away.

"We don't think she's dead," said Fitzduane. "If the pattern is any indication, she is lying low waiting to make a break for it."

"So you think she left the command bunker and is now hidden in some hidey hole under this place," said Jaeger.

Fitzduane nodded.

"So one of these days—if your theory is right—she is going to pop out of the ground and make a run for it," said Jaeger. "But when and where? And how long can you wait? I love my country, but I know its faults. The U.S. of A. likes sprints, not marathons."

GENERAL Mike Gannon was feeling progressively more impatient.

The 82nd Airborne was designed to carry out strategic missions rapidly and then be pulled out. Subduing the Devil's Footprint terrorist complex had been achieved. Keeping two brigades tied up now that the mission had been accomplished struck him as a misuse of resources.

He was itching to head back to Bragg.

"One goddamn terrorist and the entire division is tied up," he growled. "This is ridiculous. How much effort is Oshima worth? We've searched the entire Devil's Footprint complex, and diddly squat. She's either dead or she's long gone."

"She's still here, General," said Fitzduane with absolute certainty.

Gannon glared at him. Colonels were supposed to agree with generals, but this damned Irishman had his own way of doing things.

"I agree, sir," said Dave Palmer.

Gannon's eyebrows shot skyward. Fitzduane was one thing, but Palmer was his exec and definitely part of the system. He was supposed to snap out "Airborne!" in agreement and go with the flow.

"Colonel Palmer," he said. "Getting shot down and reincarnated has scrambled your brains. This division is not a democracy."

"Airborne, sir," said Palmer. He had a great deal of sympathy for the CG. Gannon genuinely cared about his men and fought to see that they were properly utilized. But on this issue he backed Fitzduane, and his eyes still showed it.

Mollified though not fooled, Gannon looked at Palmer, then at Fitzduane and the others in the group. He tapped the map. "So where is she?" he said. "And why haven't we found her? What haven't we done?"

"If she has run true to form," said Fitzduane, "she will have left the command bunker through an emergency tunnel and be holed up somewhere sixty feet underground waiting to make her move. The emergency tunnel will have been deliberately collapsed behind her. The only way we could have found her would have been by stumbling over her ventilation point, and even that would have been disguised."

"Tunnels," said Gannon in disgust. "Hell of a way to fight a war. Vietnam was full of the things, and we never completely winkled the gutsy little bastards out of them. But who'd have thought they would have built hundreds of kilometers of the things."

"The positive news, General," said Fitzduane, "is that we've got hold of the geological reports and they indicate you just couldn't tunnel as and where you like. There is too much rock. So if Oshima is sitting underground, the chances are that she is somewhere on the north side."

"So where will she come up?" said Gannon.

"Somewhere on the northern perimeter outside the minefields," said Fitzduane. "She will do it at night."

Gannon studied the map. "That's still a whole lot of territory to watch," he said. "Worse yet, it's broken ground. Not a lot of major cover, but more than enough for someone crawling on their belly. But after that, what then?"

"There will be a cache of supplies a couple of kliks away," said Fitzduane. "Food, water, weapons, and probably some kind of transport. Something easy to conceal that'll handle this terrain. Maybe a motorcycle or all-terrain vehicle."

"We can't find the cache either?" said Gannon.

"No, sir," said Palmer. "But we're still looking."

Gannon was lost in thought. He tried to imagine what it must be like to spend days underground while others hunted you. Foul air, little or no food, stale water at best, the constant fear of suffocation, darkness, no sanitation, insects, snakes, and who knew what else. A vile existence, but some people were prepared to endure it. Evidently, Oshima was prepared to endure it. You could hate your enemies and kill them without compunction, but it never paid to underestimate them.

"Run me through the perimeter surveillance."

Palmer explained the system of observation posts. Each sector was being watched by two teams, one using thermal sights and the other using night vision. In addition, antipersonnel radar equipment and chemical sensors had been set up. Theoretically, a snake should not have been able to slither through without being detected, but Gannon knew that completely sealing off an area in reality was close to impossible. People got tired, equipment failed, batteries had to be changed. Even if you put a soldier every couple of yards, a skilled operator could get through.

"How long will she wait?" said Gannon.

"Forty-eight hours minimum," said Fitzduane. "Up to a month if she has to. Her main problem will be water, but she's had plenty of time to prepare so there's probably a tank of it down there. But my guess would be that she'll try and move out sooner rather than later. If she gives us too much time we could just get lucky. Also, our chemical sensors will have more to work on. She could well have carbon filters down there, but every day the stench is going to get worse."

Gannon walked around the map. It was hard to fault the staff work, but something—some assumption—just wasn't right. Reluctantly, he admitted to himself that Oshima was probably still around and that she was certainly worth taking out of the loop.

But something was wrong. It came to him.

"Your surveillance is based on the assumption she's going to emerge outside the perimeter?" he asked.

Fitzduane nodded.

"And outside the perimeter minefields?" said Gannon.

"Affirmative, General," said Palmer.

Gannon shrugged. "Maybe," he said. "But if I was her, I would come up *inside* the minefield. Especially if I knew where the mines were laid."

"Tiptoe through the tulips," said Fitzduane. "Only, the next in line gets blown up."

"I've got another point," said Gannon. "This meticulous surveillance is all very well if the Tecuno plateau remains its normal equable self—hot days and cold clear nights. But if the weather takes a turn? If Oshima isn't alone?"

"It could get messy, sir," said Palmer.

"Colonel Fitzduane?" said Gannon.

"It will be our mess," said Fitzduane.

"Does 'our' include Lieutenant Brock's Scouts?" said Gannon.

"I guess it does, General," said Fitzduane. "Instant compatibility, you might say."

Gannon smiled thinly.

CHAPTER TWENTY-EIGHT

LIGHTNING LANCED OUT of the sky and the battlefield radar blew in a shower of sparks.

"What the fuck!" said Brock. "Whose side is this guy on?"

The sky flared again and again and the deafening cracks of thunder cut in so fast that Fitzduane had the sense of being directly bombarded. The sensations were primeval, terrifying. He wanted to crawl under cover, to pull the blankets over his head. This was not a thunderstorm. This was not weather. This was violence on an almost supernatural scale. And he had no blanket. Conditions in the observation post were basic.

A scorpion raced across the ground, stopped to stare at them, then headed down into a hole.

"Did he say something?" said Lonsdale.

" 'Follow me!' " said Cochrane.

Lightning cracked into a massive boulder off to the right. The huge rock cracked in two with a smell of ozone. One side swayed and then rolled over toward the Scout fire team. There was a single short scream and then a brief silence. Brock, bent double, headed toward the noise.

The thunder cut in again, and Fitzduane could hear the sound of shouting. He checked his watch. It was 0323. Something was moving up ahead and to the right. They were in an observation post on a slight rise overlooking the minefield and it was beginning to look as if Oshima was making her run. Unfortunately, she had picked her time all too well. Air was grounded, communications were haywire, and the array of vision and detection equipment was effectively neutered.

Nature was effortlessly sweeping aside their technological advantage.

The entire ground in front of him was beginning to move. The wind gusted and screamed. The surface was being blasted into the air and there flung against—

and into—anything that protruded. Sand and grit stung his face, clogged his mouth and nostrils, and cut down his vision.

There was the sharp, deadly crack of high explosives, and then secondary explosions. The thunder of the storm was so loud and so close that at first Fitzduane was unsure whether he was hearing nature at work or the killing blast of a mine. The secondaries suggested a mine. Someone had stepped in the wrong place and the explosion had set off grenades they were carrying.

Oshima was out, but her people could not see much better than they themselves could. Still, they had some advantage, because the wind was coming from behind them and lowing almost directly towards the observation posts.

Lonsdale, lying beside him with the .50 Barrett, fired.

Fire blasted back, its sounds of origin blending with the storm. Beside them a trooper slumped, his face black with blood. Further aimed bursts searched out the paratroopers' position and filled the air with splinters.

The terrorists must have fixed their position from their exit hole. A flash of lightning revealed that the screaming wind had blown away much of their cover. The camouflage netting was gone. The carefully covered mesh of their hides had been scoured clean of earth and now served only to identify their position.

Fitzduane searched for a target. He caught a blur and opened up with two aimed shots. The blur dropped and he fired again. Muzzle flashes and incoming showed he had missed.

The flying sand seemed to part in front of him, and he saw a black shape emerge out of the storm. He slid back behind the parapet as the hand grenade blew. They were being pinned down and flanked.

Lonsdale rolled backward, his Kevlar split open and blood oozing from his skull.

Fitzduane rolled out of the observation post and sought out the grenade thrower. What kind of force were they up against? He realized that he had assumed that Oshima would either be alone or accompanied by only two or three followers. Could he be wrong? Had some external force managed to infiltrate? Were they being attacked from behind as well?

He knew that a line of observation posts overlooked the minefield and that there were hundreds of troopers within rifle shot and thousands more on the secured base, yet for all practical purposes he was virtually alone.

He wriggled forward, trying to detect movement. The wind was gusting. Sometimes he could see little further than the hand in front of his face, and then the wind would ease for a moment or gust in a different direction and he would be given a brief, tantalizing snapshot before the image was lost again.

He moved his right hand forward and felt flesh.

Pain screamed up his arm. He was being bitten.

The sky lit up and showed a face in front of him. The man's teeth were embedded in his hand.

Fitzduane lashed out with his left hand and caught the terrorist on the side of the head. The man's mouth opened in shock and Fitzduane felt his right hand come free. The cessation of pain as the man's teeth relaxed their grip was immediate and overwhelming.

He tried to grab his rifle, but his right hand would not seem to do his bidding. The terrorist leaped forward as Fitzduane was rolling to one side.

The attacker missed Fitzduane but lashed out with his knife as he landed. The blow cut into Fitzduane's webbing and made a long thin diagonal cut across his torso.

Fitzduane unclipped a grenade and, using both hands, smashed the metal sphere into his attacker's face.

The man grunted and fell back.

Fitzduane raised himself over his attacker and hit him again and again in the face with the grenade. He could feel the man's bones breaking and the grenade getting slippery with blood. Each blow made his injured hand hurt agonizingly, but the intensity of the pain made him hit all the harder.

He dropped the grenade, found his rifle, put the muzzle against the side of the terrorist's head, and pulled the trigger. The man's body jerked and he was completely still. Half his head had been blown away.

Fitzduane lay back panting. He flexed his right hand. It hurt, but his hand would now work. Compared to the intensity of the agony the terrorist's bite had inflicted, the duller pain was almost welcome.

A figure rushed out of the swirling sand to Fitzduane's left. He was running hard. Fitzduane caught the silhouette of a Kalashnikov and fired two rounds from his rifle. The 5.56mm rounds hit, Fitzduane was certain, but the terrorist kept on coming. Adrenaline and desperation drove him. Waiting for days to break through the cordon of paratroopers, his body was now nearly unstoppable.

Fitzduane fired two three-round bursts and the terrorist stumbled and fell to his knees.

There was a vivid flash of flame and the terrorist was flung backward as a .50 explosive round hit him.

Fitzduane saw Lonsdale slumped against a rock, the Barrett wavering in his hand. Half his face was obscured with blood. Fitzduane moved forward and as Lonsdale began to collapse, then helped him to the ground. Brock appeared and slid into the observation post. He took one look at Lonsdale and pulled out a field dressing.

"Oshima?" said Fitzduane.

Brock made a gesture. "At least two got through on the right," he said. "Thirty meters way. Cochrane and a fire team have gone after them."

The storm was easing. As suddenly as it had started, it was vanishing.

"I'm calling in a blocking force," said Brock, "if this fucking thing now works." He keyed the radio.

Fitzduane was gone.

DAWN was breaking.

As he ran, Fitzduane tried to put himself in Oshima's position. She had broken through, but where would she go?

The electrical storm had passed and communications were now working. Cloud cover was still low, and rain was forecast. The air effort was cranking up, but it would be hampered.

Scout Platoon was spread out in a loose V. The lead runner, Specialist Tennant, had sworn that he could see two people running up ahead, and Fitzduane was following. Personally, he had not seen anything, but in the absence of any other lead, Tennant's certainty was as good an option as anything else.

They were running east. That meant that they were running into the rising sun, and that one thought alone persuaded Fitzduane that Oshima could well be up ahead. She left little to chance, and the fact that any pursuers would have the sun in their eyes as they followed would be something she would think of.

There was a good case to be made for abandoning the search and continuing it later on by air, but the sheer scale of the terrain made Fitzduane reluctant to concede Oshima any advantage. The Tecuno plateau consisted of thousands of square kilometers of brutal terrain, and if Oshima really did manage to shake her pursuers, she could hide indefinitely.

It had occurred to Fitzduane that his assumption that Oshima would move from the air base tunnel to a cache might well be oversimplifying. If Oshima had prepared a series of underground hides, then locating her would be well nigh impossible. There was too much ground to cover. A hide could be stood on by a searcher and still not be detected.

All Oshima had to do to gain was to elude her pursuers for a few hours, and then the advantage would pass to her.

The light increased, and Fitzduane strained to see what was up ahead.

Suddenly, he thought he could see something. He wiped the sweat from his face and tried again. This time he was sure. Over a thousand meters ahead, he could see the faintest shape of a running figure. There were supposed to be two, but he could detect no sign of a second figure.

It was running down an open, boulder-strewn valley. The hills on either side looked as if they had been made by some giant dumping buckets of jagged rocks at random. The nearest incline was about eight hundred meters away.

It went against all Fitzduane's training to move exposed through such terrain, but if they wanted to keep up with their quarry there was no other option.

He longed for the reassuring shapes of a couple of Kiowas, but several had sustained damage in the storm and one was not due for another half hour.

Up ahead, Tennant stumbled and fell. Two seconds later, the second runner collapsed.

"SNIPER!" he shouted.

As he fell to the ground, he saw that the man immediately in front of him had been hit by the third shot. He crawled forward. The trooper had been struck at an angle below the breastbone. His face was gray, and as Fitzduane approached, blood frothed from his mouth and he died. The man's name was Zalinski. He was one of Scout Platoon's snipers. His M24 lay beside him.

Fitzduane searched the high ground. The wound on the dead trooper looked as if it had been made by a 7.62mm. Three shots and three hits suggested a custom sniper rifle and a shooting talent enough to yield a world of woe. The angle suggested the hills to the left.

The jagged rocks offered endless options.

All around him paratroopers were firing single shots at possible firing positions in the rocks. Using iron sights at that range, they would be lucky to score a hit even if they could see a target. But a round could get lucky. At least it would help keep the sniper's head down.

If they did nothing, they were going to get picked off one by one.

Bent double, using the cover of the return fire, Brock ran up.

"Shit!" he said quietly when he saw Zalinski. He looked at Fitzduane. "I hope that damn woman's worth it."

Gallo was about twenty meters away. He studied the distant rocks, then closed his eyes.

Brock said nothing. He watched the performance and then crawled toward Gallo. The man's eyes opened. "Got him?" Brock asked.

"Think so," said Gallo. "The tall butte is my twelve. Go to ten, drop twenty meters and look at the ledge below the skyline."

Brock had picked up the dead paratrooper's M24 and was studying the rocks through the telescopic sight. "Negative," he said.

"Fucker's pulled back," said Gallo. "Wait one and you'll see."

"Hold your fire," shouted Brock. The command was passed along the firing line. He pulled a set of spotter's binoculars from his pocket and called Fitzduane over, and tossed the glasses in his direction.

Fitzduane moved to within ten meters and took the glasses. He did not like coming even that close, since bunched-up targets brought out a mean streak in hostiles. On the other hand, countersniper work was a collaborative effort.

Brock and Gallo were glued to the eyepieces of their rifles. Their problem now was that their angle of vision was severely restricted. A spotter would cover a wider field and then talk the shooters onto target. He would keep an eye out for other opposition.

Fitzduane focused where instructed. Thirty seconds later, he saw movement twenty meters to the right of where Gallo had originally indicated.

The enemy sniper was moving every couple of shots.

"Right twenty," said Fitzduane.

Gallo fired, followed a fraction of a second later by Brock.

Fitzduane saw a slight movement as a long black shape dropped off the ledge.

"He's dropped his rifle," he said.

Gallo's eyes were closed. "We got him," he said.

Fitzduane scanned the rocks. There could be another sniper, but only two had got through and one was ahead. He thought of Oshima increasing her lead in front of them.

"We're going on," he said to Brock.

Brock opened his mouth to say something and then thought better of it. "Airborne, sir," he said.

He rose to his feet. "Move out," he said.

The survivors of Scout Platoon rose to their feet. He had logged three dead. The RT operator had taken a round, making it four.

Fitzduane was already running.

Brock and his men followed on. They left the bodies where they lay. Brock felt numb. Hate drove him on. Hate for Oshima and, as of the moment, a profound and irrational hate for Fitzduane.

The interlude had bought Oshima thirteen minutes and had cost five lives.

Up on the ledge, Jin Endo lay sprawled with a 7.62mm round through the bridge of his nose and the back of his skull missing.

Brock's round had torn out his throat.

Up above, the vultures were already circling. Soon two extra black dots swept toward the corpse but kept on going.

OSHIMA crested the hill and looked backward. In the distance she could see her pursuers. They were now too far behind to catch up, she was certain. She turned and ran for a further ten minutes. She stopped at a pile of rocks and began to pull them aside. Behind the rocks there was earth and then camouflage netting.

She worked furiously. Soon a 250cc motorcycle was uncovered. The fuel tank was full and the panniers were full of supplies. There were other caches up ahead. She now had everything she needed to escape.

She unclipped field glasses and surveyed the terrain. The paratroopers were still out of sight, probably still sweating up the hill in their heavy equipment.

The sky was overcast. The weather was still on her side. All she could see were black specks in the distance.

Vultures heading for Jin Endo and the paratroopers he had killed. It was a good end and he had served his purpose, but Oshima felt a slight twinge as she remembered his devotion and his ardor. Endo had touched her. It was as well he was dead.

Oshima kicked her motorcycle into life and headed off down into the gorge. She had picked the route carefully. The rock overhung the gorge for some considerable distance and made the dry wadi in the bottom invisible from the air. She had outdistanced her pursuers behind her and was now safe from discovery by aerial reconnaissance. She was going to make it.

One woman and the might of the famous 82nd Airborne Division, and she was going to triumph.

She entered the gorge and felt the protection of the rock above fold over her. The sky was blotted out.

"WHERE?" said Gannon.

Palmer indicated the spot on the map.

"Fitzduane know?"

"Airborne, sir," said Palmer.

Gannon walked away from the map. Weather conditions were lousy and the wind was higher than he liked. But this damn terrorist was the core of all this bloodshed, and there was nothing worse than a mission half done. Politicians liked to call a halt before the job was finished, but about the only good thing he could find to think about the Devil's Footprint and the Tecuno plateau was that there were absolutely no politicians around.

"What do the air force say?" said Gannon.

"You know the C130 jocks," said Palmer. "Anywhere, anytime."

"Let's do it," said Gannon. He walked toward the door. Behind him, Palmer was already on the radio passing the word.

The C130s were going hot. Inside, paratroopers were racked like peas in a pod. The dirty yellow sand of the Tecuno plateau filled the air as the four turbo-props cut in.

Gannon missed the red earth of North Carolina. Fort Bragg was not everyone's idea of the place to be, but if you wore a maroon beret it was something special. Soon someone else would get the division, and hell, he was going to miss the place. Jumping out of perfectly good aircraft was just something that got in your blood.

Gannon turned around. "Dave?" he said.

"Sir?" said Palmer.

"Last jump you made you never quite got around to putting on your 'chute," said Gannon. "How would you like to make one the old-fashioned way—like we taught you?"

Colonel Dave Palmer grinned. "Not sure I remember, General."

"Let's go," said Gannon. "I'll remind you on the way down."

Kitted out, Gannon and Palmer waddled up the ramp.

Black and green faces stared at them.

Gannon scanned them. They looked frightening. God knows why you would want to love these aggressive young people, but he did. They kept the MPs run off their feet, drank like camels, turned Fayetteville into something out of the Wild West, and fucked anything that moved.

But they kept the faith. Not too many people seemed to do that these days. His gaze stopped at one face that did not normally belong.

"Padre," he nodded.

"General," said the padre. Under the camouflage he was looking decidedly guilty. He had not been rostered.

Gannon studied him. "Just remember to catch Colonel Palmer," he said.

"Airborne, General," said the padre with relief.

"When he hits the ground," said Gannon.

"HOOAH, SIR!" said the padre and a planeload of paratroops.

The ramps came up. The C130s rolled.

THE copilot got out of his seat reluctantly but without demur. The two-man Kiowa Warrior crews were a tight team. He did not grudge the Irishman his seat, but he was concerned about letting his crew chief down.

"Your friend still tracking?" said Fitzduane as he buckled in.

"Roger that, sir," said the crew chief as the Kiowa took off. "Call sign Viper Two."

High above, Viper Two focused his high-resolution TV camera on the speeding motorbike until it vanished under an overhang.

Fitzduane listened to the communications between the two helicopters while watching the ground recede in the distance.

Brock's face was an unreadable mask. Cochrane raised his weapon in farewell.

"The target's vanished, sir," said the crew chief.

Fitzduane's heart gave a lurch.

"Have you ever flown *really* low, sir?" said the crew chief.

"I hate heights," said Fitzduane.

"A lot of Airborne do," said the crew chief. "Funny thing, when you think about it."

The Kiowa roared over the crest of the hill and then dropped down as it headed into what looked from the helicopter's perspective like a tunnel.

"Relax, Colonel," said the crew chief. "Unless you get claustrophobia."

"I should live so long," said Fitzduane.

Flying five feet off the ground, the Kiowa Warrior entered the gorge and vanished under the overhang.

High up above, Viper Two flew in parallel.

In the distance up ahead, Viper Two could see the shapes of a flight of C130s.

As he flew closer he could see that the sky was filled with the 'chutes of the Airborne.

THE dry riverbed twisted and turned, and Oshima fought to keep her speed up over the irregular surface. The rock had been worn smooth enough, but the surface was strewn with pebbles and boulders. The noise of the motorbike echoed off the rock walls and pounded back at her.

The silencer had been punctured in a skid a few kilometers back, but the deafening noise was something she could live with. It would only be a temporary inconvenience. In a few minutes she would be in her hide for the day and then could repair the damaged machine at her leisure.

She sideslipped around a patch of gravel and with relief saw the light of the open space ahead. The riverbed widened at this point and the gorge fell away, but shortly afterward there was a cave system. A quick dash across the open space and then she would be under cover.

She skidded to a halt under the final protection of the overhang. The noise was still deafening.

She looked ahead. The open space seemed to be clear.

Out of routine, she looked behind.

As she looked, a helicopter flew around the last bend and hovered a hundred meters behind her.

Oshima's mouth went dry. She made an animal sound and gunned her machine into the open space. She was a small target traveling at speed, and if she moved very fast and zigzagged she could still get away.

She was halfway across when a salvo of 2.5 rockets blew the rock away from under her.

Oshima flew through the air and crashed onto the ground. Dazed but still conscious, she saw that the natural amphitheater made by one side of the gorge and the riverbed was ringed with paratroopers.

She tried to move, but her legs would not respond.

She raised her head and saw that one leg was twisted and broken. The other limb was missing below the knee.

A figure had dismounted from the helicopter and was walking toward her.

Oshima struggled to draw her pistol, but her hand arm would not respond. She raised her arm, and her hand just hung there from its broken wrist.

The figure came closer, and now she could recognize him.

Fitzduane.

She tried to move her left hand, and with relief felt some movement in the fingers.

She eased them around to the small of her back and felt for her backup pistol.

She saw Fitzduane bend down and pick up something. He made a move, and she saw the scabbard cast aside and the blade glint in the sun. Her *katana*, kept always strapped to her back and now torn loose in her fall.

How many people had she killed with that blade? Too many to recall. One of them had been Christian de Guevain, Fitzduane's closest friend. It would be good to add Fitzduane himself to the list. If he was going to use the sword, then he would have to come close, and she could not miss.

Oshima was still bringing the pistol around when Fitzduane raised the sword and severed her head.

✳ CHAPTER TWENTY-NINE

FITZDUANE JOGGED THROUGH Arlington Cemetery.

Autumn was in the air. It was cooler to run. That evening he would board the aircraft that would take him back to Ireland with Kathleen.

It was a nice feeling. He would miss America, but it was time to go home. Home. The best of words. The best of places.

At home you could build. In life, so often you had to destroy. You might not want to, but that was just the way it was. You had to fight to preserve what was worthwhile. And fighting, no matter how you did it, meant destruction. But there were times when, despite the consequences, you had to take a stand.

Freedom was not free. That pretty much said it all.

He saw Cochrane as he approached Nick Rowe's grave. They ran the last few hundred yards together in an easy silence.

Fitzduane placed several stones on Nick Rowe's headstone.

"From the Devil's Footprint?" said Cochrane.

Fitzduane nodded.

They walked together. Arlington was quiet and nearly empty and very beautiful.

"Well, you got me fitter," said Cochrane.

Fitzduane laughed. "How is the fight going to save the Task Force?"

"Lots of promises and little action," said Cochrane. "Counterterrorism isn't much of a vote-getter, and the average person thinks it's covered."

But it isn't, thought Fitzduane. And with the Cold War over America was dropping its guard. Forgery, economic terrorism, infiltration, selective assassination, the threat of weapons of mass destruction, the emergence of a whole host of new nuclear nations, fundamentalism in its various forms, Third World countries wanting a piece of the pie the easy way. There were some seriously bad people out there.

The list of real and immediate threats was a long one. But the new dangers were complex, interwoven, and frequently not readily apparent—unlike the clear-cut simplicity of the Cold War. And people wanted to get on with their lives, collect the peace dividend, and hope for the best.

Only a few really understood.

Human nature.

"We're getting through to some people on the Hill," said Cochrane, "and it doesn't take too many to make a difference. Meanwhile, we'll hang in there. We'll just show up."

Fitzduane smiled. "I guess that's how this country got started."

He shook Cochrane's hand. It was a stronger grip than he remembered.

"Hell of thing, Lee," he said. "You *are* fitter."

"Keep the faith," said Cochrane.

"There's not really much else when you come right down to it," said Fitzduane. "But right now, Lee, stop plotting. I'm going home."

They ran together to the Iwo Jima memorial and then headed their separate ways.

✳ ACKNOWLEDGMENTS

THE MORE I RESEARCH, the more I learn that however dramatic any individual work of fiction, the adventures of many of the men and women who are kind enough to help me in my writing make my work pale in comparison. There are some extraordinary people doing extraordinary things in this world of ours. Fortunately, enough of them are doing enough ordinary things as well for this world of ours to keep running.

Either way, these acknowledgments are my inadequate way of saying "Thank you."

To those I cannot name for reasons we all understand—especially my friends in Mexico—I thank you also. To those I have forgotten in print, I plead human frailty. But my thoughts are with you.

I should add that my specialist advisers have been outstanding. Any errors are mine. For reasons of space, I have used literary license to shorten the paratrooper jump sequence.

Particular mention is due to Doug Miller of Purple & Green Consulting of Maryland, who designed the Fast-Attack Vehicle—the Guntrack—featured in this book. The U.S. equivalent is the remarkable Chenowth, a company run by Dr. Max Orme Johnson.

I would also like to pay tribute to the Irish Rangers—roughly the equivalent of Delta and the SAS. The Rangers really do exist and they turn up in the most interesting places.

The ingenious Calico, Fitzduane's weapon of choice in this adventure, is made by Michael K. Miller's company, Calico Light Weapons Systems.

Col. Bob Dilger is someone I never did manage to meet. Based upon what I have heard about him, the expression "The Right Stuff" comes to mind.

There is no significance to the order of these names except its approximation of the chronology of my travels.

WASHINGTON D.C.

Brig. Gen. Frank Brusino; Brig. Gen. Samuel Cockerham; Lt. Gen. James H. Merryman; George (Jacques) O'Hara; Eric Forrest; Philip O'Rourke; Michel Verdon (Les Halles); Mike Dolan; Bill Jarrell; John Sacharanski; Seannon Fallon; Col. Andy Fallon; Christi Neuenschwander, Dawn Igler; Melissa Temerak; Vaugn and Diane Forrest; Congressman Duncan Hunter; Congressman Jim Saxton; Congressman Sonny Bono; Congressman Michael Forbes; Congressman Bill McCollum; Congressman Bob Doran; Congressman Randy "Duke" Cunningham; Congressman Charlie

Wilson; Congressman Philip Crane; Robert "Corky" Coleman; Yossef Bodanski; Don Morrissey; William R. Pitts; Fredrick Downs, Jr.; Geoff Friedman; John L. Dalton; Chris Johnson; George Ealing; John Roos; Glenn W. Goodman, Jr.; Lt. Col. Bob Edgerton.

FAYETTEVILLE/FORT BRAGG AND THE 82ND AIRBORNE DIVISION

Maj. Gen. George A. Crocker; Mrs. Clouston; CSM Steven England; CSM Myers; Maj. Rivers Johnson; Col. T. R. Turner; Col. David H. Petraeus; Col. Frank Helmick; Lt. Col. Tony Tata; 1st Lt. Jerry Perkins; 1st Lt. Steven P. Basilici; Sgt. Helm; Sgt. Mark A. Sapier; Spc. Richard Rasmussen; Spc. Julie Hottle; Spc. Michael Simco; Spc. Clutter; Warrant Officer Pat Riordan; Robert Anzuoni; Maj. Joe Andrzejewski; Sgt. David Bailey; George Howard; Pete Peterson; Capt. C. H. Ennis; 1st Sgt. McCorquodale; Sheriff Earl "Moose" Butler; Roxanne M. Merritt; John and Patti Looby; J. B. Amaker; Keith Idema; Ed Rivas; Bill Pegler; Ken Cummins; Joe van Cleve; Capt. L. W. Bailey; Pete "The Pirate" Carolan; Col. Wayne Morgan; Ron Burnett; Dr. David Silbegeld, Lt. Col. U.S.A. Retired; Stanley R. Benz; Curtis L. Spurling, Business Development, Teledyne Brown Engineering; William F. Atwater, Director/Curator, U.S. Army Ordnance Museum.

U.S. EMBASSY, DUBLIN

Col. W. T. Torpey; Margo Collins; Jean Rylands; Lynn Cassel.

LIVERMORE

Dr. Edward Teller; Dr. Bruce Tartar; Dr. John Hunter; Gordon Yano; Dr. Harry Cartland; Dr. Jay Davis; Dr. David Dearborne; Dr. Thomas Karr; Tom McEwan; Dr. Kathleen Bailey; Bill Cleveland; Dr. Rick Twogood; Mark Eckhart; Liz Curran; Dr. Alan Mode; Paul and Karin Maslin; Craig Savoye; Dr. Woody Clark; Bruce McFarlane; Ellen Placas; Neil Grecian; Fred Cole; Chief Ron Scott.

A NOTE ON THE ''SUPERGUN'' FEATURED IN *THE DEVIL'S FOOTPRINT*

I have been following the supergun story for some years and in April 1996 was part of a small group invited by inventor and designer, Dr. John Hunter, to watch Livermore's SHARP launcher fired. SHARP stands for Super High Altitude Research Project and it is the largest hydrogen launcher of its kind in the world. It is a linear descendant of Dr. Gerald Bull's HARP project, which pioneered barrel-based launchers in the 1950s. Dr. Harry Cartland currently runs the project. In his spare time, he runs, climbs, and jumps out of aircraft.

SHARP works! Seeing the 400-foot-long "gun" being fired is quite an experience. It is every bit as dramatic as you might imagine.

As I write this, SHARP has shown us a completely new low cost way of accessing space. The commercial company is called JVL—The Jules Verne Launcher Company—as a tribute to H. G. Wells, who first conceived the idea of using a gun to reach escape velocity and space. Fiction is turning into fact. Yet again, we fiction writers have a hard time staying ahead of the game.

But please note, the real SHARP and the new JVL are not "guns" as such at all. The long barrel prompts the name, but the correct term is *launcher* and they are about the most environmentally friendly launchers yet devised. Their fuel, hydrogen, turns to water.

The supergun in this book is inspired by fact—but it is fiction.

THE LIVERMORE TEAM PIONEERING "THE GREATEST GREENEST GUN IN THE WORLD"— AND MAKING HISTORY—ARE AS FOLLOWS

Dr. John Hunter and Dr. Harry Cartland; Fred Reinecker; Lou Bertolini; Warren Massey; Gary "Drew" Hargiss; Ken Haney; Ron Greenwood; Bill Fritz (Bechtel); Matt Traini; Paul Heston; Fred Allen; Dale Johnson; Chuck Cook; Jaime Lister; Sal Longo, et al. at Aberdeen Proving Ground; Jorgen Groth of Terma Electronics; Chet Vanek of Vanek Prototype; Kevin Bowcutt; Harry Shortland; Jim Rowe; Dan Schumann; Chris Steffani; John Benedict; Ed Zywicz; Mike White, et al. at the Johns Hopkins Applied Physics Laboratory; Chuck McClinton, NASA-Langley; Fred Allen; Arlin Houser; Bob "Killer" Kwasney; Gary Anderson; Dave Foltz; Carlos Perez; Dan Phillips; Ray Gobel; Gary Lehmann; Jim Armstrong; Bob Kost; Edna Martinez; Tim Sammons; Mike Doman; Ed Utiger.

WITH SPECIAL THANKS TO

My assistants, Susan Byrnes and Margaret Callahan; my agent, the redoubtable Robert Gottlieb of William Morris, and his assistants, Laura Madonna and Martha David; my editor, David Highfill; his assistant, Lorraine Martindale; Ron Swanson; Gabrielle Kelly; Dr. Joe Sperazza; Kathy and Jim Meister; Oliver Wiley; Chris and Jane Carrdus; Bob and Anne Fulton; Scott Gourley; Larry Hama; Tom Constantine and Jim McGivney of the DEA; Jimmy Fox; Rich Greene; Deputy Inspector Bobby Martin; Al Martin; Arnold Schaab; Bob Stein; Lloyd Morrisett; Jonathan and Bibi Conrad; Bob Hunter; Steve and Bonnie Kane; Marly Rusoff; Michael Kaplan; and one of the most delightful and attractive people I have met in a long time, Patricia Burke of Paramount's New York office.

WHICH LEAVES THE THREE MUSKETEERS (of which more anon . . .)

Commissioner of Police John Pritchard; Dennis Martin; and Jimmy Miley

Until the next time

Victor O'Reilly (currently working on *Satan's Smile*)

e-mail: voreilly@iol.ie

or 100126.1425@COMPUSERVE.COM *or* Web page: http://www.iol.ie/voreilly